RAIDING WITH MORGAN

RAIDING WITH MORGAN

JIM R. WOOLARD

KENSINGTON BOOKS
http://www.kensingtonbooks.com

KENSINGTON BOOKS are published by

Kensington Publishing Corp.
119 West 40th St.
New York, NY 10018

All Kensington titles, imprints and distributed lines are available at special quantity discounts for bulk purchases for sales promotion, premiums, fund-raising, educational or institutional use.

Special book excerpts or customized printings can also be created to fit specific needs. For details, write or phone the office of the Kensington Special Sales Manager: Kensington Publishing Corp., 119 West 40th St., New York, NY, 10018. Attn. Special Sales Department. Phone: 1-800-221-2647.

Kensington and the K logo Reg. U.S. Pat. & TM Off.

Library of Congress Control Number: 2013920824

ISBN-13: 978-1-61773-268-3
ISBN-10: 1-61773-268-0
First Kensington Hardcover Edition: May 2014

eISBN-13: 978-1-61773-269-0
eISBN-10: 1-61773-269-9
First Kensington Electronic Edition: May 2014

10 9 8 7 6 5 4 3 2 1

Printed in the United States of America

RAIDING WITH MORGAN

PROLOGUE

"Morgan's coming! Morgan's coming!"

Ty Mattson felt the fool the moment he shouted those words. He was yelling for Boone Jordan, a Mexican War veteran and the calmest man in all of Elizabethtown, Kentucky. The redness faded from his cheeks as a chuckling Boone Jordan stepped from the stall he had been mucking. Mr. Jordan's peg leg stirred a tiny cloud of dust on the floor of the livery stable. "Is he in sight yet?"

Gulping breath, Ty halted before the livery owner. "No, they say he may pass through here tomorrow or the next day."

"I heard about the telegram the dispatcher at the L and N Depot received during the night," Boone said. "Not to disappoint you, lad, Morgan's main column won't attack Elizabethtown. A scouting party or foraging detail may come nosing around, but not the main column."

Ty frowned. "How can you be so sure?"

Boone leaned on his pitchfork. "Morgan will follow the road through Lebanon and Bardstown, even if it means a fight with what Union blue bellies are blocking his path. It's the shortest

1

route to the Ohio River. He's aiming to cross the Ohio at Brandenburg."

"Then he won't attack Louisville or Elizabethtown like many people claim?"

Boone stroked his bearded chin. "Naw, if he captured a city the size of Louisville, he couldn't hold it. Federal forces are after him like bees swarming on honey and they'd surround him in a day or two. He'd lose his whole command. And Elizabethtown is out of his way now. He has no interest in burning the L and N trestles at Muldraugh Hill again. He has bigger game in mind. He means to invade Indiana and Ohio and raise hob as long as he can before recrossing the river."

Ty didn't doubt Boone Jordan's reasoning, but he was mighty curious as to how the livery owner could be so certain about Morgan's intentions, while no one else seemed certain about anything where the infamous raider was concerned. "How did you learn what General Morgan's real plan is, Mr. Jordan?"

Boone's response shook Ty from brow to toes. "Your father told me."

"My father lives in Texas," a bewildered Ty said. "He's been there all my life. How would he know what's happening in Kentucky?"

Boone stood his pitchfork against the wall of the stall he was cleaning. "Old Joe can finish the mucking out. Come back to the tack room with me, lad. You're old enough and have a right to the true story of Owen Mattson."

Ty stuck tight to Boone Jordan's heels, heart pounding like a smithy's hammer. Maybe he would finally learn something about his father, besides what little his grandmother had told him: how his father had gone off to fight in the Mexican War, leaving behind Ty's pregnant mother, who had died giving birth to him. According to his grandmother, his father had chosen to remain in Texas after the fighting ended. To the best of Ty's knowledge, his father had never attempted to contact his grandparents by messenger or mail after that fateful decision.

Ty never ceased wondering why his father had abandoned him. Did his father even know he was alive? Was it too much to hope Mr. Jordan might at last provide the answers to his many questions? Was his longing to know the truth finally, truly over?

The oversized tack room smelled of leather, horsehair, neat's-foot oil, and fried lard. Saddles rested on sawhorses and bridles; harness and headgear hung from wall pegs. A cast-iron stove occupied the wall opposite the doorway, with its stovepipe piercing the wall through a tin vent hole. Two ladder-back chairs flanked the small wooden table, where Old Joe and Mr. Jordan ate their meals and enjoyed their evening ration of corn liquor, behind closed doors—what with Elizabethtown being a strict Baptist community that denounced, each and every Sunday, the partaking of distilled spirits.

Boone pointed to one of the chairs at the table. "Have a seat, lad." Pivoting on his peg leg, the livery owner dropped into the chair across from Ty.

"I suppose I better start at the beginning. Your father and I went off to Texas in 18 and 46. We enlisted at Lexington, Kentucky, in John Hunt Morgan's company. Morgan was a captain then. Once the tussle with Mexico was finished, your father and I decided to settle in Texas. It may sound cruel and cold to you, but your father knew your mother had died during childbirth. She was a beautiful woman, and it sapped the will out of him for months. He—"

"Did father know I survived?" Ty interrupted.

"Don't get impatient with me, lad," Boone Jordan said with a gentle smile.

"I'm sorry I was rude, Mr. Jordan. I've asked that question since I was old enough to understand what few tidbits about my father that Grandmother shared with me."

Boone Jordan sighed, extended his arm and clasped Ty's shoulder. "Owen knew you survived. Enoch and your father had a falling-out before he left Kentucky, but your grandmother defied his orders and wrote your father and told him."

"Then father never wanted to lay eyes on me, to claim me for his son," Ty blurted out, choking back a sob.

"Hear me out, lad," Boone said. "Don't judge your father too harshly until you do. All right?"

Ty nodded his head and bit his lip to make sure he remained silent. He might not like what he was about to be told, but he wouldn't bawl like a child and disgrace himself. He was nearly seventeen years of age—too old to break into tears in front of Mr. Jordan.

"Owen mourned your mother for years," Boone said. "He talked of returning to Kentucky. Then we joined the Rangers, so as not to starve, and we were soon chasing Comanche warriors over most of Texas. We were scouting on horseback nearly every waking hour. Years went by and your father started talking of some day owning a ranch of his own. He hardly mentioned Kentucky, lad. I think so much time slipped away, your father was terribly embarrassed that he had ducked his fatherly duties."

Boone leaned back in his chair. His gaze was fixed on Ty's face. "There was also your grandfather to be dealt with, if he came home. Now, Owen fears nothing. He saved my life when we were caught in that Comanche ambush at Blue Springs. Sure, I lost part of a leg, but I'm still waking to daylight."

Brain whirling, Ty hung on Boone's every word.

"What Owen didn't want was a brawl with your grandfather. Enoch objected to his marrying your mother. Your grandmother told Owen in her letter that your grandfather had disowned him, had legally denied him his rightful inheritance, and had himself appointed your guardian by the Elizabethtown courts. If Owen ever set foot on Mattson property again, your grandfather vowed he'd shoot him."

Boone Jordan's heavy brow knitted together. "Lad, I wager you know nothing about Owen being disowned, the guardianship, or your grandfather's threat, do you?"

Flabbergasted, Ty could only shake his head. His grandmother hadn't told him—that he understood. Victoria Mattson seldom went against the wishes of her husband. Her single letter to his father constituted a lifetime of rebellion in the strict household of Enoch Mattson.

Which left his grandfather. Why had he opposed his father's marriage? What had been wrong with his mother? Did he ever intend to inform Ty of the guardianship, which legally had eliminated any claim his father had on him? How could his grandfather hate his own son that much?

Boone Jordan sat quietly, allowing Ty a chance to digest and accept what he'd just learned; here was knowledge that would change how Ty thought and felt forever. Ty's first question was no surprise. Boone would have asked the same one in his place.

"How did you find all this out, Mr. Jordan? Did Father tell you while you were in Texas together, or did he write to you?"

"No, he told me in person."

Boone saw Ty's face droop from shock. He grinned as Ty grabbed the edge of his chair with both hands. Somehow the youngster kept his composure, which impressed Boone mightily. This lad had promise, real promise of perhaps becoming the man his father was.

"Owen is riding with General Morgan's cavalry right now, today," Boone continued. "He joined the general in Tennessee, a year ago June. We became friends with General Morgan while serving under him in Mexico. Your father is assigned to the general's personal staff. I wrote your father after I returned to Elizabethtown. That's how he knew I'd taken ownership of my uncle's livery stable after he passed away. Owen sought me out after General Morgan's men captured Elizabethtown last Christmas."

"Did he want to see me?"

Boone Jordan showed no annoyance with Ty's abrupt inquiry. "Yes, he did. He just didn't dare show himself at your grandfather's door in anything other than a blue uniform. An ardent Union sympathizer, like your grandfather, would have started shooting the minute he saw a Confederate cavalryman in his barnyard, son or no son. You deal with Enoch Mattson, you better walk the same path or suffer the consequences."

"You're right, Mr. Jordan. Grandfather had the house shutters battened. He and the neighbors were armed and ready. Lucky for us, Morgan's man didn't come out north of town and pester us."

"That wasn't luck. It was your father's doing. He asked General Morgan for orders that the home and property of Enoch Mattson was not to be looted or burned, and the general thinks enough of Owen he issued such orders."

"So, even though grandfather despises him, father protected him from any harm at the hands of Morgan's men."

"Not exactly, it was more that he was preserving the Mattson acres and its Thoroughbred horses for his son, the future heir."

An entirely different picture of his father was rapidly forming in Ty's mind. What did his father look like? What kind of uniform did he wear? How did he talk? How did he walk? Why did General Morgan hold him in such high regard? How much did he honestly care about his only son?

A craving swept through Ty with the force of a tidal wave. Suddenly the most imperative need in his whole existence was to meet his father face-to-face, and he couldn't wait until the war was over. What if his father died in battle?

To search for his father, he needed a horse and a gun. Blue and gray soldiers and marauders—with no allegiance to either side—roamed the Kentucky countryside, killing, burning, and looting at will. No sane soul dared travel afoot and unarmed. It was doubly risky to travel alone, as Ty would.

He ruled out one possible source of a horse and gun. While he wasn't happy with how his grandfather had come between him and his father, Ty was loath to steal from the person who had boarded and provided for him since birth. He couldn't countenance being branded a common thief by the Elizabethtown Baptists, to the embarrassment of Church Elder Enoch Mattson.

Ty swore Boone Jordan was inside his head with him. "Want to meet your father, do you, lad?" Boone asked.

"Yes, sir, more than I want to breathe. But I can't go off hunting him without a horse and gun. Grandfather won't give them to me willingly, and I can't rightly steal from him."

"By damned, you are Owen Mattson's son, all right. He can't steal from others, even if he's starving."

Boone smiled slyly. "Well, young feller, maybe I can be of help to you. You'll be seventeen in a few days. In a year you'll be eighteen. Your grandfather can't keep you out of the blue-belly army once you reach the draft age of eighteen without breaking the law of the land. We both know he won't do that. Maybe you should have a say as to what your future will be. If you're grown enough to don a uniform and tote a rifle, and I believe you are, then you're old enough to decide which side you want to fight with. Follow me, lad."

Peg leg thumping the floor, the livery owner skirted the stove. With a loud grunt, he pulled a wooden crate from behind it. "Grab the other end. Help me slide this crate over by the table."

Full of unbounded curiosity, Ty could hardly wait for Mr. Jordan to unbuckle the crate's leather straps and lift its lid. "Been a while since I poked around in here," Boone said, "but I believe we have everything you need."

First out of the crate was a wide-brimmed hat, with the right side pinned to the crown by a brass star. Ty's astonishment grew, the deeper Boone dug. A pair of spurs, with huge silver rowels and tiny bells, and leather jackboots, which tied above the knee, followed the hat. Next out was a holstered revolver with waist belt, a leather shoulder bag, a pair of woolen trousers, and, finally, a cotton shield shirt.

"I judge you to be about my size. The clothes and boots should fit okay."

"Are these the clothes and revolver you wore in Texas, Mr. Jordan?"

"Yep, this is Ranger garb. Gano's Brigade of Texas Cavalry rides with General Morgan. You meet up with Morgan's column and you'll be a dead ringer for those crazy Texans."

Boone lifted the revolver and drew the weapon from the cavalry holster. "This is the most important thing on the table. You recognize it, don't you? I owned a matching pair of 1858 Remingtons. I sold your grandfather the other revolver last summer. It's the pistol he taught you to shoot with. Enoch bragged this winter how accurate you'd become at target practice."

Ty didn't bother interjecting that his grandfather hadn't shared that positive opinion of his target shooting with him. Compliments from Enoch Mattson were scarce as a barn cat with five legs and cow horns.

"Lad, I don't preach," Boone said. "I'm not by nature a preacher. I'll make an exception this one time and share the cardinal rule of the Rangers with you. Unless it's orders from a senior officer, never let anyone—under any circumstances—separate you from your weapon. Part with your gun and you're as good as dead. Many a Ranger is alive because he stuck to that training. Will you promise me that?"

At Ty's nod, Boone Jordan laid the revolver aside, rapped the table with his knuckles, and rose from his chair. "Let's mosey out to the stock pen. You can't meet up with Morgan's cavalry afoot. Those Texas rowdies would laugh Owen Mattson's son clean out of Kentucky."

There was a single horse in the stock pen. That animal was a big, rangy pure gray gelding, except for a large splotch of black on his left cheek. "Reb ain't fancy like those Denmark Thoroughbreds your grandfather and General Morgan swear by. Reb was crossbred. That accounts for the long face, wide forehead, and big ears. What counts is he's deep in the chest and long of hip and strong in the pasterns. Plus he's gun broke and will jump a fence or hedgerow, if asked. He's the kind of animal your father and I sought with the Rangers when we had to ride miles each day. Trust me, he's the perfect horse for you. He'll outlast a Denmark Thoroughbred."

Ty clutched the top rail of the stock pen with both hands, hard enough to splinter wood, and pretended he was studying Reb. With the horse and gun, even the clothes he required to seek out his father, he realized with a start the consequences of what he was planning. If Ty abandoned his grandfather without any warning and against Enoch Mattson's wishes, he would most likely be disowned, as his father had been. It was a huge step to abandon a safe hearth and regular meals in a war-ravaged state. The other side of the coin was the fact that if he stayed home, he couldn't avoid induction into the same blue-belly army his father was fighting.

Boone Jordan saw Ty's white-knuckled grip on the top rail and the hard knot at the hinge of his jaw. "It's a big decision, lad, a very big decision, and you're the only one who can make it."

Somehow Ty kept his voice steady. "Do you believe I can find my father on my own, Mr. Jordan?"

"Yes, I do, lad. You're a skilled rider. You can shoot and you've traveled the road from Elizabethtown to Brandenburg on horse-buying trips with your grandfather. When you're in a hurry to be someplace, knowing the way is all-fired important."

"How soon should I leave?"

"Right now, lad. The sun will be down shortly. If General

Morgan's in Lebanon today, he'll be in Bardstown tomorrow and Brandenburg the next morning. You need to make sure you join his column on the Brandenburg Road, near Garnettsville. The meadows along the road there are large enough for his night camp. You'll need to ride straight through the night or risk being caught between Morgan's column and the blue bellies pursuing him. I don't want you shot dead or starving in a Federal prison."

Ty loosed a loud sigh. In the end, it was a surprisingly easy decision. "I couldn't forgive myself if I don't try to locate Father. Maybe he won't be as glad to see me. I'll chance that for just one look at him. I've dreamed about him my whole life. I can't wait any longer."

No smile of satisfaction appeared on Boone's face. He was praying silently that his allegiance to Owen Mattson hadn't condemned a young man he loved dearly to an early grave. He was also aware that Enoch Mattson might well force him out of business if his ire reached explosive proportions.

With a somber nod, he said, "I'll return your wagon and horse in the morning and tell Enoch where you've gone. He'll be furious, but it'll be too late for him to stop you. Come inside, lad, we need to figure out the best way for you to leave town." In the tack room, Boone fired a coal oil lantern and separated the woolen trousers and shield shirt from the other items on the wooden table. "Put those on, lad. They won't attract undue attention."

While Ty changed clothes, Boone stuffed the jackboots, spurs, holstered revolver, and wide brimmed hat into a hundred-pound hemp grain sack. He passed the leather shoulder bag to Ty. "That won't attract much attention, either. In the bag, you'll find balls, percussion caps, a powder flask, and extra cylinders for the Remington. The bag is as valuable as your revolver. Don't take it off, even to sleep. Once you're well past Enoch's gate, you can finish changing yourself into a Texan."

Boone selected a Mexican saddle, with double cinches, and a bridle from the livery gear lining the far wall of the tack room. "Lead Reb inside and saddle him. Talk soft and easy and he'll follow you like a child. Temperamental he's not. I'll sack up a cache of grub for you."

Old Joe had fired the lanterns hanging at the front entryway of the stable, providing Ty enough light to work by in the growing dusk. Reb was the docile animal Boone described. Ty had him saddled when Boone Jordan emerged from the tack room with a hemp bag in each hand.

Boone headed for the street and stopped just inside the livery's lit doorway. "General Judah led his cavalry on a wild-goose chase to Leitchfield, thinking Morgan would circle to the west without crossing the Ohio. That leaves a detail here in town and a few commissary wagons with the blue bellies assigned to them along the north road. You drove past them in your wagon coming to town. If they stop you, say your wagon broke down and you borrowed a horse from the livery to take home the supplies your grandfather ordered tonight, so he won't be angry with you."

Boone took a deep breath. "You best be going, lad. If you hear riders approaching from ahead or from behind you, abandon the road and hide as best you can. Don't trust anyone—man or woman—until you find Morgan's column. You hear a challenge from a sentry, then yell out that you're Owen Mattson's son. Given how you'll be dressed, he'll have his sergeant take you to him."

Ty followed Boone into the street and mounted Reb. The livery owner tied the hemp bags together with a leather cord and slung them over Reb's withers.

"How will I recognize Father, Mr. Jordan?"

"No different than looking in a mirror, lad. You spy a man your size, with ox-yoke shoulders, red hair, green eyes, a mouth full of white teeth, and voice deep as a well, you've found your father."

Ty shook the hand Boone Jordan offered. "Thanks for everything, Mr. Jordan."

"My pleasure, lad, my pleasure," Boone said.

Ty reined Reb toward the Brandenburg Road. He didn't turn and wave good-bye.

He feared he would lose his nerve at the last second.

PART 1

North to Glory

We are bound for the Ohio in a bold bid to carry the war and its bloodletting and destruction into the enemy's lair. We will etch the terror and fright of our passage in the minds of every man, woman and child we encounter as well as those who hide in fear of us. The fame and glory garnered by our victories will shine forever in the hearts of our southern brethren and earn us the hatred of northern sympathizers. May the Lord ride with us.

—Journal of Lieutenant Clinton J. Hardesty, Morgan's
Confederate Cavalry, 7 July 1863

CHAPTER 1

Ty came fully alert as he approached the Yankee commissary wagons flanking the north road. In broad daylight, the Union detail had paid him scant attention, treating him as just another unarmed young lad driving a farm wagon to town for supplies. Ty worried that they would have pickets out ready to challenge anybody traveling by horseback after dark; and if they stopped him and insisted on searching his feed sacks, he was a goner for certain.

He advanced Reb a few steps at a time and watched for shadows around the flickering campfire visible through the trees lining the road and the openings between the parked wagons. When he thought he'd gone as far as he dared, without being seen, he halted Reb and considered what to do next.

There were no sentries in sight. Music from a fiddle floated on the night air, interrupted by laughter at the end of each verse of whatever ribald song the Yankees were singing. The commissary soldiers were apparently comfortable that they need not fear attack, as the fighting had moved well to the north of their position. Ty suspected the blue bellies had found a source for corn liquor, for their singing was stunningly loud, boisterous, and off-key, best characterized as a rambunctious jamboree.

He tapped Reb's side with his toes. The big gray moved out at a steady walk. Ty counted on the noise at the fire to muffle the soft pad of his shoed hoofs. The trees bordering the road thinned out and Ty gained a clear view of the open meadow and the four wagons resting there.

The seated revelers surrounding the fire didn't interest him. What did was the circular stack of rifles in front of the middle wagon, well out of their reach, and the absence of saddled horses. With no sentries in sight to challenge him, Ty made his decision. He couldn't risk being searched.

He touched Reb with his spurs and scrunched down in the saddle, his cheek touching the gelding's mane. They shot past the Yankee encampment, a gray blur against the trees on the opposite of the road from the wagon yard. He and Reb were into the night before any Yankee who spotted them could gain the attention of his fellow songsters. Ty was still finding it hard to believe that the officer in charge had posted no sentries.

Ty galloped Reb for a half mile and then reined him into a ground-eating trot; a pace the gelding could sustain for miles, if asked. By roughly nine o'clock, the heart-wrenching sight, which he wasn't sure he could handle without breaking down, loomed at the roadside: the archway and gate of the Mattson estate. He went past the padlocked gate without slackening Reb's pace. He'd made his decision and there was no turning back. Nonetheless, though he avoided tears, his heart was burdened with the knowledge he'd willingly closed the door on the past he'd known since birth for a future that could put him in great danger with the prospect he might be felled by a blue-belly bullet.

Around midnight, he halted Reb long enough to don the balance of his new Texas clothes and strap the Remington about his waist. The change made him more confident of facing whatever might pop up the balance of the night and beyond. He wasn't a trained soldier, but flight was no longer his only means of defense.

A ravenous hunger laid hold of him. He rummaged inside one of Boone Jordan's feed sacks and found cloth-wrapped cold fried chicken and soft bread. He ate a large portion of each on the move. After his meal, he and Reb paused at a small stream and enjoyed a drink of water. Come morning, he must locate an isolated spot, where the big gray could rest and graze.

A bright moon painted the roadway silver-gray and Ty had no trouble choosing his course when it forked twice in the next hour. In the middle of night, he slowed Reb to a walk and began thinking about the coming dawn. Odds were that the quiet black cocoon he was riding through would be dispelled by other travelers, not just all kinds of nature. He was fully aware that his revolver, horse, boots, and spurs were possessions his enemies would prize and gladly kill to obtain.

With the first peek of daylight over the eastern horizon, the deep woods fell away and Ty made out farmhouses, barns, outbuildings, most back from the road a piece, and the shadowy contours of planted fields and pastures. A rooster crowed and Ty heard the lowing of cows waiting to be milked.

Hounds began braying and Ty clucked Reb into a trot again. Soon lamps shone in upstairs and kitchen windows and smoke drifted from chimneys. The Kentucky countryside was awakening at a rapid clip.

Ty was fast approaching Buck Grove, a hamlet consisting of four houses, a gristmill, crossroads store, small wayside tavern, blacksmith shop, and two tobacco warehouses. Ty knew from his observations when traveling with Grandfather Mattson that tobacco was grown and harvested in the area. It was cured in the Buck Grove warehouses, and transported by wagon to Brandenburg Station, the L and N Siding and Depot south of Brandenburg, for shipment to the Louisville tobacco auctions. He was glad he would bear northeast from Buck Grove to Garnettsville, bypassing the siding and depot, for that was where he was most likely to find Yankee forces.

A pack of barking dogs rushed forth just short of Buck Grove. Reb ignored the spineless hounds without a single hitch in his gait. A hammer was banging on an anvil at the smithy, and the only person Ty saw on Buck Grove's single street was a small boy playing with a hoop in a side yard. It had worked with the blue bellies outside Elizabethtown, so before the hounds roused the curious and sparked a general alarm, Ty had Reb gallop full tilt again. He was through the small hamlet and beyond before a single adult citizen realized he and his mount had come and gone other than the drum of hoofbeats.

A while later, he was beginning to feel drowsy after a solid night in the saddle and started casting about for a daytime hide-away, if one could be found. He kept shaking his head to ward off his sleepiness. To keep his mind and hands occupied, he ate more chicken and bread.

The road dropped into a small valley before climbing a siz-able hill. The rat-a-tat of hoofbeats on the far rise of the hill snapped Ty's head up. One horse did not present a substantial threat; a large number was to be avoided until he'd identified who rode them, and maybe even then.

By sheer chance, unfenced woodland, which had escaped the axes of many generations, dominated Ty's right flank. With open fields to his left, he spurred Reb amongst trees with butts bigger round than flour barrels. An open glade filled with tall saplings loomed. Ty halted Reb in the towering trunks just beyond the glade.

He couldn't see the Garnettsville Road from the saddle. Satis-fied the gelding was hidden well, he dismounted, drew his Rem-ington, and angled back toward the dusty thoroughfare afoot.

The hoofbeats grew louder as the riders crested the hill to the north. Ty scrambled forward in a crouch, counting on the inter-vening trees to shield him until proper cover presented itself.

Spying an open section of the Garnettsville Road, he plucked his hat from his head and went to ground behind the leafy brush that plugged the gaps between the tree butts. He carefully parted branches with his hand and, sure enough, the oncoming horsemen would pass in plain sight without being aware of his presence.

That was, unless Ty moved and exposed himself. He mouthed a silent prayer of thanks that his grandfather had insisted he master the art of staying absolutely still in a game blind during long stretches of their deer-and-turkey hunts. Just a scratch of the nose was forbidden there.

The armed horsemen were nothing like the organized cavalry Ty had read about in history books. He couldn't imagine a more motley bunch of combatants. Not a single piece of their apparel, hat, or weapon matched. Ragged beards and untrimmed hair proliferated. Other than a creek bath by accident, none appeared to have washed clothes or body in a coon's age. Ty couldn't tell bare skin from filth.

The bunch of them were riding nonchalantly, slugging liquor from clay-fired jugs and laughing and ribbing each other. Ty assumed that the two fine-limbed bay horses without riders at their rear, with better bloodlines than their current mounts, had been freshly stolen.

These ragamuffins were classic examples of the irregulars—misfits and miscreants who bore no allegiance to either the Yankee or Confederate flag and preyed on the weak and defenseless. They had no purpose other than feathering their own nests at the expense of the innocent. Grandfather Mattson swore such men pursued nothing except their own drunken, lecherous pleasures. They were the riffraff whom loyal soldiers detested.

Ty counted eleven riders. A clipped order halted the irregulars smack in front of him. Two of the ragamuffins stood in their stirrups and stared into the woods.

Had they spotted him?

The same chilling fear that he'd felt the night the panther had screamed within an arm's reach of him birthed an ice-cold trickle of sweat in the small of his back; the urge to flee tightened his leg muscles.

Gripping the butt of his Remington with all his might, Ty clamped his jaw so tight that his teeth hurt. He hadn't run that night, despite the threat of a clawed mauling. He'd wet his drawers, but he hadn't panicked. He hadn't run, for fear the panther would hear him and determine his precise location and attack. Ty willed himself to follow that same strategy now. If he fled, the irregulars would spot him and make quick work of him. To them, taking a life was as easy as spitting downwind.

Relief nearly keeled him over when another clipped order drew the staring riders' attention to the point of their column. The irregulars lifted their assorted weapons in unison, yelled, "On to Buck Grove," and trotted south, stirring a thin veil of dust behind them.

Ty wormed his backside against a rough-barked tree and relaxed before he started choking, for lack of air. Since he had left Elizabethtown, his luck defied belief, especially for a soul who frequently dozed off in church and earned a stiff elbow to the ribs from a certain grandfather. The careless Yankees had let him slip by without a challenge; Buck Grove had been asleep; he'd heard approaching horses, not yet in sight, soon enough to take cover in a most convenient stand of timber, with sufficient cover, in the midst of plowed fields. Could that kind of good fortune continue until he rendezvoused with General Morgan and his raiders?

Despite the slight breeze that rustled tree leaves, he heard what he'd missed before in all the excitement: water purling, deeper in the forest. Pleased his pants were dry, despite his fright, he hitched his feet under him, hiked to where he'd hidden Reb, and sought the source of that mouthwatering sound.

The three-foot-wide stream, spring fed to be running full in the middle of the summer, passed over a solid limestone bottom, making for clear drinking water year-round, except for winter freezes. Such streams wet the whistles of serious game hunters throughout Kentucky.

Reb needed no invitation. A sharp tug of the head freed his reins and the big gray dropped his muzzle to drink. With a quick, cursory look upstream and down, a dry-tongued Ty laid his hat on the bank and flopped on his belly to follow suit. The coldness of the water numbed his lips and throat with the first swallow.

A crunching of leaves preceded startling words from a high-pitched voice. "You son of a bitch, you're one of the bastards who stole Paw's mares."

Ty lifted his head and looked straight into the barrel of a cocked flintlock rifle that was held firm and steady by a buck-skin-clad female. She had brown bangs and purple eyes brimming with anger and hate. *Jesus Jump, taken by surprise by a sprig of a girl with pimpled cheeks, not more than thirteen or fourteen years old at most!* The barrel of the flintlock trained on him seemed longer than she was tall. He fought back a disgusted snort and waited for his accuser to speak again.

"Get up. We'll march back to our farm and ask Paw what he wants done with you. Don't matter whether he chooses a noose or a bullet. Horse thieves are no more account than hog shit on a boot heel. You scrape it off, however you please."

Ty rose slowly to his feet, raising his hands to prevent his captor from thinking he had any intention of bringing his holstered Remington into play. Much to his chagrin, her short arms showed no sign of tiring from holding the heavy flintlock on him. He needed to talk his way out of this predicament, or else.

"Girl, I didn't steal those mares. A bunch of free-ranging marauders took them. They went past on the road out there not fifteen minutes ago. They let out a wild yell, 'On to Buck Grove,' and hightailed it south. I'm traveling north, not south. They outnumbered me and I hid in the woods until they were out of sight."

"That's a mighty lame tale, if you ask me. How do I know you didn't stop to water your horse and mean to catch up with them later?" Her purple eyes narrowed. "On second thought, you being so big and all, I believe I'll shoot you in the leg, take that horse, and let you lie right here while I fetch Paw."

Ty suspected what he said next would be the most important thing he ever uttered and might be his sole chance to prod this steely, outraged, purple-eyed female into freeing him. He had no way of determining if she and her pa favored the cause of the Confederacy. His Texas clothes clearly indicated which side he rode for. If her father supported the blue bellies, his fate was sealed, no matter which fence he jumped. He prayed the biblical axiom "The truth shall set you free" resonated somewhere in the heavens.

"I'm no marauder. I'm Private Ty Mattson, of General John Hunt Morgan's Confederate Cavalry. I'm to report to General Morgan at Garnettsville as soon as possible."

Skepticism replaced anger in the purple eyes watching Ty. "Do you have written orders? My paw was a soldier in the Mexican War. He says a soldier on duty doesn't do anything without written orders."

She was smart and not easily fooled. Ty didn't doubt that if so inclined, she would shoot him. He decided to throw all his cards on the table. He needed to be convincing, and then make his move and risk being killed far from the battlefield, the sorriest excuse imaginable for a yet-to-be Morgan raider.

"Miss, I am what I claim to be. I didn't steal your horses, and I'm not a marauder. I don't have written orders. My destination is General Morgan's camp at Garnettsville and I don't dare disobey him. I'm going to mount up and ride out of here. You may shoot me, if you wish. I'll not be cast aside like hog shit for no man . . . or woman."

The purple eyes softened. Was that a twinkle Ty saw?

"Why, you're the most brazen man I've ever met," the sprig of a female said, lowering the hammer of her flintlock. "Damned if you ain't."

The smile she flashed Ty was genuine. "You don't look like those turds that took Paw's horses. You're too prettied up and clean. And, for certain, you aren't a blue belly. Paw and I don't favor any of those shooting each other—and with him missing a leg, he ain't about to join in."

Butting her flintlock, the sprig laughed deep in her scrawny chest and said, "Off with you, Private Ty Mattson. Just make sure you ride straight past the next place with a white barn. No reason for Paw to learn I had my sights on a possible horse thief and didn't fetch him home. Paw's judgments are less lenient and a heap harsher than mine. He might hang you just so he'd feel better about losing his prize mares."

Ty lowered his hands, scooped up his hat and Reb's reins, looped the reins over the gelding's head, then mounted. Without saying a word, he turned the gray, pointed him toward the Garnettsville Road, and rode into the shielding trees. Keeping his eyes straight ahead, he was thankful he'd never had to share a table with her unnamed family.

Hadn't Boone Jordan, reflecting on his Texas years, warned that a man fast and loose with a rope was to be respected and avoided?

Be best to add his children, too. Ty thought, for he sensed the young female's decisions matched her father's more often than not.

Once clear of the woods, he urged Reb into a trot. He took time, then and there, to thank the Lord for allowing lady luck to share his saddle.

He surely owed her a big kiss for not deserting him.

CHAPTER 2

"Halt or be shot from the saddle!"

Ty brought Reb to a standstill with a light squeeze of the reins. The Texas drawl, reminiscent of Boone Jordan's, soothed nerves strung to the breaking point after hours of hiding from irate locals pursuing the marauding irregulars, a mail carrier, a doctor in a buggy, a Yankee patrol, a peddler with pots and pans clanging together on the canvas walls of his cart, and two Union Army freight wagons. But all that lonely, stealthy riding was behind him. He'd found General Morgan's raiders!

"What's the password?"

At close range, the road was darker than the back side of a fastened belt. Ty could not spot the sentry stationed in a copse of oak trees. Ahead, a mile up the road, he made out what seemed a thousand flickering campfires. It was the smell of wood smoke on the evening breeze that had kept him riding after sunset.

"Whoever you are, you best speak up. I'm short on patience."

What to say?

Ty tried a few responses in his head before he remembered Boone Jordan's instructions. "My name is Ty Mattson. I'm

25

Owen Mattson's son. He's assigned to General Morgan's staff. I'm here to join him and fight the Yankees."

The hidden sentry snorted and laughed deep in the belly. "By damned, that's a new one, huh, Frank? What do you think we should do with him?"

Frank stepped from the trees. "Forget that he don't know the password, Harvey. He isn't dressed like no Yankee spy. He's outfitted like you and those hotheaded Texas braggarts in Gano's Brigade. Any which ways, we don't want to chance upsetting Captain Mattson. Let's escort him to Lieutenant Shannon."

"I'll take that pistol, Mr. Ty Mattson," Harvey said.

Ty chanced angering the sentries. "I'd prefer to keep it. Father trained me never to hand over my weapon, no matter the circumstance," he lied. "He'd have my hide."

"Brassy young sprout, isn't he?" Harvey said.

"Yep, but that clinches it for me," Frank said. "That's what Captain Mattson preaches when he drills us. Step down, Mr. Ty Mattson. You can bring your horse. You don't mind, we'll amble along behind you. Walsh and Parsons, you stay put. Harvey and I will risk a tongue-lashing for not disarming him. If you've lied to us, sprout, this-here rifle barrel of mine is going to raise a tall knot behind your ear. You'll hear bells for a coon's age. You first, Mr. Ty Mattson."

When they reached the fringe of Morgan's camp, the sentry named Frank took the lead. They wound through countless fires, their passage attracting little attention.

Ty studied each mess as they went by. Unlike the spanking blue-belly uniforms with shiny brass buttons he had observed in Elizabethtown, the most common uniform for General Morgan's troopers was a nondescript grimy gray. Here and there, an occasional mess was outfitted in spotless white linen, showing much wear, or blue homespun.

He saw troopers in ankle-length dusters, frock coats favored by gentlemen, and short jackets. A greater number had no coat whatsoever. Wide-brimmed hats, like his own, slouch hats worn by farmers and field hands, a few derbies, even a stovepipe hat, like that worn by President Lincoln in a newspaper picture, comprised the headgear of the dining companies. Weaponry of different calibers and loads ranged from pistols and rifled muskets to shotguns. Though they were mounted cavalry, few troopers possessed swords.

Whatever similarities these troopers shared with the motley irregulars he'd encountered were negated by the cohesion of the messes and their adherence to a higher authority. He was in the midst of an organized army with a shared allegiance to a particular flag, not an undisciplined cadre of thieves and murderers.

Beautifully proportioned Thoroughbreds and saddle horses of different breeds grazed in the Garnettsville meadows, with a few grass-fed work animals wide as barn doors. Ty grinned. Obviously, Morgan's fast-moving riders couldn't always be choosy. If you could saddle it, you best ride it or risk being left behind.

The ages of the supposedly seasoned cavalrymen fascinated Ty the most. While officers tended to be older, into their late twenties and thirties, the bulk of the troopers weren't much older than he was. A few actually appeared younger. Learning that, he felt a little less out of place. He'd been afraid he would be the youngest pup in a pack of old wolves.

The smell of roasting meat and pole bread had Ty's stomach growling. He'd polished off the cold chicken and hardtack biscuits provided by Boone Jordan that morning, devouring a four-day supply in two. It was a mistake he wouldn't repeat, for he was in no position to beg for food and didn't know when he would eat next.

Ty's destination was the largest house on Garnettsville's single main street. Troopers jammed the porch and front yard of the Rainer home, a white-painted, two-story frame dwelling. Moving bodies passed each other behind parlor windows. Mounted messengers came and went in rapid succession. Ty figured he was approaching General Morgan's temporary headquarters. Nothing else would account for such frenzied activity.

Five Morgan troopers were seated around the fire in the woodlot on the right side of the house. Sentry Frank announced himself and a trooper on the near side of the crackling fire stood in response. "State your business, Sergeant Lockhart."

"Lieutenant Shannon, I'm fetching a squirt we captured on the south road, sir."

At first, Lieutenant Shannon was a shadow against the light of the flames. When he came forward, Ty made him out by moonlight and the yellow glow spilling from the windows of General Morgan's temporary headquarters. The bareheaded lieutenant was broad-shouldered, with wavy black hair and midnight eyes. His Texas garb and scorched face bespoke a horseman who had spent considerable years where the blazing sun threatened to burn holes in the ground. Huge LeMat revolvers adorned both his hips. Those pistols, the intense midnight eyes, and the slight swagger in the lieutenant's stride convinced Ty that he was about to be confronted by a dangerous, no-nonsense soldier capable of swift, forceful action.

Without so much as a nod in Ty's direction, Lieutenant Shannon said, "Sergeant Lockhart, this captive is a stranger in our camp and he's armed. Please explain your violation of brigade regulations."

Questioning his own wisdom, Sergeant Lockhart shuffled his feet. "Sir, he's no Yankee. He's dressed like you. He says he's Ty Mattson, Captain Mattson's son. He told us Captain Mattson trained him not to surrender his weapon or he'd be punished. That's the same thing the captain pounds into us at drill. Sorry, sir, but I believed him."

"We'll discuss this matter at length later this evening, Sergeant, and determine if punishment is warranted. You may return to your post."

Lieutenant Shannon finally acknowledged Ty's presence. He

minced no words. "Sprout, the question is what to do with you. Maybe you're Captain Mattson's son and maybe you're not. He's never mentioned a son, which seems mighty strange, if you ask me. The captain is not in camp to vouch for you. He's at Brandenburg with Tenth Kentucky, securing boats for our crossing of the Ohio. It'd be best for both us if I follow regulations. Hand over that revolver. We'll put you in manacles. You can ride in a commissary wagon until we reach Brandenburg."

Ty had no desire to part with Reb and his Remington and be imprisoned until tomorrow morning or longer in a bone-hammering army wagon traveling rough-rutted roads. Yet, he was bound there unless a superior officer intervened.

Grandfather Mattson's favorite dictum—"Don't swim the stream when there's a bridge handy"—seemed the best course to pursue. Ty knew of only one senior officer who could rescind Lieutenant Shannon's orders.

"General Morgan will vouch for me," Ty said.

Perplexed, Lieutenant Shannon's fingers stopped short of Ty's revolver. "He will, will he? Have you ever met the general in person? Has he even so much as laid an eye on you?"

"No, sir. General Morgan has been a friend of my father's since the Mexican War," Ty answered. "I'm certain my father mentioned me to him."

Lieutenant Shannon's sun-scorched face leaned within an inch of Ty's nose. Silent seconds ticked away. The lieutenant straightened. "All right, General Morgan will decide whether or not you're to be treated as a prisoner. I won't risk insulting Owen Mattson by refusing his would-be son. Just remember, General Morgan is busy issuing orders for a midnight march. His subordinates may turn us away. That happens, it's the wagon bed for you. Understood?"

Ty nodded. He'd thrown his eggs in a single basket of his own choosing and would suffer the consequences without complaint.

Lieutenant Shannon extended a hand. "I'll have that pistol. I

don't disobey orders. Private Hargrove, tend to this lad's horse."
Sliding Ty's Remington behind his silver-buckled belt, Lieutenant Shannon said sharply, "Follow me, Mr. Ty Mattson."

Wending his way through the crowd occupying the porch of
the Rainer home, Lieutenant Shannon managed to squeeze Ty
through the front door. Inside, the parlor reeked of dried sweat,
horsehair, cigar smoke, and coal oil fumes. Both Ty and Lieutenant Shannon were taller than almost all of the gathered
troopers. Their height gave them a clear view of what held the
troopers' attention like a magnet gripping iron. A rectangular
table blocked the doorway accessing the kitchen and behind it
sat General John Hunt Morgan.

Ty couldn't help staring. He had heard and read of General
John Hunt Morgan's daring raids behind Union lines, his spec-
tacular victories over superior forces, his numerous narrow escapes from pursuing blue-belly cavalry, infantry, and militia, but
the significance of those feats paled upon sighting the general in
the flesh.

General John Hunt Morgan was strikingly handsome and
dressed in a civilian suit of black broadcloth. A black hat, right
side pinned up by golden wreath-around-a-tree embroidery,
rested on the table at his elbow. His hands were small and white
for a cavalryman. He had a fair complexion, and his mustache
and imperial beard were finely trimmed. Dark auburn hair
framed his high forehead. His keen gray-blue eyes sparkled with
mirth, and the smile that greeted those stepping before him to
report and receive orders displayed perfect white teeth.

In a makeshift war room, ripe with tension and tiptoe hurry,
he affected a casual air that relaxed his junior officers and their
subordinates; yet he kept the proceedings moving at a steady, decisive pace. In Ty's mind, Morgan was exactly as the Northern
and Southern newspapers described him: the dashing, mounted
cavalier who rivaled Francis Marion, the "Swamp Fox" of Revo-

lutionary War fame. There was no in-between ground with John Hunt Morgan. Like the pro-Union reporters stated repeatedly, you either loved him or hated him.

Ty doubted that General Morgan would have time to bother with him. Preparing for a midnight march after a full day in the saddle was exhausting enough without adding the burden of a minor affair to his plate—one that could wait until morning.

Fortunately, Lieutenant Shannon didn't share his doubts. The lieutenant waved one of his huge revolvers back and forth above his head for what seemed an eternity. A bespectacled, blond-bearded lieutenant, the sleeves of his Zouave jacket studded with bright coral buttons, was bent over a mound of papers at the end of General Morgan's table. He eventually spied the waving revolver. Recognizing Lieutenant Shannon, he pointed to the corner of the room directly behind him.

"We'll have our audience with General Morgan," Lieutenant Shannon said, pushing into the crowd. "Lieutenant Hardesty is Morgan's adjutant. He has his ear."

Once key orders were issued, an astonished Ty watched the Rainer parlor empty in less than a half hour, except for Lieutenant Hardesty and General Morgan's grizzled black servant, Old Box, lingering with a last pot of coffee for his master. Lieutenant Hardesty signed a concluding document and stored his steel pen and capped ink vial in a leather case. Signaling to Lieutenant Shannon and Ty, he said, "Please state your business, Lieutenant."

"We need to talk briefly with General Morgan, sir."

"Is it really important, Lieutenant? Can't it wait until the general gets some much-needed sleep?"

Expecting Lieutenant Hardesty to protect his worn-down superior officer, Lieutenant Shannon assured him, "It's a personal matter that involves Captain Mattson."

The mention of Captain Mattson's name alerted General

Morgan, who placed his coffee cup on the table and glanced over his shoulder. "Captain Owen Mattson, is it? Come around here, where I can speak with you, Lieutenant."

Ty's hopes soared. Either his father was a sincere friend of the general's or was held in utmost esteem as a member of the general's personal staff. Maybe it was both. Still, his knees were shaking something awful when the general greeted him with his lady-killing smile. Ty discovered that standing before a great military leader was very intimidating, if not downright frightening.

"Well, out with it, Lieutenant," General Morgan ordered, "or we'll be in the saddle again without any rest tonight."

"Sir, we captured this sprout on the south road. He claims he's Captain Mattson's son. While he's never met you in person, he says you know of him and can vouch for him."

General Morgan frowned and said, "No, I don't know of him. Owen has never acknowledged having a son."

Ty's heart sank. It was a night in manacles for certain, and possibly nothing to eat, to boot.

General Morgan's keen gray-blue eyes locked on Ty. "But with that crazy red hair and green eyes, he could be Owen's offspring. What's your assessment, Sergeant?"

"Sir, he certainly has Captain Mattson's hair and eyes, and he's dressed like the rest of us Texans fighting with you. Might interest you that he talked the sentries into keeping his pistol."

General Morgan's smile vanished. "Are you that clever, young man, or our sentries so lacking in training and good judgment?"

Ty prayed his explanation didn't spark the reprimanding of Sergeant Lockhart. He spoke slowly to keep a tight rein on his nerves. "Sir, after I told the sentries my name, they asked for my Remington. I told them Father trained me to never relinquish my weapon. Sergeant Lockhart reminded the other sentries that Captain Mattson preached just that during drill, and they let me keep my weapon."

32

General Morgan smiled. "Given Owen's zeal for training and his reputation, I can imagine that happening. Don't be too hard on the sentries, Lieutenant. We'll arrive in Brandenburg just after daylight. I'm placing this young man in your custody. He may have use of his horse, but not his revolver. If he is Owen's son, it will be interesting to observe how well he follows in his father's footsteps. He has some mighty big boots to fill, mighty big."

With that, General Morgan's amused chuckle of anticipation ushered Ty and Lieutenant Shannon into the night; with each stride, Ty's worry mounted.

Just how big were Owen Mattson's boots?

CHAPTER 3

By midmorning of the next day, Ty Mattson was miserable.
Except for a few minutes after midnight on the evening he
departed Elizabethtown, and a brief respite following his audience with General Morgan and a hasty meal late yesterday
evening, he hadn't slept a wink in sixty-plus hours. Every solitary
part of his body screamed for rest and sleep.

Even worse, throughout the night, he rode at the tail end of
the column with Lieutenant Shannon and the rear guard. The
dust churned up by eight-thousand-odd hoofs filled the air with
a thick, stifling dirt fog, which filled his ears, nose, and eyes. The
dust covered his hat and shoulders and crept inside his shirt. He
kept his mouth moist by sucking on a small white stone provided
by the lieutenant.

He vowed he would acquire a bandana before he swallowed
another morsel of food. Better yet, though the chances were little to none for an individual not listed on the muster roll of any
company in the column, Ty still wondered, what was required to
gain the privilege of riding in the van instead of the rear?

The length of Ty's ride since Elizabethtown added to his discomfort. He'd never spent more than an entire morning in the

saddle. On horse-buying and horse-selling jaunts to Lexington, Louisville, Georgetown, and Brandenburg, he and his grandfather had traveled by horse-drawn buggy. Livery servants had handled the loose animals both ways. The friction between his woolen trousers and saddle leather galled his thighs and spawned blisters on his hindquarters. He marveled that General Morgan's troopers spent day after day in the saddle. There had to be some secret to their lower-body parts tolerating excessive time on horseback; at the first opportunity, ignorant Ty wasn't above asking Lieutenant Shannon what that secret was.

Being new to the rapidly changing nature of a military campaign, Ty had no inkling how much his tiredness and discomfort would be rendered inconsequential when they crested the steep hill overlooking Brandenburg. Ty had known from early childhood that he was gifted with exceptional eyesight. He possessed the ability to discern at great distances and in great detail things that were fuzzy and indistinguishable to others.

The events unfolding below his perch on Brandenburg Hill thrilled him to the bone. The hoof-churned road beneath them descended sharply into the cluster of buildings and homes bunched at the waterfront. At the bottom of the town wharf, the thousand-yard-wide, muddy current of the high-running Ohio stretched east and west for miles. Across the river loomed the immediate objective of General Morgan's army—the lush shore of Indiana, punctuated by farmhouses, with orange haystacks in golden fields, and swatches of trees and underbrush, which were light green along the shore and dark green on the overlooking ridge.

Ty spotted troopers on the Indiana bank, but no horses. The dismounted troopers were hurriedly taking cover in the nearest stand of trees. On the near bank moored at the Brandenburg Wharf was a packet steamboat, JOHN B. MCCOMBS painted on a sign atop its wheelhouse, and a smaller steamboat, the *Alice Dean*, both with stilled paddles. Their gangplanks were empty.

Neither cavalrymen nor horses were being loaded. The troopers had sought cover with their mounts behind town buildings and in the woods bordering Brandenburg.

A sharp report echoing through the river bottom accounted for the unnatural lack of activity on the near bank. Ty tensed in the saddle. He'd never witnessed armies firing at each other. Truth was, he was pure green when it came to soldiering. He'd never been shot at, nor had he ever shot at another human being.

A small ship steamed from upriver, black smoke spewing from its single stack. Ty had gleaned sufficient nautical terminology from the volumes in Grandfather Mattson's library to categorize the fast-approaching vessel. The snub-nosed craft was armored with iron plating. Three howitzers protruded from embrasures cut through the iron plating and the heavy oak timbers beneath it. It was a Yankee gunboat, a bulldog whose bark preceded a dangerously sharp bite.

A bluish white, funnel-shaped cloud spouted from the gunboat's left bow as she launched a shell that had troopers cringing as it hit and exploded in the middle of Brandenburg's main street. The gunboat then snapped a shell at the scrambling troopers on the opposite bank. Ty was absorbing a vital lesson in how the fortunes of war turned with the flip of a coin. General Morgan's ferryboats were as vulnerable as sitting ducks to shellfire. One small gunboat was holding a two-thousand-man army at bay, allowing Union forces in hot pursuit to gain ground and imperil the success of Morgan's mission.

"Where are Captain Byrnes and our artillery?" Lieutenant Shannon inquired aloud.

Round shot began pelting the gunboat—solid balls sending up tall geysers of water or thudding against its armor, shells bursting in flashes of red flame. The Confederate balls were coming from two 12-pound howitzers positioned on a rising eminence along the Ohio, north of Brandenburg. Ty couldn't tell if Captain

Byrnes's shells were inflicting any real damage on the snub-
nosed ship, but they were forcing it to change course frequently
to present a moving target and interfering with the accuracy of
its howitzers.

After an hour of exchanging fire, the Federal gunboat withdrew up the Ohio. Its retreat was akin to a dam bursting. Horse
holders hustled to the wharf and the ferrying of the horses belonging to the troopers on the Indiana shore commenced.

Lieutenant Shannon tracked the withdrawing gunboat with
his telescope. "She was the *Springfield.*"

"Yes, sir," Ty agreed. "The letters on the bow were awfully
small and one of our rounds splintered the wood there, but you
could read them if you looked close."

"That was half a mile away. You can see that well, lad?"

"Yes, sir, I can see individual feathers on birds at fifty yards,"
Ty said with no hint of the braggart in his voice. "A farmer is
hiding in that big white barn across the river, well over to our
left. The peak of his straw hat is showing above the bottom sill
of the hayloft door."

Lieutenant Shannon trained his telescope in that direction.
"By damned, he's there, all right. Eyesight like yours, lad, could
be plumb useful to General Morgan's scout company and advance guard. I'll make mention of you in my report."

The lieutenant's observation pleased Ty greatly. He had
wracked his brain during the entire night ride trying to determine how an untrained, inexperienced, would-be cavalryman
might be accepted into the ranks of General Morgan's raiders.
Maybe his keen eyesight was his ticket to enlistment.

An officer riding a Denmark Thoroughbred joined Lieutenant Shannon and Ty. "Lieutenant, you may send word to the
general that mounted vedettes are patrolling the Brandenburg
road at five hundred yards, and sentries are guarding the road at
one hundred yards. Per his orders, they will remain in place until
they're called to board the last ferry departing the wharf."

The large-mouthed, fish-eyed officer cleared his throat, hawked, and spat. He surveyed Ty from hat to spurs and said, "I've been meaning to ask, Lieutenant, who's this Texas pup? You find him hiding under a rain barrel in Garnettsville?"

"No, sir, Captain Bell, he found us," Lieutenant Shannon said. "He claims he's Captain Mattson's son."

"Aw, owl shit, Shawn," Captain Bell said, forgetting rank for the moment. "That's the biggest whopper I've ever heard. If Owen had any offspring, he wouldn't be drifting around the country unclaimed. Owen wouldn't abide it."

"Well, Clute, we'll find out shortly, one way or the other," Shawn Shannon said.

"Sweet Jesus, I hope I'm there when they meet up," Captain Bell said. "I'd fork over a year's pay just for the chance to catch Owen speechless for the first time in memory."

Ty assumed from Captain Bell's depiction that Owen Mattson was a man seldom surprised by circumstance or the men around him—the unflappable officer always in control—the exact opposite of how Ty saw himself. He was beginning to wish he'd stayed home instead of diving into this sea of uncertainty.

While Ty both wanted and dreaded the initial meeting of father and son, that meeting couldn't happen any too soon. The tight knot in his belly would gnaw at his shaky confidence until he learned how his father reacted to his sudden, unsolicited appearance.

"Come along, lad. We'll squeeze past the troopers clogging the road and wait for General Morgan at the wharf," Shawn Shannon said, pulling Ty's Remington from his belt. The lieutenant rolled his fingers, reversing the pistol, and offered the weapon to Ty, butt first, a clever maneuver foreign to Ty, one that reinforced how unschooled he was with firearms.

"No need for anyone to think you're a prisoner," Lieutenant Shannon said by way of explanation. "Either you're Owen's son or the gutsiest spy I've ever encountered."

Lieutenant Shannon dispatched a messenger to inform General Morgan as to status of the rear guard, and stationed Ty and himself at the railing of the wharf, where they watched officers guide men and horses across the gangplanks of the two steamers for the balance of the afternoon. A scrawny, white-goateed private missing his teeth kept them from starving. He delivered a rasher of salt pork, pole bread, and a flask of brandy mixed with milk.

"That's Private E.J. Pursley," Lieutenant Shannon said. "Can't hit his own ass at close range with a pistol, but he can find vittles in the middle of Texas brush country."

At five o'clock in the evening, Ty was standing on the ground, leaning against Reb, half asleep, when the lieutenant announced the First Brigade was on Indiana soil, which meant the other half of General Morgan's command remained in Kentucky.

The two steamboats initiated the ferrying of the Second Brigade. Cannon boomed and all eyes swept upriver. The *Springfield* had returned with a second Federal gunboat. The troopers waiting to board the *Alice Dean* froze into stone, awaiting orders whether to continue loading or seek cover. One wrong move or word might well turn a controlled situation into absolute chaos.

A thunderous voice sang out: "Hold your ranks! Hold your ranks!" The waiting line of horse holders eased apart, creating an aisle for a captain mounted on a chestnut gelding, with a blazed face and four white stockings.

The captain continued to shout orders as he advanced. "Hold your ranks! Control your animals! Ignore the gunboats! Captain Byrnes's artillery will deal with them."

The rider drew abreast of Ty and Lieutenant Shannon. He sat his horse with uncommon grace. Somehow, he seemed familiar to Ty.

The captain removed his hat and acknowledged the troopers softly hailing him. The exposed red hair, emerald green eyes, and white teeth visible when he smiled jolted the sleep from Ty and brought him up on his tiptoes. He was exactly as Boone Jordan had described him, right down to square shoulders and well-deep voice.

He was staring at Captain Owen Matson.

His father.

CHAPTER 4

Ty realized his father was staring back at him.
Dare he speak?

He opened his mouth. Excitement had knotted his tongue and he couldn't utter a sound. His father dismounted and led the chestnut onto the gangplank of the *Alice Dean*. Then he was gone, lost in the mass of horses crowding the steamship's stern.

"You sure you're Owen's son?" Lieutenant Shannon asked. "He didn't show any sign he recognized you."

Ty recovered from the shock of seeing his father in the flesh, fulfilling a lifelong dream at last. To get that close to him again, he couldn't lose the trust of Lieutenant Shannon. "Lieutenant, the only way you'll understand about Father and me is to hear me out."

Smiling, the lieutenant said, "I bet it's a corker of a tale, and I've time to listen. Have at it, lad.'

Ty decided the best place to start was by explaining his talk with Boone Jordan that had set him chasing after his father. The lieutenant proved a rapt listener. He was much more interested in what Ty had to say than the artillery duel between the *Prince-*

43

ton, her cohort, and Captain Byrnes's howitzers, which ended with the Federal gunboats churning upriver into the dark night.

By the time Ty finished, Lieutenant Shannon's head was shaking, not from doubt, but from wonderment. "Wildest story I've ever heard. Your grandfather and your paw have to be the two most stubborn people from Kentucky ever, and that's a bunch of folks."

"What do I do now?" an uncertain Ty asked.

"You best stick with me. Owen and I are on detached duty with General Morgan's staff. We're the general's eyes and ears when his command's on the move or engaging the enemy. He can't always rely on his young messengers. I'll escort you to General Morgan's headquarters, wherever that might be tonight. Sooner or later, Owen will report to him. That suit you?"

"Yes, sir. I don't relish stumbling around in the dark, asking directions to Father from armed strangers."

The ferriage of the Second Brigade lasted until midnight. Late in the evening, General Morgan and his personal entourage arrived at the Brandenburg Wharf. Messengers, dressed mainly in farm clothes, a few too young to shave, and one a mere stripling, if Ty guessed correctly, all led their mounts aboard the *John B. McCombs* with the horse-handling skill of veteran cavalrymen. If there was a place for those puppies in Morgan's ranks, there had to be one for Ty, too.

Black servants traveling on foot, wearing captured blue uniforms, carried items in hampers, baskets, and cloth bags. Apparently, General Morgan didn't completely forgo the comforts of Hopemont, his Lexington home, while serving in the field.

General Morgan was leading a handsome charger. Ty learned later the gelding was Glencoe, the general's favorite saddler. Lieutenant Shannon came to attention and saluted. Not being a trooper, Ty doffed his hat and stood ramrod straight.

General Morgan returned the salute and said, "You still have your young charge in tow, Lieutenant. I believe that's a pistol hanging from his belt. You've confirmed his identity?"

"To my satisfaction, sir."

"What about with Captain Mattson? Has be been introduced to his mysterious son?"

"Not yet. I've learned the boy's story of how he got here. Owen's in for quite a surprise, sir."

General Morgan threw back his head and laughed. "Oh yes, but isn't he now! Lieutenant, thanks for finding a spot of humor in a long, long day. I'm pushing inland once I'm across the river and we have ships to burn. Please remain with the rear guard and confirm their destruction to me personally. Captain Bell is in command."

Ty was initially appalled at the thought of burning the two steamboats. The flaking paint and dull varnish of the smaller *Alice Dean*'s wheelhouse and superstructure revealed her age, an old Federal mail packet that had plied the waters of the Ohio for a considerable number of years On the other hand, by her spotless hull, white painted wheelhouse, polished woodwork, shiny brass fixtures, and powerful boiler, the larger *John B. McCombs*, with her spacious passenger cabin and cargo rigging, was a vessel that had cost tens of thousands of dollars to build.

To destroy either of them willfully seemed a terrible crime to Ty. Grandfather Mattson considered private property a sacred possession. The burning, looting, or theft of another person's property was tantamount to murder. But while appalled, Ty wasn't naïve.

If the steamboats weren't destroyed, what guarantee was there the pursuing Yankee cavalry wouldn't make use of them? As long as Union horsemen were stranded on the south bank of the Ohio, General Morgan's lead on them would increase by the hour—each hour gained being a decided advantage for his invading force.

Lieutenant Shannon and Ty crossed the river on the final passage of the *John B. McCombs*. Reb took the boat ride like he was grazing on fresh grass. Ty was beginning to respect the gray's demeanor. While nothing disturbed him—cannon fire, the proximity of other horses in a crowded cargo bay, shadows in the night—Reb was alert and ready to respond to Ty's wishes at the slightest tug of his reins. Ty owed a big debt to Boone Jordan's knowledge of horses.

A new development awaited them on the Indiana bank. Captain Clute Bell, fish eyes big as saucers in the deck lamps of the *John B. McCombs*, met them at the foot of the gangplank. "Been a change of plans, Shawn. Captain Ballard is an old acquaintance of Colonel Duke's. On the strength of Ballard's promise to sail the *McCombs* upriver to keep the blue bellies from seizing it, General Morgan decided to spare his ship. Our orders to burn the *Alice Dean* stand."

A half hour of hard work freed the two packets of Rebel horses, troopers, and equipment. The *John B. McCombs* departed for Louisville at full speed. The captain of the *Alice Dean*, a diminutive, spade-bearded individual in frock coat and leather-billed cap with gold piping, was forced from his cabin at gunpoint; his ranting curses bluing the air.

"Wouldn't want to meet up with him again if he held the gun," Captain Bell said. "There's a lot of heat in his boiler."

The *Alice Dean*'s layers of old paint and varnish erupted into flame at the touch of a match. Her superstructure virtually exploded when the fire reached her upper decks. In minutes, the packet boat was a great, raging torch. The glare from the burning boat illuminated the Ohio for miles, turning night into day for those watching on the Indiana and Kentucky banks of the Ohio.

Lieutenant Shannon was the first to hear the nasty whine of a bullet. A soft *plopping* tweaked Ty's ear. Then rifle balls were zipping by. The shrill whinnying of a horse in pain excited the confused troopers. A trooper at water's edge warned, "It's the blue bellies. They can see us from Brandenburg."

"Mount up," Captain Bell ordered. "We've finished our business here."

Ty needed no additional urging to fly into Reb's saddle. They raced for the woods beyond the effective range of the sniping blue bellies, unaware that the *Alice Dean*'s captain and his crew were venting their frustration by chucking rocks after them until they realized the Union bullets were just as deadly to them and sought cover.

At Captain Bell's command Ty slowed Reb to a walk. The boat fire on the river was bright as lanterns amongst the covering trees. Lieutenant Shannon winked at Ty. "Something's wrong with your hat, lad."

Ty plucked his hat from his head. The brim was flat all the way around. The brass star, which had pinned up the right side, was missing. Ty gulped. That soft *plopping* he'd heard was a bullet snipping the brass star from his hat a mere four inches above his ear.

His jaw quivering, Ty made no mention of the near miss to Lieutenant Shannon. No matter how hard he gripped his saddle horn during their ride to General Morgan's headquarters, he couldn't keep his hands from trembling.

Welcome to the war, Mr. Ty Mattson.

CHAPTER 5

Bugles awakened Ty with the first trace of light in the eastern sky. He felt as if he hadn't slept a solitary wink. The sultry air of the barnyard smelled of horses and the smoke of cooking fires. He rolled over and rubbed the gumminess from his eyes, lingering too long in his gum poncho, single-blanket bed to suit Private Pursley, who shook him with a knotty fist, though Ty was clearly awake.

Ty gained his feet and found Lieutenant Shannon and six troopers watching him with bemused smiles. The slim trooper with the waxed mustache, which filled his nostrils and circled the corners of his mouth, said, "Sort of laggardly for Owen Mattson's son, ain't he?"

"More than likely he's trainable, Cally," Lieutenant Shannon said. "Ty, we arrived too late for introductions last night. Private Cally Smith here is from Georgetown. He was in the marble business with his father. The two hefty jaspers that wear out horses are Privates Ad and Ebb White. They're from the Tennessee border and are best known for the quality of their corn squeezin's."

Each messmate nodded as he was introduced. "Corporal Sam Bryant, in the spotless uniform and ruffled shirt, owns a candy store with his family in Lexington. These two bashful Texans are Privates Given Campbell and Harlan Stillion. They followed me into this cussed fighting. They charge blue-belly companies for the sheer hell of it. You already know Private E.J. Pursley. There may not be much of him, and he's old as dirt, but he's the finest camp cook in this-here army. He can have your mouth watering with a stalk of rhubarb and a pinch of salt."

"What's in that skillet, E.J.?" asked Ebb White.

"You're mighty lucky this morning, gents. Colonel Johnson's foragers happened on a gristmill five miles east before daylight. The owner refused payment in Richmond greenbacks, so our boys burned his mill and helped themselves to five barrels of flour. And while the bunch of you sawed logs with Satan, I raided that big chicken coop over behind the hay barn. So you're about to enjoy E.J. Pursley's New Orleans 'waker upper.' Flour and eggs mixed with water and seasoned with salt and a dab of bacon fat. The Creole girls thought it was the hair of the dog after drinking too much champagne."

"You going to talk us to death or feed us, E.J.," Cally Smith said.

"He's right, E.J.," Lieutenant Shannon said. "If we don't hurry it up, we'll be short on time for saddling."

The messmates joshed and jabbered throughout their breakfast, eating from tin plates with twined forks. To Ty, they appeared a close-knit mess that avoided fussing with rank or authority when the occasion allowed. They would not readily accept strangers. You were one of them when they invited you to join their mess, not because of an officer's order.

Cally Smith said out of the blue, "That a Remington pistol you're toting, lad? Like to have a look at it, if you don't mind."

Ty hesitated, not certain how best to refuse. He preferred not to be disrespectful to any trooper, regardless of rank, but he wasn't about to relinquish his revolver to someone who was not a superior officer, and he'd met just fifteen minutes ago, come what may.

Ty's hesitation riled Cally who was seated next to him and saw nothing wrong with what he thought was a harmless request spawned by his natural curiosity about firearms. "Pass it along, pup," Cally said sharply, thrusting his hand toward Ty. "I won't steal it, for God's sake."

Almost before he realized what he was doing, Ty reached beneath his tin plate, grasped the butt of the Remington, yanked it from his holster, and cocked it as he aligned its sights with Cally Smith's chest.

"Seems to me you've prodded a young rattlesnake mighty touchy about his pistol, Cally," Given Campbell said in his burry drawl. "Down Texas way, that can get a man killed right quick."

Cally leaned backward, glaring at Ty.

"Ask yourself, Cally," Lieutenant Shannon said, tone soft and patient, "would you have dared demand that of his father?"

The anger ran out of Cally Smith fast as water thrown from a fire bucket. The marble merchant raised placating palms and said, "No offense intended. I was out of my pen."

Ty holstered the Remington and offered Cally Smith his hand. "No offense taken, Private Smith. I'm new to the cavalry. I've no real training and I'm not always certain what's expected of me."

Ty and Cally shook hands and exchanged smiles. It was a satisfactory resolution in Shawn Shannon's mind to a minor set-to, one that could have resulted in bad feelings and grudges, the bane of the battlefield. He wouldn't forget, though, that Ty Mattson had shown a lot of sand for his age.

"Empty your plates, boys. By all that commotion at the farmhouse, General Morgan's about to make an appearance."

General John Hunt Morgan appeared fresh and rested despite the ordeal of his march across Kentucky. He spoke from the farm porch with an inclusive gaze filled with such personal warmth that each officer and trooper believed he was being talked to personally. "We are on Indiana soil at last, are we not?"

Hats flew and lusty cheers rang out in every corner of the barnyard. Positioned at General Morgan's side on the covered porch, Colonels Basil Duke and Adam Johnson, commanding officers of the First and Second Brigades, joined in with much verve.

General Morgan called for quiet. "We face a momentous task. Our orders will take us to the far corners of Ohio. The enemy soldiery will outnumber us twenty to one. Telegraph lines stretching across the country in every direction will constantly report our movements. Railways will bring assailants against us from every quarter. We will have to run this gauntlet for six hundred miles. It will be a long, hard, dangerous ride, but never forget for a moment that General Bragg is counting upon us. President Davis is counting upon us. The entire Confederacy is counting upon us. We must not fail. Defeat and disgrace are becoming to no man and to no country."

General Morgan paused, and then he flashed his famous smile. Nodding at Colonels Duke and Johnson, he said, "To horse, gentlemen. The enemy expects us. Let's not disappoint him."

The speech sent Ty's blood racing. He couldn't wait to engage the Yankees. He felt sorry for the hundreds of troopers who weren't present and would be told of this magnificent speech secondhand, for any man hearing it in person would deny their leader nothing—even if it meant sacrificing his own life.

After a final round of cheers for General Morgan, the barnyard became a swarming beehive. Orders for the day were issued and mounted messengers hustled from camp to deliver them. Mess gear disappeared into storage trunks. Cooking fires were doused and canteens filled at the nearby creek. Horses were saddled and cinches double-checked. Firearms received a final inspection for clear barrels and proper charges.

"Is your Remington revolver fully loaded, Ty?" Lieutenant Shannon inquired.

"Yes, sir, it is," Ty said.

"Take the cap from the ball beneath the hammer so that chamber can't fire by accident. When you're riding hard, you'd be surprised how easy it is to shoot yourself in the leg or kill a fine horse. I saw it happen, same as your father."

Lieutenant Shannon watched Ty remove the cap. "Did Boone Jordan supply you with extra cylinders?"

"Yes, sir. They're in my shoulder bag, but I haven't loaded them yet."

"Load them with powder and ball, but not with caps. Capped cylinders bounce against each other in your bag and they might fire off a round."

Ty absorbed Lieutenant Shannon's instructions with the concentration of a green recruit. Everything the lieutenant taught him diminished the chance he would embarrass his father.

He finished loading the chambers of his spare cylinders with powder and ball, returned them to his shoulder bag, and hoped he wasn't being too forward when he asked, "Where's Captain Mattson this morning, Lieutenant? He wasn't at General Morgan's headquarters, was he?"

"No, he's out front. He'll be where the next battle will be fought. That's his prime skill. Seeing the elephant close enough to look him straight in the eye is second nature to him."

Ty had no clue what the lieutenant meant by "seeing the elephant." But in light of General Morgan's speech, he didn't think much time would pass before he did.

The stripling messenger Ty had watched board the *John B. McCombs* ahead of General Morgan fetched Lieutenant Shannon his written orders for the day. The lieutenant read the single sheet of paper and motioned for his messmates to gather around Ty and himself. "We've been assigned to the Fourteenth Kentucky Cavalry Advance Guard, under the command of Colonel Richard Morgan, General Morgan's brother. Colonel Morgan will lead the advance. We're to join Quirk's Scout Company. Given and Harlan, you'll feel right at home with that bunch of rowdy roughnecks. Our next objective is Corydon, Indiana. Ty, you can ride with us, if you prefer."

Ty gladly accepted the lieutenant's invitation. He didn't want to be detailed to the rear guard or another mundane function buried in the column. He'd already eaten enough dust for three lifetimes.

The road to Corydon wound through alternating patches of ripening corn and woodland, rowed trees defining individual properties. Each farmhouse encountered was carefully scouted, though the occupants had fled in haste, leaving doors wide open. With the locals aware of the horse-stealing talents of the raiders, good horses were scarce in number. Nags were plentiful.

"They learn we're coming by saddle telegraph. They run for the nearest cave or town," Cally Smith said. "Mean and decrepit as we appear, I believe I'd be right on their heels, was I in their shoes."

Ty found the dust from trailing after thirty horses versus two thousand was child's play. His thighs and buttocks still ached, but much less after just a few hours out of the saddle. He was certain the pain would return as the day advanced and his raw blisters burst anew.

Lieutenant Shannon's verbal instructions and training continued as they rode. "Ty, whenever we meet the enemy, you're to remain in the rear, and I mean what I say. I don't want you wrapped in a burying blanket when your father comes calling. Understood?"

At Ty's nod, the lieutenant asked, "Is your horse gun broke?"

"Yes, sir."

"Have you ever fired a revolver from the saddle of a horse?"

"No, sir."

"On the outside chance you might find yourself in a skirmish with the blue bellies or their home guard militia, shooting from a standing horse is the same as target practice on the ground with your arm fully extended. From a running horse, you rise slightly in the stirrups for better balance with your arm half extended, body turned toward the target. Again, whether at a trot or gallop, shoot with your arm half extended and body turned toward the target. And always remember there's a horse under you. Many a green trooper gets excited in battle and shoots his own horse in the head."

Lieutenant Shannon swiped sweat from his forehead with the back of his hand. "There won't be time for any serious field training, fast as we'll be moving day and night. I'll stick to what will keep you alive, the same as Owen would."

The terrain gradually melded into rolling hills overshot with ravines and abrupt changes in elevation. Every sharp rise of ground or hairpin turn in the road was a mystery as to whether the enemy lurked ahead. With church bells in Corydon pealing a warning to the local populace, the scout company finished climbing a low hill, about two miles short of the city.

At the bottom of the hill, a patrol of home guards in slouch hats and cotton frocks reined their horses about and spurred madly to the north. A half mile ahead of them, a solid barricade of logs, wormwood fence rails, and rocks festooned with gun barrels on the far side blocked the road—the first sign of organized resistance in Indiana.

Lieutenant Shannon and Ty rode forward alongside Colonel Richard Morgan. "Colonel, this young man has remarkable eyesight. Ty, who's manning that barricade?"

Ty took his time, wanting to insure the information he passed to Colonel Morgan was accurate. "There are about four hundred of them, which I can see They're mostly militia in field clothes and mechanic's overalls, armed with squirrel guns, muskets, and an ancient blunderbuss matching the one on the wall in my grandfather's library. His father brought it to Kentucky from the old country."

Colonel Morgan whistled between his teeth. "That's the most succinct observation I've ever heard from a scout without a telescope. Who is this young man, Lieutenant?"

"His name is Ty Mattson, sir."

Colonel Morgan enjoyed a barking laugh. "Oh, Captain Owen Mattson's mysterious, unclaimed son, huh? General Morgan mentioned his presence at our morning staff meeting. Staff officers are betting each other on what will happen when the two meet each other."

Ty was beginning to wonder if every member of General Morgan's staff hadn't heard he and his father's story. Maybe he should have stayed home and joined the blue-belly army; there he would have been a common soldier, like everyone else, and not the object of so much public speculation, which made his stomach downright queasy.

Captain Thomas Hines, of Quirk's Scouts, reported for orders. "They're untrained militia," Colonel Morgan informed him. "We'll notify Colonel Johnson's Second Brigade and call for support, if needed. The speed afoot of retreating home guards is legendary. They've never held against us. Prepare to charge, Captain Hines."

Quirk's Scouts, followed by the Fourteenth Kentucky, eighty-seven total troopers, descended the hill in ranks of four at a trot. At the bottom, they fanned out with the widening of the road and spilled over into the planted fields bordering its hard surface, forming a line forty yards wide and three troopers deep, cornstalks slapping against the chests of the trotting horses.

Instigated by Colonel Morgan, the cry of "Buglers, blow 'Charge!'" sounded clarion clear, a fateful command that unraveled the peaceful, hot, sun-bright morning with brain-numbing speed.

Ty was in the extreme rear, per Lieutenant Shannon's orders, with every honest intention of remaining there. He was standing in the stirrups for a better view of the barricaded militia when bugles echoed in the valley: the front line of troopers broke into a gallop and Reb lunged ahead without any warning. Nearly unseated, he grasped the saddle horn with both hands, giving Reb a free rein. In five strides, the gray gelding was running at a full gallop and Ty was charging the enemy, orders be damned.

He sawed on the reins, but Reb had the bit in his teeth, determined to catch his hoofed cohorts. Ty's initial fear ebbed and he carefully drew his Remington, fingers locked on its walnut grips. Clods of dirt torn loose by the racing animals in front of him peppered his face and eyes, and he dropped beside Reb's neck. Under the same earthen assault, Reb didn't falter. Boone Jordan hadn't told Ty about Reb's whole history, but the horse surely had been a cavalry mount in the past.

Ty was suddenly spurring Reb, completely immersed in a reckless, dangerous, and spontaneous undertaking that might cost him his life any second. Screeching rebel yells rose from the ranks of the raiders. Ty drew breath into lungs starved by excitement and joined them.

Lancing flame erupted the length of the barricade blocking the road; wisely, the home guard had waited until the onrushing enemy was virtually in their laps before firing their first volley. At close range, the barricade seemed too high for a jumping horse to clear. Not a single raider tugged on his reins.

Ty watched leaping horses fall short, smash into the breastworks, and slew sideways in a mass of thrashing hoofs and flailing human arms and legs as their riders struggled to avoid the crushing impact of a nearly two-thousand-pound animal. Other horses cleared the barricade without difficulty, their riders firing downward at defiant militia while in the air.

Ty sensed Reb gathering his legs beneath him; then the big gray soared upward. He leaned forward, too busy maintaining his seat in the saddle to search for targets beneath the gray's belly. Reb's rear hoof clipped the top rail of the barricade. They landed with Ty still in the saddle and galloped onward through terrified home guards desperate to avoid Reb's iron shoes.

The scurrying crowd bumped into each other, and the gathering crush of bodies slowed Reb to a walk. Fingers trying to drag Ty from the saddle clutched his sleeves and pants leg. Realizing he would quickly be overwhelmed on the ground, Ty fired a bullet into the crowd and wheeled Reb on his rear legs, scattering home guards like windblown leaves.

A coal-black gelding cut in front of Reb, his rider's huge nine-round LeMat pistols shooting left and right simultaneously. Somehow Lieutenant Shannon's shout was louder than the roar of guns. "They're blowing 'Recall.' Follow me."

The killing whirlwind on horseback cleaved a clear path to the home guard barricade. Ty was so anxious to escape capture, he even forgot his Remington contained four live rounds. There was no hoof clipping of the top rail this jump.

Hunched low in the saddle to present the smallest possible target, Ty and Shawn Shannon maintained a full gallop until they were beyond rifle range.

Now that the excitement and uproar had ended, the danger was past, and they were safe, Ty was shaking all over.

"Well, lad," Lieutenant Shannon called out, grinning. "You've looked the elephant in the eye. Right big, ain't he?"

CHAPTER 6

Ty's adventures wielding a pistol were finished for the day. General Morgan arrived and agreed with Colonel Johnson, of the Second Brigade, that the Corydon breastworks were too high and too well defended for mounted cavalry to breach. The resulting strategy was the encirclement of both flanks of the barricade, while an on-foot frontal assault, supported by two howitzers, occupied its defenders.

At Lieutenant Shannon's suggestion, an intrigued General Morgan agreed to Ty serving as his "eyes" from the low hill overlooking the battlefield. Ty had stopped shaking from his close brush with death and looked forward without any qualms to watching the conclusion of the battle from safer ground. A hero he was not.

The home guard center repulsed two charges by dismounted raiders before they wilted under heavy cannon and small-arms fire and their flanks collapsed. Realizing their situation was hopeless, the green militia enlistees panicked and fled, discarding weapons, accouterments, and any other possession that might hinder their hasty departure. Ty cheered with General Morgan and the general's fellow officers at the sight of so many Indiana citizens in full flight.

After a quick reconnaissance of the battlefield by their subordinates, Colonels Duke and Johnson informed General Morgan that preliminary counts, yet to be confirmed, indicated raider losses of eight killed and thirty-three wounded and the taking of 340 prisoners. The front lines of the raiders were at that moment in hot pursuit of the retreating enemy not already under guard.

"Gentlemen, mount up," General Morgan said. "We have a town to subdue, prisoners to parole, and dinner to find."

The subduing of Corydon proved a minor affair. With the field secured, a Parrott gun battery was established within easy range of the town. Two shells were fired. One was a dud. Ty saw the second explode in the center of town's main street. He didn't discern any real damage for General Morgan, but the single explosion was sufficient. Colonel Lewis Jordan, of the Indiana Legion, hoisted a white flag and surrendered the town.

The first pubic building spotted by the raiders, a small Presbyterian church, was converted to a field hospital for the wounded. The Confederate dead were placed beneath white sheets in the church's fenced yard. Prisoners being excess baggage for Morgan's rapidly invading command, home guard captives were herded into lines at the limestone courthouse for paroling without arms.

Shouts of indignation on the part of Corydon citizens attracted Ty's attention. Raiders were helping themselves to horses and emerging from retail establishments carrying pants, shirts, boots, and hats by the armfuls, with the complaining sellers dogging their heels. Four Indiana merchants stepped in front of Glencoe and confronted General Morgan.

A florid-faced older male in a black suit, starched snow-white shirt, and red string tie spoke for the four of them. "By what right do your men take what they want and offer worthless Richmond greenbacks or no payment at all in return?"

General Morgan stood in his stirrups and pointed to the hundreds of troopers occupying the town's entire center. "They, sir," he said, "are my authority."

Dropping back into the saddle, General Morgan said, "And what might your name be, sir?"

"Urea Haggy, sir."

"What's your position in this community, Mr. Haggy?"

Skeletal chest puffed, voice dripping with pride, Urea Haggy said, "I'm Corydon's sole banker."

"How fortunate, Mr. Haggy. You are the proper person to carry our demand to your fellow businessmen. My scouts reported there are three gristmills in the Corydon area. It is one o'clock by your courthouse clock. The ransom for each mill is one thousand dollars to be paid by two o'clock. If the monies aren't forthcoming to the minute, we will burn the mills. Understood?"

"But those mills are no threat to you or your men," the outraged Haggy protested vehemently.

"Banker Haggy, you Northerners have enjoyed a full belly and full larder far from the fighting. But the bloom is off the stem. Henceforth, we will provision ourselves from your rich land. Every horse, mill, bridge, trestle, depot, telegraph wire, Federal greenback, morsel of food, and ton of forage are now fair game. We will allow you to experience—as we Southerners have—the harsh bite and deprivation of conflict."

Peering about, General Morgan located his adjutant. "Lieutenant Hardesty, where are we dining?"

"The Eagle Hotel, sir. First-class fare, according to the locals."

Focusing his icy glare on the Corydon merchants again, General Morgan said, "That's where you may bring the ransom. One hour, gentlemen, one hour." His casual, dismissing wave infuriated Urea Haggy. The banker huffed and fumed; but aware any further protests would be of no avail, he shooed his companions toward a brick bank building across the crowded street, which displayed his name in gold-painted script on the front window.

With no specific orders, Ty reined Reb behind Glencoe and Lieutenant Shannon's black gelding. The gist of the general's lecturing of the Corydon citizenry stuck in Ty's craw, for it declared a major shift in tactics for his raiders.

Ty was better educated than some of General Morgan's officers. Grandfather Mattson had an extensive library and the Cincinnati, Louisville, and Lexington newspapers were delivered weekly to the family manse at his grandfather's expense. From the time Ty was twelve years old, his grandfather had insisted that Ty read and digest the papers' contents and be prepared to discuss them at dinner and in the evening hours before bed. Their discussions ranged from the selling prices of Thoroughbreds in the three cities to the seasonal status of the hemp and grain market.

With the advent of the conflict between North and South, the war became a daily topic for the grandfather and grandson. Ty learned early on that Grandfather Mattson believed guerrilla warfare behind established lines of defense was an abomination and violation of the proper conduct of war. To him, General John Hunt Morgan and his raiders were loathsome; they were an affront to decency, deserving nothing but the lynching rope.

Though he didn't dare admit it openly, Ty admired the exciting and daring General Morgan. He could hardly wait for the details of Morgan's latest venture behind enemy lines. He frequently met his grandfather's courier at the bottom of the lane.

Ty didn't sway Grandfather Mattson's opinion whatsoever when he read to him how Morgan's troopers respected civil property and didn't result to horse stealing or general thievery.

They destroyed warehouses containing military stores, depots, telegraph poles, railroad trestles and rolling stock, tore up iron rails and burned wooden ties, and misdirected troop trains with fake telegraphic messages—military tactics designed to disrupt the Union's means of communication, reinforcement, transportation, and supply. Unless they armed themselves and joined the home guards or local militia and stepped into General Morgan's path, civilians were in little danger of harm.

But as Ty had heard just minutes ago, those tactics had undergone a major transformation with the raiders crossing of the Ohio River into Indiana. Horse thievery, ransom for money, looting, and mill burning were now permissible with the blessing of General John Hunt Morgan himself.

Much as Ty wanted to succeed as a soldier and not embarrass his father, the thought of what was in store for the peaceful countryside of Indiana and Ohio made him shudder.

The fare of the Eagle Hotel, if not "first class," a term new to Ty, was certainly belly-filling and tasty. The hotel owner—gray-haired, big-nosed, bull-necked, wearing a stained white apron tied off at the waist—refused to serve uninvited and what would be nonpaying guests, according to the rumors Ty was hearing.

"George Kintner feeds only those welcome at his tables. I leave you to my daughter. Sallie may do as she wishes," the hotel owner said, disappearing into the kitchen.

Sallie Kintner was a yellow-haired, charming gal in her early twenties. She pooh-poohed her father's rude exit and announced, "Dinner is served "

The kitchen door swung open and waiters appeared with platters of roasted beef and fried chicken, large bowls of boiled potatoes and pole beans, and smaller dishes of cove oysters, maize pudding, and sliced cheese. An abundant supply of freshly baked bread, butter, and beef-dripping gravy, along with pots of black coffee and pitchers of milk, reached the table next. Twelve hungry males ate as if they hadn't tasted food for a year of Sundays.

General Morgan was his usual warm, engaging self after the ice-veined confrontation with Urea Haggy. He soon learned that Sallie and her father were originally from Virginia, and Sallie was not totally hostile to the Confederate cause.

Charmed by John Morgan's openness, Sallie Kintner served him an Eagle Hotel delicacy: mint-flavored pudding with dried apples. "I certainly hope you fare better than General Lee and your soldiers at Vicksburg."

"How do you mean that, my dear girl?"

Sallie hesitated, and then said, "Oh, my, you haven't heard. General Lee has been defeated at Gettysburg, and the Confederate Army besieged at Vicksburg surrendered to General Grant."

"Are you sure of what you say, young lady?"

Placing her coffeepot on a nearby sideboard, Sallie walked to the hotel lobby and returned with the latest editions of the *Indianapolis Star* and the *Corydon Weekly Democrat*. One glance at the headlines and dispatches from the Union War Department confirmed her truthfulness.

The instantaneous change in General John Hunt Morgan's demeanor astonished onlookers. His eyes clouded and the corners of his mouth tightened. His crestfallen, mournful expression revealed a side of their commanding officer that his staff had not been permitted to see.

Their superior sat silently for a long minute. Straightening his shoulders, he gathered himself and perused every single face in the room. "Gentlemen, this is news we prayed we'd never receive. The righteous cause so dear to our hearts has suffered a serious blow. But make no mistake, that cause is not yet hopeless. It falls to us to do our duty and force our enemy to commit as many soldiers and militia to forestalling our campaign as possible. We must terrorize and frighten the populace into demanding our capture—a clamor so loud it reaches President Lincoln's desk. The longer we force the enemy's attention on us, the more time our beloved country has to regroup and prepare for future battles. Are you with me?"

The depressed atmosphere of the room vanished. Chins lifted, backbones stiffened, jaws jutted, and heads nodded, including Ty's. Morgan's key men, thanks to the persuasive power of their leader, were able to set aside the bad news for now. They were full-bellied and eager for the saddle once more.

"Fellow officers, I believe that speech deserves a round of applause."

Heads swiveled and there in the dining-room doorway stood the parent Ty was seeking. Captain Owen Mattson initiated the applause as he walked straight to Ty's table.

"Good afternoon, son," Owen Mattson said, extending his hand. "You must be Ty. You were riding Boone Jordan's gray gelding, with that black splotch on his face, at the Brandenburg Wharf—and you're the only other redhead in the room."

Ty was taken aback. He'd often thought what might happen when he caught up with his father. How would they be introduced? What would they say in greeting each other? Would his father know him for certain?

His father's simple greeting and offering of his hand answered those questions with such lightning speed that Ty had to swallow hard to free his tongue. Remembering his grandfather's dictum that no Mattson tendered any man a limp wrist, he secured a good grip on his father's palm and matched his strength. "Hello, Father."

Owen Mattson's warm smile told Ty he was pleased with his son's handshake. Ty was thrilled that they seemed to be starting off on the right foot. He had a thousand questions to ask, but none would come to mind. He was so excited.

His father filled the void. "I understand, Lieutenant Shannon, that you took my son to meet the elephant this morning."

Unsure whether or not his best friend approved of his untrained son being part of a cavalry charge under fire, Shawn Shannon was quick to answer. "He was safely in the rear, Owen, and that horse of Boone Jordan's grabbed the bit on him. He done fine, though, once we were in the thick of it."

The conversation so important to Ty was interrupted by the abrupt appearance of hard-breathing Urea Haggy with two tin boxes. The entire room watched with considerable interest as the banker, looking harried and distraught, bargained with General Morgan. As the haggling progressed and became contentious, the banker's normally florid face turned the deeper brick red of a bonfire. Eventually an agreement of $700 per mill, rather than $1,000, was reached. Urea Haggy's explosive, snorting sigh of relief told everyone present that was the exact amount in his tin boxes, and not a penny more. Morgan's laughing officers showed no mercy. Haggy was hooted out the door.

A grinning General Morgan was on his feet. The room stilled. "Gentlemen, to horse," he ordered. "We have miles to ride yet today."

The hotel emptied with a rush. The general's personal groom held the reins of Glencoe, Reb, Shawn Shannon's black gelding, and Owen Mattson's blaze-faced chestnut at the foot of the hotel's front porch. "They been groomed, watered, and fed per Captain Mattson's orders, General Morgan, sir," the black youth said with a prideful smile.

Ty's respect for his father gained a notch. Amidst the tension of the raiders' occupation of Corydon and the luxury of a hotel's hot meal, his father had seen to their horses first. It was a lesson he would take to heart. If he wanted to be a real cavalryman like his father, Reb came first, before his belly and other needs.

Stepping aboard Glencoe, General Morgan said, "Captain Mattson, since the would-be Ty Mattson is with you and not in handcuffs, I assume you have claimed him for your own. Please bring him to my tent this evening and we'll discuss his future with my command."

Ty was ecstatic. All in the same day, he'd looked the elephant in the eye, found his long-missing father, and been invited to a meeting with General Morgan that might enable him to enlist with the raiders.

He'd never been happier in his whole life.

CHAPTER 7

The raiders rode within sixteen miles of their next objective, Salem, Indiana, by late afternoon and went into camp with two encircling lines of pickets. Cooking fires were soon ablaze for hungry troopers who had gulped whatever food they could scarf up while on the move throughout the day.

Ty discovered that he was hungry, despite the big hotel meal in Corydon. When E.J. Pursley saw an opportunity to fill bellies, he seized it. Under his direction, his mess had absconded with cakes, candy, and peanuts from a Corydon confectioner; they took bacon, ham, and cheese from a Corydon grocer, and fresh eggs and root cellar potatoes from empty farmsteads. He served his feast from three skillets on two fires, designating Ebb White a temporary cook.

Their horses watered, fed, curried, and tethered, Ty and his father ate their fill with the others, hedging against the usual lack of vittles that occurred during a lightning-fast cavalry raid. Then they retired to the edge of the firelight, where their horses were picketed. They sat on gum ponchos draped over their grounded saddles

"Boone Jordan's gray held under fire, did he?"

"Yes, sir. He wouldn't be left behind. Mr. Jordan didn't mention Reb was cavalry trained and he caught me by surprise."

"I'm just glad you weren't hurt," Owen Mattson said, patting his son on the knee.

Aware his presence was so new to his son that Ty might dissolve into a bundle of nerves trying to sustain a conversation, the elder Mattson said, "Ty, maybe it would help us get acquainted faster if I told you my history with your mother and your grandparents. Then you can ask any questions you like. That all right by you?"

A relieved Ty sighed and said, "Yes, sir."

"Son, I love your grandfather, always have and always will. He taught me right from wrong with no in between. He provided me the same wonderful book and practical education he did you. He introduced me to horses and taught me how to breed, train, and care for them. We never exchanged a contrary word.

"On my twenty-fifth birthday, he sent me across the ocean to buy horses of Arabian blood in deserts where horse racing is king. On my journey, I met explorers, sheiks, and soldiers of fortune, who had fought in wars on four continents. I encountered a world where no two days were the same, where life was chancy and dangerous, where the enemy might be the next person you met, as every male bore arms.

"When I returned home to Elizabethtown, I wasn't the same man who'd left thirty months earlier. I realized a life in which each day is planned in detail had no appeal for me. I craved the danger and uncertainly of living amongst the horse-loving sheiks that inhabit deserts and fortresses as old as time itself. There I was the outsider who had to prove his worth every minute of every day. It was like drinking fine wine from a glass with no bottom.

"Ty, your grandfather is a hidebound but loving parent. I was restless and bored and stayed over once too often to bet on the races after a horse-selling trip to Louisville. Enoch Mattson breeds, trains, and sells horses, and follows the results at the rac-

ing tracks, but he is too Baptist to race or bet on them personally. He took exception to his son engaging regularly in what he
deemed sinful behavior and threatened to disown me.

"That's what started the serious trouble between us. I re-
sented his having the gall to tell a grown son what he could or
could not do. Your grandmother tried to smooth things over.
Your grandfather refused to talk to her, and the three of us went
weeks without speaking at the supper table."

Owen Mattson sipped water from a canteen, spat, and offered
Ty a drink. Ty was immersed in his father's story and nearly
choked on a single swallow. He cleared his throat and nodded he
was okay.

"It was my love for your mother that brought everything to a
head," Owen Mattson said. "Your mother was a red-haired, be-
witching, high-strung girl. I fell in love with my first glimpse of
Keena McVey at her father's Louisville tavern and boarding-
house. Bran McVey's Iron Gate was the favorite gathering place
for horse owners, horse lovers, jockeys, and those anxious to
learn the favorites for upcoming races. When she was six years
old, Keena lost her mother to fever, and Bran McVey didn't re-
marry. He saw that Keena never knew want. He enrolled her in
the Louisville Female Academy and insisted that she graduate.
Your mother always said the most enjoyable moments she spent
with her well-to-do, snobby classmates in three years was her
piano lessons in a private room.

"After her graduation, Bran McVey tried his best to make a
schoolteacher of his daughter. Your mother refused. After three
years of boredom at a female academy, a schoolroom offered the
same dull bill of fare to a tavern rat like Keena McVey. She
ragged on her father until he agreed to take her aboard as a partner in the Iron Gate. It was a decision he never regretted. He
was soon bragging that his daughter was the belle of the
Louisville racing scene. Horsemen and their wealthy guests,
knowing the Iron Gate respected proper decorum, came from

far and wide to listen to Keena McVey play the piano and partake of the most famous menu in the city. Your mother and her servers were treated as ladies and nothing less, without exception, or you were shown the back alley—same as any customer who overimbibed. The Iron Gate was the place to be seen in Louisville."

Owen Mattson sipped more water. Ty was sorry for the brief delay. "I was searching for a table the last night of racing season and, by sheer chance, met your mother face-to-face. I'd observed her from a distance, and not being acquainted with anybody close to her, circumstances didn't arise that would allow me to meet her properly. Our coming together by chance in the middle of the crowd that evening probably wasn't what some called 'proper,' but I looked into Keena McVey's violet eyes and sparks flew both ways, burning a hole in my soul.

"She treated me to a smile that melted my heart and curled my toes. I wasn't going to miss my chance. I sucked up my courage, bowed at the waist, and proclaimed, 'Miss Keena McVey, you're the most beautiful lady in God's realm.' Her response was what every man longs for in his dreams. 'And you're Owen Mattson, of Elizabethtown. You're respected for your knowledge of horses, Mr. Mattson, and not many men are built like you or look like you. You are a man I've asked about and wanted to meet, without appearing too forward.'

"Ty, your grandmother was prone to say certain things were meant to be. Your mother and I talked until dawn, after the Iron Gate closed. In a mere month, I was asking her father for her hand in marriage. Bran McVey trusted his daughter's judgment and gave us his blessing.

"I never lied to your grandparents. Your grandfather was livid when I told him of my pending marriage to the daughter of a tavern owner. Keena's education, her musical talents, the fact she was co-owner of a respected Louisville business establishment, frequented by the governor of Kentucky, fell on deaf ears.

Enoch Mattson refused to admit anyone to his home associated with the serving of alcoholic spirits, the same as he threatened to bar a son who imbibed and gambled."

Ty watched a grim sadness wash over his father's face. "His reaction didn't surprise me. Your grandmother was weeping, and it near tore my guts apart that if I married Keena McVey, I'd most likely not see either of them again unless it was your grandmother on the sly. Lord, how she would have loved your mother's high spirits and her music.

"I left that stone wall of silence behind me for good. Bran McVey had always wanted to own racehorses. He provided the money and I provided the horse knowledge. We bought a farm, south of Louisville, and established Iron Gate Stables. That fall, your mother became pregnant with you. It was a happy, busy time for us. Then came the war with Mexico. Your mother was familiar with my adventures in the Arabian Desert. She understood my restless nature, and that nothing would keep me from fighting for God and country. I enlisted with John Hunt Morgan's cavalry unit in Lexington and headed west. I wasn't worried about leaving your mother in her condition. I had faith in Bran McVey to care for the two of you until I returned.

"But as they will, things went awry while I was off glory seeking. Your mother died giving birth. It was weeks before I learned that. I couldn't desert the army, and Bran McVey was now in full charge of you, so I wasn't terribly worried about your welfare. The situation quickly took a second turn for the worse. One afternoon, Bran's buggy horse ran wild as he drove to Iron Gate Stables. The buggy crashed into a fence post and Bran was killed.

"Bran's sole living relative was his brother, Dagon. By Bran's will, Dagon inherited a one-third interest in everything his brother owned. Dagon managed the taproom at the Iron Gate. He had a wild eye and a loose wallet. He did make one good decision. Being a bachelor who liked the ladies his brother wouldn't admit to the Iron Gate, he had no intention of assuming responsibility for a child not yet a year old. He hired a wet nurse and together they traveled to your grandfather's farm.

"According to your grandmother's letter, it must have been a onetime occurrence, never to be repeated. Dagon banged on the front door with that big brass knocker Mother loved to hear announce guests. Your grandfather answered the door. Without any exchange of greetings, Dagon set your bassinet on the stoop and told an astonished Enoch Mattson, 'Here's your grandson, Tyler Owen Mattson. His mother's dead and his father's in Texas, killing stinking Mexicans. You raise him. I don't have the time or the interest.' And with that, he climbed into his buggy and whipped his horse down the lane, fearing your grandfather might fetch a gun and shoot him."

Ty was brimming with questions. "What happened after Dagon left?"

"Well, for certain, your grandfather's bobber had gone under. An upstanding Baptist elder didn't dare shun his own blood. He could disown a straying son, but renouncing a helpless infant would subject him to public scorn. That's a fate worse than death for a hard-shell believer."

The cooking fires were smoldering embers and General Morgan was expecting them. Ty hurriedly asked, "What became of Dagon McVey?"

"I hired a friend, a Louisville lawyer, to investigate the status of Bran McVey's holdings after Bran's death. By Bran's will, I wasn't given a stake in them. Your mother was granted the other two-thirds interest, not held by Dagon. Upon her father's death, that portion passed to you. Bran's faith in his brother was misplaced. Soon as Dagon had control of a substantial sum of money, gambling became his prime interest. Unfortunately, he was a poor judge of horseflesh and a sucker for a hot tip from hangers-on, who knew even less. His debts totaled in the thousands after a single racing season. He ducked his creditors for a while but those he owed grew tired of his excuses and came calling with drawn pistols.

"That's when the money-grubbing leeches grabbed control of the Iron Gate. They cut the spirits with water and cheapened the food, wanting to gain a quick, fat purse. Without the draw of Keena's piano, Bran McVey's charm, and the superb menu, the quality people drifted away. The end wasn't pretty. Bran McVey's assets—the tavern, the farm, and the horses—sold at sheriff's sale for far less than what they were worth. Dagon was found severed in half on the L and N Railroad tracks. The authorities ruled his death a suicide. Given the ruthless bunch of scalawags he dealt with, I believe he had help."

Lieutenant Shannon approached Ty and his father with a tin cup in each hand. "Coffee laced with Corydon's best brandy," he said, "courtesy of E.J.'s private stash. It's time, Captain. General Morgan's messenger said he's ready for us."

Accepting the offer of coffee and brandy, Owen Mattson said, "Give us a couple of more minutes, Shawn."

Ty found E.J.'s mixture quite tasty. His ears perked anew when his father said, "Ty, I had good reasons for staying in Texas after the war. It wasn't that I didn't want to claim you or raise you. With Dagon's demise and the loss of the McVey fortune, I decided the safest and best place for you was with your grandparents. I was a poor ex-soldier in a Texas known for its Comanche, cattle rustlers, horse thieves, outlaws, and cutthroats. I rode with the Rangers and arrested or killed all of their kind at one time or another. My knowledge of horses gained me partnerships in a cattle ranch and a freighting company. We lost the ranch to rustlers, twisters, and droughts, and the freighting outfit to renegades with red, brown, and white skins."

Owen Mattson drained his cup and stood. Ty did the same. "Ty, Texas is more dangerous than the Arabian Desert for a stripling with no mother and a footloose father with empty pockets. Trust me, I haven't liked being separated from you all these years. You know your grandfather as well as anybody. If you live with him, it has to be on his terms. I can't, so I stayed away."

Owen Mattson's smile was a mile wide. "Maybe it will all work out. I suspect your grandfather reared a son for me that I'll be proud of when this campaign is over. Now, before we try our general's patience, let's see what he has in store for you. Just be prepared for anything. John Hunt Morgan is a very resourceful military officer."

Ty tried to keep his mind clear during their walk to General Morgan's tent. It was nearly impossible. Questions that had kept him awake many sleepless nights and questions that wouldn't have dawned on him to ask had been answered in one conversation with his previously missing father. It would take a while to come to grips with all he had learned.

His father had gained in stature in his eyes. Owen Mattson was not afraid to put forth the truth. He hadn't asked Ty to forgive him for skipping his son's life until today. And Ty hadn't expected he would.

The past was the past. Whatever future he shared with his father commenced with Captain Owen Mattson's wish to have a son he could be proud of when General Morgan's great raid was over. If Ty wanted his father's respect, he must earn it. That's how it worked with the descendants of Enoch Mattson. Nothing was free. It was a hard road to travel. Ty knew in his heart that he preferred that path to anything else.

Or he'd have no pride till his dying day.

CHAPTER 8

A t ten o'clock, the waiting line at General Morgan's tent had dwindled to a few officers. The general reposed in a canvas folding chair. His adjutant, Lieutenant Hardesty, was seated at his elbow behind a portable writing table.

A slender, narrow-shouldered male garbed in a rumpled black suit, sporting a severely receding hairline, sunken eyes, and shallow cheeks, was tendering his daily report to General Morgan.

"That's Lightning Ellsworth. Morgan's telegrapher," Lieutenant Shannon whispered in Ty's ear. "See that battery box under his arm. He can loop into any telegraph line, listen awhile, and then impersonate the fist of any stationmaster exchanging messages, military or civilian. Colonel Duke claims Ellsworth is worth an armed division. He's so confused the Union Cavalry, the Yankees think we're four thousand strong."

When their turn came, Ty's father and Lieutenant Shannon saluted and stood at attention. Ty had the sense to sweep his hat beneath his arm.

"Captain Mattson, it's too late for much talking," General Morgan said. "I have need of your son's services. His rare eyesight was most helpful observing the battle for me today. He showed courage and excellent horsemanship under fire. I would like to assign him to my personal staff with the rank of corporal. He will have access to my personal string of horses, as you and Lieutenant Shannon do, to keep a fresh animal beneath him. If your son is agreeable, Lieutenant Hardesty will prepare the paperwork and the appointment will be effective immediately."

Ty couldn't have dreamed a better outcome for the meeting. Instead of a regular trooper eating dust, he would be a junior-staff officer reporting to the raiders' commanding officer. Astonished by General Morgan's offer, he gave no thought to his meager military experience. Nor did he have a clue as to how a general's staff functioned on a daily basis.

What did hit home was the fact General Morgan had extended his offer without consulting Ty's father. Ty glanced sideways. His father showed no sign he had any objection to what the general was proposing. But then, it was General John Hunt Morgan doing the proposing.

"He'll be well watched after, Captain," General Morgan said. "He will report to Lieutenant Hardesty at dawn with his horse and his weapon. You and Lieutenant Shannon will continue to ride with Quirk's Scouts and the Fourteenth Kentucky. Unless there's a situation that calls for you to report to me earlier, do so at Salem. Gentlemen, good evening."

Dismissed, the two veterans and newly appointed corporal took their leave. "Ty, let's put your thinking in proper order. Shawn, chime in when you see fit. Your duty is to do General Morgan's bidding. Whatever his orders, don't hesitate to carry them out. You will accompany him throughout the day, until he dismisses you. He will decide where you mess and where you sleep.

"General Morgan naturally prefers the head of the column. His servants and grooms travel between the First and Second Brigades. Pay attention wherever you are to who's about and what's happening. Graves are filled with larking and gawking soldiers, seldom those who stayed alert. A surprise bullet from a bushwhacker hidden alongside the road kills you same as a bullet from the rifle of a blue belly barricaded in front of you. Anything else, Shawn?"

"Don't wear Reb out. Switch horses daily with another saddler in the general's gather. Lane Farrell was a Ranger colonel. He enjoyed his old age because he lived by two simple rules. Never be the one to lose the grip on things. And if you find yourself outnumbered, a hasty retreat bespeaks wisdom, not cowardice."

The advice and counsel of his father and Shawn Shannon clarified Ty's role on General Morgan's staff and guaranteed he would report in the morning with a modicum of confidence and free of the shakes he detested. For that, he was thankful.

The fires of E.J. Pursley's mess were gray ashes. "Ty, the sinks are beyond the trees yonder, if you have need of them. I'll spread our gum ponchos and blankets."

Ty had a true need. He picked his way through the narrow woods on a path beaten down by many boots. In the quiet night, he could hear his lungs pumping. A yard from the far edge of the trees and the acrid-smelling latrine, a voice close enough that Ty could almost reach out and touch its owner said, "Didn't have a clean shot at Mattson this morning, did you?"

Ty froze, every muscle rigid. *Mattson? Did that shadowy figure say "Mattson"?*

"Naw, he's not a man to stay still for very long," a voice that rasped like a saw cutting dry wood answered. "He was never in a position where it would look like the blue bellies nailed him."

"Anybody catches you in the act, you know Morgan will hang you. You certain Mattson can't recognize you?"

"Cousin, I'm beginning to believe I made a mistake telling you my intentions. Mattson never laid eye on me back in Texas. I was hiding under the porch the day he shot my daddy and grandpa, and my real name's not listed on the muster rolls. Come along and keep your trap shut."

Ty lingered until he was positive the two shadowy figures were well beyond earshot. He had no doubt they would have killed him if they had caught him eavesdropping on their conversation. He relieved himself, buttoned his trousers, and retraced his route to camp, one careful step at a time.

Ty believed every word he had heard. The speaker's threat to kill Owen Mattson had the undeniable ring of truthfulness. Revenge had spurred many murders throughout history.

Worse yet, how could the threatening trooper be identified? Ty had not seen his face in the dark and hadn't learned his first name, let alone his last.

He could be anybody. He could shoot his father from long range or walk right up and shoot him in the back, if he became desperate and was willing to sacrifice his own life.

Ty would warn his father that someone was out to kill him. He would at least know to watch those around him. But no one could watch every direction at once during a battle.

He wished he'd stopped short of the slit trenches. But then he wouldn't have learned his father was in danger. He couldn't keep from groaning aloud.

The happiest day of his life was ending on a sour, perhaps deadly note.

CHAPTER 9

Owen Mattson and Shawn Shannon were snoring merrily away. Since the night talkers had walked in the opposite direction, Ty decided he could tell his father the bad news in the morning. Totally exhausted, he slept soundly, without tossing and turning as he worried he might. Ty awakened clearheaded when the first bugle blew "Reveille."

To his surprise, his father's saddle, gum poncho, and blanket were missing. He rolled out and joined his messmates at E.J. Pursley's breakfast fire for a quick meal of bacon, pole bread, and black coffee. He knelt beside Lieutenant Shannon with a full plate and cup. "Father's gone already?"

"Yep, a courier delivered a message from Colonel Duke at four A.M. Your guess is as good as mine as to where he headed. He didn't say and I didn't ask. With Owen, you let him do the telling, when he's good and ready."

Ty lowered his voice and repeated every word he'd overheard at the latrine. A frown creased the lieutenant's sun-scorched features. "No names, but you're sure they were Texans, and Owen shot and killed the one's daddy and grandpa?"

"Yes, sir."

Lieutenant Shannon finished his coffee. "Owen maybe can provide a name. He shot a number of men in the line of duty as a Ranger. I'll wager he didn't put down a father and son together but once. Still, knowing a name isn't worth much if you can't tie it to a face. Gano's Brigade has a hundred-plus Texans on its rolls. Ty, sometimes you have to pray the luck of the draw saves you. This fellow could be killed or captured before he has a chance at Owen."

E.J. Pursley collected their plate and cups. Ty and the lieutenant retrieved their saddles and bridles and toted them to the picket line. "We'll stay on Reb and my Buster until Salem and swap horses there. We best hustle along," Lieutenant Shannon said, nodding at the growing light in the eastern sky. "General Morgan will be finishing breakfast, and then it's straight to the saddle for him with the last bite."

General Morgan's tent was being struck when they arrived. Lieutenant Shannon gave Ty one final piece of advice. "We don't know how long this godforsaken war will last, where we'll fight next, or who we'll engage next. Riding with Morgan, you can observe how a whole cavalry division functions. You can't have too much knowledge serving in a general's personal entourage. The more you learn, the better you can serve, and a promotion or commendation might come in right handy before the shooting stops." With that, Shawn Shannon pushed ahead to join the advance guard.

Ty reined Reb to the rear of the officers following General Morgan. Lieutenant Shannon's advice was sound as usual. By listening to the verbal exchanges between General Morgan, Colonels Duke and Johnson, Lieutenant Hardesty, line officers, and the youthful couriers who came and went, Ty acquired a basic knowledge of the workings of the division's two brigades when on the move.

Scout patrols rode the point beyond the advance guard, assessing the terrain, avoiding ambushes, and locating local guides they thought could be trusted. Meanwhile, flankers moved out four or five miles on each side of the main body. Each morning, the captains of companies appointed a man from each mess to sally forth in search of provisions. With two thousand troopers to feed and supply, these flankers traversed every country road in search of horses, food, and forage. Rarely did a healthy horse escape the flanker's roundup. The flankers rejoined the column between ten and twelve o'clock, with their booty of riding stock and sacks full of light bread, cheese, butter, preserves, canned peaches, berries, and wine cordial from family pantries, canteens of milk from springhouses, and ears of corn from barn cribs for horse forage.

Hearing the exciting and glowing reports of the couriers and the upbeat responses on the part of General Morgan and his fellow officers, Ty came to realize that while he hadn't suffered from privation or hunger when residing with his grandfather, the veteran raiders had spent two-plus years fighting in Kentucky and Tennessee counties where rural areas ravaged by war and hunger were commonplace. Even coffee, a main staple of soldiering, was scarce as dragon's teeth. For them, Indiana was the golden horn of plenty, with the riches free for the taking.

With two decent routes accessing Salem, General Morgan separated his two brigades—Quirk's Scouts leading one, the Second Kentucky the other—in a race along parallel roads to their objective. A detachment of two companies was sent westward to create a diversion in that direction.

It was Lieutenant Hardesty, ignoring the summer heat that would be insufferable by midafternoon, who answered Ty's question about General Morgan's tactics in splitting and weakening his division in hostile country.

"He's mastered the art of guerrilla warfare. He's most concerned about the Yankee cavalry chasing us. By cutting telegraph lines after Lightning Ellsworth spreads false stories as to our whereabouts, and by dividing us into sections, he confuses the local forces. The militia and home guards don't know where to concentrate and effectively oppose us. The Yankees are equally confused. They don't know where the general's headed, or where his main body is located at any given point in time. Watch his strategy succeed as we move toward Ohio. The locals are too weak to slow us down, and by burning bridges and trestles and making off with every horse that can carry a man, we make it damnably difficult for our pursuers to catch us from behind."

They approached Salem whose church bells pealed continuously, a musical accompaniment so familiar along their line of march that many raiders swore every day was Sunday. General Morgan dispatched couriers to his separated brigades, gathered them together and advanced them at a trot. Lieutenant Hardesty positioned Ty beside the general. Ahead of them rode Lieutenant Welsh and a party of fourteen scouts, followed in turn by Major Webber and the Second Kentucky. Ty was certain his father and Shawn Shannon were with the scouts. They always seemed to be where it was the most dangerous, no small worry for Ty. Now that he had a father, he loathed the thought of losing him.

Major Webber's orders were to let nothing stop him, and nothing did. A detachment of enemy militia numbering 150 waited at the edge of Salem. Buglers blew "Charge" and Lieutenant Welsh and his fourteen scouts spurred their horses into a gallop and dashed down on them. The disorganized defenders' shaky bravery evaporated and they raced pell-mell for the safety of Salem's buildings. Their precipitous flight unnerved additional militia lined up in the town square; they took to heel, aiming for the far side of Salem, feverishly discarding muskets suddenly too hot for fingers to hold.

As the last of the fleeing home guards exited Salem, a full company of the Washington County Legion, commanded by Captain John Davis, marched carefree as you please into the town square to pick up arms and ammunition promised them by

Union brass in Indianapolis, only to discover that weapon-bearing Rebels had them in their sights. The ease of capturing the Hoosiers provoked raucous laughter, which rolled through Salem's streets in waves. Ty saw one Southern trooper fall from the saddle, holding his stomach.

Lieutenant Hardesty stationed Ty on the brick sidewalk of the Hiram Brightway House, General Morgan's temporary headquarters, with instructions to observe the activity of the town square and be prepared to answer any questions that might be forthcoming from the general.

The square filled with troopers from both raider brigades, and the outright civilian pillage, which had concerned Ty in Corydon, began in earnest. Salem was a community of abundance, and Morgan's men were determined to treat the Northerners they hated the same as Generals Sanders and Grierson had treated Southerners during their brutal cavalry raids into their home states. To that end, the emptying of every mercantile store and business in Salem was paramount; yelling raiders descended like a swarm of locusts to pick them clean. Ransacking Rebels appropriated saddles, replacement clothing and boots, weapons, ammunition, blacksmith tools, horseshoes, medical supplies, and an infinite variety of foodstuffs—items that filled the needs of cavalrymen constantly on the move.

The theft didn't end there. Salem's loaded counters, shelves, and storerooms were an irresistible temptation for troopers long accustomed to doing without, and who had missed their chance at Corydon. What followed made the Corydon looting petty in nature. He watched troopers impress buggies, carts, and market wagons and stuff them with books, stationery, cutlery, bolts of calico, silks and satins, hoops, and other female garments. Raiders brazenly robbed Salem citizens of money, tobacco, and everything else that suited their fancy. Cally Smith ambled past Ty with sleigh bells draped over his shoulder. Not even caged canaries, ice skates, and chafing dishes were safe.

Ty could understand the taking of items required to keep men riding and fighting, but from his lessons with Professor Ackerman, a longtime student of military history, he was aware that the Corydon and Salem pillages were beyond the pale of civilized warfare, as was stealing from unarmed prisoners of war and civilians.

Though it went against his grandfather's passion for the sanctity of private property, Ty was sure he could steal whatever he required to stay in the saddle and support General Morgan. He would touch nothing else. That went too much against the Mattson grain.

Black smoke billowed beyond the buildings on the southern and western sides of the square. A sergeant, who was headed for the Brightway House, bragged the railroad depot, along with two bridges and wooden ties piled with iron rails, were afire.

After ninety minutes of watching, Ty sensed a changing mood amongst the looting troopers. The source of the change was easily pinpointed. Bottles of corn liquor were flowing from one hand to another like water over a dam. A fight between two troopers attracted a crowd and prompted a wild spree of loud betting as to the winner. A barber, apron tied about his neck, sailed from his shop and landed facedown in the dusty street. Ty hated snitchers, but he was bound by duty to insure that General Morgan was aware of the deteriorating situation in the square.

Thankfully, only General Morgan, Colonels Duke and Johnson, and Lieutenant Hardesty occupied the front room of the Brightway House. The absence of other officers allowed Lieutenant Hardesty to note Ty's presence without delay. "Yes, Corporal?"

Conversation ceased and all eyes fixed on Ty. "It must be a thing of great importance for you to interrupt General Morgan's meeting," Lieutenant Hardesty said.

"Yes, sir. I believe you need to check the square. Troopers are drinking heavily and fighting amongst themselves."

"Thank you, Corporal," General Morgan said, turning to his

colonels. "Gentlemen, our planning is complete. We have the ransom for the mill and we've burned what we can to slow our pursuers The boys have obviously had their fun. We best clear out before they turn mean. I don't want any citizens to suffer bodily injuries, if it can be avoided."

Ty waited and followed General Morgan's party from the room. The sight of General Morgan allowed provost guards and bellowing sergeants to restore order in the square. Stolen wagons, buggies, and carts holding stolen goods were lined out for departure.

"We'll have a baggage train a mile or two long trailing after us," Colonel Duke predicted.

"If it starts to slow us down too much," General Morgan said, "I'll issue orders to abandon the whole shebang."

Ty departed Salem mounted on a bay, with one white stocking, provided by General Morgan's groom at the direction of Lieutenant Shannon. "His name is Duke," the groom said when handing him the reins. "No need to worry. I take good care of your Reb."

General Morgan opted for a two-horse buggy with fringed top cover to escape the heat. Two troopers swooped past his buggy with bolts of calico tied to their saddle horns, streamers of bright-colored cloth unfurling behind them. Not the least perturbed, General Morgan laughed and waved to them.

Ty stood in his stirrups for a last look at Salem. For a few seconds, he thought he was accompanying a different army, as a large number of troopers had donned stolen linen dusters in an attempt to keep hoof-stirred dust from coating their sweat-laden uniforms.

The black smoke from the roaring fires in Salem stained the entire western sky. Ty sighed. Whether done in the guise of war or not, rebuilding the destroyed structures would require much expense, time, and labor. He felt a twinge of sorrow for Salem's citizens.

Ty's father always seemed to arrive faster than a lightning bolt. He was aboard a seal-brown gelding, with a black mane and tail. "Sooner or later, there will be hell to pay for what we're doing. We have stuck a big stick in a very large hornet's nest. People are capable of anything when they're infuriated and scared. Mark my word, they will know we're coming, and they will stop at nothing to impede our progress until the Yankees overtake us."

"Do you think the Yankees will catch us before General Morgan decides to cross the Ohio again?"

Owen Mattson looked Ty straight in the eye. "We're in a tight race, a mighty tight race. Odds are, we'll be lucky to escape with our lives and avoid a Yankee prison."

While he had the opportunity, for there might not be another one for who knew how long, Ty said, "I overheard a conversation at the sinks after our meeting with General Morgan that I must tell you about."

"I talked to Shawn Shannon earlier. He told me what happened," Owen Mattson said.

Not wanting Ty to be distracted by the incident and neglect his duties, Owen Mattson continued speaking. "Trust me, the man you overheard isn't the first who's wanted to kill me for whatever reason, so don't spend time worrying about what he's supposedly planning to do. Never waste time fretting about anything until actions match words. Understand?"

Ty could only say, "Yes, sir."

Since he lacked his father's courage, that advice didn't alleviate Ty's fears. However, it was obvious from the tone of his father's voice that the subject was closed for now.

And a good trooper obeyed orders.

Or tried to, as best he could.

PART 2

FOR THE OHIO

We crossed the Ohio-Indiana border and arrived at
Harrison, Ohio this morning. We have covered 188 miles
in 6 days since departing Brandenburg. Our most pressing
need around the clock is suitable horses. By my rough estimate, we have impressed 1,850 mounts since crossing the
Ohio. The exchange has been so rapid troopers are far past
weeping over the loss of their beloved Thoroughbreds. To
their disgust, their replacement mounts of indiscriminate
breed last but a day or two, some not that long. Ahead
awaits our greatest and most demanding challenge to date,
a challenge that will test the stamina and lungs of every animal we ride, for General Morgan has decided we must
skirt well-armed Cincinnati to the north in the dark of
night, a beastly venture.

—Journal of Clinton J. Hardesty, Morgan's Confederate
Cavalry, 13 July 1863

CHAPTER 10

Ty leaned from the saddle and emptied his stomach in spasms of violent retching. Lieutenant Shannon reined close and studied his contorted features, especially the dark spittle dangling from his chin. "You sick, Corporal? Your face is yellow, green, and three shades of blue."

Ty fought for breath. "Ebb White gave me a wedge of Mule Harness to chew. He told me it would keep the dust from drying my mouth out."

"Ebb's been chewing that black tobacco for years. If a mule isn't used to it, it will make him blanch. I haven't seen you spitting any."

Ty's innards growled something awful. "He claimed real chewers don't expectorate. They swallow the juice."

"Yep, they do after their stomachs grow an iron lining," Shawn Shannon said with a hearty laugh. He reached into his leather shoulder bag and produced a handful of smooth white stones. "Like before, suck on one of these. They won't make you sick, and be leery of that corn likker Ebb's got hidden somewhere. That stuff will put a hammer inside your young brain for days."

Ty's naiveté disgusted him. He had disgraced his rank. Despite E.J. Pursley's warning shake of the head, he'd made himself ill trying to stick his chest out in front of his messmates. Hadn't Grandfather Mattson taught him stupidity comes at a cost most don't want to pay?

The morning wasn't a total loss. The yellow ointment Lieutenant Shannon obtained from a Salem apothecary had soothed the fiery pain besetting his blistered hindquarters and thighs into a dull ache. The cure had been a simple matter of asking for help without fear of embarrassment.

The road to Harrison, Ohio, descended between two bluffs to the Whitewater River. A stout bridge of heavy oak timbers spanned the fast-flowing waters. White church steeples, cornices of brick buildings, and a courthouse cupola caught Ty's eye during the raiders downhill ride.

Iron shoes pounding the planks of the bridge reminded Ty of rolling thunder. The raiders entered Harrison at a trot without opposition. Once General Morgan's entourage was across the river, he dropped back alongside Ty and Shawn Shannon. "Lieutenant Shannon, you and Corporal Mattson observe the destruction of the bridge. Rearguard scouts reported General Hobson and his four thousand troopers are only five hours' riding time behind us. Once this bridge is down, they will be hours finding a ford suitable for their artillery."

General Morgan winked. "Those Union boys don't like to move too far in advance of their heavy guns."

After the column's wagons had crossed, troopers covered the near end of the bridge with straw and brush. The dry, weather-beaten timbers caught fire with a sudden *whoosh*, flame shooting fifty feet into the air. Finding the heat was so intense, Ty and Shawn Shannon eased their horses back a fair distance.

Ty had come to trust Shawn Shannon to keep private whatever he said, the same as he did with his shortly-known father.

"Maybe I'm not meant to be a soldier. Burning valuable property and stealing just don't seem right to me, and I don't think I'll ever feel any different. Does that make me a bad soldier?"

Lieutenant Shannon stepped down from his horse and knelt to watch the blazing fire. Ty dismounted and knelt beside him. "Corporal, I've been campaigning against either Mexicans, Comanche, or Yankees for half my years. Yet, I've never come to like or enjoy the killing, the burning and looting, and the shabby treatment of those not wearing uniforms. I've never taken pride in any killing. Trouble is, you usually don't have a choice about joining the war. You join the army that believes the same as you. If you refuse to fight, you'll hang or rot in prison.

"What keeps my bobber afloat is that everything about war isn't mean, ugly, and bloody. Every now and then, you can smile and chuckle. Remember that ham factory in Dupont. We swiped two thousand hams. When have two cavalry brigades ever ridden away from a looting and not a single trooper could complain he was left out? How about that wagon full of lager beer at New Alsace? Dry as we were, swallowing road dust, wasn't it grand to see foam on every lip as those kegs passed the length of the column? Then there's Cally Smith. Remember how he thought he was drinking brandy, which was actually sweetened laxative? He was off his horse running for the bushes from Salem to Vienna. He turned dead white. I'll never forget his moaning that he'd shat out everything up to his throat! And if he stopped talking, his tongue was gone, so just shoot him."

Ty had to smile and chuckle.

"Maybe the best was General Morgan's ruse outside Lexington," Lieutenant Shannon said. "You weren't with the van that morning. You were serving as courier. We rounded a bend in the road and encountered three hundred home guards resting in a grove of oak trees. Their horses were tied to the trees and a fence rail bordering the road. The old captain asked one of our men who we were and he shot back Wolford's cavalry. The old captain was delighted to see blue-belly Kentucky boys and asked where Wolford was.

"Ty, John Hunt Morgan is a mighty clever rascal. He rode up, introduced himself as Colonel Frank Wolford, First Kentucky Union Cavalry, and asked the captain what he was planning to do with all those horses and men. The old captain stated that John Hunt Morgan and his horse-thieving raiders were in the area, and they were hoping to give him what-for if they found him.

"Out of the blue, the old captain made a fatal mistake. Recognizing veteran cavalrymen when he saw them, he asked General Morgan to show his greenhorns a military drill. Our general declined, claiming his horses were too tired. The old captain told him to take his horses, and our dear general gladly obliged him. The Hoosiers actually helped switch our saddles to their fresh mounts."

Ty had heard what happened next at the nightly mess fire. A firsthand account from an eyewitness made it even funnier. "We raiders mounted up and General Morgan took the point. Promising to execute an evolution the Hoosier captain had probably never seen before, the general told those home guards to line up on both sides of the road. Like sweet lambs headed for slaughter, they followed his orders. General Morgan whooped at the top of his lungs and we lit out at a gallop. Those green Indiana boys were absolutely dumbfounded, and we were out of range before a single one of them could fire a shot."

The collapse of the burning Harrison Bridge timbers accompanied by rising clouds of steam stilled Ty and Shawn Shannon's schoolboy laughter. Shawn Shannon sighed, mounted Buster, and waited for Ty to swing aboard Reb.

"Ty, it will help if you keep in mind your father's words after that nasty brush we had with Federal troops at Tebbs Bend before you joined us. Owen said then, 'It's too late to jaw about who's right and who's wrong in this war. We fight it out to the end, win or lose, live or die, no matter who suffers or what's destroyed. We're riding a wagon rolling downhill with no brakes, and there's no stopping it.' Corporal, we best hunt up General Morgan."

Ty couldn't refute his father's observation. He was in that runaway wagon with every other member of General Morgan's column. He had taken an oath and was honor bound to perform the duties assigned him. There was no allowance for a queasy stomach or sympathy for those caught in the column's path. His personal feelings were a minute pockmark on the entire face of the war.

Given Campbell and Harlan Stillion joined Ty and Shawn Shannon as they rode into the center of Harrison. The last of General Morgan's troopers were winding through town, enjoying a final binge of looting. Now that they sensed the greatest danger to their health was past, Yankee citizens could be spotted at doors and windows, watching the departure of the hated secesh.

"Ever notice," Given Campbell said, "that the young gals are braver in showing themselves while we're still out and about than their fathers. Why do you suppose that is, Harlan?"

Harlan Stillion stroked his bearded chin. A mischievous glint shone in his deep brown eyes when he said with a chuckle, "Maybe cause we're so handsome and daring?"

Given Campbell grinned and said, "You've come along right smartly since our prowling days at Fort Davis. Women just can't restrain themselves when their young hometown boys are off fighting far from home and a dangerous-looking man shows up on horseback, with guns hanging from his waist and saddle. It don't matter what flag he's serving. The sight of him stirs them something awful. It's like watching a moth drawn to a flame, ignorant of the fact he could be snuffed like a candle if he comes too close. Look ahead there, that's what I'm talking about."

Two Morgan troopers were lounging in their saddles beneath the second-story veranda of a large private dwelling. Two yellow-haired lasses hung over the railing above the men; their delicate cheeks, pretty necks, and hands smooth as fresh cream gleamed in the morning sunshine.

"Young ladies, may I have your names?" asked the bolder of the two Morgan men.

Given Campbell's rampant curiosity about anything having to do with the fairer sex provoked a tightening of reins and his horse halted. Not wanting to miss out on the fun, his fellow riders followed suit. The watching raiders constituted a small crowd, when Cally Smith and Sam Bryant drew alongside Ty's mount for the day.

"Come on, you Ohio lovelies," the bold trooper persisted. "What's the harm in my knowing you two by name?"

Eyelashes fluttered on the veranda and the two young Harrison gals stifled a rash of giggles. The bosomy girl on the right caved in to a show of male attention after months of boredom in a town filled with upright Bible pounders, lecherous old codgers, and boys too young to appreciate feminine charm if someone smacked them upside the head.

"Why do you want to know?" one of the young gals asked.

"Well, I can't make up my mind which one of you is the prettier, so I believe I'll come back after the fighting's done and marry the one of you whose name I like the best."

The girl on the left broke in, saying, "Well, I've never heard a brasher thing in—"

"Janine and Trisha Collins," the girl on the right said, tossing proper etiquette to the wind. "I'm Janine and she's Trisha."

"Janine," the other sister cried, stamping her foot. "Papa's going to be terribly upset if he hears you acted like a brazen hussy in front of total strangers."

"Don't you dare let her interfere, Janine," the bold raider said, straightening in his saddle. "My name is Trace Franklin. I hail from Lynnville, Kentucky. The word of us Franklin men is revered for its unfailing honesty. I'll be back with horse and buggy and flowers and coin in hand to court you. You tell your papa you'll be well cared for and no man will ever respect a woman more."

With a smile broader than the Ohio in flood, Trace Franklin continued, "Had I the time, I'd mosey up there and collect a kiss to seal the bargain."

A serene expression of pure joy softened Janine Collins's creamy face. Blowing her suitor the kiss he desired, she said, "I'll be here waiting for you, Mr. Trace Franklin, of Lynnville, Kentucky. Just don't you take up with another gal and leave me high and dry. Write to me now."

Trace Franklin saluted Janine and said, "On my word, I will grace your doorstep a second time. Good day, my love."

Trace Franklin and his companion spun their mounts and trotted down the street. Enthralled by what he'd observed and heard, Ty turned to Given Campbell. "Do you suppose they'll ever see each other again?"

"I've never claimed to be an expert in understanding the romantic inclinations of God's greatest creatures, especially the young ones, though some have attributed that skill to me. But I can safely say that if Mr. Trace Franklin survives the peace, he'll share more than a blown kiss with Miss Janine Collins."

"Let's move along," Lieutenant Shannon ordered.

Once the detail was in motion behind Shannon, the affable Given Campbell, riding beside Ty, chuckled and said, "It can be much more interesting when two sisters want the same man."

"How do you mean?"

"Twin sisters at Fort Davis fell wildly for the same Texas Ranger with every inch of their beings. They looked so much alike, you couldn't tell one from the other. The Ranger married Sarah Anne. He went off right after the ceremony with his Ranger company, hunting Mexican bandits. While he was away, his new bride was killed in a Comanche raid on her home place on the Staked Plain. When the Ranger returned home, unbeknownst to him, the other sister, the sole member of her family to survive, loved him so much she assumed her dead sister's name and spared him the grief of losing a wife he'd worshiped."

An incredulous Ty couldn't resist interrupting to ask, "Did he ever learn the truth?"

"Yes, a fever put Corinne down three years later. On her deathbed, she told him how she'd switched places with her dead sister."

"Did he forgive her?"

"Yes, he'd suspected the truth, but he was so happy with her and how much of herself she'd given to him, he'd stayed his tongue."

Still questioning if Given Campbell might be toying with his bobber, Ty said, "Did someone tell you this story, or did you know the Ranger and the twin sisters personally?"

Given Campbell nodded and said, "I knew them, knew all of them dear as you can. I've often wondered how I was lucky enough to have the opportunity to love two of the grandest ladies ever to draw a breath on this earth. Never stop seeking the love of a good woman, lad. Seek it like other men foolishly seek gold. You'll be much happier than they ten times over."

And with that, Ty Mattson, of Morgan's Raiders, departed Harrison, Ohio, impressed once more by how little of real life he'd experienced growing up in the safe confines of the Mattson manse in Elizabethtown, Kentucky.

General Morgan allowed his command a three-hour rest, four miles east of Harrison. A temporary camp was established beside a stream flanking a large pasture that fronted a field of corn ripe for the picking. Many troopers helped themselves and fed their horses.

A surprise awaited Ty when he and Shawn Shannon rejoined

General Morgan's staff. Owen Mattson had swapped his Texas garb for cotton pants and shirt, a slouch hat, and flat-soled brogans. Three additional troopers wore the same farm clothing and stood with him before General Morgan.

Once within earshot, Ty heard General Morgan say, "How many of Burnside's men are holding Cincinnati? How are they positioned? How many troops are arriving from Kentucky? How prepared are they to pursue us? What's the mood of the city? That's the information we need you to obtain."

A lump clogged Ty's throat. His father was being dispatched on a spying mission into the very heart of the enemy's lair. If captured, his fate was prison and a hanging rope.

Four horses best described as healthy nags—they, at least, walked sure-footedly—were brought forward. Colonel Johnson said, "Captain Taylor, you lived in Cincinnati for a number of years and will take the lead. Given Lightning Ellsworth's confusing transmissions and our subsequent cutting of the telegraph lines feeding Cincinnati, the place will be a well of confusion and fear, creating enough diversion for you to sneak through at night. We'll rendezvous east of the city at the Great Miami River Bridge."

"Mount up, gentlemen," General Morgan said. "Off with you and good luck."

Owen Mattson winked at Ty in passing. The bulge beneath his father's cotton shirt didn't lessen Ty's concern. Four pistols against thousands of weapons were outrageous odds that begged disaster.

"Don't fret yourself, Corporal," Lieutenant Shannon whispered. "If Owen can steal a rifle from a sleeping Comanche in broad daylight, those Yankees will never know he was amongst them in the dark."

Ty wasn't certain he shared Shawn Shannon's confidence. Maybe he would if he'd experienced his father's years in Texas. His father seemed to have a penchant for seeking danger, a desire foreign to him. Ty didn't believe he was a coward. Yet, despite the success of that wild, unintentional cavalry charge at Corydon, he had no inkling if he was capable of such bravery the next occasion he was under fire. Being shot at for real took some getting used to, if one ever did.

General Morgan cleared his throat and raised his arm to insure he had everyone's attention. "It's vital that Burnside expects us to attack Cincinnati and stay put. We will move that direction with the main column. Our scouts will make a feint toward Hamilton and convince the Union forces there that we are headed in their direction. We need to buy enough time to slip between the two cities without a major engagement. If we're successful, we will be able to outrun our pursuers to the ford at Buffington Island, on the far side of Ohio. The waters there will be too shallow this time of year for Yankee gunboats out of Louisville and Cincinnati."

Flashing his irresistible smile, General Morgan said, "Gentlemen, we're in for the ride of a lifetime, longer than anything we've ever attempted. Keep the column closed up as much as possible. I pray I'll see all of you again. Sergeant Rainey, have the buglers sound 'Boots and Saddles,' if you please."

General Morgan hadn't lied. The following thirty-five hours were the most taxing that Ty had ever experienced. When the skirting of Cincinnati finally ended at four o'clock in the afternoon of the following day, he was so exhausted that all he remembered of the overnight ordeal in the saddle were bits and pieces hard to pull together in their proper sequence.

He remembered the moonless darkness they rode through, mile after mile, that made shadows of the troopers ahead of him and behind him; men tumbling from the saddle and refusing the order to remount, willing to risk capture for a few hours of sleep; horses collapsing and dying under their cursing riders; kneeling troopers holding burning splinters, searching for horse slobber to guide them, as the straggling column crossed numerous roads running southward to Cincinnati; the ring of shod hoofs on cobbled streets and their thud on a plank highway; a voice he recognized, the rasping, sawlike voice from the sinks; his disappointment when it faded without his identifying its owner; the huge red flare spawned by the firing of the Great Miami River Bridge; hands tying him to saddle horn and stirrups; burning sunlight that parched his throat and forced his eyes closed; the smell of meadows lush with summer hay; being untied and lifted from the saddle; the rubbery squeak of a gum poncho beneath him, cool water on his lips; the return of black velvet darkness.

CHAPTER 11

The scaffold is a stark, skeletal structure, with a wooden crossbeam looming above it that holds four nooses. A large chattering crowd surrounds the elevated platform, waiting for the unfolding of the spectacle, which they long to witness. Owen Mattson and his three fellow spies, hands tied behind their backs, climb the twenty wooden steps that lead to eternity.

Owen Mattson turns to face the crowd, red hair a touch of fire against the bright blue sky. He smiles as the uniformed Yankee officer reads a proclamation sentencing him and his companions to death by hanging. The smile is still on his face when the hangman lowers a black hood over his head, followed by one of the carefully knotted nooses. The crowd bushes as the trapdoor beneath the four spies springs open.

Ty's arms thrashed wildly and he awakened with his mouth poised to scream. Hands clasped his shoulders and his father said, "Easy, son. That must have been a damn bad dream."

Ty came to his senses and hastily wiped the tears dampening his cheeks from finding his father was alive and unharmed and back in uniform. "I dreamed you were being hanged for spying on the blue bellies."

"Naw, Cincinnati was stampeded. I've never seen that many soldiers and people running amok. Not a soul had any interest in us."

Owen Mattson examined Ty's wrists. "Shawn always was good with leather thongs and knots. Didn't chafe your skin overly much, either."

"I will thank Lieutenant Shannon straightaway," Ty promised. "Did you gather the information General Morgan wanted?"

"Yes, we did. All told, including cavalry, regulars, home guards, and militia, General Burnside has approximately fifty thousand effectives spread out behind us in the city, the countryside, and on the river. Plus every single one of them wants a piece of our hide."

The sheer number of enemy available to pursue them staggered Ty's mind. The jaws of a giant trap were closing on them. How long could they continue to elude forces of that size?

Ty pushed himself into a sitting position. Not knowing when he might have the opportunity to speak with his father again, he said, "I couldn't see him in the dark, but I heard that voice from the sinks sometime during the night."

"Could you make out anything he said?"

"He was angry. He warned his cousin that if he fell off his horse one more time, he'd damned well finish the war in a Yankee prison camp. He called him 'Cousin Elam.' "

Owen Mattson smiled. "Now we have a name. The Second Brigade led the advance from Harrison through the night. He's a member of Colonel Gano's Texas Brigade, not the Texas detachment in Colonel Duke's First Brigade. I'll have Lieutenant Hardesty check the muster rolls of Gano's companies for the name 'Elam.' Maybe we can flush out our would-be assassin before he makes his move."

Ty said a silent prayer. Until the threat hanging over his father's head was eliminated, he would be on edge day and night. "Do you have any idea who he might be? Lieutenant Shannon thought you might."

"Yes, Jack Stedman's son. Jack and his father, Frank, headed a ring of cattle rustlers in Southwest Texas. They drove off a herd after killing the crew at the chuck wagon and the two nighthawks. I was delivering a prisoner to Three Forks for the Rangers and buzzards led me to the provisions wagon. The camp cook survived his wound long enough to identify Jack. Being miles from any help, I covered the dead crew best I could, tied my prisoner to the wheel of the wagon, with a cache of corn biscuits and water, and followed the stolen herd south toward the Rio Grande. To make a long story short, I caught up with the herd. I knew the Stedmans by sight. Through my field glasses, I saw Jack and Frank break off from the herd, so I trailed them. Turns out, they had a cabin in the hills outside Parker City.

"They were sitting on the porch slugging whiskey and having a high old time while their gang drove their stolen herd across the border. It was windy and threatening rain. I rode up with a linen duster draped across my saddle horn and a pistol in each hand beneath it. I didn't waste their time or mine. I told them they were under arrest for murder and cattle rustling. They gawked at me for a few seconds, and their eyes got big. Frank dove for a rifle leaning against the wall beside him and Jack drew his pistol. I shot and killed both of them through the folds of the duster—Jack first and then Frank. Not what I wanted to do, but they gave me no choice.

"I'd trailed them for three days and I was getting worried about my prisoner back at the provisions wagon. I carried their bodies inside the cabin, torched it, and rode out of there. I never laid eyes on Jack's son."

Ty wasn't the least bothered that Jack and Frank Stedman might have been inebriated and perfect dupes for his father's trick with the duster. What chance had they given the cowboys they'd killed? Still, he saw clearly how Jack Stedman's son would nurse a lifelong grudge against the man who killed his father and his grandfather and burned the family cabin. Ty was beginning to appreciate the truth of Shawn Shannon's assertion that Owen Mattson was "a good, hard man."

Dawn light bloomed. Troopers were up, grumbling and moving about. Smoke from cooking fires lingered over the bivouac. Thirsty and hungry horses snorted and pawed the ground. "Boots and Saddles" would sound within the hour.

Ty's father helped him to his feet. "Private Pursley has some of that Dupont ham boiling in a pot and loaves of three-day-old hard bread warming in a pan. I smell coffee, too."

"Don't complain a lick," Private Pursley warned his messmates. "Wasn't for me, you'd be eating field corn and happy to have it. Where's Cally Smith?"

"With the blue-belly cavalry," Ad White said. "He refused to get up after falling off his horse outside Glendale."

The loss of Cally and his sense of humor saddened Ty.

Shawn Shannon said, "That's a crying shame. Didn't someone try to tie him in the saddle?"

"He fought us off, Shawn. We couldn't stay with him any longer without falling behind the whole column."

Shawn Shannon grimaced. "Cally was one of many to fall out and be captured. Lieutenant Hardesty reported that today's muster by company sergeants showed one out of every five troopers missing from the rolls. We're wasting away pretty quick."

"You attended General Morgan's staff meeting, Shawn," Ad White said. "How far are we from the ford at Buffington Island?"

"Best estimate is one hundred miles," Shawn Shannon said.

"Good God, Shawn," Given Campbell said. "Didn't you calculate we rode ninety miles avoiding Cincinnati? I don't know if my tail can stand another one hundred miles without a month's rest in a feather bed, with a fair maiden tending to my every want and need."

After the mess finished laughing, Shawn Shannon said, "Owen, I haven't had a chance to tell you yet. We're accompanying Colonel Dick Morgan on a little twenty-mile ride down to the Ohio this morning. General Morgan wants a report on the status of the river."

Ty enjoyed the ride to Ripley, Ohio, with the Fourteenth Kentucky and Quirk's Scouts. Everyone involved was refreshed and invigorated after a full night's sleep. They sang as they rode, as if there were no organized opposition or bushwhackers within miles. Troopers had confiscated two violins, a guitar, and a banjo. They accompanied the Kentuckians as they sang "My Old Kentucky Home," "Juanita," "Arkansas Traveler," "Hills of Tennessee," and their favorite, "Lorena." The war seemed a long way off for a few hours.

The view from the hills overlooking Ripley shattered their festive mood. The Ohio, a wide expanse of brown, fast-moving, roiling water, was almost at flood stage—a most unusual occurrence for the month of July—and the local ferries were under heavy guard.

On the return trip, Ty was riding between his father and Shawn Shannon. "There's nothing closer now than the Buffington Island ford, providing we can beat the gunboats there," Owen Mattson said. "If we don't, we'll have to keep moving upriver to get beyond their reach."

Shawn Shannon said, "Every hour we spend on Ohio soil is to Burnside's advantage. We'll keep losing men we can't replace, and he's yet to bring his full might to bear. I'm glad I'm not the one who has to deliver this news to General Morgan."

The somber mood of their return ride was brightened briefly at Winchester, where boys from the Fourteenth Kentucky tied American flags to the tails of six stolen mules and galloped them through the town's main street, rebel yelling to scare the locals. They were drawing down on Locust Grove, their rendezvous point with the main column, by six at night.

Though it was probably a waste of breath, given Ty's next-to-nothing chance of spotting Jack Stedman's son amongst the

Texan members of Johnson's brigade, he couldn't resist asking his father, "What did the Stedmans look like?"

"No different than most men, from the neck down," his father answered. "What distinguished them was their pale blond hair, wide foreheads, bear trap jaws heavy on chinbone, and gray eyes cold as dead ashes. They never showed any feelings, unless they were liquored up."

From Ty's other side, Shawn Shannon said, "We'll keep a sharp lookout, Owen. We've been lucky before in circumstances like these. Remember Buck Granger? He was wrapped up in a winter blanket, face hidden from the wind, riding past you in Wyattsville, intending to back shoot you. You saw his fancy hand-tooled boot sticking out from under the bottom of that blanket, knocked him from the saddle with your rifle, and we hauled him off to jail. I don't think Buck's shoulder ever healed right. Let me tell you, Ty, that was one wicked blow."

"He was deserving," Owen Mattson said.

CHAPTER 12

Throughout the ride from Brandenburg, enemy militia had frequently shot at the advance guard and tried to drop trees across roads to slow the raiders' progress. Ty remembered General Morgan stating at their camp outside Harrison, Ohio, that he was pleased his men were free of Indiana, where every man, woman, or child was an enemy, every hill a telegraph, and every bush an ambush.

In two days, Ohioans gave General Morgan ample opportunity to dine on those departing sentiments with a seasoning of his choice. It was apparent from the reports of officers and couriers and Ty's personal observation that the Ohio woods were swarming with militia, pressing the column from both sides. Planks were ripped from bridges, felled trees blocked narrow roads, and log blockades defended almost every crossroad and town. After exchanging a few shots, Ohio militiamen fled and escaped pursuit or were taken prisoner and paroled, slowing the column and further taxing the troopers and horses chasing after them.

The rolling terrain, dotted with heavy woods broken by ravines and steep hillsides, favored those in hiding—the bushwhackers—and they took full advantage by shooting and killing from cover that often extended the length of the column.

Ty heard a soft *thump* and the officer next to him flopped from his saddle. He tugged at Reb's reins and there at his stirrup, on the hardpan of the road, lay Captain Duke Self—he of Virginia stock and West Point, a favorite of General Morgan's, shot plumb through the heart, dead eyes staring up at Ty.

Ty shivered. He had harbored a silly, childlike belief that his father and Shawn Shannon had the capacity to shield him from harm. The blunt truth was that no one in the column was safe, ever, day or night. That admission made him want to hunch his shoulders. Mattson pride kept him from scrunching down in the saddle. He might be scared, but he was determined only he would know.

Troopers pulled Duke Self's limp form from the road. General Morgan said a brief prayer over the body without dismounting while the column passed behind him. Then they rode on. Time was too short for proper burials. Ty was reminded of Professor Ackerman's maxim that war was the mean, uncaring, selfish master of those who fought it.

Food, forage, and horses became scarcer the more miles the raiders traveled. With such a lengthy advance warning, the Ohio populous was more adept at hiding their animals. Many troopers had worn out five or more horses already, but by some miracle— and the fact he hadn't been ridden around the clock—Reb hadn't given out along the way. Ty was as attached to the big gray gelding, with the black-splotched cheek, as General Morgan was to his swell gelding, Glencoe. Ty refused to think of parting with him.

The raiders continued their eastward flight at the fastest pace possible—the pitiful crawl of their artillery, supply wagons, and buggies bearing the sick and wounded hampering their progress as much as the efforts of the harassing militia. Late in the afternoon of July 16, they ransacked Jasper, Ohio, on the bank of the Scioto River, searching for the smallest scrap of food and horses.

Ty and Shawn Shannon were near the front of the column on the western edge of the village when a scout for the Fourteenth Kentucky, fresh from a horse hunt in the nearby hills, reined to halt in front of them and saluted. "Private Justice reporting, Lieutenant. Sir, I just spotted three black Yankee horses, one a blooded stallion that would surely catch General Morgan's eye. You know same as me how much he values a fine mount, him being top officer and all."

Shawn Shannon seldom participated in the incessant foraging of the column and surprised Ty by saying, "Where are they, Private Justice?"

"A mile down the south road, sir. They're in a paddock beside a big barn."

"Are they guarded, Private?"

"Didn't spot anybody round the house or barn, Lieutenant."

"Why didn't you bring them in, Private Justice?"

"Private Burton took sick and rejoined our company, and Sergeant Warthen don't allow his men to go it alone. There must always be at least two of you in case the Yankees are armed and hiding inside, waiting to ambush us. And you don't cross Sergeant Pudge Warthen, lessen you want the dirtiest, meanest details till the sun stops shining."

Shawn Shannon scanned the horizon, turned in the saddle, and said, "There's just enough daylight left. Lead the way, Private Justice. Corporal Mattson, Privates Campbell and Stillion, after me, if you please."

Ty's inclusion was as surprising as Shawn Shannon's decision to engage in a quick foraging expedition. Had it appeared dangerous, Ty doubted he would have been allowed to accompany the others. He realized this short foray was taking place solely to present John Hunt Morgan with a surprise gift of fine horseflesh. Ty was continually fascinated by how much General Morgan's men respected him and what he stood for. Impossible as it was, he was the officer they dreamed of being.

They trotted single file along a dusty lane that wound through a series of low hills. Around an angling bend to the west, away from the Scioto, they popped into a valley of lush meadows and standing corn. The wagon-wide lane ran straight as an arrow to the flowered lawn of a two-story frame house, which was shaded by tall oak trees. A large barn sporting a high hayloft, with a stable on the lower level, sat east of the house. A one-acre truck garden bristling with precise rows of various vegetables and a springhouse were visible on the opposite side of the house.

A substantial farm by any definition, Ty decided, too valuable to leave unattended, unless its owners had fled the premises out of fear for the havoc Morgan's men might subject them to. The desertion of property before the raiders' arrival had been a common thread of their long ride. The foragers had come to expect the tranquil scene before them.

When they reached the fringe of the lawn fronting the house, Shawn Shannon ordered the raider detail into a line abreast with Ty on the extreme right; they advanced at a slow walk. The paddock fence attached to the woods side of the barn, where the black head of a single horse lolled over its top rail, was solid of post and cross member and painted white. Ty immediately took note of the fact two of Private Justice's three horses were missing from the paddock.

Where were they?

A shot rang out, echoing throughout the valley. Private Justice grunted, grabbed his upper chest, and slipped sideways from his saddle.

"Over there," Given Campbell yelled, pointing toward the springhouse with one hand and drawing his pistol with the other.

The stable door of the barn swept open and a black stallion emerged at a gallop, bareback rider whipping hard with the reins. The big black swept around the paddock and headed for the woods beyond a pasture abutting the barn. His flight was directly away from Ty's position on the end of the raider line.

Ty didn't hesitate. He was closest to the galloping stallion. Without a direct order from the officer in command, or so much as asking permission, he booted Reb after the black and his rider.

Pistols barked behind Ty. No one called for him to halt and he concentrated on what lay ahead of him. Bending low over Reb's neck, he spurred the gray into a full gallop. The former cavalry mount loved a good run and Ty felt his stride lengthen. The black stud beat Reb to the woods by a fair margin after Ty lost ground reining the big gray around cattle grazing in the pasture.

Unsure of what awaited him within the trees, Ty sank lower yet in the saddle, drew his Remington, and reined Reb into the woods, where he'd last seen the black's rump. He was relieved to find they were following a game trail wide enough and worn down enough to provide sufficient space and solid footing for the flying Reb.

Though he lost sight of the fleeing Yankee, he could hear the beat of the black's hoofs. A low-hanging branch tugged at his gun hand, but he shook it aside without losing his grip on his weapon. After a quarter of a mile, the trees to either flank seemed to be tightening around Reb; Ty wondered how long the chase could continue.

There was a break in the trees and a threatening gap filled with running water opened beneath Reb. Without breaking stride, the gray vaulted the high-banked stream and landed on his feet with a soft thud while Ty's heartbeats were louder than thunder in his chest, even after the woods swallowed them again.

The drumming of the black's hoofs gradually sounded louder and Ty knew he was gaining on the streaking Yankee. Beyond a sharp bend in the narrowing pathway, he saw a swatch of red and realized it was the back of the Yankee's shirt.

The chase ended as abruptly as it had begun. The Yankee twisted in the saddle to check how close Ty was to him and a tree branch jerked him from the saddle. The red-shirted rider landed shoulder first, with a ringing scream of pain.

The Yankee was groaning and trying to get to his feet when Reb slid to a halt before him. Ty saw no sign his adversary was armed; but following Shawn Shannon's training, he covered the Yankee with his Remington and said, "Stand up, turn around, and look me in the eye, you bastard of a blue belly. Make a wrong move and you'll rot where you fall."

Ty had a yarn of Ebb White's to thank for his choice of words in this instance and he used them with conviction. Private Justice had been shot from ambush—someone had to be held accountable.

The Yankee struggled to his feet and steadied himself, then slowly turned. A grown, potentially dangerous adult enemy didn't confront Ty, but rather a ten-year-old boy quite big for his age. The youngster's ginger hair was ripe with twigs and leaves. His left cheek was badly scratched; tears coursed down both his cheeks. He was supporting his right elbow with his left hand.

The snort of a horse behind the lad drew Ty's gaze. The black stallion had returned unbidden. He nudged the young Yankee's shoulder with his nose and stood stock-still. Ty had once enjoyed the same kind of bond with a Denmark Thoroughbred from his foaling.

Ty found himself in a quandary. He should drag this pup and his pet stallion back to the farmyard and let Shawn Shannon deal with them. Instead, he hung fire in the saddle and stared down at his prisoners.

"What's your name, Yankee?"

"Benjamin, Benjamin Larkin," the crying lad squeezed out. "Are you gonna kill me . . . and steal my horse?"

Ty sighed. A ton of grief might be waiting at home for this

youngster and Ty didn't have the heart to heap more on the pile. This frightened boy hadn't taken part in the shooting in his farmyard; Ty was reluctant to place any of the blame on him. As Ty had witnessed many times over in recent days, Benjamin Larkin was an unintended victim of an adult war that had left none but the lucky unscathed.

If Ty did what he was contemplating, General Morgan wouldn't have a fine mount to add to his private gather. However, with a pitched battle looming for the raiders in the near future, the black stallion had the best chance of enjoying a long life with his current master. And no one would be the wiser if Ty handled the situation with care.

Holstering his Remington, Ty said, "I mean you no harm. Can you find your way home after dark?"

The Yankee lad nodded his head and dried his eyes with his palms. "Yes, sir, I can find my way home after dark by myself."

"If you want to keep your horse, stay here until the moon is out. For certain, we'll be gone from your farm by then. You understand what I'm saying?"

"Yes, sir. Don't move until the moon is out . . . and th-thank you, sir," the young Yankee sputtered, fighting back fresh tears.

Ty reined Reb about, clucked him into a trot, and didn't look back. He heard no gunfire in the distance and knew Shawn Shannon would be searching for him. He needed to concoct a believable alternative to what he had done on the spur of the moment that fit the circumstances. The explanation that made the most sense was one that portrayed his actions in the guise of a military decision, not an amateurish weakness for the under-dog. The last thing he wanted was to appear less than a profes-sional, dedicated cavalryman to Lieutenant Shawn Shannon and his father.

He was ready for the high-banked stream and touched Reb's flanks with his spurs. The jump was no harder for the gray than before. The sun was a mass of purple and gold rays shredded by darkening clouds when Ty emerged from the woods; that sight spawned the necessary lie he was seeking.

A frowning Shawn Shannon met him a short distance from the game trail. He glanced past Ty and said, "Didn't catch him?"

"No, sir," Ty answered, appalled at how glibly he was lying to a superior officer. "It was growing dark in those trees. Near as I could figure, he dismounted and hid with his horse in a thicket where the game trail petered out. I didn't know if he was armed, so I decided that stallion wasn't worth risking my life over."

Thankfully, Shawn Shannon made no mention of Ty racing off in pursuit without orders to do so and said, "You're beginning to think like a soldier. Much as I hate losing that animal, you made the right decision. I would have done the same."

Afraid his conscience might betray him, Ty quickly asked, "What happened here?"

"I learned from the father of the house that it was the oldest brother who wounded Private Justice in the shoulder against his strict orders to stand down. The shooter escaped on one of the mares. We can't tarry here and fall behind the column. I agreed not to burn the house and the barn and kill his cattle if the father promised to summon a doctor for Private Justice. I took him at his word. Let's collect the others and move out. We'll take the second mare with us. We're not leaving empty-handed, by damned, not when leaving one of our own behind."

Though Ty wasn't proud of his lie, he'd pulled it off. With Given Campbell leading the black mare, the raiders started out on the dusty lane. Now Ty did look back, realizing that he would never know, but wondering what would become of Benjamin Larkin and his magnificent stallion.

Wondering, too, given his true loyalties, if he had made the right decision.

* * *

Upon returning to Jasper, Ty's detail learned that General Morgan, convinced Union Cavalry were gaining on his column, had ordered an all-night march. The raiders rode steadily for forty-five miles. At dawn, on the seventeenth of July, they reached Jackson, Ohio, with Buffington's Ford still fifty miles away.

Ty dismounted on rubbery legs in front of a public watering trough and a raw stink assailed his nostrils. He stood sniffing, seeking its origin. The realization his own body was the source of the foul stench disgusted him. Every inch of his exposed skin reeked of stale sweat. His perspiration-soaked shirt, plastered with layers of road dust, clung to his body and gave off a skunk-like odor.

He rolled his sleeves to the elbow and ducked his head into the cold water of the trough. The head and arm bath provided little relief. Until he had a whole-body bath and replaced his shirt, he was stuck with his own stink. No amount of washboard scrubbing with lye soap could save his garment. Ty chuckled. Were she there, his grandmother, an ardent rag collector, would burn his shirt and tattered socks together, holding her nose all the while.

The brief thought of pilfering a new shirt was thankfully curtailed by buglers blowing "Boots and Saddles." Shawn Shannon's scruples were a tad looser. He hustled from the Jackson Mercantile with three spanking-new long-sleeved cotton shirts. He presented a fresh shirt to Ty and his father and said, "No quibbling. I'm not so much of a Baptist I can't steal on occasion. I'm tired of stinking like a polecat at mess. My mother did teach me some semblance of dignity."

The punishing journey they were enduring turned many of General Morgan's troopers surly. The bridge and mill destruction, fanatical looting of stores and robbery, and bullying of noncombatants intensified as the raiders passed through Wilkesville, Langsville, and Rutland. While they avoided the killing of civilians, it saddened Ty that the conduct of some of Morgan's men now matched that of the detested irregulars.

The attempt by the raiders to steal a horse at Rutland tested the admirable restraint of even General Morgan himself. Two raiders had their eye on a mare belonging to a frail, gray-haired female of considerable age. Instead of following their orders to turn over the animal, the old woman, to the astonishment of the two raiders, walked the mare from its stable straight into the parlor of her home, bolted the door behind her, raised a front window, trained a shotgun on the would-be thieves, bared toothless gums, and threatened, "You ain't taking my grandson's horse. Damned if you are. I'll blow both of you apart first."

The swarthy raider drew his pistol and dismounted. "Tell you what, you old crone. You fetch that mare to us straightaway, or you can die with her when we fire the house."

Having just delivered a message to General Morgan, Ty was with the general when he chanced upon the scene. The holed-up grandmother spied Morgan, cackled, and yelled, "Maybe that fancy-dressed officer on that tall gelding will light the match for you, you Rebel bastard."

Unconcerned as to what officer the grandmother was referring to, the two raiders scuttled sideways, increasing the distance between them, forcing the grandmother to choose between them for her prime target.

The second raider drew a bead on the open window with his rifle. "You foulmouthed old biddy," he raged, spittle flying from his lower lip. "If you don't throw down that cannon, me and Pollard here will burn your barn and kill your grandson, too. We don't have time to fool with the likes of you."

The two raiders were overwrought from the strain of continuous hours in the saddle and unwilling to accept a comeuppance from anybody aligned with the enemy, including a ninety-pound grandmother. The independent streak of Morgan's troopers frequently had them but a single step from insubordination. Ty wondered, how would these exhausted troopers, with weapons drawn and sighted, their tempers on the shortest possible leash, ready to snap, react if called to task by any officer?

General Morgan halted Glencoe directly behind them. Sweat cut runnels through the dust rimming the general's cheekbones and drizzled into his beard. Anger spawned a wide red welt at the edge of his uniform collar, and the coldness that Ty had witnessed at Corydon froze his countenance into hard planes. Having never seen the general hopping mad, Ty didn't know what might happen next.

Lieutenant Clinton J. Hardesty was on the opposite flank of Glencoe and Ty saw his look of grave concern. Always watching out for his superior's welfare, Adjutant Hardesty shouted, "Make way for General Morgan! Make way for General Morgan!"

The effect of Hardesty's shouts on the two raiders was instantaneous. They lowered their weapons and spun on their heels. They snapped to attention and saluted when they realized General Morgan had halted and was staring at them with obvious disapproval for what could only be their bullying of the shotgun-wielding grandmother. They stood stiff as plank boards—neither raider wanting to magnify Morgan's ire. They both remembered how their leader had court-martialed troopers in the past for what he deemed excessive behavior unworthy of his command and its mission. That their immediate officer, Sergeant Pudge Warthen, might have no problem with their conduct meant not a whit. They were at the absolute mercy of General Morgan's ultimate authority.

Perhaps it was their unhesitant response to Lieutenant Hardesty's shouts and their quick salute that squelched some of General Morgan's upset. Perhaps the fact that no real harm had been done and Buffington Island beckoned from afar influenced him even more. Most important, the redness disappeared from his neck; warmth swelled in the general's grayish blue eyes; Ty's respect for his commander's self-control multiplied a dozenfold.

Leaning forward in the saddle, while he studied the raiders' expectant faces, General Morgan said, "Privates, the lack of a single horse won't cripple our campaign. And I won't have the written history of our raid record we made war on women, even when they arm themselves. You may return to your company."

With another perfect salute, the relieved privates bolted past Glencoe and lit out down the southbound road afoot, leading their horses, matching the scampering hurry of rabbits fleeing buckshot.

Always the gentleman, General Morgan then amused Ty by attempting to make amends with the female enemy the best he could. "Ma'am, I wish to extend my apology for our wrongful-headed attempt to steal your horse. You, your property, and your grandson will not be harmed. On that, you have the personal assurance of General John Hunt Morgan."

The barrel of the gray-haired grandmother's shotgun lowered until it rested on the windowsill in front of her. "That's all well and good, Mr. General. Just don't take it as a personal insult that I intend to stay right here and stand guard over Jennie until every last one of you secesh Rebels are gone from my sight."

Offering General Morgan a gummy, ornery grin, the granny continued, "But I do thank you for the opportunity to tell my grandchildren that the famous General John Hunt Morgan once apologized to me at gunpoint. Good day, sir."

And with a nod and touch of John Hunt Morgan's hat brim, the saga of the general and the grandmother became campfire legend.

Southeast of Rutland, the raiders encountered their first Union soldiers since crossing the Ohio. A smattering of blue-uniformed regulars, along with companies of home-dressed militia, waited behind a log barricade atop Bradbury Hill. Given the upward slant of the narrow roadway, the thick woods on the right, and the sharp creek bank on the left, flanking movements were out of the question. Dislodging the combined force by frontal assault meant numerous causalities and the waste of valuable hours. General Morgan opted to backtrack and take the old stagecoach road that circled the Ohio River city of Pomeroy to the north, led to Chester, and then to Portland, site of Buffington's Ford.

The road to Chester curved into a broad-mouthed ravine. For two miles, a peaceful calm existed, the only sounds those of hoofs striking hardpan, the snort of a horse, the clink of metal on metal, and the soft murmur of voices. Ty rode with his father ahead of him, alongside General Morgan.

Ty came alert when his father broke off his conversation with General Morgan, stood in his stirrups, and stared at the rim of the ravine. Ty followed his gaze and saw sunlight flash on brass buttons.

A prolonged volley of musket and rifle fire raked the column with a veritable hail of lead

Pish! Pish! Pish!

Bullets were whipping past Ty. Their flitting noise was so dangerous and so familiar that he cringed with fright.

Colonel Duke's brigade was in the van. Ty watched troopers drop from the saddle and storm into the woods to rout the militia on foot. Four of the troopers' horse holders, who were waiting in the road, sagged to their knees and toppled, freeing the reins they held. Panicked horses galloped through the column, causing havoc until they were caught or veered into the forest.

"Dismount! Fire at will!" General Morgan ordered.

Delighted to be a smaller target, Ty slid to the ground, drew his Remington, and searched the woods for sign of the enemy.

The dismounted troopers poured withering rounds into the woods on both sides of the road and then the pace of bullets nipping from the trees slackened. Ty found it impossible to spy anything within the masking trees and underbrush other than a fleeting glimpse of a rifle barrel and a hat brim. Reb never flinched, and Ty fired at five muzzle flashes across the gray's back, not sure he hit human flesh with any shot.

Straining to ignore the screams of wounded horses and the thump of falling bodies, Ty reached into his leather shoulder bag, retrieved a fresh fully-loaded, capped cylinder, pulled the Remington's ejection rod to remove the spent cylinder, and switched them, under fire, with the skill of a veteran trooper. All the while, he wholeheartedly thanked his grandfather for their hours on the practice range and his father for ordering him to cap his spare cylinders the previous evening in anticipation of serious fighting.

Still seated on Glencoe, a frustrated General Morgan turned to the rear and bawled, "Sixth Kentucky, to the front. Pass it back!"

The Sixth Kentucky swept by in single file. Owen Mattson and Shawn Shannon joined them. Ty swallowed the urge to trail after them and obeyed his orders to stay with General Morgan.

"Boots and Saddles" echoed in the ravine. Ty swung aboard Reb. The First and Second Brigades bunched up behind the Sixth Kentucky and prepared to run the gauntlet, whatever miles that required.

Off they went at a gallop. Ty reined Reb around and over dead horses and gray-clad bodies. Dead troopers remained where they had died in the road or woods. The wounded who couldn't stay in the saddle were left behind to pray they survived long enough to catch a ride with the baggage train and not fall into Yankee hands.

A hip-shot horse cut in front of Ty. Reb stumbled and the horse of the trooper following him bumped his rear. Somehow the big gray gelding righted himself without falling and answered Ty's spurs.

The ravine narrowed. Ty was sure he could lean from the saddle and touch the towering eighty-foot-high walls. Wherever a pocket or defile allowed the militia to gather in numbers, the column was treated to heavy fire. Each time, the column halted and the Sixth Kentucky aped Colonel Duke's earlier tactics by barging into the woods afoot. Though suffering casualties, they successfully scattered militiamen who were unable to withstand the charge of veteran cavalrymen.

At one of the halts, a bullet tugged at Ty's sleeve. He felt pain and touched his arm. His hand came away smeared with blood. He determined with his fingers that the bullet had gouged his skin without doing any major damage. He sighed with relief. His first shedding of blood in combat had not been fatal.

The ravine ended abruptly after five miles. The column galloped into an area of open ground. Ahead loomed lines of well-armed blue-belly regulars, supported in their rear by militia. Once in the clear with room to maneuver, Colonel Duke, confronted by a foe without cannon and bayonets, didn't hesitate. He dispatched flanking companies to the left and right, waited until they were swinging into position, and charged the enemy's center.

The entire Rebel column swept forward. Ty hadn't wasted shots on targets he couldn't pinpoint, so his Remington was fully loaded. There was no Corydon barricade to jump and they were upon the blue-belly line in what seemed a heartbeat.

At twenty yards, Morgan's streaking cavalry absorbed a concentrated volley from the poised Yankees. Troopers pitched from the saddle. Bullet-struck horses went down, throwing their riders. A bullet nicked Ty's neck. Another bullet grazed his knee. Reb's heaving breath was a pipe organ gone wild. Then the Rebel juggernaut slammed into the ranks of Yankee foot soldiers hurrying to reload their weapons and the tide turned in a finger snap.

A rifle barrel slanted in Ty's direction. The sights of the rifle centered on his chest. Ty dropped alongside Reb's neck, his pistol never losing track of the yawning muzzle's owner. The blue belly's bullet flew high. Ty pulled the Remington's trigger and blood spurted from the blue belly's throat. The brown-bearded Yankee dropped his rifle and frantically clutched his neck with both hands in a vain attempt to staunch the life-ebbing flow of blood. His eyes closed and he collapsed as Ty and Reb barreled by him.

The Yankee lines crumbled. Some blue bellies dropped their weapons and raised their arms. Most chased after militia already on the run. A host of Rebel troopers ignored buglers blowing "Recall" and kept after them, yelling and shooting like crazy men.

Ty slowed Reb to a walk. The fight was over. He had no desire to shoot fleeing Yankees or Ohio militiamen in the back.

He wasn't proud of the single Yankee he'd killed, face-to-face.

CHAPTER 13

Once the raiders had regrouped, they resumed their strag-gling march without further delay. Ty checked his wounds from the saddle. The gouge in his left arm had stopped bleeding. His neck and knee burned like crazy, but he found no trace of blood on either wound—discoveries that reinforced the true meaning of a near miss.

Ty was delighted when Shawn Shannon and his father, both unscathed, rejoined General Morgan's entourage. Concern washed over Owen Mattson's face when he saw blood on his son's sleeve. "Hurt bad, Ty?"

"No, sir, just a minor wound."

Lieutenant Shannon pulled a metal canteen from his saddle-bag. "Splash some of the White brothers' corn likker on it. It might help. It can't hurt anything."

The burning sensation on Ty's neck and knee felt cool com-pared to the raging fire the corn liquor ignited in the torn flesh of his arm. His eyes watered and he bit his lip to keep from swearing aloud. Neither his father nor Shawn Shannon reacted to his discomfort verbally, but Ty swore their shoulders were quaking with silent laughter. Once the spike in pain subsided, Ty couldn't avoid a chuckle of his own.

There was no recalling or discussion of the charge against the blue-belly regulars by his father and Shawn Shannon. Ty had come to appreciate that what lay ahead was what occupied his father and Shawn Shannon, not what had transpired. They assessed the past only in terms of what lessons they had learned and gave little thought to glory won or lost. They evinced a mature philosophy, which intrigued and inspired Ty.

Short of Chester, Ohio, a slow-running branch creek, four feet deep, bisected the road. The plank flooring of the stream's wooden bridge was missing and the struts had been partially burned, rendering it useless. Horsemen could ford easily. The opposite was true for the baggage train.

General Morgan waved the column's horsemen across, pointed at Owen Mattson, Shawn Shannon, and Ty, then said, "At the roadside, please."

The four riders gathered together. General Morgan said, "Captain Mattson, we need a bridge built in a hurry. Organize the detail and oversee the construction as you did at John's Creek. Corporal Mattson will assist you. Lieutenant Shannon, seek out the rear guard and order them to close up the wagons and buggies as much as possible and send forward any militia we haven't paroled and the three farmers we captured for guides. They can tote with the sappers and miners. I don't want to be held here any longer than necessary."

"Axmen, sappers, and miners, to the front!" Captain Owen Mattson bellowed. "Pass it back!"

The detail worked at a rapid pace. Axmen chopped down nearby trees and skinned the branches from them. Deadfall limbs were collected. The creek bed was layered with tree trunks and then interspersed with rocks hand carried by the sappers and miners. Two dozen disgruntled Ohio militiamen and the three captive farmers added additional muscle. It was hot, mean labor under a brutal July sun.

Captain Mattson and Captain Tyrell, of the sappers and miners, were right on top of the work, supervising from horseback. Captain Mattson motioned for Ty to cease helping the detail and present himself. "Corporal, scout upstream along both banks. The militia didn't burn them, so those missing planks have to be hidden close by."

Ty checked the near bank first. Thickly grown brush overhung the bank, forcing him to proceed on foot. Twenty yards upstream, a bulky shelf of rock blocked his path. He thought of turning back, but his father's orders were to check both banks. He eased into the creek, holding his Remington revolver and leather bag shoulder-high, well above the muddy water.

His boots filled with water, and he slipped around the jutting rock and encountered a sizable defile, where floodwaters had cut the dirt bank away. The heavy bridge planks were stacked on end just out of the water against the wall of the defile, a clever hiding place that could not be seen from downstream at any angle.

Ty waded out into the creek until the old bridge and those working beyond it were in sight. He yelled and waved to catch somebody's attention. A sapper spied him and yelled at Captain Tyrell and his father. No further communication was necessary. Sappers and miners hustled upstream and the planks were soon flowing downstream via a chain of strong arms. The sappers leveled the makeshift bridge with shoveled dirt and topped it with the planks, creating a solid passageway for the heaviest wagons and the column's horse-drawn cannon.

While the final planks were being laid, Ty took time to dump the water from his boots. His tattered socks were "socks" in name only. He didn't attempt to remove them and wring them dry, for fear he'd have nothing left but a handful of useless rags.

General Morgan rode alongside Reb. "Fine job locating the planks, Corporal. You've made yourself quite useful."

Ty appreciated the compliment, particularly in front of his father. He didn't want the general or his father displeased with how he conducted himself in any way. His grandfather had stressed that trust between men didn't come easy. Once established, it needed to be nurtured. Trust was the anchor for man's endeavors to survive and forge a meaningful life with his fellow humans.

General Morgan, Captain Mattson, and Ty had started across the replacement bridge when a trooper behind them growled, "Mount up, sappers. That includes you, Elam, you worthless turd. There's no need for us here now."

The name "Elam" and the cadence of that gruff, rasping voice raised Ty's hackles. He twisted about in the saddle. A trooper was holding the reins of a red roan for a sergeant with yellow epaulets on his shoulders, the insignia of the sappers. The mounting officer glanced in Ty's direction and the sight of shaggy, pale blond hair and a bear trap jaw made Ty's heart pound.

"Something wrong, Corporal?" an observant Owen Mattson inquired.

Ty faced his father. "That sapper officer issuing orders a minute ago was the same trooper I overheard at the sinks and the night we skirted Cincinnati. I know it's him, sure as sleet is ice. He has blond hair and the heavy jaw, just like you said his father did."

Ty started to turn his head for another look and his father said, "Keep your eyes straight ahead."

"But, Father—"

"Eyes straight ahead. I don't want him thinking we have any interest in him. He's riding a red roan, right?"

"Yes, sir."

"Twice this morning, out of the corner of my eye, I caught him staring at me. It wasn't a friendly or curious stare. It was one of pure hate. I had a chance to observe him later without his knowing it. I believe we've identified our would-be assassin."

"What are you going to do, now that we've identified him?"

"Nothing at the moment. I don't know his name yet, but even if I did and I confronted him, it would be your word against his as to whether or not he told his cousin he planned to kill me. You didn't see him in the dark either time you heard his voice, so you can't identify him personally, and since he enrolled under a different name, there's no written record he's of Stedman blood. He's holding a royal flush son."

"Then we're really not much better off than we were."

"Yes, we are. Knowing who to look for may give me the edge I need when he makes his move."

Ty's frustration was unbounded. He wanted to scream "not if he shoots you in the back," but he held his tongue. Stating the obvious was a waste of time that benefited neither him nor his father. What was to happen would happen. He remembered Shawn Shannon telling him how his father had said during the Comanche ambush at Blue Springs that cost Boone Jordan his leg, "An honest prayer isn't to be scorned in any situation."

Ty took that advice to heart and didn't much care if anyone noticed his bowed head.

CHAPTER 14

With opposing forces reduced to the occasional bushwhacker, the raiders double-quicked the remaining five miles to Chester, Ohio, arriving at one in the afternoon. The town straddled the Salt River. Once the advance elements were across the bridge, the raiders invested the town and prepared to defend it against an attack from the northern and eastern points of the compass, as nobody knew for certain where the Union regular forces were located.

Ty dismounted at the foot of the steep hill in the middle of Chester. The county courthouse, an imposing stone structure with entryways on three levels, occupied the top of the hill. "Must be on important business if you climb that bugger," Ebb White quipped.

The remark drew a meager laugh from a worn-down Ty. Now that the sheer excitement and terror of running the Pomeroy gauntlet and charging the Union regulars had subsided, he was spent and famished. The sight of Private E.J. Pursley and Corporal Sam Bryant bearing a stock of freshly stolen cheese, crackers, jerked beef, baked honey cakes, and jugs of hard cider set his mouth to watering. The mess cook and his helper had raided grocery baskets and boxes of goodies prepared to feed home guards gathering later in the day to blockade the town. Returned from his ride the length of the column, Shawn Shannon joined his messmates for the impromptu meal.

Sam Bryant watched his messmates feast on the baked honey cakes, shook his head, and laughed. "You boys remind me of children on their first visit to our Lexington confectionery. They spy all those cakes, pies, doughnuts, sweet breads, different colors and flavors of hard candy, and black licorice and their faces light up like the morning sun. If they're allowed, they'd eat till their bellies burst."

Ebb White agreed, saying, "Yeah, and you need enjoy that kind of hurt whenever you can. You don't have many chances at sweets no matter how old you be, not at least where I hail from."

Always seeking to lighten the moment, Given Campbell gave Sam a deadpan look and said, "Now, Private Bryant, I trust after the war, you intend to return to your candy making and making children happy. You've been with this outfit fourteen months and there's still more daylight between your butt and the saddle than the greenest cavalry recruit in the short history of the Confederacy. When you made the leap over that Corydon barricade and then back again, there wasn't a clean pair of drawers in our mess."

That observation drew a guffaw from Ty and the others that made their ribs hurt. Before the laughter petered out, Given Campbell's roving eye for feminine lovelies struck again. He fettered out three young ladies studying the raiders from the door of a black-shuttered Baptist church. "Too bad we don't have the time to introduce ourselves. But then they'd just be fawning over Ty in a whipstitch."

"What do you mean by that?" Ty responded. "Women never pay any attention to me that I've noticed."

"That's because you don't pay them any attention," Given

said. "They gape at you in every town. He'll learn, won't he, Shawn? He'll learn the pretty gals like red hair, green eyes, and square shoulders. I've watched them swoon over your father till even I was embarrassed."

Ty wasn't sure where the conversation was headed. Was he being kidded? He was glad to see his father approaching the mess. "Glad you're here, Lieutenant. You and Ty, come along with me. General Morgan is about to hold a council of war."

Ty didn't hear any laughter behind him. Maybe Given Campbell wasn't joshing with him. Maybe he should start watching for friendly females as soon as the war was over. He found that a most pleasing prospect.

General Morgan's council of war convened in the yard of a large redbrick house encircled by a porch roofed with black shingles. In attendance were Colonels Duke and Johnson, the line officers of both regiments, Captain Byrnes, the artillerist, several of the general's aides, and those officers on detached duty with his personal staff.

Ty thought General Morgan's face lacked its usual high-spirited cast. For the first time, he appeared tired and his eyes were dull. It was a shocking sight for Ty. He had begun to believe John Hunt Morgan was immune to the stresses and strains of combat that taxed and ate away the enthusiasm of mere mortals like him.

General Morgan's gaze swept over the gathered officers. "Lieutenant Shannon, please step forward."

The others parted to make way for Shawn Shannon, who saluted and said, "Yes, sir."

"Lieutenant Shannon, did you deliver my orders to Colonel Gibbon's rear guard?"

"Yes, sir. They were working hard to close up the wagon and baggage train when I rode forward."

"What is the status of the column, Lieutenant? I want the unvarnished truth and nothing less."

"It's strung out and confused, sir. Companies are strewn together, and there are additional wounded to tend. Some horses are on their knees. They won't move, even if whipped."

Ty observed officers nodding in agreement with Shawn Shannon's assessment. The raider's situation was growing more desperate by the hour. Everyone in the yard wished he were standing on the breeze-brushed bank of the Ohio instead of baking under the July sun, fifteen miles short of freedom and safety.

General Morgan said, "That confirms reports I've received since we arrived. Gentlemen, I'm not proceeding without a trustworthy guide. We will rest the men and horses and fill canteens and let the column form up until we find such a guide."

Colonel Johnson objected—his tone firm, yet obedient.

"Sir, if we delay long, we won't reach Buffington Island before dark. The advance scouts confirmed a few minutes ago that the Ohio is still running high and a crossing in the night without boats would be very difficult. The scouts say the ford is free of Yankees and their gunboats, as of right now. Daylight today may be our only chance of saving the fighting elements of your command, sir."

General Morgan shook his head. "Colonel Johnson, the men and horses need a breather, and I won't allow the wounded to fall into Yankee hands by default. We'll spare as many of them captivity as we can. We owe them dearly for their service. We will resume our march, once we rest and secure a reliable guide."

Ty swore he saw a fleeting frown of disapproval twist his father's brow. One second, it was there; the next, it was gone, as if Owen Mattson had squashed the hint of disobedience at conception. "Son, we're in for a rude Yankee welcome tomorrow. I'm afraid the renowned battlefield luck of our general is about to run dry. But our commander has spoken and we Mattsons do our duty, come what may."

Two hours later, the column was on the move again, without a reliable guide. Owen Mattson and Shawn Shannon joined the advanced guard. Ty stayed with General Morgan's entourage.

The way roughened beyond Chester. The column marched along dirt roads that wound to the crests of steep hills and then dropped sharply into ravines and small valleys overgrown by heavy brush. The troopers walked their flagging horses up the inclines and trotted them down the other side, sparing their mounts as much as possible. The squeal of dry wagon axles under great stress emanating from the baggage train sounded like screeching owls. Ty looked ahead and behind atop each crest, marveling how the column resembled an oversized worm crawling through tall grass, brown and gray skin contrasting with its sun-dappled, emerald-green surroundings.

The only rain the raiders had experienced since departing Brandenburg had been a single light shower a week past, and the ever-present cloud of hoof-stirred dust wrapped the column that afternoon, adding to the misery of troopers so close to collapse that many shifted constantly in the saddle to stay alert. A number of troopers wore stolen ladies' hats with their blue veils overlaid with bandanas, enduring the joshing and catcalls of their comrades in a vain attempt to deter the sun and the grit that miraculously coated every sliver of exposed skin.

Ty was longing to reach the Ohio. At the first opportunity, he planned to hop into its waters, muddy or not, boots and all. A mud bath beat no bath, hands down.

The memorable event of the hot, miserable trek occurred outside the hamlet of Bashan. The column encountered a funeral procession bound for the local cemetery. The boys in the advance guard halted the procession, removed the coffin from the hearse, laid it gently at the side of the road, and confiscated the hearse and the horses of both undertaker and mourners. Ty long remembered Ebb White's quip as they rode by the enraged, fist-shaking, cursing-in-God's-name preacher. "It will be the only time in the Hell-bender's ministry wounded soldiers replace a dead soul."

As they neared their destination, Ty was clinging to his saddle horn with both hands, trusting a game Reb to maintain their place in line. It was shortly before dark when the column descended from the rugged hills into a narrow valley that ran parallel to the Ohio, the site of the Buffington Bar, and the village of Portland, which hovered over it.

Every trooper stood in his stirrups, seeking to sight the flooded river. Long before the others, Ty's keen eyesight picked out the faint sheen of its dark waters.

Silly as it was, he felt the joy of the traveler returning to shore after a long voyage at sea.

PART 3

BUFFINGTON ISLAND

We have at last made Buffington Island. General Morgan's temporary headquarters is located in a large, two-story farmhouse one mile north of the village of Portland. A snore-scarred hush prevails throughout its rooms as I write in the wee hours of the morning. The men are fatigued, hollow of cheek and eye, tucked up from hunger and dispirited. We are lacking morale, gumption and ammunition. By the latest reports Captain Byrnes has but twenty rounds remaining per cannon. A sizable Yankee force is entrenched behind solid earthworks to our front beyond Portland. We know not how many blue-bellies will oppose us come dawn. We do know that they are in the vicinity in the thousands while we now number but sixteen hundred, six hundred troopers having been killed, captured or wounded since we crossed the Kentucky-Tennessee border. Our day of reckoning is upon us. We have led the enemy a merry chase, but the fox has been brought to bay, and that same enemy craves a full measure of revenge on his terms and on his ground. We will know our fate on the morrow, be it escape, death or imprisonment.

—Journal of Lieutenant Clinton J. Hardesty, Morgan's
Confederate Cavalry, 19 July 1863

CHAPTER 15

Just beyond the intersection of the Chester Road and a north-south road that ran the length of the narrow valley parallel to the Ohio, a lit lantern swung from side to side in the dark. "That's Captain Mattson's signal, General Morgan," Lieutenant Hardesty said. "He has located temporary quarters for us."

General Morgan's entourage continued on the Chester Road for forty yards and reined through the open gate of a wrought-iron fence. The farmhouse at the end of the graveled, buggy-wide lane was a towering black shadow. One by one, coal oil lamps responded to the touch of wooden matches and sprang to life, illuminating the first floor of the dwelling.

Owen Mattson met General Morgan as he stepped onto the home's front porch. "Owner's a tad up in arms, but without arms, sir," Ty's father said, drawing a chuckle from his superior officer.

Lieutenant Shannon opened the front door from within the house. A bald, rotund, beardless, middle-aged male, starched white shirt unbuttoned at the throat, suspenders dangling at his waist, stepped into the center hallway from a formal living room and said in a near shout. "I am Magistrate Cordell Bainbridge, and I will not grant Rebel trash like you the use of my home as long as I draw breath!"

General Morgan removed his hat, bowed, introduced himself, and said, "Quite frankly, I would prefer to be elsewhere, Magistrate Bainbridge, but I have no choice but to intrude on your privacy. The hour is late and I need quarters and food for my staff officers. The necessities of war demand such, not gentleman John Hunt Morgan of Lexington, Kentucky. I pray our abrupt arrival did not frighten any female residing within your abode. May we enter?"

"Man can charm a rattlesnake," Ebb White mumbled behind Ty.

Sure enough, being spoken to as one gentleman to another, not enemy to enemy, coupled with General Morgan's genuine concern for the emotional welfare of any female who might be hiding elsewhere in his home, squashed Magistrate Bainbridge's outburst. Bainbridge buttoned his shirt, looped his suspenders over his shoulders, and nodded decisively. "Sir, on those terms, I grant you the hospitality of my home for the night."

Ty was certain the fact he was speaking with General John Hunt Morgan had played a major role in Magistrate Bainbridge's acceding to the general's wishes. Ty bet that for the balance of Bainbridge's days on earth, the mollified magistrate would tell the tale of this rare event in his life to anyone with a willing ear.

As Magistrate Bainbridge escorted General Morgan into his formal parlor, Lieutenant Shannon tugged at Ty's sleeve. "Womenfolk are in the kitchen. Old Box won't catch up to us for three hours, maybe more. Get them started preparing the general's supper. Wouldn't resist a bite myself."

Ty headed down the center hallway of the Bainbridge home, noting the rich blue Brussels carpet, the diamond pattern of the silk wallpaper, etched glass of the coal oil chandelier, the large wall mirror, and the painted portrait of Magistrate Bainbridge hanging above a slim marble-topped table. Like his grandfather, Magistrate Bainbridge was a citizen of stature, power, and substance in the community of Portland, Ohio. Grandfather Mattson, however, was too strict in his thinking and lacked the necessary vanity to commission a self-portrait.

Twelve chairs surrounding a mahogany dining table, a sideboard, buffet, and china cabinet of the same polished wood, a mirror that covered half of a wall and a chandelier befitting a foreign prince graced the dining room in which Magistrate Bainbridge sustained his rotund waistline and hefty jowls.

The kitchen Ty sought was behind the dining room, accessible from both the dining space and the hallway via separate doors. A bone-tired, sleep-starved, hungry Ty didn't bother knocking on the hallway kitchen door. He swept it open and barged into the kitchen, smack into the enticing smells of roasting meat, boiling coffee, and baking pie, strawberry he was certain.

An assortment of pots, frying pans, cooking utensils, spices, and gourds hung from the ceiling over a large square, oilcloth-covered table in the center of the substantial kitchen. A cast-iron stove, with side-by-side ovens, covered the back wall. Opposite Ty was a large porcelain sink, with a sideboard supporting a hand pump for water. The third wall, outfitted with floor-to-ceiling shelves, served as the kitchen's pantry. Judging by the full larder of preserved fruits and vegetables, extensive stock of canned goods and the bursting flour and sugar bins that filled those shelves, until tonight the real war had truly been fought hundreds of miles from the Bainbridge home.

Two females occupied the kitchen. A handsome black woman, with gray hair, was slicing melon on the center table with a well-honed knife. What Ty judged a nicely shaped posterior, undoubtedly female, owing to the coal-black hair trailing above it, was bent over in front of the cast-iron cookstove. The owner of the nicely built rear and midnight tresses slid something from the oven, with mitt-protected hands, straightened, turned about, and nearly dropped her freshly baked pie upon sighting Ty. Eyes bluer than the brightest spring sky widened and pinned themselves on Ty's face. "You don't know enough to knock? Maybe you didn't have a mother with proper manners."

Ty Mattson hadn't much experience with full-grown females, but minimal exposure to the fairer sex didn't hinder his ability to discern the beautiful from the pretty, the unusual from the ordinary. He was staring at the most beautiful and most unusual female he'd ever seen. A finely sculpted nose, firm chin, rounded cheekbones, and generous mouth—full lower lip trembling at the moment—fit perfectly with her sky-blue eyes and raven hair.

He understood her trepidation over confronting him so boldly in such a sharp tone. He remembered how he had looked in the hallway and dining-room mirrors: red-eyed, bearded, shirt filthy with caked road dust, trousers bullet torn at the knee, and a body stink strong enough to gag a maggot. He regretted his holstered revolver. He couldn't appear more dangerous if he tried.

Remembering his manners at last, he snatched his hat from his head, aware that his flame-red hair would be standing straight up in bunches and do nothing to soften his image. She had to think he'd stepped from the very depths of Hell, the realm inhabited by outlaw misfits and rabble-rousers.

"Corporal Ty Mattson, of Elizabethtown, Kentucky, ma'am," Ty said, keeping his voice low and calm, not wanting his unnaturally deep voice to startle her all over again. "I apologize for scaring you. I'm afraid my hunger got the best of me."

"You didn't scare me, Corporal. We've just never had an armed Rebel scoundrel storm into our kitchen before, have we, Lydia?"

"No, Miss Dana, never," black Lydia said.

The name, elegant and easy on the ear, matched her beauty. There was nothing Ty wanted more in the whole world right then but to watch her and talk with her. But military discipline ruled. General Morgan's dinner had to come first.

Given the age of Cordell Bainbridge, Ty chanced that Dana was his daughter and not his wife. "Miss Bainbridge, your father has invited General Morgan and his staff to be his guests this evening and dine with him. Will you please serve them when you are ready?"

Dana Bainbridge placed her strawberry pie on the center table and removed her mittens. Fixing those sky blues on Ty once more, she said, "Your General Morgan must be quite diplomatic to wrest an invitation from my father without threatening him with a gun. He hates you Rebels with a passion."

Ty was totally smitten with Dana Bainbridge. A warmth and longing swept through him that made his chest ache and tightened his throat. He knew instantly how his father had felt when he met Keena McVey and realized in a flash she was the woman for him. But unlike that first meeting of his parents, there was no sign the magistrate's daughter felt the same feelings for him whatsoever. She probably wanted the unshaven Rebel lout from Elizabethtown, Kentucky, out of her kitchen—jack quick—and who could blame her?

One important thing was in his favor. She hadn't corrected how he had addressed her. For what it might be worth, if by some remote chance he somehow found himself sharing her company later, she wasn't married.

"You are lucky, Corporal," Miss Dana said. "It is my father's custom to dine after the house cools in the evening. Lydia and I were just completing our final preparation. You may inform Father and your General Morgan that we will be ready to serve them in thirty minutes. Will there be other diners?"

Ty cleared his throat, swallowing instead of spitting, and said, "Yes, Colonels Duke and Johnson and Lieutenant Hardesty usually dine with him."

"And where and what will you eat, Corporal Mattson?"

"With the cook's permission, scraps on the rear stoop, Miss Bainbridge," Ty said with a grin.

Dana Bainbridge threw her head back and laughed. "I like a man with a sense of humor. We'll do better than that for you, Corporal. Now pass the word to my father. Make sure you inform father first. We don't want him thinking he's not in charge. He has enough pride for ten of you males. I prefer a quiet evening meal without the usual shouting and haranguing with our visitors about the merits of this godforsaken war."

Ty was delighted. He was certain Dana Bainbridge was at least two years, if not three years, older than he; yet she had referred to him as a man, not a boy. Speculating about a relationship with her was undoubtedly a waste of time; but, then, weren't dreams free for the making?

"Corporal Mattson, you can't stare at me and tell my father about dinner all at once," Dana Bainbridge said with a sweet smile, "unless, of course, you carry a miracle in your pocket."

Face aflame, Ty fled the kitchen, angry with himself for lingering like a child with his mouth hanging open in awe of what his eyes were seeing, instead of paying attention to his soldierly duty.

As he expected, Magistrate Bainbridge was seated in the family parlor across the hallway from the kitchen, not in the formal parlor at the front of the house with General Morgan. The general was adamant about preventing enemy civilians from eavesdropping on his meetings with his highest-ranking officers. In fact, the sliding doors of the front parlor were closed.

Magistrate Bainbridge spied Ty in the hallway and laid his leather-bound book on a low table. "Yes, young man?"

"Sir, Miss Bainbridge would like you to inform General Morgan that dinner will be ready in thirty minutes."

"I appreciate good manners and appropriate behavior, but in this unusual situation, it would be best if you delivered her message."

Ty nodded and walked to the front parlor doors, knocked, and waited. His father slid the oak doors open gently and bid Ty to enter. Ty whispered the status of dinner to his father, who, in turn, quietly informed Lieutenant Hardesty without disrupting the ongoing conversation of General Morgan, Colonels Duke and Johnson, and Captain Byrnes.

"Gentlemen, I will not countenance an assault on the Yankee redoubt to open the ford for a night crossing," General Morgan was saying. "We would be facing unfamiliar ground and we don't know the size and quality of the enemy. Our men are exhausted, and I fear that if we are repulsed, they may panic and create a situation beyond our control."

"We could leave the baggage train, artillery, and the sick and wounded here and seek a ford upriver," Colonel Johnson said.

General Morgan rejected Johnson's suggestion out of hand. "As I said at Chester, I would not abandon a single man. We will save all or lose all."

"Your orders then, sir," Colonel Duke said.

"Colonel Duke, you will prepare your First Brigade for an attack on the Yankee redoubt at dawn. Colonel Johnson, your Second Brigade will guard the approach from Chester Road. Please send out pickets and assess the enemy's location to the west. Captain Byrnes, please station your guns so you may support Colonel Duke's morning assault. Any questions?"

When no questions were forthcoming, General Morgan said, "Lieutenant Hardesty, will we be dining soon?"

"Twenty minutes, sir," Lieutenant Hardesty said.

A wan smile creased General Morgan's cheeks. "Gentlemen, while not normally an imbiber, a taste of good brandy or sherry would be most delightful. An elected official, like Cordell Bainbridge, must have a supply of cordials for wooing votes. Captain Mattson, would you ask the magistrate to join us with a bottle of his choosing?"

"I believe Corporal Mattson is up to the chore, sir."

"Begging your pardon, sir," Ty said, "but it might be best if the request came from a captain, not a lowly corporal."

General Morgan actually giggled. "Captain, given Bainbridge's evident buffoonery, our young chap is on target."

In four short minutes, Cordell Bainbridge entered the parlor with a round wooden tray holding seven hand-molded glass goblets and a glass decanter filled with a shiny brown liquid. "This, General Morgan, is my very best cognac, saved for my most special guests."

Placing the tray on a side table covered by a knitted lace doily, Cordell Bainbridge filled each goblet with three fingers of cognac and passed a goblet to each of his guests. Ty accepted his goblet with some misgivings. To the grandson of Enoch Mattson, liquor was a forbidden indulgence, but how could he refuse it and insult Magistrate Bainbridge's hospitality? Everyone lifted his goblet with General Morgan's prayer that the war would end quickly. The memory of Shawn Shannon pouring Ebb White's corn squeezin's on his wounded arm made Ty cautious. He watched the others drink until he learned cognac was for sipping, not bolting. The first dab burned his throat a tad, but the warmth magnified a taste smooth as silk. Ty was sorry Shawn Shannon had volunteered to look after their horses and missed a delightful repast.

Apparently, if Ty was old enough to imbibe with General Morgan and his lead officers, he was old enough and important enough to dine with them, for the general himself invited Ty to join him at dinner. Ty was thrilled with the invitation. If Miss Dana Bainbridge knew anything about military protocol, a mere corporal dining with a general and his key staff might impress her favorably. Ty suppressed a temptation to smile and swagger, fearing he would appear an overjoyed child amongst mature soldiers.

The evening temperature was dropping and the open windows of the dining room allowed a cross breeze, which cooled those seated at the Bainbridge table. Miss Dana and Lydia had gone to great lengths in a hurry to accommodate the large number of unexpected guests. The two ladies served up a veritable summer feast of corned beef, both hashed and with cabbage, sweet corn, pole beans with crumbled bacon, loaf bread, still warm from the oven, a crock of butter, cider, black coffee, and strawberry and blackberry pies. The ladies retired to the kitchen, and the head of the house and his guests ate with a passion, leaving no time for idle chatter.

The quiet chewing and drinking was disrupted by a screeching yelp as the diners finished their pie. Before any inquiry as to the source of the nerve-jangling interruption could be made, the front door swung back against the hallway wall with a crash that threatened to shatter its glass panels. Shawn Shannon dragged what appeared to be a mere boy resisting his efforts into the dining room. One of his hands had a firm grip on the boy's shirt collar and the other held an ancient, single-barrel, black-powder shotgun.

"Don't know who he is, General, but he was drawing a bead on you a few paces from the window," Lieutenant Shannon said.

God forbid, dignity blown to pieces, Magistrate Bainbridge shot to his feet, napkin flying from his collar and landing in the middle of his plate. "That's my youngest son, Alex. Alex, cease that caterwauling this second. How could you contemplate such a heinous act?"

Twelve-year-old Alexander Bainbridge came to rigid attention like a disciplined soldier, eyes cold with unfathomable hatred and said, "They killed my brothers, the bastards. I'll kill them, generals and all, till they hang me for it. War or no war."

"Alex, go to your room," Magistrate Bainbridge said. "I will not tolerate this kind of behavior in our home."

To Ty's surprise, General Morgan didn't object to the dispatching of his would-be executioner to his private quarters.

Alex Bainbridge poked his nose into the air and marched from the room. Everyone heard his boots pounding up the stairs at the rear of the house.

Cordell Bainbridge regained his composure. "My sincerest apology, General Morgan. I lost my two older sons at Shiloh and Gettysburg. Alex's mother died of what I'm sure was pure grief just a few weeks after Franklin was killed at Shiloh. Alex can think of nothing but becoming a soldier and extracting a measure of revenge for his brothers. I was unaware Alex had a weapon. He was staying overnight with my brother's family in Portland."

Bainbridge harrumphed to strengthen his faltering voice. "There are no other weapons in my house, sir. You may search room to room, if you prefer."

General Morgan's response was a soothing smile. "That won't be necessary. I understand young Alex's feelings. I lost my youngest brother, Tom, to a Yankee ball at Lebanon, Kentucky, just thirteen days ago."

General Morgan's deep sigh equaled a gust of wind. "No matter who emerges the victor in this brutal conflict, Magistrate, the tragic loss of life will forever haunt those wearing both blue and gray who perpetrated it and fought it."

Magistrate Bainbridge sank back into his chair. "General, I never thought I'd admit it, not in a hundred years. You Rebels aren't so easy to hate at close range. I'd be proud to share another cognac with you."

General Morgan emptied his coffee cup, pushed back his chair, and stood. "I'm afraid I must decline your offer, sir. Much remains to be done for the morrow."

Magistrate Bainbridge rose from his chair again. "I fully appreciate that, General. There are two spare bedrooms above us. Use them, as you see fit. I will be retiring. My daughter will do so after the kitchen chores are completed. I will make sure Alex is not a problem."

"What about your family? If a battle breaks out in the morning, as I expect it will, you may not be safe here."

"General, there's a deep root cellar beneath the house. We will take shelter in it if the situation requires. I bid you good night, sir."

Magistrate Bainbridge departed with a nod that General Morgan returned. The General's eyes surveyed the room. "Lieutenant Shannon, your vigilance in the matter of young Alex is much appreciated."

"No problem, sir. He came across the cornfield behind the barn. I caught a glimpse of him sneaking to the corner of the house. He hid in the bushes along the side of the house. I waited and jumped him the second he sighted that old shotgun on the open window. You were an easy shot, with your back to him."

"The 'Thunderbolt of the Confederacy' assassinated by an Ohio farm boy while dining in a Northern Yankee home," General Morgan said. "Good Lord, how the Union correspondents would have treasured that headline."

That remark garnered a hearty laugh from everyone present. "Lieutenant Shannon, if you have not eaten, I'm certain the ladies of the kitchen will provide for you. You may tell them we are finished with their fine meal. Gentlemen, we will repair to the living room for a final review of our strategy for the morning."

Ty followed Shawn Shannon into the hallway. The kitchen door was closed. "Make sure you knock," he warned.

The evening didn't conclude as Ty prayed it would. He did learn during the second parlor meeting that the main preoccupation of General Morgan and his officers was the location of the Yankee gunboats. The current height of the Ohio's flooded waters raised the distinct possibility that the gunboats could steam upriver to Buffington Island. Even with an exclusion of the baggage train, a fording by Morgan's troopers under their relentless fire was problematic at best. General Morgan closed the meeting by repeating his firm orders to have the cannons properly placed to support Colonel Duke's assault and the entire column—every man who could stand and fire a weapon—ready for action at daybreak.

Ty hustled to the kitchen. He was too late. The stove fire was banked for the night; the cleaning up completed; Miss Dana Bainbridge and Lydia gone. He'd longed for one last look at Dana Bainbridge in all her beauty.

Shawn Shannon stepped through the rear door of the kitchen. "I'm disappointed that Bainbridge gal retired for the night so quickly."

"Me too," Ty said, wishing he hadn't.

Shawn Shannon grinned slyly. "If you hadn't noticed her with those field glass eyes of yours, I'd be worried you'd gone blind on me or you're too young to kiss a woman. Now, don't get your knot tied double on me, but I think she was taken with you."

"How could you tell that?" a doubting Ty asked.

"She asked if you were married and how old you are. That's kind of unusual for a female after a chance meeting with an armed enemy combatant you've never laid eyes on before."

"What did you tell her?"

"I told her you aren't married and that you're twenty years old."

"Why did you lie about my age?"

"I didn't want to scare her off straightaway. You mad I fibbed to her?"

"No," Ty said. "You know more about women than I do, and the odds are that I won't ever see her again, anyway."

Shawn Shannon shrugged his shoulders. "Don't discount anything in this-here world, my boy. Only the Lord knows in advance what will come to pass, and He hasn't yet chosen to tell me or you 'yea' or 'nay' in advance."

CHAPTER 16

With the conclusion of the evening's festivities and military strategy sessions, Ty bedded down on the rear porch of the Bainbridge home. His gum poncho made the hardness of the rough planks tolerable, and the roof of the porch offered protection against the heavy morning dew common to river bottoms. His thin blanket was sufficient to ward off the chill spreading through the narrow valley.

Ty was as comfortable as he'd been any other night and desperately tired, but he couldn't sleep. His chance meeting of Dana Bainbridge had started him thinking about what kind of future he might have if he survived the battle tomorrow and whatever came afterward.

Ty had willingly severed his ties with Grandfather Mattson to search for his father, which most likely meant he wasn't welcome to grace that Elizabethtown doorstep anytime soon. The key question, then, for Ty was what were his father's postwar intentions? Would Owen Mattson invite Ty to follow him home to Texas? If he did, what would they do to provide themselves sustenance and shelter? If his father became a Texas Ranger again, was Ty old enough to be sworn in with him, if the Rangers would accept him? If not, what could Ty do to make his own way as Shawn Shannon had said Ranger pay supported the officer in fair style, but often left a meager amount for the man's family.

The things Ty knew best were horses and farming. From observing his grandfather, he knew the secret to acquiring land and animals was securing the necessary credit. But what did a former Ranger and his son have to offer a bank in return for financial backing?

Ty realized that chill dark night on the Bainbridge porch that he'd been buried in the details of his sheltered life—hearty meals morning and evening year-round, library brimming with books, lessons with Professor Ackerman, evening discussions with Grandfather Mattson, colts to break and train for the races, crop fields to inspect, and a few hard chores—to the exclusion of any future planning if anything went awry. He'd forever assumed he would live with his grandfather until, as Enoch Mattson had said, "You are grown enough to sit at my desk."

Ty sighed. If his being a Rebel, and she the daughter of a Rebel hater, didn't negate a relationship with Dana Bainbridge, his prospects were so dim and uncertain that the only worse situation he could imagine was writing to her from the moon, begging her to abandon her father's cozy quarters to marry a former soldier with empty pockets and no assurance where their next meal would come from. Dreams might be free for the making, but Ty was beginning to understand that a man needed a mountain of luck for a few of them—perhaps those he cherished the most—to come true.

He eventually dozed off. Gentle fingers shook him awake. Still groggy with sleep, Ty grabbed for his Remington. "Save those bullets for the Yankees," Lieutenant Shannon said. "We'll need every one of them before the morning passes."

"What time is it?" Ty asked.

"Five-thirty," Shawn Shannon answered, "and we have our orders for today."

Ty heard the movement of troopers and horses before he saw them. Ground-hugging fog filled the river bottom and he couldn't make out the Bainbridge barn a mere thirty yards away. Dawn was a slight brightening of the sky to the east.

Shawn Shannon helped Ty to his feet and handed him a mug of black coffee, hot from the stove, a strip of bacon, and a cold biscuit. "That's breakfast. You can eat on the way to the horse lot. We need to be in the saddle in five minutes."

The coffee burned Ty's tongue and he let it cool while he chewed on the dry biscuit. He had no fondness for what the troopers called "iron rations." But he was lucky to have anything hot. No external cooking fires had been permitted since their arrival yesterday. The scalding coffee had come from the Bainbridge kitchen.

He finished wolfing down what passed for breakfast as they entered the Bainbridge horse lot, a fenced enclosure large enough to accommodate a dozen loose horses. Reb nickered upon sighting Ty and was his usual docile self, until the bit was in his mouth. The big gray's head lifted and he came alert, anxious to be saddled. It was as if the miles he'd trod to date were meaningless. Ty doubted he would ever mount a finer animal.

Owen Mattson's chestnut gelding, with the white stockings and blazed face, wasn't amongst the other horses in the lot. "Father out and about already?"

"He's with Colonel Duke's Fifth and Sixth Kentucky Regiments. They're preparing to assault the Yankee redoubt below Portland. Let's ride."

Once they were under way, Shawn Shannon located the raider divisions for Ty. Colonel Duke's Fifth and Sixth Regiments held the south line, and Colonel Johnson's Seventh and Tenth straddled the Chester Road to the west. The remaining regiments—Duke's Second and Tenth, and Johnson's Eighth, Eleventh, and Fourteenth—occupied the open area opposite Portland that extended to the Bainbridge farmstead. The baggage train was ensconced at the foot of the Chester Road, behind Colonel Johnson's line.

Clusters of weary-eyed, slump-shouldered troopers, their drooping heads matching those of their horses, fumbled with paper cartridges and ramrods in the fog, trying to be certain their rifled muskets were properly loaded. Ty saw no evidence the troopers had eaten that morning except for possibly hardtack and water. Morgan's Raiders seemed to have little fight left in them. Ty had been taught that famished, exhausted soldiers were prone to flee a battle when confronted by well-armed superior numbers.

After covering a mile and a quarter of fields covered with wheat stubble, the fog parted briefly and a twenty-five-foot-tall mound, with the conical shape of a bullet, swelled to their right.

Lieutenant Shannon halted his black horse, Buster. At Ty's quizzical expression, Shannon said, "It's one of the Indian burial mounds that dot the middle of the valley. This fog will lift, and when it does, you'll be on top of it and be Duke's and Morgan's eyes."

"How far away are the Fifth and Sixth Kentucky?" Ty inquired.

"About a hundred and fifty yards. Keep in mind that it's confirmation of what's reported that counts. A general's couriers provide him much information, some worthwhile, some useless. What counts with Duke and Morgan is not that the enemy has cannons, but how many cannons does he have and where are they positioned on the battlefield. Report to Colonel Duke first, and then General Morgan, unless Duke says otherwise."

"Where will you be?"

"Wherever Colonel Duke wants me to be. Keep a sharp lookout in all directions. Consider everything you see unusual, until you determine otherwise. Do not, I repeat, *do not* stand upright for any length of time. Don't make yourself an easy target for Federal sharpshooters."

Shawn Shannon rode forward and Ty dismounted. He thought about Reb being on a loose rein and decided the big gray, with his fearless temperament, would hold on his own.

The grass on the mound was slick with morning dew. Climbing carefully, Ty gained the crest without mishap. The rounded top of the conical mound was bigger than he anticipated and provided him just enough space to sit or crouch. If anything untoward happened, three quick steps would put him down behind the crest and out of harm's way. That was except for an unseen bullet.

The quiet was unnerving. He was alone in a sea of swirling gray mist. Visibility, though, was improving minute by minute as the rising sun backlit the fog. He stared to the south, searching for any sign of the Fifth and Sixth Kentucky. The lack of any firing by cannon or musket meant the raiders had not yet attacked the Yankee redoubt.

Oblivious to Ty's presence, a rearward-bound, wildly spurring courier went racing by the mound. What was there to report in such haste? Had the Yankees abandoned the redoubt without any resistance? Ty resisted the urge to scratch his chin. He was on station to observe, not speculate.

Not ten minutes later, the fog lifted with the speed of a slatted window blind responding to its pull rope. Ty leaped to his feet. The dismounted Fifth and Sixth Regiments were in line of battle and before them, at a mere distance of thirty yards, caught completely off guard, was a small force of mounted blue bellies that had a single cannon in tow.

Raiders swept muskets to their shoulders and loosed a full volley into the surprised enemy. Between the sporadic shots of the Yankees' return fire, Ty heard raider sergeants shouting, "Handle cartridge!" In unison, every Rebel took a cartridge from his box with thumb and first two fingers and carried it to his mouth. With "Tear cartridge!" each man bit off the paper end to the powder and carried it to the chamber of the weapon.

At "Charge cartridge!" they emptied the powder into the chamber, pressing the ball in with the forefinger. At "Ram cartridge!" they tugged their ramrod from its tube under the barrel of their weapons, seated ball and charge, with a quick downward thrust, and then returned the ramrod to its tube. With the final reloading order of "Prime!" each raider cocked his musket and applied a percussion cap to hollow metal "nipple" at the rear of the barrel. It never ceased to amaze Ty that the whole process required less than ten seconds.

The sergeants yelled, "Commence firing!" The second full volley was too much for the outnumbered blue bellies. They broke line and, in the welter of confusion that followed, their artillery horses spooked, upsetting both cannon and caisson and blocking their only escape route—a narrow section of road bordered by fences and deep ditches. The Yankees abandoned their mounts and rushed, afoot, for the bluffs fronting the Ohio.

An exuberant Ty watched the raiders charge after their fleeing foe, capture the Federal cannon, and take forty prisoners. The troopers in gray had won the first skirmish of the day quite handily.

CHAPTER 17

The bright bloom of hope faded for the Raiders with two events that occurred almost simultaneously. Cannon fire commenced behind Ty at the mouth of Chester Road. Puffs of powder smoke rose above the trees that screened him from a view of the action. Heavy small-arms fire accompanied the roar of the Federal cannons. From last evening's meetings with General Morgan, he understood how critical it was for Colonel Johnson to stand firm against whatever fire the Yankees brought to bear on his position. If the blue bellies broached his lines, they would fall upon the baggage train and wreak havoc the length of the valley.

New cannon fire from a different point on the compass rang in Ty's ears. He spun to the left toward the Ohio and there was the Yankee gunboat everyone had dreaded while praying the river wasn't high enough to permit its passage upriver to Buffington Island. Those oh-so-familiar puffs of powder smoke laced the deck of the gunship as her Dahlgren guns launched shells with a thunderous *boom*.

Turning his shoulders, Ty checked the status of Colonel Duke's Fifth and Sixth Kentucky. His jaw dropped open. Companies of dismounted, blue-uniformed cavalry were pouring from the cornfields at the south end of the valley. The Yankees in sight soon outnumbered Duke's men. From his high vantage point, Ty could see many more rifle barrels protruding above the shielding cornstalks, barrrels Duke's men couldn't detect on flat ground.

Ty caught movement out of the corner of his eye on the far right. Despite Lieutenant Shannon's warning regarding Federal sharpshooters, he rose on his tiptoes. Kepi-covered heads and blue-uniformed shoulders appeared to be floating on air above the tall corn. A thin black line, tipped with a tiny swatch of yellow, loomed above each Union horseman. The memory of how the raider column had appeared from the hilltops of Chester Road flashed through Ty's mind. He was immediately certain of what he was watching. The billed caps and the upper portions of tasseled horsewhips were the gear of Union artillerymen. Three pairs of horses, with a rider for each pair, towed a single Union cannon. A quick head count told Ty four pieces of artillery would soon be shelling Colonel Duke's outnumbered regiments.

He didn't linger to confirm the horses and cannons he couldn't yet see were actually there. He knew their number and location; all he needed to do was report to Colonel Duke.

Two newly positioned Union cannons on the Rebel's far left entered the fray. Ty spurred Reb into a full gallop. The blue-belly line was advancing afoot at a measured pace when he reached Colonel Duke. Though Duke was short in stature and finely limbed, with a youthful face despite his chin-wide beard and cropped mustache, like his brother-in-law General Morgan, Basil Duke possessed a first-rate military mind. He gave Ty his complete attention upon hearing the words "Union cannons."

"How many and where, Corporal?"

"Four pieces, sir, to our far right. They should be in action in a few minutes."

The Rebel situation worsened as Colonel Duke assessed the

potential impact of Ty's revelation. The two long guns the Rebels possessed were perched on a knoll on the raider's left flank, stationed there the previous evening to support Duke's dawn assault. The knoll was beyond the raider's foremost line at the moment. The two Rebel field pieces were blasting away as fast as they could load.

Tired of the harassing fire, fifty mounted Union troopers charged the knoll, sabers slashing left and right, and dislodged the undefended Rebel gunners. The few lucky survivors fled for their lives.

Duke motioned to his second in command. "Colonel Grigsby, mount an attack and retake that knoll."

It was too late.

Dismounted Union troopers were flooding the knoll. Colonel Grigsby led the counterattack as ordered and ran straight into volley after volley of Yankee bullets. Gray bodies jerked, stumbled, and fell into the path of those still pushing forward. The attacking raider line slowly wilted, halted, and then panicked and retreated at a full run.

Ty marveled at how Colonel Duke suddenly was everywhere at once, shouting orders, turning retreating troopers to face the enemy, and placing the balance of the Fifth and Sixth Kentucky behind and beside them to present a united front again and quell the panic before it engulfed his entire command.

Ty stayed within arm's length of Colonel Duke, awaiting further orders. Every chance he had, he scanned all directions, but he failed to locate his father and Shawn Shannon. Were they amongst the Rebel dead littering the dust and yellow stubble of the cornfields?

Ty palmed sweat from his brow and mouthed a silent prayer asking the Lord to protect the both of them. The ever-vigilant Basil Duke saw Ty's lips moving and said with a tight smile, "Say one for me, too, Corporal."

Colonel Grigsby, chest heaving from exertion, came bounding up and saluted. "Sorry, sir, their volleys were too intense to withstand."

"I allow you did your best, Colonel. Now prepare to defend the road and the ford behind us. We can't allow our means of escape to be closed off. In light of what has beset us, I must confer with General Morgan. I shall return as quickly as I can. Follow me, Corporal."

Colonel Duke pointed at the horse holders waiting behind him. "My horse, please, Private."

A skinny trooper, with a hooked nose and an Adam's apple the size of a walnut, led a mud-colored gelding from the horse line. Colonel Duke swung into the saddle with the smooth grace of the veteran horseman and spurred the gelding into a trot. Ty mounted and urged Reb alongside the colonel's gelding.

What Colonel Duke and Ty encountered after passing through the wagons lining the ford road, waiting for the opportunity to cross the Ohio, were unengaged Rebel regiments in complete disarray. Unrelenting Yankee cannon and rifle fire poured down on them from the western hills, scattering troopers and horse holders to the four winds, separating officers and sergeants from their regiments and companies. Ty witnessed troopers emptying their pockets of Federal greenbacks and other stolen items, actions that expressed their fear of what the enemy might do if they were captured and discovered them. The tail end of the baggage train was frantically reining off the ford road and madly seeking refuge of any kind in the narrow northern neck of the valley where no blue-belly weapons belched smoke and fire.

Cannon balls sounded like tearing canvas as they *zeezed* through the air. A bouncing ball struck a mounted trooper riding in circles, severing his head and right shoulder. The dead trooper's fingers clutched the reins with a fierce, unyielding grip and his body hung upright in the saddle for agonizing seconds before pitching to the ground.

Taken aback by the horror of it, Ty leaned from the saddle and retched, parting company with his breakfast. He hawked and cleared his pipes, unaware that tears were dampening his cheeks. *At least*, he thought dismally, *it's a quick death with little suffering.*

Colonel Duke ignored the unholy commotion surrounding him and angled toward the river road and the Bainbridge residence. Apparently, he believed the general could best be found there or close by. In the midst of a pitched battle, Ty found himself wondering if Dana Bainbridge had taken to the family root cellar yet?

He shook his head in an attempt to clear his mind and failed. Romantic foolishness knew no limits when lovely young females were involved.

General Morgan was standing on the Bainbridge porch with Lieutenant Hardesty, Ole Box, and two of his personal staff. Three couriers stood with reins in hand on the gravel driveway. The Bainbridge family members were either inside the house or safely ensconced in the root cellar beneath it.

A bleak-appearing General Morgan lowered his field glasses as Duke dismounted and saluted. "No need for military protocol, Basil. Where do we stand?"

Basil Duke's response was pointed and perceptive. "The Yankee cannons, gunboat, and superior numbers make it impossible for us to ford the Ohio at Buffington Bar. Our only course is to withdraw and try to ford upstream beyond the reach of their gunboat."

John Hunt Morgan was not a dithering officer. He understood that the odds had turned against him in ninety short minutes. "Retreat is inevitable. I will attempt to organize an orderly withdrawal, though some frightened teamsters and troopers have already broken rank. Basil, your Fifth and Sixth Kentucky and Colonel Johnson's Seventh and Tenth will delay the Yankee advance as long as possible, while the rest of our forces depart the field."

Stepping to the front of the Bainbridge porch, General Morgan extended his hand. "Good luck and Godspeed, Basil."

Colonel Duke grasped his brother-in-law's hand, held it for a long second and, aware that neither of them might survive the day, said just loud enough for Ty to hear, "It's been a long ride, General. The men have done us proud. If it ends here, so be it. We'll not be forgotten."

General Morgan, voice cracking a tad, said, "I, too, pray the men receive the honor and glory due them. Off with you now."

Ty prepared to follow Colonel Duke, but General Morgan noticed his lifting of Reb's reins and said, "Corporal Mattson, you will remain here. I have special orders for you."

Shifting his gaze to the waiting couriers, General Morgan barked, "Private Samuels, you will accompany Colonel Duke."

The chosen courier leaped into the saddle and followed Basil Duke. General Morgan smiled and confronted Ty. "Corporal Mattson, you will seek out Colonel Johnson, obtain the status of his command, and report back to me posthaste. Your father is with Johnson. Just look for where the action is the hottest and that's where you'll find them."

Discounting the danger of riding into perhaps the heaviest fighting, a delighted Ty saluted General Morgan and touched Reb's flanks with his spurs. As usual, the big gray shot off at a gallop. Taking the shortest route, Ty disdained the open gate of the driveway to the south and put Reb over the iron fence enclosing the Bainbridge yard.

Within a quarter mile, even the inexperienced Ty determined General Morgan's proposed orderly retreat was not doable on a large scale. The remnants of Colonel Johnson's Seventh and Tenth Kentucky were spread in thin lines, well out to each flank, trying to keep them from being turned. Union shells, grapeshot, and shrapnel rained from the high ground firmly in Yankee control; more and more blue-clad, mounted troopers swarmed Chester Road.

The Union breakthrough was precipitated by the collapse of Colonel Johnson's right flank, which provided the howling Yankees direct access to the baggage train at the rear of his troopers. Ty rode in a wide half-circle to skirt the growing mass of men, horses, and wagons milling behind Johnson's rapidly weakening front.

The continuous roar of Union cannons was deafening. As Colonels Duke and Johnson succumbed to Yankee pressure and fell back toward the center of the valley to form new tighter lines, they were subjected to a three-way Yankee long-gun cross fire from the Ohio to the east, the southern cornfields and the ridge looming above Chester Road. Ty groaned in despair. Except for Rebel rearguard action to prolong the retreat further, until they ran out of ammunition, the battle was lost.

Ty rode ever forward, cringing as a shell burst short of Reb. Shards of flaming-hot metal sought his body. Somehow he and the big gelding escaped unscathed. He couldn't begin to count the number of *pishing* bullets he had heard in the last few minutes. The smoke-fouled, blistering-hot, river-bottom air was alive with death, not caring which trooper—blue or gray—perished.

A stolen circus wagon, of all things, collided with a lumbering supply wagon; the wheels and beds of both vehicles imploded on impact. Horses impaled by flying splinters and snagged in snarled harnesses screamed in agony as their leg bones snapped and they smashed into each other. The result was a pile of useless equipment, animals, and injured and dead men that became an impediment causing additional wrecks.

Ty spotted the blazed face and the four white stockings of a chestnut horse emerging from behind what remained of the brightly painted circus wagon. He stood in his stirrups, waved with an upthrust arm, and reined Reb toward the site of the wreck. His father saw him coming and slowed his prancing chestnut.

Blood darkened Owen Mattson's shirt at the left shoulder. His hat was missing and his shirt was torn open to the waist. It was an insanely small detail to catch in the heat of a raging battle, but Ty noticed the chestnut's right ear had been shot completely away. He marveled at the chestnut's training and lack of fear. A lesser mount would have bolted from the field, bit or no bit.

Owen Mattson smiled as calmly as if he were seated at a mess fire. "Been a long morning all the way around, son."

Ty blurted out, "Are you all right? How bad is your wound?"

"It can wait until this dingfod is over. What are your orders, Corporal?"

Owen Mattson's thinking of military duty first settled Ty's quaking nerves. Now that he was with his father, he was certain that everything would be fine. "To determine the status of Colonel Johnson's regiments and report their status to General Morgan," Ty answered.

"We know more than enough to make that report. We best find General Morgan. I'm concerned about his personal safety. I won't have the Yankees trumpeting to the ends of the earth how they whipped and captured the 'Thunderbolt of the Confederacy.' Damned if I will. Where did you last speak with the general?"

"On the porch of the Bainbridge house."

"That's well north of here, near the river road, smack beside our line of retreat. General Morgan will maintain known headquarters until he's forced to abandon them. Let's ride."

The clutter of the river road worsened steadily. The wagons previously lined up nearest the ford had abandoned all hope and jammed themselves in amongst the wagons from Colonel Johnson's sector, already racing to escape the death-dealing Yankees. Having abandoned any semblance of military discipline, mounted

Rebels weaved their way through the stampeding horde at a full gallop. Ty and his father trotted their horses far enough off the road to avoid wagon crashes and the frightened troopers fleeing in justified haste.

They were in sight of the Bainbridge home when, without any warning, a rider barged into them from behind. A pistol fired three times as fast as the trigger could be pulled. Owen Mattson slumped over his saddle horn. A stunned and shocked Ty grabbed his father's shoulder and tried to keep him from falling. It was then he saw the three black holes in the back of his shirt.

Instinctively wanting to protect his father, he let loose of him, tugged on Reb's reins, and reached for his Remington. The mysterious pistol barked again before he could turn and fire. The first bullet struck Ty in the back, below the ribs, and jolted him sideways. The next bullet smashed into his left leg. He lost his balance, grabbed desperately for his saddle horn, and missed.

He hit the ground with a solid *thump*, rattling his bones and driving the last ounce of breath from him. Gasping for air, he ignored the sudden, searing-hot pain of his wounds and tried to roll onto his knees. He fell back on his side, too weak to lift a newborn baby.

He forced his eyes open. Nobody was coming to help him and his father. He watched blood seep through the hole in his pants leg, unable to do anything to stop it.

Ty felt things slipping away. What he could make out was edged in black, with the center growing darker.

His dying regret was that he'd never had a chance to hug his father.

CHAPTER 18

He was afloat in swirling pools of light and dark, first one and then the other. His senses told him nothing. He didn't know up from down, left from right. The pain came and went. If he so much as twitched, the wounds in his back and thigh turned into raging infernos that sickened him.

Once in the midst of suffering through the pain, he thought he heard a voice whisper, "Never fear, I'm with you."

Was it an angel or a tempting she-devil? Was he in Heaven or in Hell? It surprised him that he didn't really care where he was.

He had no father. He had no mother. The grandmother who raised him had gone to meet her Maker. He had deserted his grandfather without the courtesy of a simple "good-bye." He had no ties anywhere. There was nothing ahead of him but the grave or, perhaps worse, a Yankee prison camp.

On top of that, his eyes were too dry to shed tears for the longest while. He had no means of expressing his grief except for a heavy heart, which ached without relief. He wasn't certain which pain hurt the most, the real or the imagined.

He came awake at last, swimming mightily through a curtain

of cottony haze. His eyes popped open and he was staring at a whitewashed ceiling, with spidery hairline cracks. Light streamed into the room from two closely spaced windows.

Expecting that terrible pain to flare in his back, he turned his head toward the twin windows, one inch at a time. Surprisingly, he found the pain caused by the deliberate movement of his head was tolerable. He knew that moving the rest of him would invite disaster.

The door at the foot of the bed opened. He saw towels draped over a bare arm, the bodice of a red-checked gingham dress, a silver locket on a thin chain at the base of a tan throat. Then, as he lifted his eyes, he saw a familiar, blue-eyed face surrounded by raven-black hair.

For a fleeting instant, he thought for certain he'd died and was in Heaven. But that couldn't be. Dana Bainbridge had not perished with him. So he was actually alive, in a room, in her father's home? How that had come to be, he couldn't fathom. A tear he didn't dare wipe slid down his cheek and he snapped his eyes shut to hide his embarrassment.

A gentle fingertip traced the track of the tear. "You've been through a lot, Corporal Ty Mattson, but you're alive, and our doctor believes you will survive."

Embarrassed that he had shut his eyes, Ty opened them and was greeted by a female smile full of warmth. He muttered, "How badly am I hurt?"

Dana Bainbridge said, "One bullet passed through your left side, below the ribs from back to front, and the other went through your left thigh. Apparently, neither touched a vital organ or an artery. Dr. Gates claimed he'd never seen two bullets rip through a soldier in those areas and do so little damage. According to him, the friend of yours who put the tourniquet on your leg so quickly and doused the exit and entry wounds with whiskey improved your chances of survival considerably."

A suddenly excited Ty tried to sit up, demanding weakly, "What friend?"

Pain washed over him with a vengeance. Everything in the room went red. Dana Bainbridge pushed gently on his chest and he sank down into the folds of the feather mattress, stifling a sob. When she spoke, her tone was firm and straightforward. "You're not to move. You're to stay calm. If you try that again, I'll leave the room. You hear me, Corporal?"

Ty bit his lip, waited for the pain to subside, and gave her the tiniest nod in the history of the human race. He gathered what little strength he had left and asked in a mere whisper, "Who brought me here?"

Dana Bainbridge dabbed Ty's sweaty brow with a towel. "The same person who bandaged your wounds, Lieutenant Shawn Shannon. He kicked the front door open, brushed Father aside, carried you up the rear steps, and placed you in my dead brother's bed. Father chased after him, swelled like a croaking toad, preparing to launch another tirade about his home being unlawfully invaded, then the lieutenant pulled a pistol, which, I swear, was the size of a bed pillow. My father is not a coward, but he peered down that huge barrel and retreated like a scampering rabbit. I saw that happen from the hallway. I came into the room to check on you, and the next thing I knew, General Morgan was beside me. He removed his hat, touched my shoulder, and said, 'He's a special lad, the son of the finest soldier who ever served under me. Please look after him, as you would one of your own.'"

Those five words "who ever served under me" shattered Ty's heart. The whole terrifying scene was right there in front of him once again: the assault from behind, the rapidly firing pistol, the bullet holes in his father's cotton shirt, the limp slump of his father's body as he spun to defend the both of them from their attacker. Knowing his father was dead was a hammer blow that numbed his entire being. He moaned and the tears finally flowed, unchecked.

Dana Bainbridge let Ty have a good, long cry. She had needed one often in the past year, what with losing two brothers and her mother. The last loss had been the greatest. It was as if fate had forever turned against her family for no good reason.

Ty cared little if his weeping made him appear a child to a grown woman. His eyes eventually ran dry, but he was afraid to move his arm to wipe his cheeks. Dana Bainbridge did it for him with a fresh towel.

He felt a terrible tiredness and realized he was falling asleep. Before he blacked out, he hoped beyond hope that Dana Bainbridge had the answer to the most vital of questions. He beckoned with a finger and pursed his lips. She lowered her ear to his mouth.

"What happened to my father's body?"

"He's buried in our family plot, on the high ground by the river, with my mother."

Ty took great comfort in that. He had learned from mess fire conversations since joining the raiders that gray-clad soldiers were often buried quickly by the Yankees in any nearby open spot of ground, for the sake of expediency and convenience. There was little time in the aftermath of a battle to fret over identifying the fallen enemy and notifying their families.

How his father had come to be buried in the Bainbridge plot raised further questions. Why had Magistrate Bainbridge, a passionate Rebel hater, allowed such a thing? Had General Morgan and Shawn Shannon somehow been involved?

And where were the general and Shawn? Had they been killed or captured or escaped across the Ohio?

Try as he might, he couldn't fight off sleep another second. He dozed off, praying for a rest free of nightmares.

* * *

170

He awakened in a midnight-black room. He sensed someone moving at the foot of the bed. A sharp, oily scraping of metal against metal—the unmistakable sound of a pistol cocking—furrowed his brow. Feigning deep sleep, he labored to keep his breathing slow and measured. There was nothing else to do. Bedridden and unable to defend himself, he was at the total mercy of the gun holder. He caught a sharp intake of breath, not his own, and steeled his body against a bullet.

No shot rang out. Had his would-be murderer lost his nerve, or was he savoring the helplessness of his intended victim? The absolute quiet and the waiting were pure agony. His father had died without the opportunity to see and confront his slayer. Was that how his life would also end?

Despite the pain, he clenched his fists and was on the verge of shouting, "Shoot, damn you," when a second oily scraping clamped his mouth shut.

The hammer on the pistol was being lowered. Clothing rustled. Flat-soled brogan shoes squeaked. The door latch rattled. Then he was alone again, quivering from crown to heel.

Totally spent, he passed out.

A sharp patting of his cheek rescued Ty from the cozy darkness craved by the wounded. Morning daylight backlit a head with bristling white hair, lumpy ears big as Ty's palms, large-beaked nose befitting an eagle, pellet-hard hazel eyes, thin pink lips, and a protruding chin shaped like the carved beakhead of a warship. Whoever he was, he was the most unattractive individual, male or female, Ty had ever seen.

The head loomed over Ty and said, "I'm Dr. Horatio Gates. How is our young raider this morning? Hurting less, are we?"

Ty recoiled from the smell of the doctor's rum-laced breath. As Boone Jordan was wont to observe, "Regardless of their station in life, some gents can't start the day without fortifying themselves with distilled spirits." Dr. Horatio Gates was definitely one of those gents.

"Yes, sir, I believe the pain is less than it was yesterday."

"Well, by damned, I've finally met a polite Rebel. They do exist," Dr. Gates said with a chuckle.

He slid the covering blanket from Ty's bed. "This won't be pleasant, but I must examine your wounds, front and back, and change your bandages. It's been two days since I was here."

To Ty's amazement, he was wearing a clean shirt and nothing below the waist except a pair of short drawers, neither of which belonged to him. And his body reeked of cologne. He had been too preoccupied with his pain to realize someone had undressed and washed him. "Did you remove my clothes, Doctor?"

"Yes, there wasn't much left, though, after Dana finished with her scissors. That child can be right helpful. She insisted I bathe you. It was a new experience for an old sawbones like me. I usually leave the washing to nurses and others. Miss Lydia toted hot water up from the kitchen for half the morning."

"And I never knew you were here?"

"Son, if you lose a lot of blood, it takes a while to recoup. I've had patients who went days without coming to. You were unconscious just four days, by my reckoning. Now let's have a look at you."

Dr. Gates first retrieved a roll of cotton cloth, a white towel, and a quart bottle of rum from a black leather satchel resting on the floor. The physician wet the towel with the rum and laid it beside the bandage on the bed within easy reach. He unbuttoned Ty's shirt; and with a gasping Ty arching his back as ordered, the doctor removed the bloody bandage encircling Ty's middle. After studying the bullet hole below Ty's ribs, Dr. Gates said, "Excellent, no mortification of the flesh is evident and healing is under way. We need to sit you up, lad. I'll be as gentle with you as I can."

Ty moaned when Dr. Gates helped him into a sitting position, but he didn't pass out. "Same back here," the physician said. He swabbed Ty's entry and exit wounds with the rum-dampened towel, wrapped the fresh bandage about him, and tied it off.

Dr. Gates eased Ty flat on the bed and followed the same procedure in treating his leg wound. The aging physician settled on a nearby chair and downed two hefty swallows of rum. "Corporal, the bullet that tore through your thigh may have nicked your leg bone, without breaking it. I can't be sure either way. There may be enough bone and nerve damage to leave you with a slight limp. Otherwise, I expect a full recovery."

After a final slurp of rum before stashing the bottle in his satchel, Dr. Gates said, "Lad, I wasn't always a besotted sawbones residing in Pomeroy, Ohio. I practiced medicine at the finest military hospital in Washington City for decades. How I sank to where I am now is not important. What's important to you is what Dr. Frank Culver and I discovered in treating numerous bullet wounds. If those wounds are regularly cleansed with alcohol, and fresh bandages are applied, and the patient has sufficient bed rest and proper nourishment, his chances of making a full recovery are much greater. We can't explain it in medical terms, but we're convinced that will eventually happen. I will leave instructions and a supply of bandages with Dana. Old Bainbridge has an ample supply of alcohol. Dana can tend to you as well as I can. If your wounds change in appearance or begin to bleed, she can send for me."

"Then I won't see you again?" an anxious Ty asked. His opinion of Dr. Horatio Gates had undergone a major transformation in thirty short minutes.

Closing his satchel, Dr. Gates winked at Ty and said, "Corporal, it's best I'm not seen coming and going. No one except the members of this household knows you're here. The Yankees were in hot pursuit of Morgan and his men, and they had no cause to bother the Bainbridge family. Lucky for us, they established a field hospital for the wounded in Portland rather than here.

"At General Morgan's request and Dana's insistence, Magistrate Bainbridge agreed that he would harbor you for two to three weeks before turning you over to Federal authorities. That is a very generous offer, since those same authorities may frown on his hiding the enemy and seize his property."

Ty couldn't help wondering what hold Dana had on her father. He couldn't imagine the magistrate risking his wealth and stature, no matter how much he had appeared to respect John Hunt Morgan. Ty was thankful beyond measure he wasn't in that temporary Portland hospital, where the medical care from blue-belly army doctors would be much less trustworthy than what Dr. Gates was providing him.

Rising from his chair, the eagle-nosed physician cracked a smile. "I'll take my leave. I wish you the best with whatever befalls you. You can trust the Bainbridge family. They will maintain our ruse and you'll be safe here until you're out of bed and on your feet. Good day, Corporal Mattson."

The door closed behind Dr. Gates. Ty's immediate thought was *Not as safe as you think, sir.* Remembering that pistol cocking in the middle of the night gave him the shivers. He had no doubt as to who had invaded his room. The hate in Alexander Bainbridge's eyes had been hot enough to turn cold stone into molten lava.

Ty could only surmise that Alex had stopped short of murdering a helpless enemy for fear his upright, law-abiding father might throw him out of the house and summon the law. And Alex had his sister to consider. Dana Bainbridge had to love her brother, but that affection might evaporate if Alex committed a heinous act, for which there might be no forgiveness on her part ever. According to Dr. Gates, she was the main reason Ty was ensconced in a Bainbridge bedroom. She had stood up for the very Rebel whom Alex wanted to kill.

Much as he hated it, Ty had no alternative but to pray Alexander's hatred of those who had taken his brothers from him didn't trump the wishes of his father and his sister. He had no desire to cause Alex grief by telling Magistrate Bainbridge and Dana what had happened, and there was no means by which he could secure a firearm. The magistrate might endure the presence of an enemy soldier within his abode for a specified length of time; the arming of that same enemy was beyond Ty's imagination.

CHAPTER 19

A knock at the door interrupted his rumination. A foot pushed the door open and Dana Bainbridge, carrying a large round tray, popped into the room. The smell of the steaming tray's contents brought Ty upright, pain or no pain. He discovered he was hungrier than a posthibernation bear.

Dana had to hear his stomach growling. She grinned and said, "Dr. Gates says you may eat. I brought Mama's cure for whatever ails you—the broth from a boiled chicken, soft biscuits, and freshly churned butter. If you have no stomach upset today, tomorrow you may have the meat of the chicken."

She placed the tray on Ty's lap, poured a mug of broth from a china pitcher, and buttered a biscuit with a silver knife. "Can you hold the mug yourself, or shall I do it for you?"

Feeling a little unsteady, and wanting to bring her closer, Ty said, "If you would, please?"

The broth was scalding hot. Ty had to blow on it to cool it, and then drink it sip by sip. The aroma of the broth was divine—hers more so. She reminded him of the spring wildflowers his grandmother picked to decorate the front hallway and the dining-room table. Grandfather forbade posies in his library, preferring the smoky fragrance of an evening cigar, his solitary sin.

Ty finished the broth and the biscuits without a single pause. "I haven't seen anyone hungrier since Father's last winter hunt, when I was a child," Dana said. "He vowed he'd never roam the woods hungry again in any season, and he hasn't."

She lifted the tray from Ty's lap, rested it on a marble-topped table beneath the bedroom windows, pulled Dr. Gates's chair to the edge of the bed, and seated herself. "If you're up to it, I have news—not good, unfortunately—that is of interest to you. It concerns General Morgan."

"Quite frankly, I'm not expecting good news," Ty said. "The battle went against us, almost from the beginning. Did General Morgan survive?"

Dana Bainbridge pushed a lock of raven hair behind her ear, a gesture so feminine and beautiful that Ty knew he had to have her, whatever the price. Forget his Baptist upbringing. Selling his soul to Satan, the most sin-rewarding devil in Hell, wasn't too great a stretch for him.

Unaware of how much she had stirred Ty's deepest feelings, Dana said, "General Morgan is alive. He and his remaining men were captured near Canton, Ohio."

"Where are they n-now?" Ty asked, stumbling over the simple word "now."

Grab the halter, he raged inwardly. *This woman has no interest in a boyish man, other than nursing me.* If she saw Ty in that light, he had as much of a chance of sharing a life with her as the moon had of kissing the sun.

Dana hesitated and said, "Papa told me the enlisted men are being transported by steamboat and rail to Camp Douglas, near Chicago. General Morgan and his officers will be jailed at the Ohio Penitentiary at Columbus."

Ty sighed. "If he was captured with the others, Shawn Shannon is with General Morgan."

"The Lieutenant was certainly loyal to you. When I saw how hard his face was, I realized nothing was going to prevent him from carrying you straight to this bed."

"Your father didn't object?"

Dana treated Ty to a coy smile. "He did, but he doesn't always have the final say in this house. He didn't when my mother was with us, and he doesn't now. He understands my mother's sister wants me to join her in Cincinnati, where a proper education for a young lady is available. Papa can't stand the thought of losing me."

"You are something special, Dana Bainbridge!" Ty exclaimed. "I've never met a female with your kind of spunk."

Dana's head tilted. "I bet a man like you says that to every lass he meets."

"What do you mean by 'a man like you'?" a puzzled Ty said.

"Corporal Mattson, don't act as if you're not aware how that red hair and those green eyes can make a girl's heart flutter, to where she might swoon. Makes a girl wonder how handsome you are without that awful beard."

Ty was as joyful as a newborn colt. She was attracted to him as a man, not just out of sympathy for a wounded soldier. Shawn Shannon's little white lie in the Bainbridge kitchen about Ty's age was proving helpful, after all. He'd tell her the truth at the proper time. It made no sense to squash a potential romance before it had a chance to spread its wings.

Despite his excitement, Ty couldn't suppress a big yawn. Dana jumped from her chair. "We've talked long enough for one morning. We don't want to tire you unnecessarily. You rest and I'll bring you more broth after Papa's noon meal. Mama spoiled him with three meals per day. Given his belly, two would have sufficed quite nicely."

Scooping up her tray and pitcher, Dana said, "Have a restful sleep," and she was out the door and gone.

Ty missed her company immediately. Unlike the young ladies

Ty spoke with during social gatherings at the Elizabethtown Baptist Church, Dana Bainbridge was without pretense and had no difficulty relating to the men around her. She wasn't shy or backward or nervous. She was just herself, and that only added to her beauty.

Ty smiled at the ceiling. It had been a grand morning. He pushed aside his pain, the lad who wanted him dead, and the fact a day of reckoning with the Yankees was unavoidable and fell asleep, praying he would dream of Dana.

Nothing to honestly bother the Lord with, but he couldn't resist.

A different face confronted him upon awakening. This one was black and lively and so unexpected that it startled him.

"Now don't take on so, Corporal," Miss Lydia said, her wide smile puffing her cheeks. "I'm come to cut away your beard and shave you, not scare you to death."

A pan of water, a towel, a bar of soap, a pair of scissors, and a razor filled the bedside chair. A leather belt for stropping the razor was draped over Miss Lydia's shoulder. Her confident manner relaxed Ty. "I done shaved the master when that fever put him abed. I'll do right by you, too, Corporal Mattson."

Miss Lydia trimmed his beard to the nub with the scissors, wet his remaining whiskers, lathered his face and neck, and stropped the razor. Concentration tightened her mouth. She shaved him with short strokes, nicking him but twice when he inadvertently moved his chin fighting off an itch. After a final draw of the razor, she dampened the towel, wiped his face, and pulled a narrow-necked bottle from an apron pocket.

She saw the questioning lift of his brows. "Florida Water, the master's favorite," Miss Lydia said. She applied it liberally on Ty's razor-sensitive skin. He flinched and Miss Lydia giggled.

"You won't be sorry. It makes you smell good, but not ripe. Miss Dana likes it better than her brother's cheap cologne that fool doctor splashed all over you. He was trying to hide a poor washing was what he was doing."

Miss Lydia emptied her water pan out the window and placed the soap, scissors, razor, and towel into the empty pan. "We'll cut that hair another day. Then with some proper clothes on you," she said, her nose pointing upward. "You might be taken for a gentleman instead of one of those rowdy Texas outlaws that done scared the wits out of folks hereabouts."

A broad smile showed her white teeth. "Like Miss Dana say, it surely was exciting while it lasted." The smile faded quickly. "Just remember, those folks you scared to the bone will be mighty mad and upset they learn you're holed up in the master's house. They'll likely tar and feather you or hang you. I seen it done afore. They might do the same with the master. The hate for you Rebels is deeper than the roots of a tall tree on the bank of the Ohio. I heard the master hisself say so."

After dispensing that piece of sage advice, Miss Lydia hefted her pan, wriggled her fingers at Ty, and scooted through the door.

Before Ty could digest her warning and what all it might entail, Dana Bainbridge returned with another tray of food. Now she was wearing a yellow cotton dress that clung to her body in the intense daytime heat of the bedroom. Ty nearly whistled aloud. She was what Given Campbell called "a lush-figured gal."

Ty ground his teeth and pushed himself into a sitting position, the pain sharp but not making him breathless. Dana laid her tray on the bedside chair and surprised Ty by settling on the bed beside his knee.

"My, my, is this the same man I fed earlier? You certainly don't resemble that wild-bearded, gun-toting Rebel, with huge spurs, who burst into my kitchen last week."

"You can thank Miss Lydia's razor. She's quite a barber."

"Contrary to what Father thinks, she's the backbone of this family. Let me show you what I brought you."

Assuming Ty was capable of feeding himself, Dana passed him a stout mug with a handle. "You did so well eating this morning, I cut the breast of the chicken into little pieces and added it to the broth. Here's a spoon."

Dana followed the broth and breast meat with generous helpings of custard made with cream, sugar, and a dusting of ground cinnamon. Ty had never enjoyed a meal of any kind more.

A refreshed Ty stretched out after Dana fluffed his feather pillows. Without further ado, she placed the mug and white china bowls on her tray and prepared to depart.

"If you're not too tired, my father would like to speak with you," Dana said.

It wasn't something Ty was looking forward to, but sooner or later, it was inevitable. He was welcome in the Bainbridge house so long as the magistrate acceded to his daughter, a tenuous thread that he dared not stretch too thin.

"I'll be glad to talk with him."

Dana smiled, then said, "Good, but be warned. Papa will want to discuss what must be done, once you're on your feet and able to travel."

That was the subject that concerned Ty the most. How firm was Magistrate Bainbridge about turning him over to the Federal authorities? Was there the slightest chance he might be persuaded differently? Maybe have pity on a shot-up young Rebel adrift and homeless? Hadn't Ty's grandmother claimed that mercy becomes the biggest of men?

Magistrate Bainbridge was dressed in a white shirt, with a starched high collar, brown trousers, and suspenders. The bulge of his belly nearly preceded him through the door. Sweat gleamed on his bald head. Though his remaining hair was black and his eyes blue, his features were heavy and lacked the refinement of his daughter's, indicating Dana's mother was the source of her beauty.

Tugging the bedside chair away from the prone Ty to make more room, Cordell Bainbridge fell into it and wiped his brow and throat with a large red handkerchief.

Ty moved to sit up, out of respect to his visitor.

"Rest easy, Corporal Mattson, I will not linger. I believe my daughter informed you of my intentions. We will provide you quarters here until it is safe for you to be transported. We will then proceed to Pomeroy, Ohio, where you will become the property of the United States Government."

Bainbridge struck the sober face of a sentencing judge. "The Union Army will decide your ultimate fate. You will, of course, initially be classified a 'prisoner of war' and sent to a prison camp in the North."

The red handkerchief wiped skin again. "As I told my daughter, I cannot countenance participating in the escape of a Confederate soldier. I am loyal to the Union and Mr. Lincoln, mind and soul. I am a rabid antislaver. But I'm also enough of a father that I will allow my daughter certain latitude, providing it does not endanger the health and well-being of what remains of this family. My agreeing to secure medical treatment for you and serve as a private hospital without my family coming to grief, or worse, was based on my standing in Pomeroy. I sat the county bench for fifteen years and own property within the town.

"My story is that you were wounded in my yard, which is literally the truth—and, war or no war, as a humanitarian, I could not simply turn my back and allow you to die. There will be no mention made of Lieutenant Shannon and General Morgan's involvement whatsoever. That would inflame the whole countryside."

Cordell Bainbridge rocked forward and stood. "Be advised, your father's burial on my property is not known outside this house. Lieutenant Shannon hid his body in my barn and he was buried that night after dark by my freed farmhands. Lathrup is Miss Lydia's husband. He and his brother are well treated and fiercely loyal to me and will never mention it happened."

Pocketing his handkerchief, Bainbridge said, "Once again, we will leave for Pomeroy as soon as Dr. Gates says you can withstand the journey. We can't prolong your stay. It's one thing to provide critical medical treatment to a wounded enemy, quite another to appear to harbor and succor him while our boys in blue are dying on the battlefield. I'm sure you appreciate the precarious nature of my situation, Corporal Mattson."

Ty groaned as the door swept shut behind Cordell Bainbridge. There would be no reprieve. There would be no escaping across the Ohio.

The blunt truth was he did appreciate Bainbridge's position. Morgan's Raiders had earned the hatred, resentment, and condemnation of Indiana and Ohio citizens for the bodily and emotional terror they'd caused them and the destruction of their property. As his father had said when Ty was observing the cloud of black smoke hovering over Salem, Indiana, "Sooner or later, there will be hell to pay for what we're doing." Well, the bill had come due and Ty was one of those holding it.

But no matter how steep the price, he would not waste Shawn Shannon's saving of his life. Somehow he must survive.

Quitting wasn't an option, particularly not for the son of Captain Owen Mattson, General John Hunt Morgan's best soldier.

CHAPTER 20

Two weeks later, during a surprise visit by Dr. Gates, Ty gained his feet at the doctor's urging. The pain was less than he anticipated. It was a slow burning sensation that clenched his jaw, but not his fists. He swayed to and fro at first before his knees locked and kept him upright.

"That's excellent, young man, just excellent!" a delighted Dr. Gates exclaimed. "You still don't show any sign of the fever or proud flesh that frequently accompany gunshot wounds. We'll have you out of that bed, for good, in a week."

Ty gulped. Though he was sleeping through the night and eating solid food, Dr. Gates's prognosis seemed terribly optimistic. There was a heap of difference between standing and walking and eventually riding in a horse-drawn wagon.

He knew his opinion counted for naught. He suspected Dr. Gates's sudden appearance in the bedroom doorway was at the request of Magistrate Bainbridge and reinforced what he'd told Ty the prior week. Bainbridge wanted to shed the worry of sheltering an enemy who might be discovered by hostile Portland residents and county militia.

Ty had learned that the magistrate's fear for his safety and that of his family was legitimate. Dana had described to him how the Raiders had ransacked Portland homes and businesses the night before the big battle. The local hatred for the Rebels spawned by those few hours of looting—intensified by the raiders' wanton discarding of valuable personal possessions belonging to their fellow Ohio citizens on the battlefield—was at a fever pitch. Hanging was too good for any captured Johnny Reb. The true hotbloods preferred to draw and quarter him. Prison was an afterthought.

Holding Ty's arm, Dr. Gates had him walk to the door and back, a total of ten steps. He noticed Ty's limp. "Does your left leg feel weaker than your right?"

"Yes, sir, just like you said it would."

"You'll need to favor it a bit for a while. It should become stronger as you heal," Dr. Gates said. "Let's get you back to bed."

Once Ty was abed, Dr. Gates said, "Walk every morning and every afternoon. If you notice any bleeding, stop till it stops. Has Dana been changing your bandages, per my instructions?"

"Yes, sir," Ty said, suppressing a guilty smile.

The bandage changing highlighted his recovery. He took advantage of her closeness, marveling at the swell of her bosom in the scalloped hollow of her bodice, how she bit her lower lip when concentrating, how readily she blushed, the sudden gleam of her blue eyes when their conversation became animated, the schoolgirl charm of her throaty laugh, how she smelled of a fresh scent each day, how she missed nothing that happened about her or its implications. She was a female wiser than her years. Maybe too wise to entangle her emotions with those of a seventeen-year-old male with honest love for her in his heart, but the blood of her people on his hands and prison awaiting him.

Leather satchel in hand, Dr. Gates halted in the doorway, grinned mischievously, and said, "Enjoy Dana's company while you can, Corporal. Life is a short venture that rewards those who grasp the brass ring when it swings their way."

Ty was mulling over the doctor's parting words when Dana Bainbridge arrived with his dinner. By the bounce in her step, he could tell her spirits were running high. The fare for the evening was basically that of his first meal at the Bainbridge dinner table—corned beef with cabbage, corn cut from the cob swimming in warm cream, loaf bread, butter, hot coffee, and Miss Lydia's famous cinnamon-dusted custard.

Dana said, "It's time for you to eat as much as you want. We need to build up your strength."

Ty sensed a slight tension in her voice. Had something transpired that threatened to force him from the Bainbridge home prematurely? He wasn't ready to undertake a journey of any length. Another week of rest, walking, and solid food might turn the odds in his favor, if he wasn't forced to march too far afoot.

In their brief hours together, Ty had shared with Dana the story of both his finding of his father and his death by bullets from the gun of a fellow Rebel soldier, not the blue-belly enemy. Having lost close family members recently herself, she understood and they shared their pain and grief.

He found it easy to be forthright with Dana Bainbridge. She was enthralled by his recounting of how his mother and father had met at the Iron Gate, how Ty came to live with his grandparents, his father's hard, lean years in Texas, and Ty's decision to leave home and seek out his father. She laughed heartily when Ty told her of the stolen hams, the stolen beer wagon, and Cally Smith's gastric nightmare.

In turn, he listened attentively to her tales of life with a stern judge for a father, a warm, loving, "waste not, want not" mother, and three brothers. The two older brothers had stood guard over her at church, at school, and during community socials, running off suitors as she grew into a woman. She regaled Ty with tales of how Franklin and Joseph had put the school bully in his place by dangling him from a rope atop the cliff behind

Pomeroy in the dead of night, frightening him nearly to death. No outdoor privy in the city was safe and the two ornery brothers weren't particular about whether they were occupied during the overturning. Pretty young females seemed to be a target of choice. No school bench was safe from tacks. Pigtails were for yanking. No male body part was spared a rough pinching. Mouth washing with lye soap for swearing had no more effect than throwing wheat chaff into a strong wind. Halloween brought on an annual frenzy of pranks, screeching ghosts, and a parade of Headless Horsemen that shamed Ichabod Crane. Mothers kept their children away from windows from dusk to dawn, against, of course, the protests of their offspring.

These same two young hellions were perfect students in school, chased a knife-wielding robber from the Kenton Mercantile, armed with spade shovels at the age of twelve, chopped wood an entire winter to keep the destitute Larson family from freezing to death, rescued eight-year-old Bobby Lynch from a flood-swollen Ohio River, led the town carolers at Christmas, made the Fourth of July resemble a duel between military cannons with their homemade fireworks, and swore an overweening allegiance, which defied logic, to the flag of the United States.

No one would deny, though, that the entire adult population of Pomeroy, including their own father, had breathed a collective sigh of relief the morning Franklin and Joseph, both bitterly disappointed they hadn't secured appointments to West Point, took up arms with the Union Army. Their send-off on the morning packet boat had gleeful townspeople and saddened children cheering long after the stern-wheeler disappeared round a bend in the Ohio. Ty had no doubt that Alexander Bainbridge thought he had boots to fill as big as those of Owen Mattson.

Ty loved the zeal of Dana's brothers, their cleverness, their courage, and their commitment to protecting their sister. He saw himself locked in the barn on a diet of cold corn bread and water for prolonged periods, had he pulled their shenanigans on

Enoch Mattson, for his grandfather seemed to know which horse farted last in his stall.

Ty smiled inwardly, trying to imagine what it would have been like to court their sister, if the two brothers were still living at home. That would have been a unique challenge. Would he have been up to it? Maybe now, if he recovered, but definitely not before he'd fled Elizabethtown.

Dana's only sad reflection was her father's insistence that the family abandon the hustle and bustle of Pomeroy for a quiet existence in the country. She hazarded a guess that as he grew older, her father had desired to be a bigger fish in a smaller pond. She missed the gracious Bainbridge home overlooking the city and the river, as well as the family's autumn and spring excursions to Cincinnati to partake of its delicious Southern food and enjoy stage performances by actors and musicians from across the world. But as a loving daughter, she'd eventually accepted the move, as she did the other vicissitudes of life she couldn't control.

The next morning, Ty counted on the closeness and friendship they had developed and hoped she wouldn't disappoint him. Hands occupied with a fork and a wedge of bread, he mentally crossed his fingers and asked, "Am I causing your family a problem?"

Bad as the news was, Dana didn't avert her gaze. "Alex claims there's a rumor afloat in Portland that a local family is hiding a Morgan Rebel."

Ty blurted out, "Maybe Alex started it," and then he wanted to bite his tongue in half for saying it.

"Oh, my," Dana said, taking a deep breath, "I'm afraid I've been naïve Father keeps saying Alex wouldn't dare betray you, but Alex has disobeyed him before. As you well know from his attempt to kill General Morgan, Alex is consumed by his hatred for anyone wearing a gray uniform. He'll never accept the fact that it was the war, and not you personally, that took his brothers. You're a convenient and handy outlet for his vengeful feelings."

A new twist, Ty thought. If Alex hadn't the nerve to shoot him, he could recruit the local Rebel haters to do it for him. Bullet or rope, dead was dead.

Not wanting to push ahead too fast, Ty kept his voice soft and low. "Have you discussed the rumor with your father?"

Dana refilled Ty's coffee mug. "No, but he went to Portland, as is his custom on Saturdays. He enjoys a weekly game of pool and a few beers at Hall's Emporium. If the rumor is for real, he will certainly hear it there. Father says the 'Hall's gang' even knows when someone isn't feeding his horse regularly and cheerfully will let it be known far and wide. Rumors are their best friend."

"When will your father be home?"

"Late today. He lingers at Hall's longer since Mama died."

"You'll let me know if you learn anything?"

"I'll wait up for him," Dana promised, gathering together her dishes, bowls, utensils, and coffeepot. "I'm fearful of what might happen. I want no harm to come to you."

Arms full, she turned away quickly. For a second, Ty thought he saw tears welling in those lovely sky-blue eyes. Then she was gone down the rear stairs before he could respond to a sudden, overwhelming desire to yell out that he loved her.

He flopped back on his bed. He shared her foreboding. Her family had secreted him away from public scrutiny for three weeks. That couldn't continue without something going haywire, and though the evidence was skimpy, he was certain it had. Any man was entitled to only so many answered prayers and pure luck.

He felt empty of both.

Late in the evening, carrying a coal oil lantern, Magistrate Bainbridge entered Ty's room. The sight of his rigid face in the lantern's flickering wick meant he was there on what he deemed serious business. Ty knew deep in his heart that his life was about to change directions. At this juncture, it was a matter of how much, not how little.

The magistrate leaned over Ty. "We must move you to a safe location tonight. The Lebanon County Militia, the most misbegotten, foul-tempered, dim-witted, battle-leery bunch of nobodies, will commence a house-to-house search at dawn. This house will be high on their list. I made a big to-do about how they could start here if they liked, to throw them off the scent. By morning, with Dana's help, there'll be no sign you were in my house."

The magistrate looked over his shoulder. "Lathrup, bring those clothes in here."

A tall, lanky black male, with a seamed, kindly, intelligent face, appeared behind Cordell Bainbridge. Ty remembered he was Miss Lydia's husband. Lathrup was toting a pair of trousers, a pair of brogans, and a large straw hat.

The magistrate pulled the covering blanket from Ty. "Time to be up and about, Corporal. Lathrup will help you dress. Ben Jack and I will harness the buggy horses. Then Lathrup and Ben Jack will drive you to Dr. Gates's hospital in Pomeroy. Dana will pack cold food for your trip."

Lathrup's arms were strong, and his grip gentle. He held Ty upright with one arm, while he used his free hand to help him don the trousers.

"Them shoes will fit, too," Lathrup said. "They belonged to Mr. Franklin, the master's eldest. He was a big fellow like you." Lathrup laced the flat-soled brogans for Ty, for which Ty was thankful, as bending over would imperil his balance.

Surprisingly, the pain was manageable and Ty's mood brightened. Maybe the coming buggy ride wasn't as lethal for him as he'd assumed.

A black male, the same size as Lathrup, joined them. Lathrup jammed the straw hat on Ty's head; and with Ty's arms draped over Lathrup's and Ben Jack's shoulders, they descended the rear steps without incident to the first floor.

Dana Bainbridge was waiting at the bottom of the stairs by the kitchen doorway. Had Ty's arms been free, he would have attempted to embrace her, told her he loved her, and kissed her good-bye. The fact that her father was watching within earshot and might have disapproved, or he might have had his face slapped for his troubles, wouldn't have hampered him in the least.

However, his arms weren't free; and as he passed her, he looked straight into her eyes, with all the yearning he could muster, and whispered, "Write to me in care of Boone Jordan, Elizabethtown, Kentucky. . . . Don't forget, Boone Jordan, Elizabethtown, Kentucky."

CHAPTER 21

Departing the Bainbridges' farm, Ty rode the entire night between Lathrup and Ben Jack on the cushioned seat of Magistrate Bainbridge's two-horse buggy, sleeping fitfully against their shoulders whenever the road smoothed out. Dana's basket of cold beef, cheese, and bread, washed down with a jug of springhouse buttermilk, kept their hunger at bay.

Unlike many Kentuckians, Ty had no problem sharing the same milk jug with his black companions. His grandfather had trained him that every man was to be judged by how he acquitted himself, not the color of his skin, a philosophy that had caused him considerable difficulty with his pro-slavery neighbors.

They passed not a soul on the moonlit road and reached Pomeroy with dawn light washing the rock face of the high ridge that paralleled the Ohio River behind the town. Dr. Gates's two-story residence/hospital was situated on the southwest corner of Mechanic and First Streets, within sight of the riverbank. Pomeroy's streets were virtually deserted at that hour. A Federal packet stern-wheeler, boilers huffing in preparation for an early departure, was moored at the public levee.

Lathrup and Ben Jack wasted no time tying the buggy team to an iron hitching post at street's edge and hustling Ty to the front steps. Once they were on the porch, Ty stood without assistance. At the sound of the bell and the door opening, Dr. Gates, clasping his satchel, stepped from the home's dining room and pulled its doors shut behind him. Both sets of parlor doors were also tightly closed.

"Good morning, Corporal, I've been expecting you. I received an encoded telegram from Cordell Bainbridge last evening."

The Pomeroy physician nodded at Lathrup and Ben Jack. "Gentlemen, please help Corporal Mattson with the stairs. We'll put him in my private quarters up above so he's isolated from my other patients."

Three weeks abed and his wounds had weakened Ty, yet he needed less help ascending the stairs than he anticipated. His pain had diminished to a dull, manageable throb. Except for the limp he would have to deal with—and he had no idea how bad it might be—if he suffered no setbacks, he was convinced a complete recovery was possible.

Ty's destination was an upstairs room that held a single bed, a night table with a coal oil lamp, dresser with commode, wash pan and water pitcher, and in the far corner, an iron bathtub with tall legs and claw-feet. A thunder mug protruded from beneath the wooden frame of the bed.

The bed linens and covering spread were the whitest of whites, indicating a recent washing and pressing. Dr. Gates had a true fetish for patient cleanliness, which fascinated Ty.

Lathrup and Ben Jack took their leave. At Dr. Gates's bidding, Ty disrobed for a full examination of his wounds, front and back. "Remarkable, one must never underestimate the resiliency of our early years. We'll forgo new bandages. You've scabbed over quite nicely."

Ty was delighted with his prognosis. Collecting the old bandages, Dr. Gates stood and repacked his satchel. "I will have breakfast sent up," the doctor said, "then Jarvis will fetch water for the tub. I trust you will indulge me, Corporal. It's good that you're not adverse to water. Many of my patients fear bathing more than they do smallpox and diphtheria."

The Pomeroy physician withdrew before Ty could ask him how soon he might be turned over to the Federal authorities. Disappointed, he waited in his short drawers and shirt for breakfast. Twenty minutes later, a stubby, stoop-shouldered, white-bearded gnome of a man, moving with surprising quickness for his age, delivered a tray of poached eggs, bacon, fried potatoes, grits and milk in a bowl, bread, and freshly brewed coffee.

Jarvis patiently watched Ty savor every bite. "You *best* enjoy that," the gnome said. "I hears dogs won't eat the slop they call food in the Yankee prison camps."

When Ty finished his breakfast, Jarvis poured him a final cup of coffee, swept the tray from his lap, and said, "I'll be back with your bathwater afore you know it."

The gnome made a believer of Ty. The door hardly seemed to close before he returned, carrying a bucket of steaming hot water in each hand. Numerous trips up and down the stairs were required to fill the big iron tub, but stubby Jarvis was up to the task, aided immensely, Ty decided, by his thick forearms and hands with knuckles the size of crab apples and palms the size of small cabbages.

The last two buckets contained cold water. Jarvis poured them into the tub and stuck his arm into the water up to the elbow. He flashed a satisfied smile and motioned a naked Ty into the tub.

Ty crossed the room, one careful step at a time, and climbed into the tub, left arm braced against the wall. The water was still very hot, but not hot enough to burn. Jarvis passed Ty a bar of brown soap and a thick-bristled brush for scrubbing. "I'll haul up the rinse water and towels whiles you wash."

Ty soaped and scrubbed until his skin was raw red, except in the area of his scabbed wounds. He wondered as he made a last swipe of the brush how Jarvis was going to empty the tub for his dozen buckets were now full of rinse water and aligned beside the tub. Beckoning for Ty to stand, Jarvis reached into the water in front of him and his hand emerged with what Ty realized was a threaded drain plug. "The doctor man," Jarvis explained, "saw this tub in Paris and he had to have one like it. A pipe under the tub drains the water out through a hole in the wall."

The after-bath water was cold enough to provoke shivers and chattering teeth. Ty toweled off and, though he was short of breath for a few moments, climbed from the tub, walked to the bed, and donned his short drawers and shirt with little difficulty.

Wet towels looped over his shoulder, Jarvis stacked his buckets, one into the other, and backed out the door. "I'll bring you another meal this afternoon."

Ty stretched out on the bed. He found he couldn't relax and lay there, staring at the ceiling. Was he ready to undertake a journey to a prison in an undisclosed location? He had better be. That decision was beyond his control, and he had a feeling Dr. Gates would make it before the end of the day.

A sense of loss and frustration descended on Ty like a smothering blanket. His life was less certain than it had been the evening he rode away from Boone Jordan's livery stable. He had found his father and then lost him to an assassin's bullet. He did not know if Lieutenant Shannon or any of the other raiders he had fought with were still alive.

Had his father's murderer survived Buffington Island? If he had, was there a chance Ty would share a Yankee prison with him? Ty was certain he'd recognize Jack Stedman's son, even at a distance. If by chance he was so fortunate, what could he do, if anything, to avenge his father stuck in a Yankee prison without a weapon?

Other questions ate at Ty equally hard. Supposing Dana

Bainbridge did write to Boone Jordan. If personal letters were taboo in Yankee prisons, how could Ty inform Boone where he was to start written communication with Dana?

And though perhaps of lesser importance in the eyes of some, but not Ty's, what had happened to Reb? Had the big gray gelding been killed, or was he in the hands of the blue bellies? Ty had bonded with Reb, as cavalrymen were prone to do with their mounts. Losing the big gray was akin to parting with a cherished friend.

Ty had never felt so alone and helpless. He gripped the edges of the feather mattress to keep from shedding useless tears. Hard as it was to swallow, there were equally mean days ahead of him. What little he had heard about Yankee prison camps was enough to impress upon him the fact that he could possibly be in as much danger there as he'd been on the battlefield. Ty remembered Professor Ackerman's lesson that the hatred of the victor often leeched from the battlefield into their prison camps, where unarmed enemy soldiers were frequently treated with the harshness shown head lice.

He reminded himself, as he had a thousand times before, that he needed to gather his wits together and be the man his father was. Owen Mattson wouldn't fall prey to his weaknesses because things hadn't gone his way, not as long as he could still fend for himself.

Ty had his father's blood. He was, and would always be, first and foremost a Mattson. His grandfather had stressed that the family name stood for honor, trust, and courage. Cowardice and fear did not abide beneath the Mattson roof and Ty vowed aloud that he would not be the Mattson who held the door open for them.

Ty drew enough strength from that vow to hold his fears at arm's length long enough for him to drift into a much-needed, deep, restful slumber.

*　*　*

Dr. Gates and Jarvis awakened Ty, who was amazed at how long he had slept, in the early evening. They brought with them a meal of fried pork, cheese, corn bread, and coffee. It was solid fare, though Ty sorely missed the creamy taste of Miss Lydia's cinnamon-dusted custard.

Once the dinner tray was situated on Ty's lap, Dr. Gates allowed him to enjoy a few bites, and then said, "The Federal authorities will be here at six in the morning, sharp. You will travel to Cincinnati on the morning packet boat."

The Pomeroy physician allowed Ty a minute to absorb his news. "I don't know where you're bound after that." Dr. Gates swallowed hard. "Corporal, I'm sorry I couldn't do more for you. I recommended that you be paroled because of your wounds and the future difficulties you might have with that leg. Unfortunately, General Burnside's headquarters refused to parole you. Quite frankly, I believe the Union boys are still furious at themselves for not catching your General Morgan sooner. Leniency is mighty scarce for those that raised Cain with him."

Parole had not entered Ty's mind. He had no trouble grasping the blue bellies' overwhelming anger at how arrogantly the raiders had led then on a merry chase across three states. It was their hateful, revenge-seeking attitude that frightened him the most.

"I appreciate your efforts on my behalf, Doctor. I was aware soon after I joined General Morgan's forces that my service with him might be brief and come to a bad end."

Ty sighed. "Like my grandmother said, 'Life's twists and turns may not suit us, but it's up to us to weather the storm.'"

Dr. Gates extended his hand. "I must tend to my other patients. You may be our enemy, but you're a fine young man. I wish you the best. Who knows," the doctor continued with a sly grin as he and Ty shook hands, "maybe you'll pay Dana Bainbridge a visit when this miserable war is over. If you do, I'd give anything to witness the shock on old Cordell's face."

Dr. Gates's wry comment left Ty wondering what Magistrate Bainbridge would think of Ty courting his daughter from afar, which he hadn't considered before. Would he permit her to write to him?

Ty supposed there was a goodly chance Cordell Bainbridge would not tolerate Dana corresponding with a Rebel imprisoned by the blue-belly army, whose cause he fervently supported. But she had seemed adept at dealing with her stubborn, headstrong father.

After Jarvis disappeared with the supper tray, Ty whiled away the hours by daydreaming about Dana Bainbridge. Perhaps without meaning to, she had hooked Ty as deeply as Keena McVey had his father. He saw her again in detail as if she were before him—the tiny cleft in her chin, the delicate curve of her ears, the daisy-shaped blemish on the back of her left hand—for no feature of hers had escaped his notice.

It fascinated him that he could recall word for word every conversation with her. He had detected nothing then or now that indicated a lack of interest in him on her part. He believed her affection for him was sincere and honest and not motivated by pity and kindness.

He must have her. And to that end, he would pursue her by whatever means he could devise until his chances with her were dead-flat impossible, willing to risk suffering a broken heart to the grave.

He dozed off and dreamed near dawn that he was on his knees asking Cordell Bainbridge for his daughter's hand in matrimony. The magistrate was poised to answer, when bare knuckles beat a rapid tattoo on the door of his room, which boomed through the entire dwelling.

The handle turned and the door flew open. A blue-uniformed Union infantryman, armed with a bayoneted rifle, marched into the room and halted a few paces from a bewildered Ty. The footslogger was blunt at shoulder and hip and built rock solid. His eyes were the feral yellow found in mongrel cats; his nose was bulbous, red-veined, crusted, and dripping; his mouth rivaled that of the baboon. His neatly trimmed auburn beard hung to the middle of his full-muscled chest. Ty couldn't detect an ounce of fat on him anywhere.

The Yankee soldier came to attention and announced, "Lieutenant Sheldon Foote, Company B, Sixteenth Regiment, United States Infantry. Rebel name on my orders reads Ty Mattson. Would you be him?"

Ty swung his legs over the side of the bed, rocked his body, and then stood. He swallowed to steady his voice and said, "Yes, sir, I am."

A skeptical frown muddled Lieutenant Foote's rugged features. He butted his rifle, freeing a hand to drag fingers across his nostrils and sling snot against the wall. "That may be your name, but, by damned, you don't look like no gun-waving, fire-eating Morgan Raider to me. You look like you should be plowing somewheres today."

When Ty didn't respond to that degrading epitaph, the Yankee footslogger slung snot again, hawked, spat on the floor, and said, "Here's how it's gonna be, pup. I'm escorting you to Cincinnati on the morning packet. I'm going to manacle your hands. We'll do it with them in front of you for starters. You give me the slightest cause and you'll travel with your hands locked behind you, a damn unpleasant way to ride on boats and trains. You try to run on me, and I'll stick you or shoot you. Don't matter to me which."

Removing a set of handcuffs from a leather pouch attached to his belt, Lieutenant Foote, hard gaze never leaving Ty, tossed them to his prisoner. "Get dressed and put those on your wrists and snap them shut."

The lieutenant waited patiently while Ty pulled on trousers

and shoes and locked the heavy metal bracelets on both his wrists, doing his best to hide the pain in his leg. He was determined to keep Lieutenant Sheldon Foote from spotting any weakness in his prisoner that he could exploit.

Ty's caution was quickly rewarded. Lieutenant Foote slanted his rifle across his burly chest and said, "Like I told the good doctor downstairs, I'm not concerned about the healing of your wounds. My orders are to deliver you to headquarters in Cincinnati double-quick, since you're to be on a northbound train tomorrow morning. You've been assigned a new home, Mattson, what we call the 'Hotel De Gankee,' just outside the fair city of Chicago. Bein' a Southern secesh boy, I'm certain you'll enjoy its lakeside winters."

Lieutenant Foote stared straight into Ty's eyes. "Keep this in mind every minute. I'm a field-commissioned officer. Fail my duty once and I'll be broken back to the ranks. So heed my every order, or I'll leave you dead on the riverbank for the locals to bury."

With that final, explicit warning, Foote stepped aside and pointed at the bedroom doorway. "After you, Mattson."

Ty didn't let Lieutenant Foote's deliberate refusal to address him by his military rank faze him. He was beginning to realize how few personal rights were accorded prisoners of war. Professor Ackerman had noted in his studies that in many historical wars, it had proven cheaper for both armies to bury their captured enemies rather than house and feed them.

Hands braced on the walls of the stairwell, Ty negotiated the steep steps to the first floor. Dr. Gates and Jarvis nodded to him from the front parlor, but they didn't speak. Given Lieutenant Foote's zealous devotion to duty and lack of social amenities, this was probably best for everyone.

With that threatening bayonet behind him, Ty kept moving. He stepped out into a dreary morning. Fog clung to the river in silvery gray patches. Dark clouds whisked eastward, propelled by high-level winds. Damp air tweaked Ty's nose.

The scene fit his mood. He stepped off Dr. Gates's porch and turned toward the Pomeroy levee. He felt like a condemned pirate walking the plank of a British warship at sword point, a sensation that reminded him with stark clarity how precious, tenuous, and short life could be.

PART 4

EIGHTY ACRES OF HELL

We are in Union shackles facing an unknown fate. We will shortly pay dearly for acts of war that our captors have declared illegal and unwarranted. We will not encounter a single forgiving heart. For us, human kindness and mercy perished on the battlefield behind a swirling veil of cannon smoke. The Union prison camps are shrouded in mystery. Will we be treated honorably or housed like starving dogs and whipped if we bark in protest? Will we be exchanged? If not, can we outlast the war? The uncertainty tears at our nerves. Oh, how some wish they'd died with gun in hand. We pray for the best. May the Lord watch over us.

—Journal of Lieutenant Clinton J. Hardesty, Morgan's Confederate Cavalry, 30 August 1863

CHAPTER 22

Ty shivered, pulled the threadbare blanket tighter about his body, and snuggled against the backside of Shawn Shannon. The 1864 New Year's Eve blizzard raging against the single pine-board wall behind him threatened to tear the tar paper roof from the prison barrack.

His bunk was the farthest from the wood-fired boiler burning in the center of the narrow room. He was thankful he was in the middle tier of bunks, sandwiched between the solid bodies of Lieutenant Shannon and Private Ebb White. He was protected there from the arctic blasts of freezing air that swept through holes in the roof and the penetrating chill of the bare earth floor that seeped from beneath the lower ones.

Ty dreaded the coming morning. The guards had refused to buck temperatures twenty degrees below zero and the three feet of snow blanketing the yard to help the prisoners fetch more wood for the stove. When the wood box was empty, Ty would fetch wood with his fellow inmates in shifts or they would freeze to death. Lord, how he wished for the stifling round-the-clock heat of his ride with General Morgan.

Prisoners were not allowed to talk after the evening bugle.

That didn't stop Ty from hearing those suffering closest to him in the near darkness. Below him, Private Billy Burke whimpered occasionally, the result of his spending hours riding the "Mule," a wood frame near the yard gate with a narrow scantling across the top of it, his punishment for stealing a fellow prisoner's meager ration. The guards had gladly provided Billy with a set of stirrups by tying sand-filled buckets to each of his ankles. A day and night on the "Mule" left Billy sore, stove-up, and hurting a week after he returned to the barrack.

The groans reaching Ty across the narrow aisle separating the tiered bunks frequently drowned out Billy Burke's whimpers. After being caught throwing a stone at a Union sentinel, Private Ben Henry had been sentenced to thirty days with a sixty-four-pound iron ball, on a three-foot chain, strapped to his ankle. It made no difference that Private Henry was taken to the Camp Douglas smallpox hospital the next day. He was made to wear the ball and chain throughout his hospital stay. Upon his release, the iron ball slipped off the bed of the wagon returning him to Ty's barrack, severely injuring his ankle and his hip. The Reb doctor serving the camp hospital doubted Ben Henry would ever recover completely. He was left to suffer in his barrack bunk, because sick prisoners enduring infectious maladies other than smallpox filled the beds at White Oak Square Hospital.

Bad as the situation was for some in his barrack, Ty knew that the circumstance of Private Given Campbell was worse yet. Given had joined a group of conspirators that bribed night guards to look the other way while they scaled the east wall of the stockade. Their escape was short-lived, for the five of them were found hiding in the tenement slums of Chicago, three miles from Camp Douglas, within twenty-four hours. The punishment meted out after they were returned to the prison was thirty days in the White Oak Square Dungeon.

Just thinking of that pesthole made Ty's skin crawl. Accessible via a hatchway in the floor of the guardhouse, the underground room of the dungeon measured only eighteen square feet. Prisoners who survived a sentence there told of the one small barred window near the ceiling, and the solitary sink in a corner, which gave off an intolerable stench that assailed their nostrils and watered their eyes without relief. Rations were scant meals of bread and water, morning and evening. No blankets and bedding were provided. Regardless of the outside temperature, Rebels served their time in whatever clothing adorned their bodies when the hatchway door shut above their heads. Populate the tiny dungeon with up to twenty-four men at the same time and brutal brawls and fisticuffs were inevitable. The ordeal severely weakened prisoners, so after their release, death from other causes was commonplace.

"Our commandant," Shawn Shannon had warned, "isn't concerned a whit about how many of us die from a stretch in the dungeon. Why should he be? It helps do away with the biggest of his problems."

Ty wanted no part of the "Mule," the ball and chain, or that foul dungeon. On the advice and counsel of Shawn Shannon, he had been very deliberate with his every move since arriving at Camp Douglas, Lieutenant Sheldon Foote's "Hotel De Gankee." He was never late for morning roll call; and when the guards chose to make fun of his troublesome limp, knowing Ty didn't dare retaliate, he kept his lips buttoned and a bland expression on his face, though his innards burned hotter than Hades.

A Yankee sergeant, who laughed nasally, snarled, "Too bad those big shoulders will never have a chance to lift you over the stockade, secesh. You'd be running for a week to get there with that gimp leg." That sergeant came the closest of any of the blue-belly guards to riling his feelings.

That was, until earlier this New Year's Eve, when Ty had been visiting the sinks before the blizzard struck in full force and ran smack into his father's murderer. All of Morgan's men, other than his highest-ranking officers, had been imprisoned at Camp Douglas. Ty had watched for Jack Stedman's son from the second he walked through the stockade gates—no small feat, what with White Oak Square containing sixteen barracks that held nineteen hundred men.

The sinks for each set of four barracks were constructed over sewers, with forty funnels from each sink connected to a soil box. Each funnel fit one man. To discourage escape attempts, Camp Douglas regulations mandated that a prisoner visiting the sinks during nighttime hours, no matter the weather, had to strip to bare feet and underwear before stepping from his barrack. If his sink was crowded with long lines, a prisoner sought relief at another, as public urination was forbidden and the guards were diligent about watching for such acts and quick to administer a whipping or paddling.

Long lines had forced Jack Stedman's offspring to seek accommodations at a sink other than his own, fostering the unexpected encounter that set in motion a chain of events that ensnared Ty like the jaws of a metal trap clamping on his ankle.

The Stedman son was in a powerful hurry to answer his need; he and Ty bumped into each other in the sink doorway. For two long seconds of lantern light, Ty looked squarely into a pair of cold gray eyes before he was shoved aside. In that short span, he caught the other vital features of the hurrying figure—pale blond hair, wide forehead, and bear trap jaw heavy on chinbone—that confirmed what he'd seen. He'd found his man. He was here in White Oak Square. He hadn't died on the battlefield, been sent home with the severely wounded, or been amongst the 103 Rebels that had escaped the first week of December.

Ty didn't hesitate or look back. He let the wind swing the sink door closed behind him and scurried across the ice-covered parade ground, arms spread wide to keep his balance. His feet growing numb, he hustled inside his barrack and made straight

208

for the warmth of its boiler, stomping his feet and rubbing his hands together. Lord, but he was wracked with chills, through and through.

"Damn cold pee, huh, lad?" Private E.J. Pursley quipped, holding out Ty's shoes, shirt, and pants.

Never to be outdone, Private Cally Smith asked from his bunk, "Didn't freeze your vitals, did you? They're mighty important to us young fellers."

"They would be, if we ever saw anything besides stockade walls every morning," Corporal Sam Bryant said. "I didn't believe before they stuck us in this godforsaken pox pit that you could die of boredom, but I'm about to change my mind."

"Oh, pshaw, Sam," Ebb White countered, "you'd miss our chess games right off the mark, don't tell me no different. I'm the only man in creation you can checkmate."

"Truth is, Ebb, I'd swap the rest of my days for a Yankee pardon and one more kiss with Kaitlin Fowler in her father's hay loft."

The barbed teasing and romantic lamentations of his messmates seldom taxed Ty's patience. Upon his arrival at Camp Douglas back in September 1863, he'd been delightfully overwhelmed to learn that, except for Ad White and Harlan Stillion, his mess had survived the fight at Buffington Island intact and he would be sharing the same quarters with them. Tonight, though, he was only half listening to their jabber. He was desperate to talk with Lieutenant Shawn Shannon about the incident that happened a few minutes ago at the sink.

Ty dressed in a rush and headed for the far end of the building. Shawn Shannon, who'd lied about being an officer to travel to Camp Douglas with his messmates, liked to distance himself from the guards who lingered about the barrack's boiler, a strategy that also made a bunk available for a sick Rebel closer to the barrack's sole source of heat.

Lieutenant Shannon was reclined on their middle-tier bunk,

reading a book by candlelight. His midnight eyes fixed on the rapidly approaching Ty. "Barracks aren't on fire, are they?"

Ty ignored his question, rose on his toes, leaned close so as not to be overheard, and, voice brimming with excitement, said, "I just saw Jack Stedman's son, father's killer, in the sink."

"Are you certain it was him?"

"Yes, he's the same sapper sergeant Father and I identified while we were bridging the creek outside Chester, Ohio."

The seven o'clock evening bugle blew, signaling that all candles and lanterns were to be extinguished and all conversation was to cease. The sharp tone of Ty's voice told Shawn Shannon he wouldn't be put off until morning, not about something of such importance to him that it was threatening to pop his cork.

Shannon laid his book aside, snubbed out the candle, and threw his legs over the side rail of the bunk to make room for Ty. "Climb up here beside me. If we talk in a whisper, the wind and the roar of the boiler should keep the guards from hearing us for a little while."

When Ty was settled on the paper-thin, straw tick mattress, Shawn Shannon said, "Now, if you've found the right man, what do you intend to do?"

"I'll see him hanged or kill him myself," Ty answered vehemently.

"Ty, let's set things straight. The Yankees won't hang him, unless he confesses, which is not likely to happen. We have no witnesses that saw him shoot Owen. You didn't see him do it, and when I got there, he'd already disappeared into that mad scramble of wagons and vehicles and horsemen fleeing the blue bellies. Even if we did have witnesses, think about it, why should the Yankees care if a secesh trooper killed one of his own in the heat of battle? On the other hand, you murder Jack Stedman's son or kill him in a fair fight, either way they'll gladly make an example of you and hang you in front of the entire garrison."

In the ensuing silence, Shannon could practically hear gears spinning inside Ty's mind. He knew what was coming. The keen edge in Ty's voice deepened. "I'll see him dead, one way or another, and they can bury me with him. I'll keep a stranglehold on the bastard's throat till the Lord or the Devil, I don't care which, pries my fingers loose."

Lieutenant Shannon took a deep breath. Any objection on his part to what Ty was proposing was pointless. Owen Mattson had made life-endangering decisions with the same kind of rock-hard conviction that ruled out waffling, self-doubt, and recrimination. The Mattson bones of fate had been cast upon the blanket, and they weren't to be touched again, period.

"Ty, did he recognize you?"

"I doubt it. He was in a heap of hurry to keep from wetting himself in front of everybody."

"That's good. He's a coward and a back shooter. He figures you know who he is, he might swallow the dog—take the Union Loyalty Oath—and agree to fight the western Indians with the Yankees. And if he does, he's beyond our reach faster than the flare of a dying match."

Shannon squeezed Ty's forearm. "I want Stedman's bush-whacking turd of a son to pay the piper as much as you. Promise me, you won't seek him out without talking with me first. I'll back you, but I want a chance to tell you if I think you're taking the wrong path. Then I'll step aside. I won't try to stop you."

It was an offer Ty didn't dare refuse. He was fully aware he lacked the rough-and-tumble fighting experience of his father and Shawn Shannon. He'd participated in two full-blown horse-back charges, firing with his pistol from the saddle. Never had he engaged another man, blow for blow, to the death as they had. In close quarters, he was an amateur with gun, knife, and fist.

"How would you go about it?"

Rubbing his cheek with a knuckle, a relieved Shawn Shannon thought a long moment, then said, "First we learn as much as we can about him. I'm acquainted with the Rebel master sergeants responsible for each of the barracks. I have a hunch our man is like a bear with a sore paw dealing with enlisted men and a handful of grief for his master sergeant. I'll ask about him as one officer talking to another. Then we'll talk again. How's that—"

A rough growl arose by the boiler. "I hear any more chatter, we'll fall out and sit bare-assed in the snow till it melts beneath you."

The Yankee officer's threat echoed through the barrack and captured the ear of every prisoner. The long room grew quiet—so still that Ty swore he heard one of the prisoners bunking below him gulp. Not a single Rebel wanted to endure that particular punishment a second time. The weather ten days past had been right balmy compared to the howling New Year's Eve blizzard that continued to breach the walls and roof of the barracks. Thawing out a pair of frostbitten haunches was a unique agony, one that made the toughest of men well up and cry.

Shawn Shannon shushed Ty with a finger against his lips. Shooed away from the boiler by the guards, jovial Ebb White joined them and the trio rolled into the blankets for the night.

Still wound up, Ty lay awake long after his bunkmates were asleep and snoring. He prayed devising a plan to confront Jack Stedman's son wouldn't prove as frustrating as another endeavor of his had been, to date. The sighting of the White Oak Square Post Office as he passed through the camp gate the first time five months ago had squelched temporarily the dread of his coming imprisonment and thrilled him to the bone. He soon learned mail and packages were delivered daily from all points of the compass, north and south, and that the post office sold postage, paper, and pencil to those prisoners with the necessary funds. But the cost of postage for a single letter—three cents in Federal stamps and ten cents in Confederate—and that of paper and pencil seemed an insurmountable sum to a penniless prisoner such as Ty. The post office did forward outgoing mail minus the Confederate stamps, leaving the collection of the ten cents due to the final post office delivering it to the addressee. So, for want of three 1-cent Federal stamps and paper and pencil, Ty was against the wall when it came to writing letters.

Shawn Shannon kept him from becoming a beggar. When he asked Ty with a devilish glint in his eye if there wasn't someone, anyone he wanted to write to—and learned of Ty's impoverished state—postage, paper, and pencil were quickly in Ty's hands at the cost of a conspiratorial wink from the lieutenant.

Ty seated himself at one of the long wooden dining tables, laid a sheath of blank business forms looted from the various blue-belly towns the raiders had visited to use for stationery, wet the tip of his pencil, and discovered he didn't have the foggiest notion how best to write to Dana Bainbridge.

Every opening line he pondered sounded immature or presumptive. He sat thinking far too long. His courage deserted him and he decided to contact Boone Jordan, instead. Maybe she had written a note or letter to Mr. Jordan in the meantime that showed a desire on her part to stay in touch and perhaps help him determine his status with her. Was he a wounded veteran deserving of her friendship and kindness, or was he a potential lover and husband?

He felt like a coward as he wrote:

15 October 1863
Dear Mr. Jordan:
    Having been captured at Buffington Island, I am imprisoned at Camp Douglas outside Chicago, Illinois. I wish to inform you that Father was shot and killed during the battle, not by the enemy but by one of our own men. His loss cannot be measured. The same assassin wounded me. I recovered except for the limp in my left leg.
    Despite what has transpired since we parted company, you have my eternal thanks for helping me run off and meet Father. I will be a bigger, better man, though I shared his

life for only a short time. He was all I hoped for in a father and much, much more. He made me proud of my heritage and showed me by example how a true man comports himself. I swear I will survive the war and make him proud of me.

Lieutenant Shawn Shannon, the officer that kept me from bleeding to death and saw to Father's proper burial, shares my barrack. He is cut from the same cloth as Father and watches out for me when he can.

In closing, you may receive a letter addressed to me from Miss Dana Bainbridge, of Portland, Ohio. If you do, please forward it at your first opportunity.

Best regards, your friend,
Ty Mattson
P. S. I pray nightly that Grandfather will see fit to forgive me.

Cautioned by Sam Bryant that Yankee clerks censored every word of outgoing letters, Ty avoided any mention of the progress of the war in the South or the miserable conditions at Camp Douglas. Prisoners could ask relatives and friends to ship them clothing, food items, and monies, with no guarantee against the guards stealing a portion for themselves. Some prisoners complained that jealous and nosy clerks kept their sweetheart's love letters from them. Ebb White summed up the mail situation in his succinct fashion, "Put stamps on your letter and hope for the best. How else can we reach beyond the stockade?"

Then the waiting had started for Ty. He hated standing in long lines during mail call, but it did give purpose to his countless, idle hours, since he was not good at chess, hated checkers, and quickly read what few books his fellow prisoners had received from home. Daily Chicago newspapers purchased from the civilian sutlers by Cally Smith and Sam Bryant augmented the holdings of a barrack library with but two short shelves. The marble and candy enterprises of the Smith and Bryant families had continued to be profitable, despite the war, and their parents and numerous relatives became a steady source for hard candy, dried fruit, tobacco, cigars, and other treats. With delivery from Lexington and Georgetown, Kentucky, requiring only three days, packages arrived at Camp Douglas for Cally and Sam at regular intervals.

As the weeks slid by, the short mail delivery time between Kentucky and Chicago nibbled at Ty's patience more each day. Had something happened to Boone Jordan? Not being a young man, had he perhaps passed away? Or had he fallen ill and become bedridden? Mr. Boone was a bachelor, with no siblings, and his last blood relatives, his aunt and uncle, were deceased. That left Old Joe, who was illiterate and would not think of checking for mail at the post office without instructions.

Ty stewed and fretted morning, noon, and night. Still hesitant to write directly to Dana Bainbridge, he duplicated his letter to Mr. Jordan from memory, again cursing his lack of intestinal fortitude with each scratch of his pencil, and sent it off. If Mr. Jordan failed to respond by Thanksgiving, he vowed to bite the bullet, fire off a short note to Dana—for a long letter was too frightening to undertake—and learn the truth of his situation with her. He was teetering on the brink of a sheer cliff.

It was all in or nothing before he lost his mind.

CHAPTER 23

A few days later, Shawn Shannon had pulled Ty tight against the rear wall of the barrack, where the other prisoners milling about couldn't overhear them. "Lad, I'm not faulting you for being moonstruck over that Bainbridge gal. You walking about with your head down and chin dragging the ground snapping at anyone that comes near you, I won't tolerate. You get real love foggy and speak to a guard that way, you'll end up riding the 'Mule' or worse. Are you listening to me?"

The bluntness of Shawn Shannon's query straightened Ty's backbone. He avoided Shawn's probing gaze, shamed by how far into the doldrums he'd fallen. Without appearing like a whining weakling, he wasn't quite sure how to tell the lieutenant that it wasn't just his unfulfilled infatuation with Dana that had squashed his spirits.

The monotony of prison life was almost unbearable. Every day was the same. Roll call was one hour after the sunrise bugle blew. Providing no prisoner was late or failed to respond to the calling of his name, prisoners were dismissed for breakfast. With the slightest infraction, the entire prisoner population stood in line without moving in fair weather, rain, and snow for as long as their captors saw fit—sometimes for up to three hours.

Once the roll call was completed to Yankee satisfaction, the prisoners cleaned the camp barracks and policed the grounds. They then had one hour for breakfast. The first fatigue of the day commenced at eight o'clock when assignments ranging from the digging of ditches for new waterlines, extending the height of the stockade, or emptying the soil boxes of the sinks were given to the prisoners. Recall at twelve o'clock preceded dinner by thirty minutes. The afternoon fatigue reported at one o'clock and lasted until the five o'clock recall for supper. Lights went out with the seven o'clock bugle.

The unvarying daily routine, coupled with constant confinement in an enclosed area under guard around the clock, bored and unnerved Ty to where he had to fight the urge to scream aloud and take his frustration out on the smirking guards, no matter the consequences. Before Camp Douglas, he would have scoffed at the suggestion a man could feel lonely and isolated if like-minded peers surrounded him. One glance at the seventeen-foot-high stockade, with its guard towers, dispelled that notion double-quick.

Nattily dressed male and female Chicago citizens gawking and pointing at Rebel prisoners on weekends from a high platform built for them outside the stockade wall reinforced Ty's gloom. Hearing their tinny laughter made him feel like a striped monkey in a cage wearing a dunce cap.

Shawn Shannon clasped Ty's shoulder. "Lad, are you listening to me?" he repeated.

Ty blinked and nodded. "I am now, sir."

"Then get your head up and keep it up. You may have forgotten you're an officer. Well, I haven't, and I expect you to conduct yourself accordingly. Wherever we are, we set the example for others to follow. We don't mope about like tarred and feathered dogs. Not a single Morgan man is ready to admit he's been defeated in spirit or the flesh. We'll either escape or walk out of here with our heads held high when the fighting stops. I don't know which way it will be, or when it will happen, but it will. That's what I want you thinking about every waking minute. That's what will see you through, not your pining away in a stupor while you wait for a letter that may never come. Put this thought under your hat for safekeeping—You have no chance with her at all if you finish the war in a pine box. Are we on the same page now, Corporal?"

Shawn Shannon's lecture jerked Ty from his doldrums and changed his demeanor and behavior in a hurry. It was as if his dead father had spoken to him. During the day, he hid his innermost feelings behind a smile and make-do attitude, showed due respect to the guards, and volunteered to help Private Pursley in the kitchen. He enjoyed that chore, though his ears did suffer for a fortnight when the white-goateed cook exploded in a fit of profanity after a rumor floated through the barrack that come winter the boilers would be used for cooking instead of stoves to save on firewood.

The red of E.J.'s cheeks matched that of a male cardinal. Without his cursing missing a beat, he slung cookware about in frenzies that endangered the unwary. Shawn Shannon took mercy on the entire barrack by dousing E.J.'s ire with a promise that greasing the palms of the guards could keep his stove burning indefinitely. No one was certain Shawn's promise would hold water, but in the humble opinion of all who dined at Private Pursley's table, the ensuing peace and quiet qualified Lieutenant Shawn Shannon for sainthood in a faith of his choice. If there was an upside to E.J.'s carrying on so, he had given everyone within earshot a new definition of the word "pride."

At night, Ty stayed as still as possible between Shawn Shannon and Ebb White. It was then he let his longings off their daytime leash and prayed without uttering a sound. He prayed Dana would write soon. He prayed Boone Jordan was in good health and had received his letters. And Ty prayed that the livery owner would decide on his own to inform his grandfather that he was alive. The guilt Ty felt for abandoning Enoch Mattson in the cold-blooded way he had was growing in his gut faster than spring mushrooms.

Ty's self-imposed deadline of Thanksgiving descended upon him quickly. Thanksgiving was a Federal holiday the Confederacy did not officially observe. Nonetheless, it proved an exciting week for Ty. The day before the holiday, Wednesday, 25 November 1863, a date he never forgot, he at last heard his name during mail call. A quick glance at the return address told him the letter was from Mr. Boone. He distanced himself from those remaining in line, in order to claim a little privacy, and, with pulse thumping, opened the envelope. Did it contain a letter from Dana Bainbridge?

The envelope held only a note from Boone Jordan. Ty's keen disappointment was offset by the knowledge that he had successfully contacted the forwarding point for mail he had given Dana. Half the line of communication between Portland, Ohio, and Chicago was open.

The delicate script of Boone Jordan's note puzzled Ty until he started reading:

> *15 November 1863*
> *Dear Ty:*
>
> *Forgive me for not answering sooner. I suffered a black spell and was abed for some weeks. The spell numbed my fingers, and when I could move about, I had to search out Mrs. Kincaid from across the alley to pen my note.*
>
> *I was saddened by the news of Owen's death. At the same time, I'm happy you spent a few weeks with him. I hope your leg is better. I have not received any letters to be forwarded to you.*

*If you need money, food, clothing, anything, and can re-
ceive those items, please advise. I will have Old Joe check the
post office every other day.*

Your friend,
Boone Jordan

Suppertime was near and he returned to his barrack as fast as
the thick, shoe-clinging mud of White Oak Square allowed. He
had serious thinking to do before lights-out. Though he had finally
heard from Mr. Jordan, did he want to write to Dana, anyway?

He had learned Shawn Shannon and Given Campbell wouldn't
hesitate. They lived by the creed that when the opportunity arose
to make an attractive female aware of your interest, do so straight
out. Fuss and fume like backward Ty and you chanced losing her
to a bolder man. If a man's intentions were rebuffed, he need remember that maybe the next gal *would* be interested and perhaps
even prettier.

What had initially appeared as selfish and ungentlemanly behavior on the part of Shawn and Given, which defied proper
decorum and ignored female sensitivities, was appealing more to
Ty every minute. Pining away through the night for a female
who might well be glad she was free of the nursing demands his
care had placed on her, and the disruption he had brought to her
home, had him dreading lights-out.

A step from the door of his barrack, he decided to take the
plunge. He was sick of being an embarrassment to himself. He
would write to her yet today, if that were possible. But E.J. Pursley had another chore lined up for his assistant cook, and it pre-
cluded any letter writing on the eve of Thanksgiving.

A barrel of sugar had been delivered to the barracks, instead
of a barrel of flour. Sugar being a scarce commodity, the resulting excitement had the entire barrack in an uproar. Ty was es-

corted to the kitchen. The door opened a crack. He was shoved inside and the door locked behind him.

Flour-smudged apron tied about his waist, Ebb White was rolling pie dough on the center table. E.J. was stirring a big pot on the six-oven stove. He beckoned to Ty and said, "Over here. Grab a pan and make a flour and water slurry like I taught you."

"What are we making?"

"Vinegar pie, the delicacy those boys out there crave after their corn bread, and since there's no meal to be had for corn bread, they're a tad worked up."

The vinegar pie recipe was quite simple. E.J. combined sugar, water, vinegar, and eggs and brought them to boil, added butter, and then folded in Ty's slurry, stirring slowly till the mixture thickened. From there, E.J.'s filling was poured into pans of every size and shape lined with Ebb White's dough.

The kitchen couldn't contain the aroma, once a smiling E.J. nodded for Ebb to open the door, resulting in a prolonged cheer, which rattled the rafters of the barrack. Loud as it sounded, Ty doubted a Rebel war-concluding victory could have been any louder.

The prodigious pie eating was one for the ages. Ty witnessed a classic example of how scarcity primed a prisoner's belly for sweets. The hungry camp guards went along and the feasting lasted well after the lights-out bugle. Ty was so tired and full that climbing into his bunk was akin to scaling a mountain.

On Federal Thanksgiving Day, deluging rainstorms canceled afternoon fatigue and enabled Ty to climb into his bunk with paper and pencil. The events of the previous evening had granted him plenty of time to reconsider his decision. His resolve didn't falter. After all, his father hadn't wasted any time pursuing his mother Keena, had he?

He wasted paper in the beginning, then he laid down his feelings straight from the heart:

26 November 1863
Miss Dana Bainbridge:

I'm writing to you from the Camp Douglas Federal prison to thank you for the care you gave me during my convalescence at your family home. You eased my pain and lifted my spirits. While my present circumstances are tolerable, I long for my freedom.

It is my intent to call upon you once the war is concluded. Not being a man inclined to waste words, you have won my love and I dream of a life with you nightly. I know now how my father felt when he first met my mother—that he was the luckiest man on God's earth. My prayer is that you will find me a worthy suitor.

My address is Corporal Ty Mattson, 14th Kentucky Cavalry, c/o Camp Douglas, Chicago Illinois.

Longing to hear from you,
Ty

He read the note through twice and determined that fooling with the wording would detract from its sincerity. He sealed it and attached the required Federal and Confederate stamps, which Cally Smith had loaned him.

He had enough loaned postage remaining to answer Boone Jordan's letter. He informed the livery owner that his health was the same as before; and while he had written directly to Dana Bainbridge, he still requested that Mr. Boone continue to check for mail addressed to him in his care. Lastly, Ty thanked Mr. Boone for the trouble he had taken to answer Ty's previous letters and wished him a speedy recovery from his black spell.

Ty made no mention as to whether or not Mr. Boone could forward clothing, monies, and other sundry items. Though he needed a good winter coat, like those that other affluent Kentucky Raiders besides just Cally Smith and Sam Bryant were receiving from their relatives and friends, he was acutely aware that Mr. Jordan was far from being a wealthy man. The single man of substantial means he knew was Grandfather Mattson, and Ty was a long way from daring to ask favors of him.

He carried his letters to the post office and slipped them into the mail slot that accessed the drop box inside the front door. He had taken the initiative and was certain the waiting would be easier for at least a little while.

Or so he would pray.

CHAPTER 24

"General Morgan escaped! General Morgan escaped! General Morgan escaped!"

The screeching Billy Burke, recovered from his session riding the "Mule," burst though the barrack door during noon dinner, waving the latest copy of the *Chicago Tribune* high over his head.

The Camp Douglas raiders had gleaned from the local papers that General Morgan and a number of high-ranking Rebel officers had been sent to the Ohio Penitentiary in Columbus, a steep-walled, heavily guarded institution. The verbal picture painted by the news sheets of their commanding officer's rude treatment and his cell, eight feet by ten feet, containing a metal bed with no mattress and slop bucket for bodily functions, seemed unnecessarily harsh to the Confederate troopers, who had enjoyed serving a leader wise enough to seek indoor accommodations and avoid the hard ground they were forced to endure.

"How'd the general escape?" an impatient Cally Smith demanded.

The onrushing Billy Burke halted, caught his breath, and, speaking in short squeaks, said, "He and six of his officers discovered an air chamber below their cells. They chipped through the concrete floor of their cells to get into the air chamber and tunneled through the foundation of their cell block out into the prison yard. They used ropes to climb over the outside wall."

"How'd they scale the wall without being seen?" Sam Bryant wondered.

"*Tribune* claims it was a dark, rainy night," Billy said. "The prison dogs were asleep in their kennels and the patrolling wall guards were huddled in their towers to keep dry."

Ebb White roused a cheer for General Morgan by chuckling and observing, "Same old 'Thunderbolt of the Confederacy.' Caught the Yankees with their pants down round their knees and their dirty drawers showing. The man has a genuine knack for making downright fools out of wrongheaded blue bellies, don't he now?"

"Have any of them been captured yet?" E.J. asked.

"Nary a one, so far," a gloating Billy pronounced, raising a second boisterous cheer for Morgan and his fellow escapees.

The dinner conversation centered on the general's daring feat. Shawn Shannon listened a short while, turned to Ty beside him, and said softly, "They're caught up in the idea that, if the general did it, they can tunnel under the wall here and escape. They forget that all but very few who've already managed that are recaptured in a few days and sentenced to the dungeon. They're also forgetting what can happen to them, besides the dungeon, for just planning an escape if the Yankees find out. Remember the day Commandant DeLand made the lot of us stand in formation and watch three prisoners tied up by the thumbs for threatening to hang a prisoner they thought was planning to rat them out with the guards. You remember that day, don't you?"

Ty most certainly did. The groaning and pitiful hollering of the three suffering prisoners had turned his stomach. After they pleaded repeatedly that they were innocent, a frustrated Commandant DeLand finally had them taken down. One untied

Rebel fainted and the freed raider trooper next to him threw up on his own chest. The commandant then gave a lecture that no prisoner reporting escape plans to the guards was to be touched or threatened. He dismissed everyone with a promise that unless the guilty Rebels turned themselves in at his headquarters, he would bring them back with orders to stand in the cold until daylight. Fortunately, the guilty Rebels went to Yankee headquarters later that evening and confessed. They were punished, as the innocent had been.

Shawn Shannon chewed a piece of beef gristle and swallowed with a hard gulp. "These boys don't realize they face an even bigger challenge, once they're outside the stockade. You can bet that money was smuggled into General Morgan. After he escaped, someone provided him civilian clothing, fed him, bought train tickets for him in advance so he could move fast, and probably provided him fresh horses after he crossed the Ohio. A clean escape that sees you back to the Confederate ranks is harder than our boys believe. You need help from friends and supporters in the right places, with waiting arms and deep pockets, willing to risk imprisonment for your freedom. General Morgan has them. We don't."

"If they understood that, do you think our boys would quit trying to bribe the stockade guards and stop digging tunnels?"

"Not hardly, they can only stand so much haranguing and needling from the guards, lousy quarters, short rations, and constant rumors that we might be exchanged, which never amount to anything. An idle prisoner becomes dangerous if his patience wears thin. And believe me, lad, their patience is thin as a knife blade. Sooner or later, some incident of consequence is bound to ring Commandant DeLand's bell and the repercussions won't be pretty."

Shawn Shannon's predicted incident occurred on the second of December 1863. Right before midnight, the beating of drums followed by rifle fire awakened Ty and his bunkmates. In the distance, a booming cannon of a voice said, "Prisoners outside the wall! Prisoners outside the wall! All companies report for duty!"

Billy Burke leaped from his bunk and scampered for the door. He grabbed for the latch and froze when Shawn Shannon said, "Don't open that door. That's an order, Private Burke."

A puzzled Billy Burke spun about and peered though the feeble light of the darkened barrack. "Who gave that order?"

Shawn Shannon dropped to the floor and approached Billy. "I did. Listen to them calling back and forth. Those guards are jumpier than a long-tailed cat in a room full of rocking chairs. Open the door and they'll likely think you're meaning to join in the escape, and bad things happen in the dark. We'll stay put and listen. We'll know soon enough what's happened."

On that count, Lieutenant Shannon was wrong. Punctuated by beating drums, blowing bugles, shouting guards, and an occasional rifle shot, the commotion beyond their barrack continued well into the middle of the night.

At dawn, the door swung open without a knock, as usual, and two guards, strangers to the barrack, swept inside. The taller Yankee was burly and walked with a swagger. His stringy brown beard was spotted with gray streaks, despite his relative youth, and his black jagged teeth hinted at breath that would gag a maggot. Eyes the color of sun-brightened sand canvassed the room and the burly guard's lip-curling smile was that of a dog preparing to devour a meaty bone. "There's a hundred less of you filthy scoundrels to deal with. That's good for us, and bad for you. You'll pay dearly, me buckoes, for the sins of others."

The two guards framed the door. They carried bayoneted rifles, the first Ty had seen at Camp Douglas. The blue bellies were truly upset.

Sneering, the black-toothed Yankee said, "Fall out, you Rebel scum. You're about to receive part of the bill for last night's shenanigans. Leave your coats. We want you to enjoy the chilly weather."

The muttering, coatless prisoners marched out of the barrack and gathered together. At a nod from one of the guards, a civilian carpentry crew armed with claw hammers, crowbars, and spud bars marched into the barrack. The sound of wood planks being ripped up incensed the watching prisoners.

E.J. Pursley's dander was on the rise, like a freshly fired steam boiler. "The bastards are tearing out the floors."

The burly guard, whom the Rebels took to calling "Snag," since his teeth reminded them of rotting stumps sticking from swamp water, snorted triumphantly. "You gray lice won't be hiding any more tunnels from us."

"That dirt floor will be a mud sty in a week!" E.J. fumed. "Won't be nothing dry in there, and a doctor will tell you that makes for a lot of sick soldiers."

Snag glanced at Shawn Shannon. "Shut the old goat's face or he'll be eating a rifle butt for breakfast."

Having dealt with an irate E.J. in the past, Shawn grabbed him by the shoulders and pushed him amongst the gathered prisoners. "Ebb, keep a grip on him. He opens his trap again, gag him."

The carpentry crew emerged and walked to Barrack Nine next door. Snag announced roll call and daily fatigues were canceled. He dismissed the shivering Kentuckians with a warning. "Wait until tomorrow morning. It'll be the nastiest roll call in Camp Douglas history and I've seen some hell bangers, me buckoes."

What awaited the Rebels inside was a spirit sinker. All the separating partitions had been torn down, turning the barrack into one long, narrow room. Except for the planks beneath the tiered bunks, the floor was bare dirt. E.J. saw one bright spot. "Leastways, the blue bastards didn't haul off my stove and pans."

"Just wait," Ebb White cautioned. "They figure how much it will devil you to lose them. Snag will be here with a dozen volunteers. That feller has a ton of spite in him."

Anticipating the worst at morning roll call, the Kentuckians spent a restless night. They suspected something unusual was in the wind when they were marched from White Oak Square to Garrison Square in front of Colonel DeLand's headquarters and found the non-Kentucky Rebels from Prisoner's Square were already lined out for a joint roll call. The two groups had always been held apart from one another, a tribute to the feistiness of Morgan's raiders.

Yankee lieutenants and sergeants set to work searching the prisoners. Personal possessions from knives to money, even family photographs, were confiscated. Cally Smith noticed that some searchers were compiling a list of what they took and others weren't. Cally and Sam Bryant were lucky. Their sutler checks and cash monies were inventoried, though that was no guarantee they would be returned at a future date.

Commandant DeLand's officers saved their most blatant confiscation for last. His officers undertook a second pass through the lines and removed every good coat, replacing them with thin cotton pepper-and-salt jackets and an equal bunch of thin black spade-tailed gentlemen coats. The indignant well-to-do Kentuckians accepted the replacement garments with clamped lips and murder in their hearts. Ty shared their angst, but he was left hoping for any kind of winter coat.

Perched upon the top step beneath the roofed veranda that stretched across the front of his headquarters, Commandant De-Land raised his arms for silence. When he was certain he had the attention of the entire assemblage, the colonel said in a forceful, clear baritone that everyone, whether clad in blue or gray, could hear, "You secesh are prisoners of war and will be treated accordingly. Henceforth, you will be provided minimal clothing, survival rations, and a roof over your heads. No more, no less. You will suffer. You will not enjoy luxuries while our brave Yankee soldiers perish with less, from famine and disease at your Andersonville Prison Camp. Expect little from your captors, knowing it will be less. Understand that we will do as we please with you. You are dismissed."

Those fateful words struck home when the Kentucky Rebels returned to their barracks. During their absence, a squad of Yankees and civilian workers had searched their quarters and had removed all the good clothing they had found, with the work hands stealing what stored foodstuffs they could carry off. Plus they had torn up the flooring under the bunks. All axes, wood saws, and spades were confiscated, depriving the Rebels of their means for cutting wood and cleaning their quarters. A few yard rakes went untouched, inspiring a remark from the belligerent Snag a few days later that they were left for the Rebels to "comb their hair with."

As the weeks of December 1863 unfolded, Colonel DeLand's retaliation for the Rebel's tunnel digging and Confederate abuse and neglect of Yankee prisoners of war elsewhere intensified. He shut down the general stores of the civilian sutlers, the Southern prisoners' prime source for cider, eggs, milk, canned fruits, boots, underclothing, postage stamps, envelopes, and paper. The closing of the sutler stores forced the Kentuckians to purchase these items from the camp's Yankee commissary where any excess supplies were scarce and prices much steeper. Ty was ecstatic when he learned of the alternate source for postage stamps. He couldn't imagine a worse situation than the inability to answer a letter from Portland, Ohio.

The attitude of the guards hardened with that of their superior. Freshly armed with six-shot revolvers, they stood for little back talk and were prone to punish the slightest offenses by demeaning the Kentuckians in front of their fellows. The guards' favorites were to order the guilty prisoner to swing from ceiling rafter to ceiling rafter aping a chattering monkey until they dropped from exhaustion or to crawl the length of the barrack floor, barking and howling like a dog, until his knees were bloody and his voice too hoarse to utter a sound.

Not all December days turned sour for the Kentuckians. Given Campbell returned from his stay in the dungeon, leaner of body, but with his wit intact, instantly boosting morale with his impersonation of the guards, especially an undersized, stuttering Yankee who had gray hair, gray skin, gray eyes, sharply pointed nose, small yellow teeth, and weak chin. To everybody's amusement, Campbell nicknamed the short blue-belly "Mouse." Snag and Mouse were such exact opposites that the sight of them together provoked laugher throughout the barrack. Everyone was pleased to have Given Campbell back amongst them.

The highlight of the month was E.J. Pursley's corker of an 1863 Christmas dinner. For over two months, E.J., not trusting sutler checks, given the worsening atmosphere of the camp, had purchased commissary checks instead with funds contributed by his affluent messmates and other well-to-do Kentucky residents of Barrack Ten. He had kept them hidden in a flour barrel.

The white-goateed, toothless, aging ladle wielder—once the youthful, renowned chef in parlors of joy throughout New Orleans—had shared recipes with the Union commissary cooks to the delight of their officers and called in his chips for the big feast. E.J., Ty, and Ebb White spent the entire day before Christmas in the cookhouse baking pies and plain and sweet doughnuts, while holding those craving sweets at bay with sharpened knives.

It was a Christmas miracle of sorts that Snag and Mouse were on leave for the holidays. After a full night of cooking, sanctioned by salivating guards, Ty, Shawn Shannon, Sam Bryant, and Given Campbell served their guests biscuits, tea, beans and bacon, buttered baker's bread, toasted molasses, boiled onion steeped in water, cheese, peach pie, onion pie, and doughnuts, the most sumptuous prisoner feast in the short history of the camp. The absence of beef and pork, real meat, dulled not a single appetite.

The small joys of Christmas faded on the last day of the year. In early December 1863, President Abraham Lincoln had pro-

232

claimed amnesty for all Confederate soldiers below the rank of general, and the camp guards took great delight in telling the Rebels that the president had changed his mind and ruled his proclamation did not extend to prisoners of war. Upon hearing the news, most of the Kentuckians agreed with Ebb White's assessment, "We'll be whipping boys for the blue-belly guards till the last shot is fired on the battlefield, and I don't think the fighting will be over anytime soon."

The prospect of little improvement in the Kentuckians' situation for months, perhaps years to come, was reinforced when the raging blizzard roared in from Lake Michigan on New Year's Eve, 1864, doubling their physical miseries.

Long before dawn, any thought of revenge against Jack Stedman's son or romancing Dana Bainbridge deserted Ty Mattson's shivering body. Body warmth and food were first and foremost in his mind and his life.

No matter how frustrating it might be, everything else had to wait.

CHAPTER 25

The arctic weather that lasted through mid-January didn't deter Commandant DeLand from implementing new directives from his superiors designed to continue the Union program of retaliation and prevent future escapes. The guards were instructed to shout only one challenge to prisoners seen near the fence or outside the barracks at night and to shoot at any prisoner who didn't respond. The rule continued that a prisoner visiting the sinks had to remove his clothes, no matter the weather. Two divisions of fifteen Yankee enlisted men, each with one officer and one corporal, patrolled the grounds and barracks during daylight hours. The patrols inspected prison quarters twice per day to search for tunnels, broke up congregations of Rebels inside and outside the barracks, and watched their fellow guards, reporting any dereliction of duty on their part. Patrolling Yankee officers were given the authority to arrest Union soldiers for lingering amongst and talking to prisoners.

To further confine prisoners to White Oak and Prisoner's Squares, Confederate sergeant majors were barred from leaving White Oak and Prisoner's Squares to draw rations from the camp commissary. The guards assumed that task, and when shortened rations were delivered consistently, prisoner complaints fell on deaf ears. Newsboys selling papers were banned from the camp. The directive limiting all prisoners to one written letter of two pages every thirteen days lowered camp morale to the deepest point yet, though a few prolific letter writers like Cally Smith and Sam Bryant had the wherewithal to bribe the guards on the sly to deliver their outgoing mail to the Chicago post office.

The delivery of coal for newly introduced coal stoves and the removal of its ashes added to the grime, vermin, and rat droppings already ground into the mud-enriched dirt floors of the barracks. The ongoing shortage of rations and the outlawing of stoves for cooking provided boiled food, which made for a dietary blandness that turned meals into cheerless affairs. The daily ration consisted of beef, light bread, and soup one day, then just beef and bread the next. Fresh beef was delivered each morning, but a dejected, stove-banned E.J. Pursley hated preparing it. The beef he received was always neck, flanks, bones, and shanks, the poorest-quality cuts, for the civilian contractors sold the choice cuts to Chicago butchers.

Ty kept his sanity by daydreaming of Dana Bainbridge and her beauty. One snowy, boring afternoon, Shawn Shannon asked out of the blue what his future plans were and Ty's lack of shyness for once startled him. "I will win Dana Bainbridge's hand and marry her, whether her father approves or not."

"And then what?"

Ty had to acknowledge that his future planning beyond marrying Dana was more than a tad fuzzy. The proverbial question was how could he and Dana fashion a life together? He was clueless as to his status with his grandfather. By law, he was slated to inherit his grandfather's property and assets, but that might be ancient history by now. Though he knew his grandfather loved him in his own rigid, high-principled way, Enoch Mattson's personal philosophy made it doubly difficult for Ty to draw close to him again after abandoning him with no worthy explanation. Was there any forgiveness in Enoch Mattson's heart? There had not been a smidgen for his dead father.

So where did that leave him? Nowhere, most likely.

Shawn Shannon read Ty's puzzled look. Aware of Ty's awkward Kentucky situation, he decided to offer a possible solution to his dilemma, one he'd been biding time with. "If there's nothing for you at home, you might consider traveling to Texas with me. I own part of a parcel of land that can support a herd of cattle. My uncle owned a bank and a mercantile store before the war and made himself some money. I'm Uncle Paige's closest living relative. I was tired of fighting Comanche and chasing down outlaws for pocket change, so Uncle bought the land and we were about to become partners in a cattle ranch when the war broke out. Uncle is a tough old bird and he'll be there when I return."

"What about my limp? I don't know how long I can stay on a horse, any given day. I might not be much use to you as a cowboy."

"Uncle Paige and I share big ideas. Uncle believes there'll be a big demand for beef in Northern cities after the war. He intends to take full advantage of it. But while he'll front the money, the rest is up to me."

Shawn Shannon stopped talking, nodded his head, and then smiled. "Ty, you're a well-educated young man. It will take a few years, but we'll build a sizable spread. I don't like paperwork, money handling, or watching the market. You'd make a good ranch manager, and Uncle has other holdings that will need tending as he ages. If you want to try the cattle business with me, once we're shut of this place, I've a place for you in Texas.

"Who knows," Shawn Shannon said with a chuckle, "maybe that gal of yours would enjoy a new style of life? Texas is a different world from Portland, Ohio. What do you think?"

Ty was too stunned to answer. Before his father's death at Buffington Island, he had often thought of returning to Texas with him, providing he measured up to Owen Mattson's standards. Now Shawn Shannon was offering him a chance to do just that, with the promise of a livelihood that would financially support a wife and children. It was the opportunity and adventure many a man dreamed about but seldom realized.

It was Ty's turn to smile. "I won't know until I ask her, will I?"

"That's great. You can take your father's place."

"What do you mean 'take your father's place'?"

"I intended to make the same offer to Owen. I just never got him to stand still long enough in one place so I could discuss it with him. If I can't have him for a partner, his son will do just fine."

Ty frowned. "Did you say 'partner'? I thought you said 'ranch manager' before."

"I did. That's for starters. If you work out, there'll be a full partnership for you when Uncle Paige passes. I wouldn't have insulted Owen with anything less."

The evening bugle sounded. Before Ty could thank him, Shawn Shannon waved him off and said, "We'll talk in more detail later. One more thing for now, I know you haven't heard from that Portland gal yet. Don't give up on her. That gleam in her eye when we talked about you was a lot more than female curiosity. Awe struck, I'd call it. Like she'd finally met in the flesh the type of man she always wondered about."

Despite the penetrating cold and hunger pangs, Ty slept well after his excitement abated. Shawn Shannon had unexpectedly become his potential savior. His ranching venture offered Ty the solid footing he'd been missing since his father's murder. Moreover, Shawn didn't believe Ty was being naïve in pursuing Dana Bainbridge.

His final waking thought was of his grandfather. Perhaps with his improved stature, he could muster the courage to write to him, knowing that rejection wouldn't devastate him, as he'd feared it might.

The next morning, Cally Smith brought vital news to Shawn Shannon. Cally and Sam Bryant had a knack for circumventing the ban on contact with Union soldiers and extracting information from their officers and guards. Their ability to fulfill the monetary promises associated with their bribery was legendary.

"Lieutenant, we've been hearing a lot of hammering and sawing over in Prisoner's Square beyond DeLand's headquarters. I learned from that Yankee Danby that the blue bellies are building a larger, higher stockade, with a guard walk, and that's just the half of it. They're planning to lump all of us prisoners together there in one new, huge Prisoner's Square."

"Just how big will the new square be?" Shawn Shannon asked.

"Danby saw the drawings. This sucker will run two city blocks from north to south and two blocks from east to west, a space of about forty acres. He says it will hold twelve thousand prisoners."

"Good gosh!" a listening E.J. Pursley exclaimed. "Are they building new barracks for that many?"

"Nope, not all of them," Cally said. "They're cutting our barracks into sections, putting them on rollers and wheeling them to the new square."

"That will be come spring, right?" Ty asked Cally.

"Nope, this month and next. DeLand won't risk having the spring thaw slow him down."

Shawn Shannon said, "They expecting help from us?"

"Danby claims they are, but the other boys in White Oak Square say they're not helping them move us from one bad spot to another. DeLand can hire Chicago contractors, for all they care."

"Well, by damned," E.J. said, "I'll move if they give us back a floor before everyone of us is toted off to the hospital."

Breakfast call and more pressing issues stilled conversation about Colonel DeLand and his new square. Given Campbell was plagued by fever and a hacking cough. Ebb White's stomach refused to hold food. Four members of Barrack Ten had smallpox and two others symptoms. Treatment for them was nil, as the beds of both the White Oak and the Smallpox Hospitals were jammed with patients. Eyewitness reports confirmed that measles, mumps, pneumonia, and sinus infections were ravaging the camp. It was a common occurrence to open the barrack door and spy four Rebels in butternut clothing carrying a wrapped body to the camp graveyard.

Though Ty had been vaccinated, he feared smallpox the most. Hardly an afflicted soul returned from that hospital. Still without a winter coat, he kept his two blankets wrapped around him night and day, and he cleaned his plate at every meal to conserve what remaining strength he possessed. The portions on his plate grew ever smaller, due to the growing shortage of rations, and it became more difficult to keep from shivering constantly.

Back from one of his visits to their neighbors, gadabout Sam Bryant revealed that prisoners in Barracks Four and Five were killing the big gray rats roaming the camp, dressing them out like deer, and boiling them for supper. One Kentuckian had bragged to Sam that boiled rats tasted like tender chicken. Lieutenant Shawn Shannon, the highest-ranking officer in Barrack Ten and an ex-Texas Ranger—not one whom the 144 Rebels housed there wanted to reckon with—drew the line and backed E.J. Pursley's condemnation of rat meat. The barrack would boil shoe, boot, and belt leather for a meal before eating rodent fare.

Disregarding the weakened and diseased condition of its charges, Yankee brass commenced the transfer to the new Prisoner's Square in mid-January. The Rebels in the old Prisoner's

Square refused to assist their captors, as had the Kentuckians, slowing the arduous process of rolling the White Oak barracks to their new locations to a crawl.

As night fell a week later, Barrack Ten was amongst those still en route. Quick to pounce on the opportunity to make life insufferable for the Kentuckians, Snag ordered the guards to bar Morgan's men from sleeping in their old quarters.

Sergeant Clarence "Snag" Oden took particular pleasure in jabbing the air with his bayoneted rifle and announcing, "Grab what you want from inside, but be quick about it. We'll see how many of you rock-hard raiders freeze to death and leave your rations for others. They'll love you for dying. Make do, me buckoes, make do."

The blustering, Chicago-born, authority-protected bully was unfamiliar with outdoor survival and underestimated the skills of woods- and plains-born men. In short order, a makeshift tent city composed of mattresses, blankets, and the bottom planks from barrack bunks mushroomed before his eyes. Unused coal was interspersed with stove wood and ignited in front of the temporary shelters to fight the raw chill of the wind. A supper of cold beef, cold bread, and hot coffee filled as many bellies as possible. Much to Snag's chagrin, the experienced raiders had put themselves in the best position for lasting until morning.

The cold, the thick mud, and the scampering herds of huge rats made for a memorable night. Around two in the morning, Shawn Shannon awakened Ty and handed him a tattered winter coat, which Ty hastily donned. Shannon was dressed in a leather jacket, which Ty hadn't seen before.

"Two of the boys with pneumonia passed away," Shannon explained. "Snag will puff his chest and credit the cold, but they could've lasted till morning if they'd been healthy."

The raiders were glowering at the guards and hustling to start new fires and prepare some kind of breakfast on a greatly reduced supply of coal and wood when civilian contractors with teams of horses swung through the gate, eliciting cheers throughout their ranks.

"About time General Orme showed the sense of a Kentucky raccoon," Given Campbell said. "I need be careful, though, not to flatter the old fart overly much."

As usual, Given Campbell's biting humor drew laughs and brightened the morning, but gloom soon reared its head again. Snag Oden killed the good mood of the prisoners nearest him by bellowing at the top of his lungs, "Dump the stoves out of those barracks, that will ease the pull for the horses!"

An outraged E.J. Pursley, standing between Ty and Shawn Shannon, not more than ten feet behind Snag, shouted in return, "Wait a by-damned minute. There was nothing said about dumping my stove, you big shit."

As Snag's head turned, Shawn Shannon stepped in front of the outraged E.J. "Who said that?" an equally outraged Snag demanded, walking with his usual swagger toward Ty and Shawn Shannon.

"Keep your trap shut, E.J.," Shannon said over his shoulder.

Expecting to encounter a cowering prisoner, Snag stopped six inches from Shawn Shannon's nose, bayoneted rifle resting butt first on the ground. "I aim to stick whoever said that," Oden seethed.

A stony expression tightened the skin at the corners of Shawn Shannon's eyes and mouth. Ty's breath caught. He admired the lieutenant's skill at suppressing his anger, but he worried that one wrong word might give Snag reason to employ his blade, which he had done before and killed a prisoner.

Shawn Shannon's black-as-midnight eyes bored into Snag's and Ty saw him flinch. Ty wondered if the bully realized he'd bitten off a mighty big chunk of trouble.

When Shawn Shannon spoke, he kept his voice so low, only

Ty and possibly E.J. could hear what he said. "You hear me out, Sergeant, or I'll take that rifle away from you before you can blink and slice you open from belly hole to breastbone. For the sake of your life, don't try me."

Doubt slackened Snag Oden's features. His rifle was butted, not held at arms across his chest, where he could fend off a move to snatch it away from him. The bully licked his lips, a sure sign he understood he'd mistakenly confronted an extremely dangerous man. His bluff had been called, perhaps with fatal consequences for him, and he found himself afraid to twitch or yell for help.

"Sergeant, I've no desire to embarrass you publicly by questioning or disobeying your orders," Shawn Shannon stated quietly. "But understand this. You can move the stove from our barrack, but we will carry it to its new home. It will not be confiscated as others have. Do we have an agreement?"

Grateful for a way out of the danger he'd blundered into, Snag nodded and fled, just short of breaking into a run, yelling orders to make it appear he was dealing with an emergency regarding the horse teams. There was not a hint of swagger left in his gait.

E.J. had overheard the conversation. "Pshew, I was certain I'd gotten you into serious trouble with that big devil. I'll watch my tongue from now on, I promise. And thanks for saving my stove."

Shawn Shannon chuckled and said, "Wait till you find out you're carrying one end of that heavy beast by yourself. You may regret thanking me then."

Reflecting on the incident later, Ty thought of how unselfish Shawn Shannon had been in putting himself at risk to save a friend and subordinate from harm. The lieutenant had done so without hesitation. What Ty had come to respect the most about his father and Shawn Shannon was that each possessed a well of courage they drew upon when they found themselves and those close to them in dire straits. The depth of that well, Ty reasoned, was the true measure of one's manhood.

He prayed that he'd have the courage of his father and Shawn Shannon when someone he'd befriended or loved needed him desperately. He realized that was a mighty tall order to fill; and to be on the safe side, he prayed twice again.

CHAPTER 26

The last week of March began on a high note for Ty and his mess that broke the monotony for a few hours of the same faces, the same daily inspections, the same detail duties, the same washing and wrapping of their disease-felled comrades for burial, and the same tired jokes.

Early that particular Monday afternoon, Sam Bryant returned from mail call, bearing an envelope and express package addressed to Ty. Even the sight of Boone Jordan's return address, instead of Dana Bainbridge's, hardly diminished his excitement. News and goodies of any kind from beyond the stockade were as cherished as gold coin; and having nothing better to do, Sam Bryant, Ebb White, and Given Campbell gathered about Ty to share his good fortune. An under-the-weather Shawn Shannon watched from his bunk.

Ty laid the package on his bunk and ripped open the envelope. Maybe there was a letter from Dana inside?

He hid his disappointment from his messmates when he discovered the envelope contained just a letter from Mr. Jordan, written again for him by his female neighbor:

20 March 1864:

Dear Ty:

I hope this letter finds you well. I learned from Jayson Crowder's father that money and clothing could be sent to Confederates held in Union prison camps. You will find twenty dollars of Federal greenbacks in this envelope. Lew Crowder told me his son wrote that many of you boys lack winter coats. Therefore, I am forwarding you a wool coat by express delivery. I hope it reaches you. No mail addressed to you received here as of this date. We check the post office every week. My health is much improved.

Your friend,
B. Jordan

Ty wasn't concerned that Boone Jordan's greenbacks weren't in the envelope. The Union censor had written the dollar sign followed by the number twenty and his initials on the front of the envelope. The money had been deposited in the prisoner's bank maintained by the camp commissary officer in Ty's name. At his discretion, he could spend the money on credit at the commissary or obtain sutler checks for an equal amount.

He put the envelope in his pocket to retain written proof of his bank funds, unwrapped the express package, and held up his new coat. The coat was made of black wool and sported brass buttons, deep front pockets, and the wide lapels and hood of a military greatcoat.

"Hell's bells, Corporal," Given Campbell said, "there's boys would pay dearly to wear a coat like that to the sinks if they weren't afraid the guards might shoot them. Good thing is, with us stuck in Chicago, you got plenty of winter left to enjoy it. See how she fits."

A grinning Sam Bryant held the coat for Ty and said in a servile voice, "Your garment, sir!"

Ty slid his arms into the coat's sleeves and Sam slipped it over his shoulders and drew the hood over his head. The coat fit perfectly.

"Looks like someone surely knew your size," Given Campbell said. "If there's a finer winter-courting coat anywhere else, I ain't laid eye on it. I know a sprightly gal that would love to snuggle against a wool coat like that. She'd be the same way with you, Corporal, if you weren't so filly shy."

Ty laughed along with everyone else. He owed Boone Jordan a huge thanks for his gifts. The greenbacks were a virtual fortune for him to relinquish. As a livery owner in a small city, cash was a scarce commodity for him in peacetime, more so in wartime. Both Union and Confederate forces had pressed his horse stock on occasion without offering to pay a thin dime. The stalling and feeding of town horses, when he didn't have horses he had bred and broken to sell, barely kept a roof over Boone Jordan and corn liquor in his jug.

Ty didn't want the fun of celebrating his new coat to end. He was sure Mr. Boone wouldn't think what he had in mind was a waste of his money. "Private E.J. Pursley," he boomed, "front and center! That's an order."

E.J. marched from the kitchen with a frown on his face, brandishing a large knife. "Which one of you jackanapes wants to interfere with my cooking?"

"You cook the same lousy rations every blessed day. We can't be interrupting much," Cally Smith deadpanned. "Ty gave the order, you old buzzard."

Learning that garnered a toothless grin from E.J. "Yes, Corporal?"

"Can you secure a pass to the commissary?"

E.J.'s eyes twinkled. "What's your game, Corporal?"

Prudent Ty was determined not to spend more of Boone Jordan's gift than necessary. "I received twenty greenback dollars in today's mail and this coat. I want to celebrate being warm for the first time in weeks with a meal befitting a prince, something better than just beef and bread, thin soup and lousy coffee. Can you do it?"

The twinkle in E.J.'s eyes became shooting sparks. Nothing excited a chef like a culinary challenge. "The lieutenants aren't as strict as they were back in the middle of the winter. Cally can buy a pass to the commissary for him and me with a small bribe. Do you have cash money?"

"No, credit at the commissary. Will they let you buy under my name?"

"They will if Cally has an envelope with your name and the amount written on it. The commissary sergeant has permitted that kind of purchase in the past. He's a gem for a Yankee. Money talks right smart to him and you get what you pay for."

Ty said, "Just remember, I want something special and we'll fire up the stove for you. I want a meal that hasn't been cooked to death on top of the boiler."

"Have no fear, Corporal, I know what you're after," E.J. said, handing his knife to Billy Burke. "Come along, Cally. Put your best conniving smile on your ugly puss. It's time for a little real grub."

Given the monotony of being confined to the barrack by days of rain and eight-inch-deep mud that made fatigue work impossible, E.J. and Cally were as full of joy as schoolboys racing for the door.

"If those two tadpoles don't trample each other or sink out of sight in the mud," Given Campbell said, "E.J. might fill a plate right smart for a change."

Billy Burke said, "What about Snag and Mouse, Corporal? Won't they make us put out the stove? They've done that in the other barracks."

"Naw, they don't come on duty until the midnight watch, and Sergeant Winters has the biggest sweet tooth in the whole Union Army."

With nothing to do but wait, barracks life returned to normal. Cards, checkers, and chess resumed. Books with their covers worn away occupied a few heady souls. Quiet conversations centered on life after the war ended and they were freed, who had escaped Camp Douglas and their fate, where General Morgan was campaigning, the progress of the war outside the stockade, the wild ride across three states with General Morgan, the fighting, drinking, and looting escapades that accompanied it, the best weapons for killing men and four-legged animals, how the pretty girls of the North compared to those of the South, memories of family and siblings, and a keen subject discussed in the quietest of tones: the illnesses of their comrades.

Amongst the disease-stricken Kentuckians scattered throughout Barrack Ten, at least one man per bunk was unable to eat solid food, or was so overwrought with pain and misery he was unaware of the excitement spawned by Ty's new coat. In a usual day and night, two or more of their lot would perish. Ty had taken his turn with the burial detail and was learning firsthand that the aftermath of war for the wounded and the diseased was crueler than the battlefield.

Ty was sincerely concerned about Shawn Shannon. The lieutenant had remained in his bed during roll call that morning. He had mentioned a fierce headache and hadn't communicated with anyone since.

Ty approached the lieutenant's bunk and found Shannon lying absolutely still, gaze riveted on the underside of the bunk above him. "How you feeling?"

Only Shawn Shannon's eyes moved. "Bad pain in my lower back now and my head is about to split open."

Ty's heart froze for a beat. Headaches and back pain were symptoms of smallpox. Another symptom was a sore throat and Shawn Shannon's voice was very hoarse.

"Have you been vaccinated, Lieutenant?"

It was an effort, but he managed to say, "At Union gunpoint

on Valentine's Day, like the rest of you. But I'm not certain it took. The dose tore my stomach up and I squeezed as much of it out of my arm as I could."

Ty gulped. He had done the exact same thing in hopes of calming his own innards. Yet he had no smallpox symptoms, to date. He leaned over Shawn Shannon. "Show me your arms."

"No need to, Ty. I don't have any bumps anywhere that I can find. How about on my face?"

Leaning forward until his nose practically touched the lieutenant's chin, Ty studied his forehead, cheeks, and the skin of his neck. "No, not a speck of black. Nothing."

"That's good. No sense getting up a fret over nothing. I've been sick this way before. I remember hurting damn near everywhere for three weeks. The Rangers used to call it 'Comanche Revenge,' when your bowels let loose and joined in."

Ty straightened, praying silently with his fingers crossed that Shawn Shannon had correctly diagnosed his condition. Beyond Ty's open admiration for him, the lieutenant had become a substitute father, whom Ty relied upon to tell him what to watch out for and how to conduct himself. And while it hinted of selfishness on Ty's part, he was depending on Shawn Shannon's offer of employment after the fighting ceased, an opportunity to make a fresh start in Texas. He couldn't foresee a long ride on his own to find Uncle Paige Shannon. For all he knew, Uncle Paige wasn't aware Ty existed.

A ruckus at the door indicated Cally and E.J. had returned with the supper fixings. Shawn Shannon cleared his throat the best he could and said, "Go have your fun. The boys need it something awful."

Ty joined the mass of prisoners blocking the door. A frustrated E.J. Pursley, both hands holding large hemp bags, yelled, "Out of my way or I'll feed the Yankees instead of you louts!"

At the kitchen door, he turned and said to those trailing after him, "Cally, Ebb, and Sam will help me with the cooking. Ty, you stand clear. This is your surprise supper. You paid for it."

Waiting became doubly difficult when expectations grew in concert with the rich odors soon wafting from behind a kitchen door no one dared open, for fear he might be greeted with a skillet to the skull. Someone opined aloud he smelled roasts of beef cooking, not bones, shanks, and flanks. "And what's that baking? It surely isn't plain bread. Too sweet for that."

Wild guessing as to what exact dishes E.J. planned to serve helped while away the time. The seven o'clock bugle echoed within the stockade and, as expected, Sergeant Fletch Winters filled the doorway. A hush silenced the barrack. Had Ty's assessment of the sergeant's sweet tooth been accurate?

A vast sigh of relief shot through the room when the squat Sergeant Winters lifted his snout, sniffed like a quartering hound, grinned, and dashed for the kitchen door.

"Seems we'll have a guest for supper," an astute Kentucky private observed.

There was no need for a call to dinner. An audience of seated prisoners, with forks poised and appetites primed, greeted Sam Bryant and Ebb White and their steaming platters of roast beef and onion-garnished potatoes. Next came warm baking pans, which brought tears to more than one eye. After months of going without, the Kentuckians could finally partake of honeyed corn bread, a dish they'd been fed from the cradle and craved like no other. Crocks of fresh butter, jars of pickles, a round of cheese, and pots of black coffee, blistering hot on the tongue and sweetened with sugar, completed the main course.

E.J. Pursley loved building suspense at the dinner table and withheld dessert until all the plates and cups were clean to bare metal and his diners were leaning back and grunting their satisfaction. He nudged the kitchen door open with a baking pan held high in the air, hiding its content as long as possible. "Was you New Orleans gals, I'd expect a kiss from every cussed one of you."

He set the pan of oven-browned rolls of dough, with an orange filling, in the center of the table with a flourish. "Peach roll, boys. May be hard for you to believe, but besides the gals, the mayor of New Orleans kissed me on the forehead before he took a single bite. Dig in, boys."

No further encouragement was needed. Because the peach roll disappeared so quickly, Ty thought somebody would surely do without, but E.J. delivered another pan and started it around at the opposite end of the table. "A true cook sees no one is denied."

It was a grand evening from start to finish, and it wrapped up with a toast to Ty's thoughtfulness and generosity by Given Campbell, which left Ty blushing. The only sour note was the absence of Shawn Shannon, who was much too sick to laugh or eat.

Lieutenant Shawn Shannon's condition worsened during the night. By morning, he had developed a fever; his throat was no better; a headache pounded between his ears. Ty found the dreaded black spots on the lieutenant's cheeks. Aware smallpox had an incubation period, he asked, "How long have you been under the weather, Lieutenant?"

"About ten days," Shawn Shannon croaked. "I held it off until night before last."

Ty's worry about the lieutenant ballooned. "Dr. Craig is due in an hour. I'll bring him to you."

Gray-haired, with handsome features, kindly blue eyes, an erect carriage, despite his profession, and personally stone-cold sober, without a trace of alcohol on his breath—a rarity with wartime physicians—Dr. Amos Craig arrived on schedule. After he had treated Kentuckians for various ailments he had treated before, he came to Shawn Shannon's bunk at Ty's request. The Confederate physician's examination required less than a minute.

"He has smallpox," Dr. Craig said. "I'll send an ambulance for him. Several patients died the past three days and we have open cots at the hospital."

Without warning, Shawn Shannon heaved up in protest, for he loathed the Smallpox Hospital as much as Ty did. His strength failed him and he toppled back into his bunk. Dr. Craig closed his bag, turned to Ty, and said, "It's his best chance of surviving. We have medicines that help you fight the disease. They may well work with him."

Though he shared a sincere friendship with the remaining Morgan men and was battle scarred, it surprised Ty that the prospect of barrack life without Shawn Shannon petrified him. Not until that moment had he realized just how much he leaned on the former Texas Ranger for inspiration and counted on his ability to read men and their intentions and keep their prison existence on an even keel. He'd watched Shannon's extraordinary calm prevail in tense situations and restore order again and again—a trait vital to survival in an overcrowded stockade housing eleven thousand frustrated Confederate prisoners of war.

"Can I visit him?" Ty pressured the doctor.

Dr. Craig frowned. "Possibly, but be advised, we don't encourage visits. We isolate patients to isolate the disease. The exceptions we normally make are for the nurses."

Ty was assisting E.J. in the kitchen when the ambulance came and Shawn Shannon was away before word reached him. He spent the balance of the day in a grumpy mood, which had his fellow prisoners avoiding him. He sought his bunk right after supper and endured a restless night. What if he never saw Shawn Shannon again? Had he been yanked from Ty's life as swiftly as Jack Stedman's bullet had taken his father from him?

He vowed he would ignore the horror stories he'd heard about the Smallpox Hospital and somehow obtain a visitor's pass. If Shawn Shannon was meant to die, Ty refused to countenance letting him die with his final wishes unheard. He owed the former Ranger more than he could repay in a dozen decades.

Ty believed a man was privileged to meet and know but a few people who profoundly impacted his life, and he needed to cherish, thank, and remember each one of them. The Lord had gifted him with three such men: his father, his grandfather, and Shawn Shannon. And he would do anything to help Shawn Shannon stay alive, including praying with all his heart for his recovery.

When he dropped from his bunk the following morning, Ty's legs felt weak for a few steps. He was on the morning detail with Given Campbell. Their assignment before roll call was to fetch a barrel of water for the sinks. The shinbone-deep mud of the prison yard added to their burden. Before they reached the sinks with the heavy barrel, Ty's strength evaporated. A case of the blind staggers beset him and he came within a whisker of passing out on his feet.

The weakness of limbs persisted. During roll call each morning, Ty requested and received permission to leave the line. He rested in his bunk until breakfast. Once at the table, he discovered he had no appetite, so he limped back to his bunk and tried to catch some sleep.

On day four, his forehead became damp with a feverish sweat and chills continued to wrack his body after he donned his winter coat. He remained prone the entire day, unable to consume any kind of nourishment. By the next morning, he felt a tad better and secured a basin, intending to wash his face and hands at the outside water hydrant.

Ebb White stopped him at the door. "Let's have a gander at your face, Corporal."

Rough fingers pulled and probed at the skin of Ty's cheeks.

"You can barely see the spots, but you're coming down with the pox. You don't dare wash. Get back to your bunk and stay off your feet till Dr. Craig makes his morning rounds."

Ty couldn't determine whether he should be afraid or excited. If Dr. Craig confirmed he had contracted the disease, the problem of visiting Shawn Shannon was resolved. On the other hand, many people died of the pox, and it was not a pretty death, if there was such a thing.

The doctor confirmed Ebb White's diagnosis and squashed Ty's misgivings. "You have a light case of smallpox. You should recover. I'll call for an ambulance."

Ty almost smiled. He was undoubtedly the first prisoner in the history of Camp Douglas delighted that he was bound for the Smallpox Hospital as a patient.

Leaving his new coat in Given Campbell's custody, Ty donned the tattered garment Shawn Shannon had provided him earlier and waited at the door for the smallpox ambulance. He spied the vehicle at a distance, for it was painted a brilliant red to distinguish it from regular prison vehicles and warn the healthy to stand clear, a waste of paint given the prevalence of the affliction throughout the barracks.

Seven others joined him for the trip to the hospital. They were counted at the guard post, passed into Garrison Square, where a Yankee doctor reexamined them, and then driven through the south gate out of Camp Douglas to the hospital, standing seventy yards away, near the Douglas Institute and Monument.

The passengers tumbled out of the ambulance under their own power and sought the warmth of the hospital stove to escape the raw cold of the late-April wind blowing off Lake Michigan. To the stockade-imprisoned Ty, the open expanse of the lake's blue waters was breathtaking. It was his first clear, unimpeded view in seven months of how beautiful the outside world was.

Ty was the last prisoner up the porch steps. He went through the door with a hurried stride. There, across the room, beside the stove fire they sought, dressed in the brown smock issued to Rebel nurses and puffing on a corncob pipe, stood Jack Stedman's son.

CHAPTER 27

Ty looked left and right and saw open doors in both directions that led to additional wards. He chose the ward to his left, walked past the stove down the center aisle between patient cots, and kept his gaze focused straight ahead. He gave no indication he'd recognized his father's murderer.

The hospital's atmosphere was meaner than Ty had expected. It was a ghoulish nightmare of humans in wretched physical condition, eerie mutterings, and ghastly smells. Flies covered patient faces and hands awash with swollen pustules. Groans and grunts mixed with the ravings of patients bereft of their senses. A black patient begged the wall next to his bunk not to hang him. A brute of a fellow sobbed uncontrollably. A slim patient with red hair like Ty's was proposing marriage to an invisible sweetheart.

The rancid smell of infected flesh, unwashed bodies, filthy blankets, untended spit boxes, slop buckets waiting to be emptied, and dried urine and feces on patients too sick to visit the slop buckets made Ty's stomach turn. He squelched a powerful urge to flee and take his chances in the barracks—no paradise, either, but heavenly quarters compared to where he was standing.

Ty's strength was sufficient to undertake a search for Shawn Shannon. If Dr. Craig's diagnosis was wrong and he was to perish in that god-awful place, it would be next to a friend.

With a stroke of luck, he found the lieutenant next to the exit door in the last ward at the north end of the hospital. Though the lieutenant's features were haggard and swollen, he managed a wan smile when he spied Ty. "Come closer, you young pup," whispered Shawn Shannon, his voice a forced wheeze. His own vigor fading, Ty seated himself on the wooden rail of Shawn Shannon's cot.

"Are you here to visit?"

"No," Ty answered. "The doctor says I have a light case of the pox."

"That's good to hear," Shawn Shannon said. "No sense both of us dying in this rotten Yankee armpit."

The lieutenant's assertion that he was anticipating death had Ty shedding tears before he could hold them back. Thoroughly embarrassed, he quickly swiped his cheeks dry with his sleeve and hoped Shawn Shannon, whose own eyes were shut momentarily, hadn't noticed. Ty did keep his voice from cracking. "What did the doctor say?"

With monumental effort, Shawn Shannon, voice barely audible, said, "My vaccination didn't take. I have full-blown pox. The kind that sends you to meet your Maker."

Those words shattered Ty's heart. He and the lieutenant had been wrong in washing and squeezing the vaccine dose out of their arms. To feel better immediately, they had endangered themselves—risky behavior in light of Shawn Shannon's usual levelheaded approach to things.

To keep himself together, Ty put his mouth to Shawn Shannon's ear and said, "I won't leave you. I promise."

Ty wasn't good at thinking in other men's shoes and had no way of knowing if his presence meant that much to the grievously ill Shawn Shannon, a strong man capable of dealing with his demise in any circumstance. Maybe he preferred that Ty let him die peacefully without drawing undue attention to his plight.

Shawn Shannon's blanket fell away and his hand clasped Ty's forearm, grip weak but solid with no shaking. His lips moved and Ty lowered his head. "Thank you. That would be the same as having Owen with me. I need to sleep, pup."

The lieutenant dozed off with the speed of a rock striking the ground. Ty sat watching him. He had just received the biggest compliment of his life. If everything else he was to experience journeying to the grave went haywire, he would savor Shawn Shannon's sentiments with each step he took.

Ty pulled his legs beneath him, preparing to stand, and a hand grabbed his sleeve. A woozy Shawn Shannon wanted to say something else. Ty leaned down again. "A few of the Reb nurses are planning to escape soon. . . . Jack Stedman's ugly boy may be one of them. . . . I overheard them. They thought I was delirious. After dark, take the stiletto hidden in my boot. Keep it out of sight, no matter what. Trust no one, ever."

The lieutenant's warning wasn't lost on Ty. If he needed a knife handy, Shawn Shannon was telling him acute danger lurked within the hospital. He couldn't help but wonder if a chance to escape was the reason Jack Stedman's son had become a volunteer nurse. It was common knowledge in the barracks that the absence of a stockade fence at the hospital had helped Confederate nurses escape in the past.

Ty remembered Jack Stedman's son had seen him with his father at the bridge building outside Chester, Ohio, and when he'd ambushed the two of them at Buffington Island. If he didn't recognize Ty straightaway, but heard the Mattson name aloud, or saw Ty's name, regiment, and rank on the hospital roll, he would quickly identify him and realize he hadn't killed both his victims as he'd intended. The question was, would Jack Stedman's son still want to extract a final measure of revenge from the Mattson family? Given his determined tone months ago at the sinks following Ty's meeting with General Morgan, Ty was certain he wouldn't hesitate, given the opportunity.

Movement behind him drew his attention. He looked over his shoulder and a Confederate burial detail was lifting a body from a close-by cot on the same side of the ward as Shawn Shannon's. Exhausted and emotionally spent, he lurched to his feet. "May I lie down there?"

Ty couldn't help but notice the straggly blond hair of the brown-smocked nurse with his back to him. The nurse turned about and Ty had his second up-close look at his archenemy since arriving at Camp Douglas. Bleak gray eyes as cold as wood ashes studied him from brow to heel. A smirk curled the lips of the bear trap jaw. Ty felt in his bones that his would-be assassin had already identified him. Shawn Shannon's stiletto would be his bedmate as soon as the night lanterns were out.

Ty kept a straight face and repeated his question. "May I have that cot?"

The smirk on the bear trap jaw widened. "She's yours," the rasping voice forever etched in Ty's memory said. "I'll tell Lyle, the ward nurse, and the doctor where you are."

The burial crew departed with their burden, followed by Nurse Stedman. The fact he hadn't been asked his name confirmed Ty's suspicions. Jack Stedman's son knew who he was and where he was, making him an inviting, bedridden target, bringing home Shawn Shannon's warning full bore.

He limped to the empty cot on wobbly knees. His little remaining strength was fading rapidly. He lifted the cot's filthy blanket and discovered it was ripe with black scales from the deceased's body and damp sticky spots he couldn't identify. He gagged and would have thrown up if he'd eaten breakfast.

Had Ty not wanted to stay near Shawn Shannon, he would have sought another cot or accommodations in another ward. He removed his tattered winter coat, eased down onto the canvas cot, and pulled the crusty blanket over him. He wrapped the sleeves of the coat around his neck, covering his nose in a vain attempt to distance himself from the gut-wrenching stink, fully appreciating in retrospect the stark cleanliness of Dr. Horatio Gates's Pomeroy hospital.

He looked up and saw the sky, courtesy of two holes in the roof big enough for him to crawl through. One of the two ward stoves was missing a flue pipe, indicating cold nights awaited him until the Chicago weather warmed considerably.

During his walk through the hospital, Ty had spotted a few patients who appeared to have light cases of the pox similar to his. That wasn't true of the patients on either side of them. Both were desperately ill, pestered by swarms of flies, talked incoherently, and stank like week-old fish. Death was near for them. Ty had been in tight, demanding situations while riding with General Morgan and had survived two gunshot wounds. Nothing had prepared him for this ugly scene.

He was thirsty as a caravan camel abandoned in the middle of the desert, but he did not ask for water after hearing Nurse Lyle warn other pox victims that they were killing themselves by drinking it. Dinner was served from a small table in the middle of the ward by Reb nurses and a Yankee steward called Croswell. The slim meal consisted of a slice of baker's bread and weak coffee for those able to sit up and eat from a tray. The nurse assisted the worst cases and provided them a cracker or roasted potato.

Ty struggled into a sitting position and found he had a decent appetite. He wolfed down his food. Afterward, he made himself as comfortable as he could and tried to sleep.

He sensed he was out of sorts. The light-headedness that had beset him earlier returned. He didn't feel sick, but he feared he was going out of his mind when the rain stains on the walls transformed themselves into armed assassins. He closed his eyes and was jolted by a vision of his own funeral—a freshly dug grave surrounded not by family members and friends, but by a slack-faced Confederate burial detail. A different funeral vision intervened and he was in the graveyard of the Elizabethtown Baptist Church, the crowd composed of church elders and parishioners listening raptly to a solemn, pastoral eulogy beneath a bright sunny sky. The name on the gravestone read, *Enoch Wentsell Mattson*. Ty popped his eyes open and the would be assassins were gone, replaced on the wall by the outline of a woman dressed in black, with a black mourning veil hiding her face.

Ty's body quaked. He kept his eyes open, wanting nothing more to do with visions of funerals and mourners. Was what he'd imagined a portent of the future? Would he die at Camp Douglas and be dumped into a mass grave? Had he lost his grandfather? Was Dana Bainbridge the mourning woman? If so, how had she learned of his death?

It was too much to grasp at once. To keep from screaming aloud, he concentrated on an entirely different subject—the stiletto in Shawn Shannon's boot, thrilled he could center his whole attention on something real.

Mind locked, feelings numbed, he stared at the holes in the ceiling, waiting for lights-out. At midnight, a tall beanpole in a Yankee uniform extinguished the wicks of the two oil lanterns hanging from ceiling beams. Ty scanned the ward and noted that Nurse Lyle and the guards were out of the room.

Not trusting his legs, he rolled off the cot and came to rest on his knees. Fortunately, the patients between Ty's bunk and Shawn Shannon's were either asleep or too sick to care what Ty was about.

As weak as a newborn calf, the crawling Ty reached the lieutenant's cot and pulled his boots from beneath it. Ty ran his hands over them and found what felt like a stiff rod inside the right boot. His probing forefinger encountered a hard knob. The stiletto was sheathed in a cloth pouch sewn into the leather. He knew instinctively that locating the stiletto on the outward side of the leg allowed a right-handed person to retrieve it with a quick bend and grab.

With his thumb and two fingers, he slid the long, thin knife from its sheath. Careful not to cut himself, Ty inspected the stiletto. The narrow blade was razor sharp, its tip pointed as a needle, and the guard an inch wider than the blade. It was a lethal weapon, with which Ty had no experience.

At that moment, he was resting on his knees, hunched down, facing the wall behind Shawn Shannon's cot. Without any warning, someone grabbed his shoulder. Certain a guard had discovered him, Ty dropped the stiletto into the lieutenant's boot, thinking he would act delirious and avoid any stronger charge than stealing from a fellow patient, if that.

"That you, pup?" the lieutenant asked in his wheezing whisper, tightening his grip on Ty.

Ty stopped holding his breath before his lungs burst. "Yes, sir," he whispered in return, raising his head above the rail of Shawn Shannon's cot.

The lieutenant tugged on Ty's sleeve, signaling Ty needed to bring his ear closer to the lieutenant's mouth. "The stiletto is a wicked blade. Aim for the bottom of the breastbone and thrust upward hard as you can. Hit the heart and your attacker's a goner. Understand?"

"Yes, sir, bottom of the breastbone, thrust hard."

Shawn Shannon clung to Ty. "I'm poorer every hour. Don't fret over me . . . and don't quit on that Bainbridge daughter. She's got more sand . . . than the two of us together."

"I won't, sir," Ty responded. "I won't."

CHAPTER 28

Even with the stiletto at his hip, Ty's nerves were too frayed for him to rest. On top of that, the ceiling lanterns were relit to accommodate the continual coming and going of the nurses and a burial party between three in the morning and dawn. Ty was too new to the hospital to ignore what was happening around him. Four patients died in that brief span of time. One of the deceased occupied the cot beside Shawn Shannon.

Ecstatic over his good fortune, Ty didn't ask anyone's permission to move. He limped to the empty cot and settled himself on the rough canvas. The blankets he inherited were much cleaner, with minimal scales and stains. The poor fellow hadn't spent much time in the cot before dying.

Shawn Shannon was asleep and Ty didn't wake him. He winced at the severe swelling of the Ranger's face and the rattle in his throat. Ty was relieved that he hadn't yet developed the sore throat or back pain affecting the lieutenant. The bumps breaking out on his cheeks were not thick, and those scattered on his hands and the rest of his body were small in number. He did find he had to spit a great deal into the spit boxes, located a mere two feet from the top of his cot, to clear his throat.

At midmorning, Nurse Lyle, offering no objection to Ty's new location, gave him two teaspoons of a light liquid that had no notable taste. He left the medicine bottle and spoon with Ty. "Same dose, three times a day. It's called Number Two. You appear to have a light case, but you need to rest and let the pox run its course. The doctor makes his rounds in the afternoon."

The morning meal was the same as the evening before. Ty was still hungry afterward. Nurse Lyle informed him that a woman selling milk and buttermilk for ten cents per quart came within a few yards of the hospital at midmorning. At noon, a different vendor had apples and cakes for sale. Nurses purchased and delivered these items at no charge to patients with coin money. Ty had a genuine craving for milk, but his funds were resting in the commissary bank and he had no one to bring money to him. His nerves finally settled and he dozed off, smacking his lips in his sleep as he dreamed about Miss Lydia's cinnamon-dusted custard.

He slept beyond lunch. Dr. Craig awakened him during his rounds and confirmed Nurse Lyle's diagnosis. "You have a light case and should be out of here in a few weeks. Except for bodily functions, stay in bed and rest."

Ty had to ask. He nodded toward Shawn Shannon's cot. "What about the lieutenant? Will he recover?"

Dr. Amos Craig sighed. "His chances are slim to none. The pox has a real hold on him. Disease doesn't fight fair. It ravages as it pleases. Our saving grace is vaccine, when it works. When it doesn't, we have an ongoing epidemic and the healthiest and strongest of men perish with the famished and the weak. That's what makes medicine a damnably hard field to pursue, young man. Despite all our training, there's much we don't know, and a good physician wants every patient to survive. Believe you me, every patient lost takes its toll on a caring heart."

Closing his satchel, Dr. Craig said, "Make sure to take your medicine and comfort your lieutenant the best you can. No man deserves to pass away alone amongst strangers."

Over the next week, Ty hovered and prayed over Shawn Shannon like a hawk circling its prey. He sat on the rail of his cot every hour he was awake. Whether it was good for him or not, Ty had water available for him around the clock with the cooperation of Nurse Lyle. On the fourth day of the week, the lieutenant depleted his failing strength extracting a promise for Nurse Lyle that Ty was to inherit his boots. On the fifth day, the lieutenant could eat only little nibbles of cracker and lost the ability to speak. By the seventh day, Ty was certain he was no longer coherent. Not once had Shawn Shannon whined, complained, or shown his pain.

Ty watched his mentor and best friend waste away for another three days. Toward the end of the lieutenant's suffering, Ty adopted the notion that a soldier with the deep pride of Shawn Shannon, accustomed to playing a vital role in whatever endeavor he undertook, preferred death to life as a disfigured, chronically weakened shell of himself dependent on others for sustenance. That reconciliation of his feelings kept Ty from breaking down completely the morning he clasped Shawn Shannon's fingers and discovered they were cold as ice.

When the burial detail and Nurse Lyle answered his summons, he pleaded with them to let him accompany them to the graveyard. Nurse Lyle denied his request. "It's for your own good. The weather's foul and you're not well. Lad, take my word for it, the pox graveyard isn't a place for sane people. I was plagued by nightmares for weeks after one visit and I have a strong stomach. I'll have the guards tie you down, if necessary."

After the burial detail removed Shawn Shannon's body, a dispirited Ty plopped on his cot and stared at those familiar holes in the roof of the ward. Lord, how he wished he had wings to soar through them to freedom, the miseries of Camp Douglas a forgotten chapter of his part in the war.

It hurt him terribly that he was unable to arrange a proper burial for his best friend, as Shawn Shannon had his father, and he hated that Shawn's demise and quick removal transpired so quickly that there hadn't been time to arrange for a man of the cloth to say a few words over him. Ty's resolve not to cry evaporated and he sobbed with his hands covering his mouth to keep anyone from hearing.

Would he ever again experience a fortnight of more joy than grief?

With only himself to worry about, Ty's prime goal was to secure a release from the ward and return to Barrack Ten, for nursing Shawn Shannon had kept his attention elsewhere and helped him hold the stark reality of his surroundings at bay. With the lieutenant's passing, however, the horrific everyday events and conditions of the ward attacked his senses with a vengeance.

The wailing of groaning, dying men, the pleadings of out-of-their-minds patients for forgiveness of sin and a return to the bosoms of their mothers and the arms of their loved ones, and the endless procession of nurses and burial details with their crude coffins, made sleep nearly impossible. Rotting human bodies, unwashed bedclothes, human waste, and the very air of the ward exuded a raw stench that had Ty longing for the outside world with its clean bathing water and glimpses of sunlight. It intrigued him that the religious paper with the stars and stripes on its masthead delivered to each patient was used mainly for keeping flies off their faces and was seldom read, in some curious way confirming the ungodliness of the pox hospital.

The first step toward his release was a change of medicine. Nurse Lyle started him on Number One, a dark liquid with a bitter taste. "This will dry up your spots and make you hungry.

Your spots should start to scale off in nine days. Then you can return to the barracks."

A delighted Ty ate a second piece of bread and two dried apples at supper, was happy to see mealtime come thereafter, and in forty-eight hours the bumps on his face developed dark spots, a clear indication that the drying phase of the pox was under way. Dr. Craig checked on him and encouraged him to walk about the ward each morning.

The hardest part of the healing process for Ty was to fight the perpetual temptation to scratch his face and hands. Left alone, the scabs peeled off on their own, leaving small light-red places instead of pits. Ty asked Nurse Lyle for a mirror and studied his facial skin. Anybody watching would have caught his smile and figured he was a roguish young ladies' man admiring himself, which was close to the truth. Though not terribly vain, Ty was thrilled the pox hadn't seriously scarred him. Courting Dana Bainbridge with a limp was obstacle enough. To do so with a repelling face was a horse of another color, one he didn't care to mount.

A disturbance in the middle of the night created a minor panic in the southern wards of the hospital. When Nurse Lyle reported for morning duty, he gave the ward a succinct explanation. "Four night nurses are missing. The guards have search parties out in all directions. One or two usually get away."

Reports of frustrated and disgruntled guards the following day, relayed by Nurse Lyle indicated the four Reb nurses were still on the loose and were presumed to be beyond the camp's reach.

Ty wondered if Jack Stedman's son had gone with them. He cornered Nurse Lyle on his next round, described his father's killer, and asked if he was one of the escapees.

"You mean the gray-eyed bastard that lets the rest of the night nurses do the dirtiest of the work? I'd like to know myself. I'll ask, but the guards keep a tight lip regarding escaped prisoners, and nurses caught passing information about them are treated more harshly than the escaping prisoners when they're recaptured. The guards assume that if you're talking about who's already escaped, you're probably planning to make a dash for it yourself. The guards these days are ripsaws pining for dry wood. I hear General Orme's irate over escapes from here and from inside the stockade," Nurse Lyle said.

In the early-morning hours eight days later, Dr. Craig declared five patients, including Ty, fit for removal to the convalescent ward. A smiling Nurse Lyle handed Ty a shallow pan and he went to the hydrant outside the door of the ward and washed his face and hands for the first time since being diagnosed with the pox. It had been so long that watching dirt from his body turn clean water brown was nearly a divine experience.

Ty had helped Nurse Lyle tend patients as he grew stronger. As Ty made ready to depart, the overworked Reb presented Ty with four large apples and a quart of sweet milk. Ty shook Lyle's proffered hand and followed after Dr. Craig and the others, stopping to say good-bye to those who beckoned to him and wanted to thank him for his kindness and his willingness to assist the nurses on their behalf.

Shawn Shannon's boots were a little loose, but not enough to make Ty awkward on his feet. As he exited the ward, he understood why the lieutenant had insisted Ty have his footgear. There was no other means by which Ty could keep the stiletto out of sight during his transfer to the convalescent ward, for strict orders prevented healing patients from taking anything with them but their clothes and food items they could hold in their hands.

Without gawking or swiveling his head, Ty kept an eye peeled for Jack Stedman's son, but he didn't catch a glimpse of him in the wards they passed through. The convalescent ward was near the center of the hospital, leaving southern wards that Ty had no cause to visit. He sighed. If the Stedman offspring had escaped, he might never know the whereabouts of his father's murderer. Not knowing one way or the other meant he had to keep his guard up and sleep with one eye open. He was looking forward to gathering his barracks friends about him again. They offered a protective shield that might warn him of impending danger.

Ty and his fellow convalescents were promptly ushered to the breakfast table in the ward's kitchen. There were two separate tables: one for Ty's group and one for the nurses, cooks, and Yankee guards. Coffee with sugar provided by the cooks and a dab of Ty's sweet milk, which he gladly shared, provoked much slurping and lip smacking. The assembled prisoners were aware that, if the rumors were true that Prisoner's Square was on strict bread-and-water rations, they might not taste such a delicacy again for a long while.

After breakfast, a Confederate doctor new to Ty's bunch appeared and, without any kind of examination, recorded each person's name and ruled they were fit to return to camp. They were then led outside, where iron tubs awaited them in an open, roofless shed. After drawing water from a nearby well, they filled two barrel boilers fueled by a wood fire and obeyed the order to strip to bare skin. A Yankee private hauled their old duds away in a wheelbarrow. Ty was much relieved when they were allowed to keep their shoes and boots.

Once the three bathing tubs in the roofless shed were filled with hot water, the convalescents divvied them out amongst the five of them. Because Ty had shared his milk for their morning coffee, he was given his own tub. He sank into the scalding hot water to his neck, not caring if it burned him. He accepted the rags and bar soap handed him by a Yankee attendant and used both liberally and thoroughly. The thickness of the brown scum that accumulated on top of his bathwater was downright insulting to a Baptist taught from childhood that cleanliness was next to godliness.

He lingered in the tub and, out of the blue, thought how fine and wonderful it would be if he were sharing his bath with Dana Bainbridge and blushed all over. He couldn't shake his imaginary picture of how beautiful she would look nude and became rock-hard aroused. Luckily, the water turned ice cold as he sat there daydreaming and dampened his ardor before he was ordered from the tub, saving him from an acute embarrassment that he might not live down. Being the butt of raucous barracks teasing wore thin quickly. He toweled himself off, certain his nighttime dreams had forever been altered.

Ty and his equally naked companions were herded into the convalescent ward by Yankee guards and given new clothing, consisting of thin shoes without socks for those without usable footgear of their own, unlined blue pants without drawers, a quality gray shirt, and a thin black frock coat with a claw hammer tail. A red cravat tied "a la Brummell" completed their toilet.

Though he didn't have access to a mirror, Ty was certain he looked like a peacock at a gathering of somber-clad Baptists. If childhood friends Rory Howard and Abner Downs saw him now, they'd have clever Joshua Holder draw a sketch of him, have it printed into handbills at the Holder Print Shop, and distribute them the length and breadth of Elizabethtown. Sometimes it paid for certain things to happen to you far from home.

Their final hospital dinner was a bountiful dish of beef, bread, and a bowl of vegetable soup. Hawkeyed Limon Fox joked that such plentiful fare made him feel like he was eating his last meal before his execution, instead of his discharge from a doctor's care.

A Yankee sergeant and two guards were assigned to oversee the return of Ty's group to their respective barracks. They slogged up the drying road to Camp Douglas's south gate. After a cursory search by the gate guards, they were turned in to Prisoner's Square.

Ty was shocked at the changes that had occurred during his

hospitalization. The yard was teeming with milling Confederate prisoners. The barracks had grown in number, like wild mushrooms, and all seventy-one of them were ninety feet long, including a twenty-foot-long add-on kitchen. Elevated on wooden posts five feet off the ground, each barrack held 165 men. Ty learned from Given Campbell later in the day that the Rebel population of the forty-acre Prisoner's Square had surpassed eleven thousand. A gruesome testimony to stricter Yankee discipline was a "Mule" fifteen feet high and twelve feet long that required a ladder, where before it had been just five feet high.

Larger guard patrols roamed amongst the prisoners. Additional Yankees watched the yard from the guard walk of the stockade. Gas-fired reflector lamps hung from the stockade walls at precise intervals for nighttime illumination of the yard. The dreaded Deadline was still in place, but it appeared the wooden stakes circling the barracks had been moved closer to them. Taking one step beyond the Deadline, day or night, was an open invitation to a Yankee bullet.

To Ty, the brightly painted stores of the sutlers and the new photographic studio squatting on the fringes of that dreary, overrun, desolate panorama seemed as out of place as a jeweled necklace on a rattlesnake. They were striking reminders that even within walled prisons, money separated men into different camps.

Ty's homecoming began on a sour note. A step inside the door of Barrack Ten, he was accosted by a sneering Snag Oden and his bayoneted rifle. "So, that dead bastard Shannon's favorite lad has come home to roost, has he? It will be different now, you young turd. There's no one here to protect the bunch of you from proper Yankee discipline. I'm praying day and night you'll step out of line. When you do, I'll make you pay dearly, bucko."

With that warning, Snag shoved past Ty for the door. Ty gave way, not wanting to inflame the sergeant's temper unnecessarily.

The next person he encountered in the nearly empty barrack was a smiling Private E.J. Pursley. "Welcome back, Corporal," the goateed chef said. "Come to the kitchen with me. I have news that will interest you."

The empty kitchen was stone cold, the stove fire a pile of ashes. E.J. dipped a gourd into a pail of cold water and presented it to Ty. "Everybody that survives the pox is dying for a cold drink. I don't suppose you're any different."

Ty's answer was to drain the gourd dry in one long series of swallows. "Oh, my, but that tastes good. Best water I've had since the ambulance hauled me off."

E.J. refilled the gourd for Ty. They seated themselves at a small table in the corner of the kitchen, the chef's personal spot. Being the chief cook came with a few privileges—you sat there only at E.J.'s invitation.

"Much has happened in your absence," E.J. began. "Snag was delighted to hear of Lieutenant Shannon's death. He damn near exploded when Sam Bryant and Cally Smith escaped."

A surprised Ty said, "How'd they manage that? I've never seen tighter security."

"Those two boys are mighty clever when they've a mind to be. They volunteered to help unload freight wagons delivering supplies to the camp commissary. With a chance at help from two healthy prisoners in the midst of all the sickness, the Yankees accepted. Sam Bryant said Cally has an uncle and a first cousin who lives in Chicago and one of them is a freighter. Well, it was raining hard one evening and the unloading went later than usual, way past dark. The soaked Yankee guards, trusting the gate guards to thoroughly search the outgoing wagons, went for their supper. The way the Yankees figure, the freighters nailed our two bunkmates in either empty pickle or flour barrels and drove them out the gate, slick as salt passing through a goose. Nobody has seen them since."

E.J.'s devilish smile showed his toothless gums. "Couple of

the talkative Yankee guards told us what happened and said you could hear General Orme's tirade clean to downtown Chicago when the guards told him what happened. He'd had a belly of escapes and put the entire camp on bread-and-water rations for three weeks. That didn't keep our boys from having their fun. Remember the story of the Trojans and their wooden horse?"

At Ty's nod, E.J. said, "If any Yankee hadn't heard that story, Billy Burke made sure they did through the rumor mill. It didn't take but a short while for the news of the barrel escape to spread amongst the Yankees and the barracks. Now, every time the Yankee patrols are out and about, our boys chant, 'Trojan horse, Trojan horse' behind their backs. The guards look like dogs biting at their own tails until they quit trying to catch the prisoners heckling them. The problem is, they're mad enough to bite an anchor chain in half and forgive nothing. Spitting on the barracks floor might earn you a ride on the 'Mule.' "

Unaware of any escape plans on the part of his messmates, Ty asked, "How long had Cally been planning his escape?"

"For weeks, according to Sam. He gave up trying to bribe the guards and sought outside help."

"Did Lieutenant Shannon know about it?"

E.J. spat into the stove's ash bucket. "He certainly did. Cally and Sam begged him to break out with them, but he turned them down."

Intrigued that Shawn Shannon had refused to consider a plausible escape plan that included the local Confederate assistance he'd stressed was necessary, Ty inquired, "Did he say why?"

A twinge of embarrassment tightened E.J.'s mouth. "Yep, he told them he couldn't rightly leave me and Billy behind, not with Snag and Mouse prancing about hungry for an opportunity to bayonet us or have us thrown in the dungeon."

"That fits Shawn Shannon like a glove," Ty said. "He thought of his men first. He was a fine officer and a better friend."

"Yes, he was," agreed E.J. "But he's gone and the guards were afraid of him. They aren't afraid of us, which means we better keep a sharp eye out for each other. I don't want to give the cussed Yankees any excuse to bury any more of us. A rabid dog deserves better than that."

E.J. stood and hitched his rope-belted trousers a notch higher beneath his apron. With hands on his hips, he said, "It won't be the same without Cally and Sam. Those boys figured out how to enjoy themselves, instead of moping about, cursing the war, the Yankees, Jeff Davis, and President Lincoln for not exchanging us. My grandmother, the Lord God rest her soul, said that you make your own bed in this old world. You can laugh more than you cry, if you've a mind to. Seemed to her, strong folks with an honest purpose in life never had much trouble smiling and laughing at the drop of a hat. It might be helpful for us to remember what she preached."

Turning to the stove, E.J. said, "Now, let's light a fire and start the supper bread baking."

Given E.J.'s New Orleans house of joy and Texas frontier background, Ty had never imagined E.J. Pursley having a grandmother who saw through the foibles and difficulties of everyday life and could cleverly state in a few words what the great philosophers he had read in his grandfather's library spent countless words trying to do: spell out what it took for a person to be happy.

The bloated population of Prisoner's Square made it impossible for the Yankee command to assign more than six to eight prisoners from each barrack to daily work details. A free man for a few days, Ty converted a portion of his money in the commissary fund to sutler checks, purchased paper, pencil, and stamps, and penned a letter to Dana Bainbridge the very next morning.

He didn't waste words on flowery sentiments. He wrote that he prayed she was in good health, thought of her constantly, dreamed about her beauty and her laugh, and looked forward to the day when he could finally hold her in his arms. Whether she answered his letters or not, he vowed, in closing, that he would write to her as often as possible and love her forever.

He made no mention of his unsettled future. His plan to travel to Texas with Shawn Shannon had gone up in smoke with the lieutenant's passing. He had to hope in the meantime that a new prospect would emerge that would give him his chance at financial success and an opportunity to win Dana's hand. The blunt truth was he had to trust to himself and the good Lord as his father and Shawn Shannon had.

In a second letter, this one to Boone Jordan, he thanked the livery owner a second time for the greatcoat and the twenty dollars of greenbacks. He related the smallpox death of his father's best friend and his own bout with the disease. He assured Mr. Jordan he had recovered completely and awaited his eventual release from captivity. Ty beseeched him once more to continue watching for mail forwarded to him from Ohio.

Mailing letters had become an arduous chore during Ty's stretch in the hospital. By newly implemented camp regulations, the sender personally stood in long lines at the post office until his turn came and a Yankee censor read his letter, crossed out any unacceptable passages, and either rejected it or dropped it in the outgoing mail. The decision of the censors was final. Appeals were forbidden.

Ty fought to keep his spirits high when he saw his censor was a grizzled Yankee sergeant who most certainly had drunk sour milk for breakfast. He accepted Ty's letters with a shrug and no more interest than a fly for a swatter.

As he read, Ty was certain the sergeant's hazel eyes grew warm and longing. The sergeant snuffed out his smoldering cigar in a bucket of sand beside his desk, studied the Ohio address on Ty's envelope, and said, "You truly love this Northern gal, don't you, Reb?"

Not entirely certain of the sergeant's sincerity, Ty gambled that he wasn't being kidded. "Yes, sir, I intend to marry her when I'm free."

The sergeant grinned. "Felt that way about my Martha in the beginning. Still feel that way after twenty years in the same buggy together. Be grand to see her again."

Without bothering to read Ty's letter to Boone Jordan, the Yankee sergeant sealed both envelopes, checked that the postage was correct, dropped them in his basket of approved mail, extended his hand, and said, "Best of luck pursuing her, lad."

Ty shook the proffered hand. "Thank you, sir."

"Stand in my line the next time," the sergeant advised. "I'll put your mail straight through."

Boots scarcely touching the ground, a delighted Ty ambled back to his barrack. Knowing his mail would not be subjected to harsh censoring relieved his mind of any fear that the rumor about the Yankees keeping sweetheart letters for themselves to enjoy was a threat to his attempts to reach Dana.

His world appeared a tad brighter until he blundered into a deadly duel just inside Barrack Ten's front door. He slid sideways and flattened himself against the wall, separating himself from two knife-wielding Rebels. A lean string bean of a soldier, with full beard, narrow shoulders, and pigeon-toed feet, kept circling to keep his opponent—smallish, mild-mannered, affable Billy Burke—in front of him.

Ty realized his messmate was in serious trouble. The tall jasper's arms were half again as long as Billy's and his strategy was readily apparent. Slashing back and forth with his razor-sharp weapon, the shuffling string bean was forcing Billy to retreat into the corner of the room, where the attacker would have the advantage and slash Billy to ribbons.

The many Rebel onlookers watched with an amused indifference. Ty looked for Ebb White and Given Campbell. They weren't in the room and no one else was inclined to intervene and prevent the spilling of his friend's blood. That left it up to

Ty and he didn't hesitate, trusting to survival instincts honed during the hot ride across Indiana and Ohio when he was expecting the slam of an enemy bullet into his chest any second.

As the string bean, eyes locked on Billy, passed in front of Ty again, Ty stuck his leg out and tripped him, speeding his fall with a hearty shove. Billy's opponent landed on his side with a rapping thud, banging his head on the floor and losing both his knife and his wind. Ty stepped over him and swept up the long blade.

A voice near the door shouted, "Somebody snitched. The guards are coming."

Without breaking stride Ty confronted Billy, his naturally deep tone stern and ringing with authority. "Give me your knife, Private. Now."

Billy Burke instantly obeyed an order from a superior officer by reversing his knife and presenting it to Ty, handle first. Ty heard the guards demanding that the onlookers move aside and let them through. He calmly walked in the opposite direction, with the crowd parting and closing behind him. The Rebels wanted no part of the knife fight and had cared less if someone was killed, but aiding the guards was leaping beyond the pale.

Once in E.J.'s empty kitchen, Ty closed the door behind him and deposited the knives in a pantry drawer with the chef's other cutting utensils. He then stood facing the door, ready if the tall jasper and any of his friends wanted to seek him out. The guards, frustrated they couldn't locate and punish the participants in a reported knife fight, yelled for the Rebels to line up for a search of their bodies and their bunks. Such a spontaneous search for no reason that morning had let Ty know he needn't inquire about the greatcoat he'd left in Ebb White's safekeeping. Boone Jordan's gift had been warming a Union backside for days whenever the weather was cold.

The shouting and bullying by the guards in the barrack continued. Ty recalled Given Campbell's assessment of the blue bel-

279

lies' current attitude yesterday afternoon: "Ty, I didn't think it could happen, but our situation is worse than ever. You'll notice that there will be absolute silence after lights-out. Those bastards hear one word inside the barrack and they're likely to shoot through the wall. During the day, you can't walk around the yard. Unless you have a letter to mail or a written pass, you must stay in the street in front of your barrack. The guards and round-the-clock patrols delight in handing out severe punishment for the slightest offense, even if you've never heard of the rule you've supposedly broken. To protect ourselves, we say, 'Hisst! Hisst!' when we're talking if a guard comes near us, trying to overhear the conversation.

"Some of us are at wit's end. Tempers explode faster than popcorn, and we've taken to fighting amongst ourselves. You don't have any trouble spotting black eyes, busted lips, and broken teeth. It's a sorry end for men who fought side by side under enemy fire and were willing to die for one another."

"Will we ever turn on the guards?" Ty had asked.

"It's possible. There are less than a thousand of them and eleven thousand of us. Nobody has said anything to me personally, but there are rumors that a mass rush on the stockade walls is being planned. I'm keeping an ear to the ground for our barrack."

Ty was thinking again how his limp would keep him from joining any mass escape attempt, when the door flew open and two revolver-toting guards, both privates and both walking with limps worse than his, marched into the kitchen. They were from the Yankee invalid companies assigned to Camp Douglas security and frequently the meanest of blue-belly guards.

"Hiding in here out of sight, are we?" the clean-shaven invalid snarled, aiming his pistol at Ty.

Ty slowly removed his hospital-gifted coat and donned an apron before saying, "No, I'm a cook. I'm to start baking the bread for supper."

The big-eared invalid nodded and said to his companion, "I've spied him in here with Pursley and that gray coat and red cravat is the kind they give you when you leave the Smallpox Hospital. See those red marks on his cheeks. He's had the pox, all right. You touch him if you want, Horace, but I don't search anybody that's got the pox or had the pox. You do with him what you want. I'm for leaving him be."

"Hell, Mike, I ain't laying a finger on him, either. That's how I believe Jericho came down with the pox."

The main barrack room had quieted enough so that the squeal of front-door hinges raised Horace's brow. "Come on, I don't want the lieutenant harping on us for lollygagging."

Ty exhaled sharply as the two invalid Yankees exited the kitchen. Fear of the pox had forestalled a personal search of his body and clothing. Even though he kept the stiletto safely ensconced in his boot, he was thankful that he wasn't searched. Given Campbell had passed along solid reasons for him to be careful even when dealing with his fellow Rebels. Facing a knife was vastly different than disarming an attacker from behind.

Danger lurked everywhere within the walls of Camp Douglas for the careless, the unprepared, and the unarmed. Wariness was the watchword for those longing to see home again, or surviving until they found a new one.

CHAPTER 29

Another long stretch of absolute boredom, hunger, deadly disease, prolonged morning roll calls, instant inspections, and wire-tight tension—both inside and outside the barracks—stilled laughter and made smiles distant memories. Letter writing, checking for mail, cooking with E.J. Pursley, and reading the same books again and again barely kept Ty from going crazy and pounding the wall with his fists. Not even the introduction of a bathhouse for washing and shaving and gas-heated tubs for clothes washing alleviated the monotony. The high point of Ty's day was his nightly prayers for the well-being of Dana, who was the love of his life, Mr. Jordan, his grandfather, his messmates, and himself.

Barrack Ten's morale hit rock bottom on Friday, September 9, 1864. On that day, the *Chicago Tribune* announced a blue-belly bullet had killed General John Hunt Morgan the previous Sunday in the streets of Greeneville, Tennessee.

Many of Morgan's Raiders thought the announcement was a Yankee prank, refusing to believe that their beloved "Thunderbolt of the Confederacy" was growing cold in the ground like a common trooper. But additional *Tribune* articles related the details of how the general had been shot in the back in the early morning of September 4 as he walked away from Union Cavalry, which had ordered him to halt—evidence difficult to refute and confirmed by the Camp Douglas commandant.

Yankee patrol officers took particular delight in reminding the men of Barrack Ten that their untouchable, uncatchable hero leader had been consigned to future history books—which the North would write—as a fallen, fleeing raider. This spawned an ever deeper hatred of them, and the pinch-eyed, sullen faces that resulted had Ty feeling he was inside a box of matches, where the tiniest spark might ignite a conflagration the guards couldn't handle.

Though it took more time than Ty had anticipated, the guards struck the match he feared in late October. A keen night wind was blowing off Lake Michigan and the temperature had dropped below freezing.

Shouted commands and curses rent the frigid air near Barrack Ten, swelling to a volume that awakened Ty and his bunkmates. "What's that all about?" Billy Burke muttered.

"I'll check," Ty whispered.

"Just open the door a crack," Given Campbell said quietly. "Don't alert the guards you're out of your bunk."

Ty padded to the door and opened it far enough to peek with one eye into the yard. The gas-burning reflector lamps mounted on the stockade wall cast white light the length of the street fronting Barracks One through Twenty. Ty groaned. The members of Barrack Eight were seated, buck naked, in the frozen mud of the street, shaking and shivering, arms wrapped about themselves. The punishments of last winter were starting even earlier.

Ty crept back to his bunk and spoke to Given Campbell in a whisper again. "Guards have Barrack Eight sitting naked in the mud. I believe some of the guards are drunk. I'll keep watch and wake the barrack if they head this way."

By Ty's reckoning, Barrack Eight was left to suffer in the street for a full hour. As they returned to their bunks, Barrack Nine was jousted from theirs. Despite the midnight hour and their inebriation, the guards gave no sign they were tiring or losing interest in inflicting their choice of punishment for the evening.

With his back to the door of Barrack Ten, a short Yankee watched the disgruntled Rebels from Barrack Nine file out. He turned to speak to the guard next to him and Ty made out Mouse's narrow face in the lamplight flooding the street. The Mouse shouted loud enough for Ty to hear him say, "Let's roust Barrack Ten. I've been dying for a chance to whap on E.J. Pursley's skinny ass ever since he shooed me from his kitchen last summer with a butcher knife."

That threat kindled fresh hatred in Ty for the Yankees; his animosity burned his insides like scalding water. He'd had enough and seen enough of their cruelty to last three lifetimes. There would be no abusing of E.J. Pursley, not tonight or any other night. He tiptoed to the kitchen in the dark and, from memory, grasped the heavy-bladed metal coal shovel E.J. kept behind the stove.

Given the ongoing ruckus outside the barrack, Ty knew eyes were following him in the dark as he crossed from the kitchen to the front door. What he planned called for him to act alone, and he said in a low voice, "Everybody stay in their bunks. I'll yell if I need you."

He didn't know who might or might not respond when he called out, beyond Given Campbell, Ebb White, and Billy Burke. He hoped he wouldn't need his friends. He was praying he could employ the tactical strategy of stiff, unexpected resistance that Given Campbell claimed Texas Ranger Shawn Shannon had executed to quell a drunken riot in a Texas town.

Ty, of course, didn't have Ranger Shannon's revolver at his disposal, and he feared that flashing his stiletto would so enflame the besotted Yankees, they would shoot him. So it was the metal shovel that could inflict considerable bodily harm, or nothing. One thing was in his favor. He had seen from the door earlier that neither Mouse nor his fellow blue bellies were armed with bayoneted rifles, which meant he could initially hold them at bay with the shovel.

Mouse and two blue bellies were a few paces away when Ty stepped through the front door and came to rest on the stone stoop of Barrack Ten, the shovel hanging limply at his side. His sudden appearance startled the three guards.

They halted and stared at him with bleary eyes. Their revolvers were holstered. Mouse and the guard on his left held wooden paddles with holes drilled opposite the handles. The third guard bore a coiled whip.

Ty took a deep breath and silently thanked his Maker. These three were so accustomed to Rebel prisoners obeying their orders and accepting any punishment they doled out, they had grown careless. One of them should have had a pistol at the ready in case they encountered a defiant prisoner. Still, to them, Ty was but a single man, albeit a big, broad-shouldered one for his age.

Mouse tilted his head, sniffled, peered over his snout of a nose, and said, "I recognize you. You're E.J. Pursley's bread baker. We've come for that little runt. Maybe when he can't feel his butt no more, he'll apologize for chasing after me with that knife while the bunch of you laughed behind my back. Out of the way, secesh. We're coming in."

Ty stood silently without moving, waiting until he had their complete attention. "You'll have to kill me first." The guard on Mouse's left frowned as Ty swung the shovel across his chest and spread his feet. "I'll say it again. You'll have to kill me first."

Uncertainty beset the Yankees. They weren't too drunk not to realize they had nothing in their hands except two paddles and a whip; Ty could wade into them with the shovel before they could draw their pistols, not a desirable outcome, given the wicked curve of the shovel's blade.

The standoff continued for a lengthy half minute, with Ty on his toes awaiting their first move. The guard on Mouse's right broke the silence by saying in a whiskey-blurred, sputtering voice, "Hell's bells, boys, we've had enough fun for one night!"

Mouse's cheek twitched, a visible hint he might doubt the wisdom of escalating the confrontation. His grip tightened on the handle of his paddle; yet he gave no thought to drawing his pistol. He knew a tightly knit group of Morgan's men inhabited Barrack Ten and he would invite much trouble if he shot the young man whom Lieutenant Shawn Shannon had treated like a son. Lastly, he had too much price as an officer to yell for help in encountering a single Reb with a limp, who was armed with a mere coal shovel.

Mouse nodded slowly, pursed his thin lips, and said, "You win tonight, but you won't catch me without my rifle and bayonet again. You best not forget that."

Ty stayed put until the Mouse and his cohorts called it quits, sent Barrack Nine back to their bunks, marched in a stumbling shamble to the end of the street, and disappeared around the far corner of Barrack One.

When he entered Barrack Ten, he was greeted with back-slapping and congratulations from his bunkmates, as well as from men he knew only by sight.

"Cleverest bluffing of them Yankees I ever saw," Given Campbell said.

A pox-scarred private proclaimed, "Sweet as sugar pie."

Billy Burke chimed in, "I've dreamed of seeing Mouse scurrying for his hole and it's come true at last."

E.J. was one big, gummy grin from ear to ear. "Sorry to bring trouble down on you. But I'm damn glad I share a mess with a man who will stand up for an old codger against an ass that ain't big enough to paddle and do some real harm with it. Last time my maw laid into me, I hurt for most of that winter."

The statement that most pleased Ty—who had never imagined himself any kind of hero—came from Ebb White. "Your father and Shawn Shannon would be proud of you, Corporal, mighty proud."

Ty went to bed fully aware he had acquired a personal enemy in Mouse that would bear watching whenever he was in sight. At the same time, he needed to keep a steady eye peeled for Jack Stedman's son, for tonight he had experienced the depth of hatred that drove the thinking of Frank and Jack Stedman's offspring, and he was convinced more than ever that his father's murderer was somewhere inside the Camp Douglas stockade, waiting for the chance to extract a final measure of revenge.

Returned from morning detail, Given Campbell pulled Ty aside in E.J.'s kitchen. "Rumors of a mass revolt were flying fast and furious in the wood lot. Last night's escapade with paddles and whips went a step too far and even riled men I've never seen show any interest in trying to escape. Mouse and his drunken pals may have provoked what the camp commandant wants the least—eleven thousand Rebels determined to flee, no matter if some of us are killed."

Though Private Campbell was speaking softly, Ty read the excitement in his voice. "What will you do if they revolt? Will you join them?"

Given Campbell fingered his short beard. "Yes, I'm plumb tired of watching men dig through the garbage barrels searching for bones. The war will drag on for months, but we can't win. Our cause was lost at Gettysburg when General Lee squandered our finest men. I can't swallow the dog and swear the Union oath. I'm headed home to Texas, not back to our lines and the Yankee bullet waiting for me. I promised Lieutenant Shannon that I'd personally inform his uncle if he died in the pox hospital. That's a chore needs doing—the sooner, the better."

"What about Ebb, Billy, and E.J.?"

"If any of them want to join me, they're welcome. What will you do, Corporal?"

Ty considered his choices weighed his chances, and said with considerable reluctance, "I hate it here as much as you do. But with my bad leg, I couldn't keep up with you, once you're outside the stockade. I won't slow you down. I'd be excess baggage and useless to you."

"I regret that more than I can say, Corporal. I'm sorry we can't offer you a Trojan horse like Cally's. But then a pickle barrel would be a mighty tight fit for you. I don't want to overstep my authority, sir. Do you mind if I ask our messmates their druthers?"

Ty underwent an awakening with Given Campbell's use of the word "sir" when addressing him. In his military history discussions with Ty, Professor Ackerman had stressed that how an officer reacted in a dangerous situation often impacted his subordinates in unanticipated ways. His successful bluffing of Mouse and the guards had erased any doubts amongst his messmates of his ability to lead, though he was young, and they deemed him fit for command. For the true soldier, the ranking of officers, once established, determined the line of authority and insured that proper protocol was observed. Age was a moot issue.

Over the course of the day, Given Campbell talked with Ebb, Billy, and E.J. individually and reported to Ty that Ebb and Billy were supportive of the Rebel breakout, when and if it occurred. E.J.'s response was that he was a turtle afoot and wasn't inclined to trade his soup ladle for the dungeon.

A fresh rumor the next morning that Yankee howitzers were being placed outside the stockade walls galvanized the prison population. Given Campbell approached Ty before breakfast. "Just came from policing the grounds. I talked with a sergeant from Barrack Seven. He says the officers of the other barracks believe we must act tonight while Colonel Sweet, DeLand's replacement, is away. Captain Shurly is in charge and our officers don't believe he will use the howitzers against us. Tomorrow might be too late."

"Is there a plan in place?"

"Barracks One through Twenty will charge the west wall at midnight, breach it, and open a path for everyone else."

"And if the Yankees are waiting for them outside the stockade?"

"We'll overwhelm them. We may lose a few men, but the rest will finally have their chance to run for it."

Shaking his head, Ty said, "Private, we saw what happens when men charge loaded guns afoot after they lose their weapons and you'll be unarmed. I think there's a better way that will at least get you clear of the camp. I want to talk to you and Private White after roll call."

Roll call went off without a hitch for the first time in Ty's memory, perhaps because the prisoners, with what they had in mind, didn't want to agitate the guards one iota. A calm sea gave no warning that a tempest was brewing.

Given Campbell and Ebb White weren't assigned to morning detail and joined Ty in the Barrack Ten kitchen. The two would-be escapees were somewhat disgruntled when E.J. handed them knives and pointed to the bushel of potatoes Ty had purchased at an exorbitant price to break the endless cycle of boiled pork and light bread, which the chef served twice per day. Dinner had become a long-forgotten meal with the Yankees' constant shortening of rations.

"Gives you cause to be here," E.J. admonished them, "in case a Yankee patrol sticks its nose in the door."

"Keep an eye out, anyway, Private White," Ty ordered, kneading bread dough in a flat pan as he talked. "Do you two remember the conversation we had with Lieutenant Shannon last spring about what to do if the prisoners revolted en masse? Remember what he said then, Private Campbell?"

Given Campbell dropped potato peelings into a pan positioned between his knees and said, "Something about making sure you know which direction the tide is flowing before you light out."

"Well, the tide is flowing up against the west wall tonight, and didn't Lieutenant Shannon say a smart trooper might check what's happening in the opposite direction? Perhaps with the guards all looking and running pell-mell in one direction, he could sneak off in the other."

"By damned if he didn't," Ebb White exclaimed at Given Campbell's vigorous nod.

"Think along with me," Ty said. "Lieutenant Shannon and I studied the walls of Prisoner's Square from every angle. The northeast corner of the square overlooked by the guard tower juts well past the north wall of Garrison Square, and only a handful of blue bellies are ever on duty there. Once over the wall, you slip across Cottage Grove Avenue, where there are no houses, and gain the railroad running to Chicago."

"What then?" Ebb White asked. "Which direction would we take at the railroad?"

"Did Cally Smith tell you the name and address of his uncle who lives in Chicago?"

His interest in Ty's escape plan growing rapidly, Given Campbell laid his peeling knife aside for the moment. "Yes, he did. Francis Wellington Ferguson, Esquire, 999 Fairmont Square."

"Did he mention where Fairmont Square is located?"

"Three blocks north of the Colony Street Hospital. He said Colony Street runs due north from the railroad depot."

Ty shaped his bread dough into long cylinders. "Squire Ferguson being loyal to our cause, it seems to me he might be inclined to help his nephew's friends escape the clutches of the Yankees, a golden opportunity to stick his finger in their eye again."

Given Campbell chuckled. "I'd bet you're right about that. From what Cally said, his uncle hates President Lincoln like rats hate barn cats."

Ty slid his baking pan into the oven and wiped his hands on his apron. "The key question is how to get over or through the wall of the stockade. Lieutenant Shannon pointed out a man-sized door at the northeast corner of Prisoner's Square under the guard tower. He believed it's locked with a crossbar on the out-side, meaning there's no need for a keyed padlock. His idea was to put someone small, like Billy, over the wall and let him open that door."

Given Campbell could hardly contain himself. "Billy is good with a rope. We'll cut up our blankets and make one for him. He'll be over the wall faster than a treeing squirrel."

Ebb White asked, "What if Billy can't get the door open for us? What if it's padlocked?"

"We'll run back to the barrack and Billy can try to make it clear alone," Given Campbell said. "I've won money betting that boy can sneak up on rabbits in broad daylight. There's a goodly chance he can duck the Chicago Police and find Fairmont Square and Squire Ferguson's house."

Flicking peelings from his knife into his pan, Ebb White in-quired of Ty, "Lieutenant Shannon was a wily devil. Did he say exactly how he'd go about this?"

Ty started dicing peeled potatoes at the kitchen's sideboard. "Yes, send a man across the open area short of the Deadline to attract the attention of the guards in the tower, while whoever is going to scale the wall sneaks out from behind the far end of the barracks. Once the man with the rope is next to the northeast door, he waits for the commotion erupting on the other side of the square to catch the full attention of the guards above him.

The tower guards seldom lean out and check below them. With any luck, they'll be called away from their post to help with the emergency on the west side of the yard and that's when our roper scales the wall. Then whoever is breaking out with him rushes to the door. Once the door's open, they slip through, drop the bar, and skedaddle Lieutenant Shannon thought the whole thing shouldn't take more than two to three minutes, maybe less "

"Who's going to walk out along the Deadline to start the wheel rolling?" a heretofore silent E.J. inquired.

"That would be me," Ty answered. "I was to exaggerate my limp and stagger around a little, always inching toward the Deadline. We felt that would make the guards curious enough to study me for a bit."

"You sure you still want to be the decoy?" Given Campbell asked.

Ty locked Private Campbell squarely in the eye. "Yes, if I can't escape myself, I won't fail the men in my charge."

Given Campbell came to his feet and extended his hand. "Corporal, no matter what happens tonight, it was a pleasure meeting you, knowing you, and riding with you. It will be a while before I meet a better young man, if I do."

Surprised by the unexpected compliment, Ty swallowed hard and shook hands with Given Campbell. "The same here, Private."

"Before you boys start fawning something awful over each other," E.J. interjected, "there's a few things I'd like somebody to tell me. Who's heading this all-fired breakout this evening?"

"From what I'm hearing, Sergeant Blair Taylor, of the Eleventh Alabama Infantry," Given Campbell said. "The signal will be the 'all's well' calls of the guards after their midnight exchange. Taylor's men have come by some axes to chop through the west wall. We hear a chorus of rebel yells, it means the wall has been breached and it's every man for himself."

293

E.J. thumped the table with his butcher knife. "You boys are smart to listen to Corporal Mattson. I've seen a few shifty-eyed rascals amongst our own men lately that makes me suspect they're spying for the Yankees. Hear you me, the blue bellies will be waiting outside the west wall with loaded rifles."

"Our boys are so out of kilter, even if they know the Yankees are waiting on them, I don't think it would stop them. Like Lieutenant Shannon said," Ty reminded his messmates, "when the quiet and the meek are riled, along with the hotheads and the impatient, an explosion of tempers is inevitable."

Ebb White nodded in agreement and said, "What are your orders for tonight, Corporal?"

"Wait until after lights-out to make your blanket rope. If anybody notices what you're doing, say you're making a rope in case you need it. Don't tell them what we're planning. We don't need bystanders watching us once we're outside the barrack. We want them listening for the rebel yell. When we go, we'll slip out the kitchen door. You best tell Billy what's up right away."

Excruciating second by excruciating second, the day passed for Ty and his men. Not even E.J.'s excellent diet-changing meal of fried pork and potato hash and fresh bread elicited much comment.

As Ty helped E.J. clean the kitchen after supper, a thought struck him that hit close to the bone. If Privates Campbell and White escaped, all of his original messmates, except for E.J., were gone from his life. He doubted he would see any of them after the war and that saddened him. Charging point-blank into a hail of enemy fire on horseback and surviving forged a bond amongst cavalrymen that tied them together forever. While Ty had no desire to fight in another war, the pride he shared with his messmates in their feats on the battlefield made him feel a foot taller and fully grown.

In contrast to the painfully slow pace of the day and evening hours, the thirty minutes short of midnight swept by like a

speeding bullet. They bunched at the kitchen door with a shocking quickness that had Ty panting for action.

"Private Burke, don't hurry too much," Ty ordered. "It's important that your loop snags a wall stanchion the first try or two.
Private Campbell, you've been on watch at the front door, what's
happening in the streets?"

"E.J. may be right. No Yankee patrols tonight. Prisoner's
Square is empty of guards on foot."

"Then we best not linger," Ty surmised. "If the Yankees are
lying in wait, there will be a host of blue bellies outside the west
wall and fewer Yankees on the guard walk and in the towers. Private Campbell, no matter what happens, you and Private White
move from behind the far barrack the second you see Private
Burke's in position to scale the wall. Don't look anywhere but at
that northeast door."

Not wanting to pressure Billy Burke unduly, Ty made no
mention of the fact that their fate was in his hands and his roping
ability. He heard the front door of Barrack Ten creaking open,
eased the kitchen door open, and whispered, "Off we go, me
first."

Ty stayed close to the front walls of the barracks lining the
street, out of the path of silent Rebels mobbing in the opposite
direction. His objective was Barrack One, the closest building to
the northeast tower. Privates Campbell, White, and Burke
wended between barrack rows to his right and turned left three
streets over. That maneuver separated them from Ty enough
that it was unlikely the tower guards, hopefully entranced with
his decoy act, would spot their rush to the northeast door. Ty
wasn't above crossing fingers on both hands and praying in
earnest. It would be a tight affair if they succeeded.

The cloud-covered sky was pitch black, the only source of illumination being the gas lamps hanging on the stockade wall,
some of which were not lit, a lucky break for would-be escapees.
Ty peeked around the corner of Barrack One and counted the

shadowy outlines of four widely spaced bodies on the guard walk to the left of the northeast tower, half the normal complement of Yankees. The tower itself appeared to be unmanned.

He sucked air into his lungs, slid around the corner, and moved toward the Deadline, one exaggerated-limping step at a time, staggering sideways on occasion. He hoped he appeared a disabled prisoner who had found a source of liquor and overimbibed.

The guards either showed no concern over Ty's challenging of the Deadline or they hadn't spied him yet. That wouldn't do. "Hey, you damned Yankees," he shouted, slurring his speech. "You see any better than you fight?"

The heads of the guards swiveled and trained on Ty, who kept moving ever closer. "That's the Deadline straight in front of you, you drunken secesh!" one of the guards yelled, bringing his rifle to his shoulder. "Cross it and I'll shoot you dead."

Ty desperately wanted to look beneath the tower and confirm that Billy Burke was in place by now, but he didn't dare, afraid he might arouse the suspicions of the alerted blue bellies. "I'm lost and don't know where I'm bound," he called, knowing he was within two lurching steps of the potentially fatal Deadline.

Sharp thuds and the crack of splintering wood echoed within the stockade. The eyes of the guards lifted in unison and stared over Ty's head. A bugle blast rang through the night, and then a bellicose Yankee screamed repeatedly, "Guards, to the west wall! Pass the word."

Ty snuck a peek at the northeast door and his heart leaped with joy. A smallish body was snaking upward on a rope, hand over hand. Once within an arm's reach of the top of the pickets, Billy Burke lunged, gained a handhold, and disappeared slick as a scampering circus monkey, dragging his cloth rope behind him.

A single ear-piercing rebel yell was followed by a hundred more; and Ty forgotten, the guards in front of him left their posts in a mad dash. The northeast door swung open. Their plan was working to perfection.

Ty caught movement in the northeast tower. A previously unseen guard stepped from the wooden structure and pointed his rifle toward the ground, on the far side of the stockade. "Who goes there?"

Ty's spirits sank. Had all their planning and effort been for naught?

His eyes widened when the guard's arms slammed against his sides, his rifle went flying, and, with a squawk, he shot over the wall like a toy puppet discarded by an angry child. Ty chuckled. The Texans riding with General Morgan had bragged over campfires about their talents with the "lariat." He might never witness a Texan on horseback roping and taking down a steer, but he'd just witnessed a Texan rope and take down a by-God Yankee from his lofty perch.

The northeast door closed and its bar thumped into its hangars. The last of his messmates were outside the stockade, bound for Cottage Grove Avenue and the railroad.

A sporadic volley of rifle fire spun Ty about. The clash between Yankee and Rebel had taken a violent turn. Barrack Ten seemed the logical place for him to be—and quickly—in case the shooting blue bellies routed the prisoners and pursued them through the streets of Prisoner's Square.

His best attempt at a run was aptly described as a disjointed hop and skip, with his balance in constant jeopardy. The sporadic gunfire continued and the thunderous rebel yells of a few minutes ago slowly died away. Ty sensed the mass revolt was collapsing.

Short of Barrack One, he noticed a curious shadow protruded past the corner of the building. The dark extension moved; without thinking, Ty ducked as he rounded the corner. There was a swish of air and a metal object clanged against wood. Ty stumbled and went sprawling facedown into the muddy street.

He heard a man grunt and say in a voice brimming with determination, "Won't miss again, Mattson."

Ty flipped on his side. He saw light flash on metal and the blade of a shovel zipped past his hip and buried itself in clinging brown goo. He grabbed the handle of the shovel above the blade and dug frantically in his right boot for the stiletto with his other hand. The kick of a boot lanced pain down his leg and stout hands wrestled him for control of the shovel.

His probing fingers found the handle of the stiletto. Jack Stedman's son, it could be no one else, tugged hard on the shovel and Ty stopped resisting, but he maintained a firm grip above the blade. As he'd anticipated, the sudden exertion of his foe in the opposite direction leveraged him to his feet.

Ty let go of the shovel and followed after it. Jack Stedman's son wobbled backward, shuffled his feet to regain his balance, and raised the shovel above his shoulder for another strike at the charging Ty.

Ty's opponent was too late.

Ty stepped inside the arc of the descending shovel; abiding the instructions of Shawn Shannon, Ty thrust the stiletto up under his opponent's breastbone. He would stop every now and then the rest of his days and remember how easily he'd taken a life. It was akin to sticking a finger in freshly churned butter. One breath, Jack Stedman's son was alive and hell-bent on revenge. The next, he was a lifeless body propped against Ty's chest. Ty pulled the stiletto free, shrugged, and Jack Stedman's son's body fell away from him, landing in the mud with a soft *plop*.

The sheer excitement of the encounter ebbed, Ty's nerves calmed, and he thought of what must be done next. Prisoners fleeing the wrath of irate guards flooded the far end of the street. Ty drew back his arm and threw the stiletto into the dark night in the general direction of the northeast tower. Clasping the shirt collar of Jack Stedman's son, he hurriedly dragged the dead body to the edge of Barrack One and rolled it into the crawl space under the building, where it probably wouldn't be discovered before morning.

He scooped up the shovel and marched for Barrack Ten, remembering what his father had said after Shawn Shannon told of his breaking of Buck Granger's shoulder with the stock of his rifle:

"He was deserving."

CHAPTER 30

The next morning, the tally of prisoners killed and wounded as a result of Yankee rifle fire was zero dead and ten injured. Ty thought that a minor miracle, given the number of rounds he'd heard fired. The biggest toll on the Rebels was knotted heads, bruised egos, and wounded pride. The twenty-five prisoners who successfully breached the outside wall were recaptured within an hour. Sergeant Blair Taylor and six other revolt ringleaders, who were ferreted out by the testimony of bluebelly spies, were dispatched to the dungeon with a ball and chain padlocked to their ankles for good measure.

While outwardly appearing to share the bitter disappointment of those in his barrack, a warm glow of satisfaction filled Ty's heart every additional day there was no report of the capture of the Rebels having fled via the northeast door of Prisoner's Square. The process of elimination identified the escapees and Ty delighted in watching the frustrated attempts of Snag, Mouse, and their cohorts to pinpoint how three Rebels had escaped under their noses without a trace. It became commonplace for Ty and E.J. Pursley to look at each other and burst into gales of laughter, leaving other inmates to wonder if the long imprisonment finally had skewered silly the minds of Barrack Ten's cooks.

The discovery of a Confederate body beneath Barrack One launched the most thorough search for bladed weapons in the brief history of Camp Douglas. Prisoners were stripped naked and their clothing, boots, bunks, and blankets torn apart. When a Yankee patrol found a bloody stiletto between the deadline and the stockade wall, and no prisoner could be coerced into claiming ownership, Commandant Sweet, lacking credible eyewitnesses, moved on to bigger issues than the death of a single secesh. Ty prayed his father was resting easier in the grave. As Grandfather Mattson preached, justice might be a long time coming, but she always got her proper due.

Without the company of his messmates, the monotony of the daily grind behind guarded palisades overseen by enemies who detested him doubled for Ty. The one constant that helped keep his spirits from sagging into total despair was the eternal optimism of E.J. Pursley. The old chef found something positive in whatever befell them. If Snag and Mouse lingered in Barrack Ten, they weren't harassing raiders in the other barracks. If the ground froze overnight, it was easier to walk to the sinks, an important advantage for ancient legs that ached without warning. If they had but ten potatoes in the kitchen, ten was better than five. There was always a new way to season the same old fare. It was a matter of learning what new spices might be available from the blue-belly commissary. And the bottom rung was that when all else seemed bleak as warmed-over death, there was food on the table. Though short rations continually contributed to illness amongst the prisoners, no raider had yet to starve to death.

When Ty asked E.J. what he would do once they were free men, the goateed ladle wielder rubbed his chin and surprised Ty by saying, "Family's gone. I got no prospects. But that don't concern me too much. I been thrown out with the garbage before and landed on my feet. I can beg to cook at one of those fancy

Chicago hotel dining rooms, if need be. I'd have to start out washing pots and pans. That don't really matter much. Before I croak, I'll have my own stove again and hungry mouths to fill."

Adhering to E.J.'s outlook, Ty gained a smidgen of hope from rampant rumors that the Yankees were planning to institute a large prisoner exchange by the last day of the year. In succeeding weeks, Ty spent his time contemplating his future as a free man.

He wrote again to Dana Bainbridge—she was never absent from his thoughts—reaffirming his intentions and his love for her. The lack of any response to his entreaties was worrisome and kept him on edge. Had he totally misread her feelings for him? Had it been merely pity and kindness on her part, as he had feared earlier, but dismissed because his deep attachment to her foolishly led him to believe otherwise?

To keep his wits about him and not succumb to the hopeless stupor he saw turn many inmates into walking zombies, he resolved that his first destination as a free man was Portland, Ohio. He would call on Miss Bainbridge, and if she had reservations regarding his sincerity, he would overcome them. He would worry later about his ability to provide for her financially. For Ty, Dana fulfilled dreams he hadn't imagined before meeting her—dreams that were too precious to relinquish until she personally, God forbid, said she had no true interest in him.

When he wasn't dwelling on Dana Bainbridge, Grandfather Enoch Mattson occupied the balance of his private waking hours. He felt no guilt whatsoever for killing Jack Stedman's son. But the wrong he had perpetrated on his grandfather began to plague him every minute, day and night. It wasn't a matter of his writing to beg for forgiveness. The deed was done and couldn't be undone, nor could any hurt he might have caused his grandfather be erased. The question that needed answering was very simple: Was Ty enough of a man to apologize, knowing his letter might be burned without even a cursory reading?

He mulled it over another day and then seated himself at

E.J.'s private kitchen table. With blank paper in front of him and pencil firmly grasped, Ty wrote:

> *30 November 1864*
> *Dear Grandfather Mattson:*
> *I wish to apologize for deserting your home unjustly and without warning. When I learned my father, your son, was riding with General Morgan, I feared he might be killed in action before I had the chance to meet him. As Mr. Boone Jordan informed you, I departed Elizabethtown that very night and caught up with Morgan's men near Brandenburg on the Ohio River. I met Father the next day and rode with him until his death at the Battle of Buffington Island.*
> *Though he departed my life nearly as quickly as he entered it, or so it seemed to me, I cherish every minute I spent with Father. It seldom happens that a young man's lifelong dream comes true. Mine did. I pray this letter finds you in good health and your personal affairs as you want them.*
>
> *Best regards,*
> *Ty*

Ty read over what he had written three times, decided no editing was warranted, secured envelope and postage from his stash, and went directly to the Prisoner's Square post office. He stood in line until the hazel-eyed, cigar-loving Yankee sergeant he had dealt with before was available. The smoke-wreathed sergeant recognized Ty without any introduction, stamped his letter approved without opening it, affixed his initials, and dropped it into his outgoing mailbox.

Ty didn't feel the biting cold and the usual raw-edged wind barreling through Camp Douglas that afternoon during his hasty walk back to his barrack, not when he'd just dumped a mighty heavy weight from his shoulders. Shucks, even the weak late-fall sun added a cheery note to what was a fine, good day to be alive.

Three weeks later, Snag barged into E.J.'s kitchen after roll call and halted a step from Ty. With mouth exuding a cloud of sewer gas, he blurted out, "I've come for you, secesh, and I don't want a word out of you. I'm not in the mood for no questions. You're to report to Colonel Sweet this minute and I'm bound to transport you."

The disruption of Ty's normal routine didn't unsettle him. He was not the unsure, inexperienced lad who had ridden free of Elizabethtown sixteen months previous. Reb grabbing the bit on him at Corydon, his father's violent murder, and the midnight ambush by Jack Stedman's son had taught him that part of a man's attention best always be attuned to unseen developments that spring upon him with lightning quickness. He had no clue as to why the camp commandant wanted him in his office without delay. If an eyewitness to his killing of Jack Stedman's son had come forward, he might well face the dungeon, possibly a hanging rope. But then, there might be another explanation, though he couldn't imagine what it could possibly be.

The cold weather refused to abate, forcing Ty to quail within his best winter garment, a thin blanket wrapped about his body, on the wagon ride to Garrison Square and Colonel Sweet's headquarters. He wondered which Yankee bastard was wearing Boone Jordan's confiscated greatcoat. At least he was somewhat presentable in the clothing given him upon his discharge from the hospital.

His one regret as he was conveyed to an unknown fate was his failure to tell Dana Bainbridge how much he had loved her before he was whisked from her father's Portland home under cover of darkness. How could he have allowed that to happen? His father wouldn't have, and neither would he, by all that was holy, given another opportunity.

The lack of activity at Yankee headquarters surprised Ty. He had expected the beehive gyrations of General Morgan's staff meetings. A blue-belly corporal wet enough behind the ears he wasn't shaving yet was seated behind a desk piled high with bulky ledgers. The Yankee sprout's eyes jumped from his detail work when Snag said in an unnecessarily booming tone, "Reporting with Ty Mattson as ordered, sir!"

The Yankee corporal's disapproving hunch of his shoulders was lost on Snag, who left Yankee headquarters in a huff, without waiting to be dismissed. A grin tweaked the corporal's mouth. "Sergeant Oden is such an intolerable bore on every occasion. Now, to the business at hand."

Lifting a muster roll of Rebel prisoners from the pile on his desk, the corporal thumbed through the company rosters, paused, and said, "You are Corporal Ty Mattson, Quirk's Scout Company, Fourteenth Kentucky Regiment, Morgan's Confederate Cavalry, are you not?"

"Yes, sir, I am," Ty responded.

"You hail from where, Corporal Mattson?"

"Elizabethtown, Kentucky, sir."

"Your birth date?"

"July 12, 1846," Ty answered, concern growing. The Yankee brass seemed to be going to great lengths to be certain they hanged the right Rebel.

The corporal laid the muster roll aside and came to his feet. "Excellent, we have the man we want. Follow me, Corporal Mattson."

The blue-belly corporal knocked on a door with a sign reading, COMMANDANT. A firm voice with the slightest lisp bade him to enter.

Colonel Benjamin A. Sweet, beard and mustache dense and neatly trimmed, widow's peak exposing a high forehead and brown eyes shining with interest, inspected Ty from behind a massive wooden desk. Though his uniform tunic was devoid of decoration, its double row of polished brass buttons sparkled in the sunlight streaming through the window of his office.

The shaggy-haired captain with the lisp standing at the corner of Colonel Sweet's huge desk announced, "This is the secesh officer cited in the document, sir."

Colonel Sweet licked his lips, wiped them with his fingers, and, with a final glance at the sheet of paper that had triggered the meeting of a Yankee superior officer and a lowly Rebel prisoner, said, "Corporal, what I have before me is a full pardon for you and for any offenses you may have committed in pursuit of your duties as an officer of the Confederate Army. You will be pleased to know the pardon was signed by President Abraham Lincoln."

With this incredible news, Ty's knees trembled and threatened to desert him. If he had been asked to list five things he would least expect to happen to him before his death, a full pardon from President Abraham Lincoln defied odds of a million to one. Speechless, he could but stare at the bemused Colonel Sweet. He had been handed a reprieve from a sea of uncertainty.

"Corporal Mattson," Sweet said, "whoever secured this pardon for you has political clout beyond my comprehension. Pardons for Confederate prisoners of war have been nonexistent for months. You are a very lucky man to have the support of properly placed people."

Not people, Ty rejoiced, but a prime leader of the Kentucky Republican Party. Ty read every newspaper brought to his barrack and frequently purchased them from his own pocket. While President Lincoln had not carried Kentucky in the 1864 presidential election, Ty knew from his daily reading that a certain elder of the Elizabethtown Baptist Church had turned out large numbers of Republican voters in northern Kentucky counties, and the pardon on Colonel Sweet's desk had to be President Lincoln's personal thank you for such ardent support in the face of fierce political opposition.

Ty crouched slightly to steady his legs, burning with embarrassment at how badly he had misjudged the depth of his savior's love for his own blood. He would be a long while forgetting such rampant stupidity on his part.

To his amazement, Colonel Sweet had additional news of great import. "Corporal Mattson, a letter from Secretary of War Stanton accompanied your pardon. You are to be released from Camp Douglas this date in sixty minutes at high noon. For the sake of my career, it is most fortunate that my subordinates responded with alacrity to the dictates of my superiors. You will be provided a railroad pass to a destination of your choice, and any funds deposited by you in the commissary bank will be returned to you posthaste. Do you have any questions?"

"The pass won't be necessary, sir," Ty said with conviction. "Transportation will be waiting for me outside the main gate. I do have one request, sir."

Never having heard of a prisoner declining free transportation home, a most curious Colonel Sweet stiffened in his chair. "And what would that be, Corporal?"

Ty ratcheted up his nerve. What he was about to ask resulted from a snap decision. "Private E.J. Pursley, of Barrack Ten, was a noncombatant during our months in the field. His rank was honorary. He was never sworn to duty and never carried a weapon. He was, and still is, a civilian cook. With your permission, I would appreciate your freeing of him with me. He is elderly and has no home to return to after the war."

Colonel Sweet didn't refuse Ty's request out of hand. He turned, instead, to the shaggy-haired Yankee officer waiting patiently by his desk. "Captain Farrell, your opinion, if you please?"

Captain Farrell exhibited a decisive mind, which Ty suspected had earned him his promotions. "We checked our records regarding Corporal Mattson, the composition of his Confederate

Cavalry regiment, and their place of capture. Being old and a noncombatant, this Pursley should have been released at Buffington Island and sent packing. I foresee no difficulty in dismissing him as infirm, Colonel. He would be one less mouth to feed."

Colonel Sweet's ready acceptance of Captain Farrell's proposal validated his respect for his subordinate's judgment. Ty also suspected Sweet couldn't risk ruffling the feathers of his superior officers over a Rebel fully pardoned by the president for reasons no one had chosen to share with him.

"Yes, that will do quite nicely. Corporal Mattson, please report here in thirty minutes with your Private Pursley. Captain Farrell will escort you to and from your barrack."

The arrival of Captain Farrell and Ty at Barrack Ten caught the attention of Snag and Mouse. The two Yankees were there with four other guards performing a spur-of-the-moment search designed, as usual, to harass more than locate any item warranting confiscation, even by the camp's mercurial rules and regulations.

"Captain?" an uncertain Snag inquired.

"Corporal Mattson and Private Pursley have been pardoned by the president of the United States."

Ty swore the resulting expressions of Barrack Ten's main tormentors equaled that of confident political candidates so soundly defeated on Election Day they doubted their own mother's love for them. At the same time, the impact of Captain Farrell's pronouncement on Ty's Rebel inmates was instantaneous. The entire barrack rippled to attention as Ty entered E.J.'s kitchen.

"What's up, Corporal?"

"E.J., we don't have time to palaver. Grab that nothing coat of yours and follow me!" Ty ordered. "You're a free man and new employment awaits you."

Astounded but thankful, E.J. Pursley, trusting the son of

Owen Mattson would never deceive him or fun him, grabbed his threadbare coat and followed the quick-moving Ty. At the front door of Barrack Ten, Ty told Captain Farrell, "We're ready, sir."

Word of the presidential pardons spread like wildfire. So scarce was good news for any of them, eleven thousand-plus Confederates, cheering at the top of their lungs, thronged the streets of Prisoner's Square, leaving a narrow path between them for Ty, E.J., and Captain Farrell.

An emboldened E.J. Pursley took the lead. The Barrack Ten chef hadn't been the point of attention in a crowd since the spontaneous midnight street parades of his New Orleans heyday. He thrust his shoulders back, chest out, and nose up; his strut matched that of a preening peacock. Ty hadn't laughed really hard in months, but he did then, until his sides hurt. The cheering grew ever louder as the three-man procession passed through the portal accessing Garrison Square and subsided only after the tall doors of the portal closed behind them.

Ty and E.J. were ushered into Colonel Sweet's office. Captain Farrell guided them to Sweet's desk, handed them pens, and pointed to copies of discharge papers, which officially recognized their dismissal from Camp Douglas. E.J. balked at his discharge listing him as "infirm." A jab in the ribs from Ty slammed E.J.'s jaw shut and produced a series of hasty signatures.

Colonel Sweet then handed Ty his presidential pardon, a copy of his Camp Douglas discharge, and a single Federal greenback, the remaining funds from Ty's commissary bank account. "You are now civilians under the jurisdiction of the Federal Government," Colonel Sweet said, "and will conduct yourselves accordingly. Show your papers at the main gate and you're free men. The gate guards will be expecting you."

The Camp Douglas commandant didn't offer his hand and Ty didn't take offense. President Lincoln may have pardoned him, but he was still a stinking Rebel in the eyes of Federal Army personnel.

Ty walked beside E.J. across the parade ground of Garrison Square, struck by his good fortune during his imprisonment. It pained him greatly that so many of his fellow raiders had perished in ways no man should be made to die. But by prayer, luck, circumstance, and the iron will of Shawn Shannon, he was still standing and strong enough to hold his head high. And no matter how often horrifying memories of the Camp Douglas hellhole haunted him at night, he was gifted with wonderful dreams that hadn't yet come true. That prospect put a bounce in his step, lame hip be damned.

As he expected, his grandfather was outside the main gate with a horse-drawn Chicago carriage and a blanket-wrapped driver that seated four. Enoch Mattson was a mighty welcome sight in his knee-length worsted-wool coat, with the unruly red hair of the family lineage protruding from beneath a plain leather cap with a square bill. When it came to clothing, fancy was for others.

The green eyes of Enoch Mattson, which matched his grandson's, fixed an iron gaze on Ty. Ty broke the ice with an assurance and confidence he'd lacked the last time he'd spoken with his grandfather. "Good afternoon, Grandfather. I appreciate what you did on my behalf."

"Didn't amount to all that much," his grandfather responded, reaching into the carriage. "Political debts are easy to collect if done in the right manner."

The elder Mattson brought forth a packet of letters tied together with a cord and passed them to Ty. "Boone Jordan thought these might be of considerable importance to you."

Ty accepted the packet. When he read the return address on the top envelope, his racing heart nearly exploded. For there, before his very eyes, written in a neat, flowing hand were words he would forever treasure: *Miss Dana Bainbridge, Portland, Ohio.*

His watching grandfather spared Ty a torrent of unmanly tears. "And who might this chap with you be?"

Ty slipped the packet of letters inside the flap of his shirt for safekeeping and said, "Grandfather, I'd like you to meet Mr. E.J. Pursley, of New Orleans. He's our new chef."

His grandfather's reaction to the making of a decision impacting the operation of the family household without consulting him first told Ty where he stood with Enoch Mattson going forward.

"Well, gentlemen, it seems we have another train ticket to purchase. We best hurry along."

EPILOGUE

Ty dismounted, tied his horse to the gate of the iron fence surrounding the Bainbridge home, and started up the lane that looped around to the dwelling's front stoop. Tired and cramped from his ride from the depot at Pomeroy, Ohio, his limp was more pronounced than usual. His abiding fear of his upcoming call on Dana Bainbridge was that his game leg, withered frame, and the red splotches peppering his cheeks and neck made him look like the emaciated shell of a once-strong man, a far different man than the swashbuckling Rebel raider who had charmed her after barging into her kitchen in the dark of night. What kind of future did he offer a vibrant young woman in full health, with the best years of her life yet to be lived?

In her most recent letter, he'd learned that Dana's father had sent letters and collected the incoming mail for his entire household on his Saturday trips to Portland. It wasn't until after his death from heart failure that Dana had found every piece of written correspondence they had exchanged hidden away in his desk. Recent newspapers had contained fresh rumors of possible prisoner exchanges about the time of her discovery, and fearing that her undelivered letters might reach Camp Douglas after his departure, she had bundled them and mailed them to Boone Jordan per Ty's original instructions.

The fact she'd never stopped writing, despite receiving no answer from him, was what gave Ty the courage to be here at all.

He had been forthright and honest in his single letter to her since his discharge from Camp Douglas. Wanting true feelings, not pity, he'd refused to deceive her as to his physical condition. Nothing in life was ever dead certain and he was fully aware there was a chance she might reject him, once she saw him in person, which was her right. He could but hope and pray she was truly the girl who'd penned those spirit-renewing letters over many months.

Every part of him fully alert, he kept walking. Though she knew the date he was scheduled to make his appearance, no one was yet in sight on the porch of the white painted house. The high steps of its veranda loomed taller than a mountain to a bum-legged ex-soldier on the brink of exhaustion.

The front door of the house popped open and the raven-haired object of his undying love stepped from the front foyer. Ty's breath caught in his throat and his feet were suddenly lead weights that he couldn't move. She was even more beautiful than he'd remembered.

Dana Bainbridge shared none of his misgivings. Opening her arms, she bounced down the steps. Ty saw the joy in her sky-blue eyes and his doubts and fears vanished as her inviting smile filled his whole world. Then his lips were on hers and he buried himself in the warmth and lush smell of her.